ON THESE BLACK SANDS

on these black sands

AN AISLING SEA NOVEL

VANESSA RASANEN

CRAB APPLE BOOKS

Printed in the United States of America.

Crab Apple Books
P.O. Box 21034
Cheyenne, WY 82003
www.crabapplebooks.com

Visit the author's website at www.vanessarasanen.com

Cover design by Maria Spada
Map and illustrations by Dimension Door

ISBN 978-1-7327652-2-1

For my husband, who ensures the rum is never gone.
(And by rum, I mean gin.)

BLACK SOUND

DAORNA

HAVIERN

HELLES ISLAND

TYSHALY

CREGAH

PORT MORSHAN

THE COUNCIL

LOST COV

CAPROTHE

THE AISLING SEA

TURVALA

FOXHAVEN

THE COUNCIL

TO LARCSPOROUGH

PRONUNCIATION GUIDE

CHARACTERS

Declan: DEK-len
McCallagh: muh-KAH-luh
Mikkel: mih-KELL
Aoife: EE-fuh
Lani: LA-nee
Melina: muh-LEE-nuh
Cait: KATE
Maura: MOR-a
Bron: BRAHN
Callum: CA-luhm
Halloran: HA-lor-en
Csintala: sin-TAH-luh

PLACES

Cregah: CRAY-guh
Morshan: MOR-shahn
Larcsporough: LARK-spur-uh
Turvala: tur-VAH-luh
Daorna: day-OR-nuh
Haviern: hav-ee-AIRN
Caprothe: cuh-PROHTH
Tyshaly: tih-SHAH-lee
Aisling: ASH-ling
Helles: HELL-es

OTHER

Muirnaughton: MEER-not-en

The screams of his wounded men had finally begun to subside, but not enough to afford Declan McCallagh any rest. Not that he could have slept now, regardless. It had been the third attack in as many weeks, and his already battered crew had barely managed to hang on long enough to outrun their attackers.

It could have been worse. They'd avoided being boarded, raided, and forced into service in another crew—not that he, as captain, would have been granted such an offer.

Yet they'd far from succeeded in this latest battle. Nine had been lost at the onset. Another twenty-four wounded, half of those severely enough he doubted they'd live to see the next port.

They'd been caught off guard, the sails of the other ship having been spotted in the dawn's light mere seconds before the first cannon shot had been heard and felt. It had narrowly missed their bow, hitting the teal waters of the Aisling Sea instead. A warning shot perhaps, but the *Winged Serpent* and its captain, Tiernen, were not known for being merciful. Not even to fellow pirates.

While other captains had formed alliances—albeit fickle and shaky ones at best—within the pirate guild, no such accords could ever be made with the pirate lords who posed a constant threat to the smaller ships, like Declan's.

And Captain Tiernen's barbarism was that of nightmares. Crews cut down. Captains and officers brutally tortured and strung up on the rocky coastlines as a warning for all passing ships. Tiernen's signature, as it were.

Still, the *Serpent*'s gunners had missed. Whether on purpose or by accident, Declan was unsure. But it had granted his men enough time to rally and get the guns into position to fight back.

It had been for naught though.

The next attack from the *Serpent* had brought bundle shot ripping across the deck and tearing into his crew as they scrambled to get the ship into a better position to return fire. But they were dangerously low on munitions after such hard weeks at sea.

Though they'd managed to overtake a handful of merchant ships making their way south to Larcsporough, those ships had not surrendered outright, requiring the use of more powder and rounds than Declan had hoped or planned for. And none of those raids had yielded much of value. The attacks from fellow pirates had taken even more of their resources, and by the time the *Winged Serpent* had hit them upon rounding the north side of Helles Island, they'd had no chance of making much of a stand.

Declan had been forced to make the call to run instead of fight.

Now, standing in his quarters, with the strong afternoon sunlight streaming in through the windows at his back, he pushed against the worn desk and stepped back from the map, rubbing a hand across his stubbled chin.

The last three weeks seemed to have aged him more than the entire twelve years he'd spent sailing these waters. He might have been the youngest captain on this sea, but the recent attacks from the lords had him feeling twice his age.

He eyed the trio of men standing opposite him. The same weariness he bore was mirrored in their stances, as if the fatigue hung like a dead weight upon their bones. It had been growing heavier during these long weeks at sea—weeks that had felt more like months.

All three studied the map in silence as they considered every possible destination, but Declan already knew where he needed to take the *Siren's Song*. And it was the last place he wanted to go.

"We could attempt to make it to Haviern, perhaps," his quartermaster, Tommy Murphy, said, breaking the tense silence. Friends since their first stints as cabin boys at the age of ten, he and Declan had grown up on the seas together, learned each other's secrets. And tells. Seeing Tommy now gnawing on the inside of his lip, Declan knew he hadn't offered the suggestion lightly and had wanted to recommend a different destination.

Tommy pulled his cap off and scratched the back of his head as he continued to stare at the map.

The ship's helmsman, Gavin Flynn, spoke up without raising his gaze. "Even with favorable winds—and no more attacks—we'd lose half the injured by the time we arrived. We can't risk it."

Tommy looked around the room, as if checking to see if any of the crew could hear him. "We'll have to replace the injured regardless."

Declan's stomach knotted. Another captain, one like Tiernen perhaps, might have been willing to let the injured crew die at sea to appeal to his own whims. But Declan couldn't.

Gavin's chin snapped up, shock pooling in his eyes, but it was their bo'sun, Mikkel Harlan, who spoke for him, his Turvalan accent strong with his fatigue. "As true as that may be, Tommy, you know the captain wouldn't hear of it. And even without the injured, the crew is far too exhausted. I doubt they'd vote in favor of that destination."

"You know where they want to go," Gavin said, shooting a glance at Mikkel and Tommy before all three lifted their eyes to Declan, their bodies still as if he were a stalking predator instead of their captain.

There was no fear in their eyes though. While the rest of the crew might not know the reasoning behind Declan's orders, these men—the men he'd assembled for their grit and their drive and their loyalty—understood. Despite their youth, each of them had known heartache and loss, and they'd spent the last hour trying to find a way to spare him from facing his own.

Only out of sheer desperation would they suggest this destination.

Their unspoken words hung in the cabin's stale air, and Declan's gut twisted as he repeated the port's name in his mind. It would be best for his men, and after all the years of asking them to sacrifice—to risk life and limb for glory and riches—how could he refuse to do the same for them?

Yet his body protested physically at the thought of returning, of walking those cobbled streets once again, of having the scent of ancient wood and brine hit his nose. His jaw tightened as that familiar weight pressed against his chest, his throat tightening until he could barely breathe or swallow. He forced his face to remain calm, however, not wanting his men—even the three closest to him—to know just how greatly he struggled.

He felt their stares as he looked back down at the map for the millionth time, as if some ancient magic might have altered the position of the lands scattered throughout the Aisling Sea. These men would follow him wherever he dictated. He could insist they seek solace elsewhere, let his injured die on the crossing to Haviern or Foxhaven, all so he could avoid returning to those rocky black shores.

A distant scream pierced the air, pulling his gaze back up to his men, who winced at the sound. Another crew member was likely losing a limb to their overworked and exhausted carpenter-turned-surgeon. It pushed him to make a decision.

He pulled the salt-coated air deep into his chest and uttered the last words he'd ever planned to say.

"We make for Port Morshan."

Declan and Tommy stood at the railing of the quarterdeck as Gavin guided them into Cregah's main port, Morshan, the air somehow stifling and heavy despite the sea breeze greeting them. Though Tommy seemed as tense as Declan, the captain knew it was more from empathy than any trepidation of his own.

Declan had vowed never to return, and Tommy had never questioned it. This wasn't his home any longer. Hadn't been since he was a boy.

He couldn't watch as they approached the dock. The sight of this land pulled his gut into a painful knot.

He turned to Tommy. "I'll be in my quarters if you need anything."

"Aye, sir," Tommy said with a slight dip of his chin before looking back over the uninjured crew bustling to prepare to go ashore.

Declan managed to avoid the view of his past home as he made his way down the stairs and turned toward his cabin door. Once inside his room, he gritted his teeth, fisting his hands until his nails dug into his palms. The pain a welcome distraction from the one still crushing his chest. There was no time to let the past haunt him. He loosened his grip and stretched his fingers wide as he forced a breath deep into his lungs before moving toward his desk.

He'd barely moved two feet when a knock came at the door, startling him.

"What is it?" His words came out less harshly than he'd intended. This port always seemed to make him soft, and that was less than desirable for his line of work.

The door creaked open, and the bright red hair of his master gunner, Wes Keiley, appeared, followed by the old sailor's long frame.

"Apologies, Captain. We've arrived. The crew is preparing to go ashore."

Declan straightened, raising his chin. He nearly asked why his gunner was delivering this information instead of one of the cabin boys but remembered at the last moment that the lads were among those below decks clinging to life. He moved to wave the man out and acknowledge the information he'd delivered, but Mr. Keiley spoke again, raising a piece of paper in his hand. "This message arrived for you."

Declan ushered him forward and reached for the neatly folded note. It carried a scent not found aboard any ship. He started to open it but noticed his gunner still stood before him. Glancing up, his eyes met the pair already staring at him, and he gave Keiley a look that demanded the man speak.

"I…I'm sorry, Captain. Only wondered if you planned to go ashore, or if we would be shipping out soon." Hope clung to the man's words.

"We ship out at dawn." Enough time to get the wounded unloaded and taken to the small hospital in port and get the looted goods traded for the supplies they desperately needed. And maybe let the crew have a hot meal and a warm bed. Thankfully, he'd already convinced his first mate they could risk moving on despite the shortage of men if they made straight for Foxhaven, where additional crew could be recruited, so there was no need to stay any longer than necessary.

The man's face fell. "Yessir." He turned and took slow steps toward the door, as if begging his captain to reconsider their departure time.

Declan opened the note and skimmed the hurried but neat writing. He pursed his lips and bit back a curse. How she had known he'd be arriving in port when he himself had only made the decision to come here mere hours ago, he couldn't know, but he had bigger problems than to wonder about her ways.

"Change of plans, Mr. Keiley."

Declan rose as he spoke. His gunner faced him once again, a mix of dread and hope swirling around in his features, as if the two emotions were fighting to see which would be warranted for the situation. Declan might have laughed at the comical look on the gunner's face had they been in any other situation.

"Twenty-four hours. That's as much time as we can spare. We sail tomorrow night."

"Yessir," Mr. Keiley said around a smile he tried—and failed—to hide. Spinning on his heel once more, he headed toward the door.

Declan called after him, "Fetch Tommy." Years ago he would have added a "please" to the end of that as his parents had taught him, but he was no longer that kid. Time on the seas and the waves with unsavory characters and their deplorable manners had wiped clean all but the memories of his former life.

Mr. Keiley gave a silent nod and ducked through the entry, shutting the door behind him with a resounding click. Declan hadn't needed to tell Mr. Keiley to spread the word of their extended stay. He could already hear the news spreading, with cheers and whoops and hollers springing up outside his door and boots tromping as the men moved with haste to make the most of their time in port. He could only imagine how much grander their display would have been had they not been transporting their injured shipmates ashore.

Declan tried to mimic the sense of excitement he heard from his men, but he couldn't curb the dread that had burrowed into him, sending its venomous tendrils into every muscle and tendon. But he had to hide it, couldn't show the extent of his torment to anyone. Not even Tommy.

You're a pirate, damn it.

And a pirate could not be vulnerable, could not show any emotion except ruthlessness, and maybe lust, but even that was curbed by the rules of Cregah.

It might be a place of respite for them, a land where, because of the treaty signed all those years ago at the end of the Aisling War, pirates like him and his crew, could—for a price—go ashore and rest, relax, have a drink, and sleep in an actual bed if they wanted to.

But in this land run by women, the women made the rules and set the limits. Sure, the pirates got their rest, but did they get what they truly needed and wanted? There were places where they could, of course, fulfill their basest of needs. Though these needs were shared by men and women alike, in Morshan it was always on the latter's terms. Here the women were the patrons, coming to be served by the visiting pirates, not the other way around, not the way it was in other ports. But in those ports a pirate had to be on constant guard for a dagger in his back or at his throat while he was otherwise indisposed.

Whores. Pirates turned whores with this blasted treaty.

That word bounced around his head, leaving a rotten taste on his tongue despite him not having uttered it. He had been raised here, sure, and had always known life under the council and under the treaty. But from his first days as a cabin boy, he had learned things weren't always what they seemed. The pirates who sought refuge here were far from free; all were tied to the ladies of the council—even the lesser pirates like himself.

Each captain had to pay to earn admittance to the port. With either goods or services.

Whores, indeed.

He scoffed just as another knock sounded.

"Come in," Declan said as he dropped the letter onto his desk and settled himself back into the chair at his desk. He stretched his back and legs out to alleviate the soreness that had settled in. Yes, it would be good to go ashore. Even if it meant facing her and all the memories that accompanied such a reunion.

"You wanted to see me, Captain?" Tommy stepped inside and closed the door behind him.

"Aye, Tommy. I have business taking me ashore." He paused to see how Tommy would react, but his quartermaster hid any surprise well. "I assume word has spread already, but ensure Mikkel tells the men to be back on board and ready to sail after sundown tomorrow."

Tommy eyed him, the unspoken question creasing his brow.

Declan breathed deep and answered. "I know. Longer than planned. Longer than I'd like, personally. But I don't know how long this will take." He picked up the letter once again. "And with morale low, I need to give the men a bit of a breather. Last thing I need is a mutiny."

Neither of them laughed at his sore attempt at levity.

"Do we expect the council—"

"Aye." He moved a hand to his temple, hoping to ease away the threatening ache before it became unbearable. "We aren't able to pay the full tax, and I fully anticipate them calling in that debt before we leave."

He could see Tommy mulling over that information. But again, he didn't push further. Didn't need to. They both knew what the council demanded of the pirates who couldn't pay.

"The men's rest is worth the risk, I believe."

Straightening, Tommy said, "What are my orders?" asking as both his first mate and his best friend.

"Relax. Get some damn sleep and a bit of decent food. Kiss a woman if you want. Sands knows it's been too long. We'll meet at the pub tomorrow at sundown."

"Alone?"

"No. Bring Gavin with you."

Tommy's jaw set, and his brows pulled in as if he were debating whether to ask the question Declan knew was buzzing around in his head. The same question he'd been asking himself since he'd made the decision to sail here.

Am I ready to go back?

He had made peace with the idea quickly, when he'd planned to simply wait out their short stay by remaining on the ship, when he'd intended on giving the men only one night ashore.

But her note had changed everything, raised too many questions, and wiped away all confidence that he would be able to stomach this visit.

The note—despite its weightlessness—seemed to pull him under the sea of memories he'd ignored all these years. Or had tried to. The dreams had ended years ago, the anxiety attacks ceasing along with them, quicker than he'd thought possible.

Would returning, stepping foot on those black shores, bring all of it back?

Tommy glanced down at Declan's hand and the paper he held. Declan's gaze followed.

He could hand it over, let Tommy read it for himself. But something kept him from doing so. They'd been searching for years with little luck, and her note—however vague—offered their first lead in months. But he didn't know how much she knew or how much help she'd prove to be.

And he couldn't risk stirring within his friend the tiny amount of hope she'd offered, especially when it was tethered to something as shaky as his relationship with her.

Declan didn't lift his eyes when Tommy spoke again. "I'll see you at the pub then."

And with that, Tommy was gone. The door to the cabin closed again to give Declan the privacy he'd need to get his wits about him.

He turned to the small wood-burning stove behind him, which provided the only heat on the ship except for the galley, and dropped the letter inside, watching the paper catch and burn with the smell of polished wood and fresh flowers, the smell of home.

Once it had turned to ash, he extinguished the flames. It was time to leave. Time to get this over with.

Neither Aoife Cascade nor Lani Bierne spoke as they walked arm in arm, their shoes crunching over the twigs and pine needles that made up this long-forgotten path from the port city to their home at the council hall. Overhead the pine branches swayed in the summer breeze, like waving hands greeting them with their calming scent as the girls passed underneath. Aoife sensed her sister's eyes on her for the third time in the last hundred paces.

Aoife stopped in her tracks but did not release her sister's arm as she turned to her.

"Okay, Lani, out with it."

She'd given her plenty of time to come clean with whatever was on her mind. All the time they'd spent in town that afternoon and then the first forty minutes of their walk back home, at least.

"What do you mean? Out with what?" Lani's eyes brightened with what Aoife could only assume was feigned confusion.

Aoife's shoulders slumped as she let out a groan. "Oh come on! You've obviously got something on your mind. You've been near bursting with some news since we left home." She cocked her hip to one side and flashed a smirk, knowing she had her sister pegged.

"It's nothing, really." Lani pulled her arm away and started walking again, calling over her shoulder, "You coming?"

Aoife caught up within a few steps, her stride matching her sister's once again, but didn't bother relinking arms. She should drop it, trust Lani when she insisted it was nothing. Another glance at her sister, though, confirmed this was far from nothing. There was a change in the way her eyes took in the world, a change in the curve of her lips, as if a stupid grin were itching to be unleashed.

Lani's waves of red hair danced in the wind, and on impulse Aoife reached up to her own brown hair, which always seemed to be knotted instead of lying nicely like her sister's. As a kid she'd wondered how they could be sisters when they looked so little alike, with only a speckling of freckles across their nose and cheeks shared between them. It wasn't until she had matured that she realized their sisterhood was not forged by blood but by duty alone.

Still, she often found herself wishing she'd been gifted with the same features and demeanor that made Lani endearing, charming, approachable. A stark contrast to Aoife's awkward aloofness. Not that there was any need for closeness in the council hall.

"You know you think too much, Aoife." Lani's words cut through her thoughts.

"You should really try it sometime. It's good for you." She shot her sister a look before jabbing her in the ribs with an elbow, then waited for the giggles that normally ensued between them, but instead Lani breathed deep and looked away.

Aoife exaggerated her movements, looking up at the trees and then at the bushes along the path. She fidgeted with feigned nervousness.

This will either get her talking or she'll think I'm mad.

She cleared her throat, louder than necessary, but then forced her voice into a whisper. "I stole a roll at breakfast."

Lani faced her but kept walking. "What? We didn't have rolls this morning."

"When we were ten." Before Lani could question further, she continued. "I had a pet too."

Lani stopped then, wrinkles forming across her brow as she listened to Aoife's confessions with either confusion or concern. Aoife wasn't sure which.

"He was just a spider who showed up one day in my room. It's not like I had a cage for him or anything, but I named him George. He was a good listener."

Lani fought back a laugh. "Aoife. How could you? You know pets are strictly forbidden." She appeared ready to burst into chuckles.

"I know! It's why I haven't told you until now. It's been eating me up for years. Remember that day I came to dinner and everyone wondered why my eyes were all red and puffy, and I said I had gotten dust in them? Well, it wasn't dust. I'd accidentally dropped a book on George. I killed my pet. The only one I could talk to, and I'd killed him!"

"Oh, Aoife," Lani said, mock sympathy dancing within her words. "That must have been devastating."

"You have no idea how good it is to get that off my chest. It's been plaguing me for years."

Lani gave Aoife a gentle pat on the arm. "Secrets can weigh you down, it's true. They're not good for the heart." And she started back down the path.

Aoife scrunched her nose in defeat and stomped her foot—an action not suited for someone who was turning twenty in nearly a month. But she didn't care. "Gah, Lani! Come on!"

Lani skidded to a stop and turned, her resolve held tightly on her face, her eyes challenging Aoife to back down before they began to water at the corners. The shake of her head started slowly but picked up speed as the tears threatened to spill from her eyes. "I can't."

Aoife was by her side in a fraction of a second. Her heart thumped harder in her chest at the sudden shift in her sister's demeanor. "What has you so worked up? Whatever it is, it can't be good."

"Oh, but it is good. It's wonderful. Or it would be for anyone else." She dropped her chin to her chest as she spoke, allowing Aoife to wrap her arms around her and pull her close.

Warm afternoon sunlight filtered through the branches above, casting shadows in Lani's hair that normally would have had Aoife imagining fanciful stories from the shapes it created, but here, with her sister crying into her shoulder, she felt plagued by an ominous feeling that things were about to go downhill fast.

But she said it was good? Wonderful? But not for her.

Aoife's mind whirred through the possibilities. As heirs to the council, they had grown up knowing certain things in life couldn't be theirs. She considered each option, but only one seemed a likely cause for the flush in Lani's cheeks. It was a long shot, and she'd feel incredibly silly to have suggested it if she were wrong.

But if she were right…

She pulled back and lowered her head to look Lani in the eyes.

"Who?" she whispered, as if the council might have spies in the trees along the path.

Lani shook her head again, more from an inability to answer, it seemed, than a denial that Aoife had guessed correctly.

"Who is it, Lani?" she repeated, still soft but with increased urgency.

"His name is Adler."

The name didn't sound local. He couldn't be from Cregah. Which could mean only one thing.

"Which ship?"

Lani spoke around her fingers as they fussed with her lower lip. "The *Winged Serpent.*"

A gasp escaped before Aoife could stop it. "Nooooo. This is far from good and wonderful, Lan! Captain Tiernen's ship? What are you thinking?"

She didn't dare call Captain Tiernen Lani's father, despite his siring her. The title of father implied a presence in one's life, didn't it? It was a concept foreign to many children on Cregah, but especially so for the council heirs.

"Well, I didn't exactly plan it, you know. It just happened." Lani's gaze lowered to the ground as she toed the drying pine needles in the dirt.

"What exactly happened? I mean, what are we talking about? If you just looked at him, that's far from an issue. But what—"

"Six months ago, when Captain Tiernen was here to see Mother, his crew was invited to visit the palace."

"Yeah, that's nothing new, Lani. That happens all the time. They have a dinner. We eat. They talk. That's it."

Lani ignored her interruption. "He had a new crew member who wasn't like the others. He didn't shy away from looking at me like they all do. You know what it's like, Aoife. The way they avert their eyes and pretend we're not there."

Aoife did know, but she also knew why they did it. To save their skins. Self-preservation.

Adler must have been an idiot.

"He saw me, and he smiled," Lani said.

Aoife's eyes widened. "You're going to risk everything because of a smile? And a man's smile at that."

"You don't understand." Lani—tears now gone—stood her ground, her words matching her stance, armored with resolute confidence.

Aoife mimicked her sister, straightening so she could look her in the eye. "You're right. I don't. He's a man. Men are the problem, Lani. It was their warmongering that caused such destruction—scarred, broken lands and whole races wiped out. Or have you forgotten?"

Lani didn't so much as flinch or move to respond, so Aoife continued.

"You were born for something greater. All three of us were. You, me, Darienn. Even if we wanted such things—which we shouldn't—we don't get the luxury of a smile and a man of our choosing. We will eventually be paired with one of the pirate lords—"

"But I don't want to!" Lani squared her shoulders and lifted her chin. "I don't want someone who just visits me once every few months to breed like a prized cow to serve the needs of the council. I want a family and children. Multiple children. Not the one I'm allotted here as an heir. I want a life, Aoife!"

The words pushed Aoife back. She couldn't be hearing this. They'd grown up together, been raised for a bigger purpose. To lead this land and protect it so the ravages of war could never reach its shores again. It was why the first court had been instituted, why the treaty had been signed, why the whole nation had banded together and changed their ways.

They'd both learned this in their council lessons, so why was Lani now acting as though none of that mattered or even existed?

Lani released a sigh. "This is all rather rich coming from you, you know."

"What do you mean?" Though she already knew the answer before it came.

"All those novels you used to read. And would still read if your mother hadn't burned them."

"The novels *we* used to read, you mean. But those were mere stories. Fairy tales."

Lani dropped her head to the side. "Even fairy tales have some truth to them."

Aoife waved a hand between them. "Regardless, those were books.

Love has no place in our life. Your life. Here. You can't walk away from it for a damn smile."

"It wasn't just a smile. After the dinner he found me in the hallway, and we talked. Aoife, we actually talked."

Aoife's confusion rose to the surface, contorting her features. "About what exactly?"

"Life, mainly. We stole out to the gardens. Everyone else was inside or heading back to the ship or to the pubs in Morshan, and he stayed behind to talk to me."

"Because he has a death wish apparently."

"I guess he thought I was worth it, and that felt amazing."

"But there can be no future with him. You'll be twenty in a few months and taking your full place on the court. You'll be expected to—"

"I know what I'm expected to do. How many times can I explain to you? I don't want it, Aoife."

"So what are you going to do? You can't just walk out the front door. You can't request to be released from your heritage, your duty!" She nearly added herself to the list of things Lani couldn't abandon, but she choked back those words. Compared to her obligations to the council, simply staying with Aoife was far from important.

"Yes, I can. And I will."

Aoife took a half step back, as if shoved by the realization this was actually happening. "Why are you telling me this?"

"Because you forced me to." Lani's gaze and tone were sharp as her hands flew into the air.

She's got you there.

"Fair enough. But do you expect me to simply step aside and let you?"

None of this made sense. The forest around them seemed to disappear as Aoife stared at her sister, this sister who might not have even said goodbye before running off with some pirate. Aoife felt a familiar lump lodge itself in her throat. Thankfully it remained there and didn't bring tears.

"What exactly are they going to do to me, Aoife? We are a land of peace, order, nonviolence. It's not like they're executing people in the village square."

What would they do to her? This was unprecedented. No heir to the council had ever abandoned her duty. At least, none of the historical records indicated anything of the sort.

Something twinged inside Aoife, an inkling of a doubt. What if someone had? What if it had been excluded from the record? Covered up? Hidden for the disgrace it was. She brushed the thought aside as nonsense. Such deceit would never have been tolerated, let alone practiced, by the council.

"But they can't just let you walk away from your place on the council! You're coming of age in less than six months. Your ceremony is being planned as we speak! If you walk away before that, what would that do to everything we've built here? You'd risk war and the collapse of all order here for a man? A man you barely know."

"Oh, don't be so dramatic, Aoife," Lani said, her eyes darting to the treetops in exasperation.

"You're one to talk. I can't believe what I'm hearing."

"I can't stay, Aoife. I can't. I can't do what they need me to do. To be paired with one of the pirate lords? To be shackled into a loveless contract? I can't do it. Not when I have the chance to love and be loved on my own terms."

When Aoife looked in Lani's eyes again, she found tears—not of fear, but of hope. Promise. Love. She swallowed down her worry. Her sister might be foolish—ridiculous—yet some part of her own heart began to twist in yearning. What would she have done in Lani's place? If Aoife had been the one to turn a man's head?

She'd known her whole life she wasn't destined for love or family or normalcy, but for service to her land and her people. She'd accepted that. It was how things had to be to keep the peace. But she couldn't deny the look in her sister's eyes, and she couldn't cause her sister pain.

She couldn't believe what she was about to say. Didn't even know if she'd be able to utter the words at all. But she steeled herself, drew in a breath, and glanced at the trees surrounding them—as if someone might be lurking nearby and would overhear.

"What do you need me to do?" The question came with none of the courage she'd hoped to muster, but this wasn't a summer picnic they were plotting. This was treason. Or something similar.

"Nothing, Aoife. Nothing. I mean, nothing actively. Just don't tell anyone you know where I've gone. Not our mothers. Not Darienn." An image of their younger sister—still two years from her own coming of age ceremony—flashed in Aoife's mind. Darienn had a particularly cold demeanor, as if she were always plotting and scheming behind those dark blue eyes.

Aoife shuddered and let Darienn's face fade from her memory. "Where will you go though? And when is this happening?"

"The next time they're in port. I'm going to steal away while Mother's with the captain. She'll be preoccupied. And you know the others in the council lie low during those visits. Adler has been saving his money for his own sloop, and he found someone willing to sell him one next time he's in port. He spoke of his homeland across the sea, an island where his people live simply but happily."

"So why did he become a pirate if he loves his homeland so much?"

"His family needed the money after his father died. Piracy allowed him to provide for his mom and sisters."

"And he can just stop pirating now that he has you?" Aoife's muscles recoiled at the unintended harshness in her question.

"Are you trying to overthink this, or are you ruining it for me for your own pleasure?"

"No! I just want to make sure you've thought this through before you throw everything away."

Lani's shoulders slumped. "He doesn't need to pirate anymore. He's made enough in one year to help his family start their own business to support themselves. We'll get married and go back to help run their shop."

A small spark flickered within Aoife as an image of Lani's future took shape. Her sister's red hair blowing in the wind. Laughing children running around her legs as she hugged her husband. Compared to the cold stone walls of the council hall and a loveless union with a pirate lord, she began to understand the appeal. Even if only slightly. But it was a future she'd never allow herself to dream of, because it was impossible.

Still. Could she deny it for her best friend?

"Aren't you going to miss this?" She gestured to the forest around them. "Aren't you going to miss home?" She choked on a ball of emotion before she could ask if Lani would miss her.

"Of course I will. I'll miss you, our chats, and the black sands of Cregah. But I'm taking it with me." At that, she lifted a chain from around her neck. At the end of it lay a small glass vial with a cork stopper glued in place.

"What is that?"

"Adler gave it to me when he asked me to leave with him. He'd filled it with the sand from the beach. Said I could carry home with me always."

Aoife had to admit, the more she heard of this Adler fellow, the less he sounded like the men they'd been warned about for all these years. She looked from the pendant to her sister's eyes, which were gleaming with hope. Was that what love looked like?

"Okay." She sucked in a breath. "I'll help you. I'll keep your secret. Just like I did about George."

Lani pulled her into an embrace, and Aoife's insides twisted, as if trying to shield her from this, to pull her into some protective shell. She didn't want to let go of her sister, this sister she loved and adored and admired. She would do anything for her, but still, Aoife hated to lie. And she would have to now. Either she was lying to Lani now by agreeing to help, or she would need to lie to her mother and the council when Lani ran.

Which it would be, she didn't know.

The sound of Declan's boots on the cobblestones still wet from the afternoon rain showers mingled with that of laughter coming from the eateries he passed. The rich scent of sea salt and weathered wood at the docks had given way to a mix of blooming flowers, roasting meats, wet stone, and the occasional vile tang left by those who had drunk too much. Even in the light of dusk the town of Morshan looked much like he remembered—its buildings freshly painted, their upper window sills lined with flower boxes, and storefronts well-stocked with goods.

A fresh facade to hide the truth.

He shook away the memories. It did him no good to be burdened by a past he couldn't change. The sea had been his escape, but it was that constant reminder of all the dreams he'd had as a boy dashed away in a single night—the night he'd learned life in this seemingly peaceful town—more peaceful than anyone would imagine with how many pirates and privateers and generally despicable individuals found respite here—was far from safe and quaint under that shimmering mask.

A door swung open sending warm lamplight across the path and a sweaty mound of flesh toward him. Raising his arms before him he turned and, with an easy shove, sent the drunkard past him where he fell in a stinking heap upon the cobblestones, shaking with laughter despite being in the cold and the wet.

Declan winced at what fluids the man might have landed in, but he kept walking. Five hundred more paces and he'd be there. He could make this jaunt from the docks blind, but then he wouldn't be able to ward off any more bumbling buffoons as easily.

But the others he met were not bumbling, nor buffoons. Despite the streets being far more crowded than he'd hoped at this late hour, no one else made contact with him. He watched—with some amusement—as each approaching pair of eyes glanced at the dark teal fabric tied at his waist and then darted away. They stepped aside, giving him a wide berth, some choosing to tread in the swampy gutter rather than risk brushing his shoulder.

His reputation—and that of his ship—must have preceded him.

And it had only taken years of sweat, blood, and the unthinkable to make that happen. His entire childhood lost.

He turned the last corner and nearly froze. It might as well have been his first time back with how his stomach tightened at the sight of the pub sign ahead. Shaped like a weather-beaten flag in the wind, it beckoned him forward, its distressed lettering calling his name.

Literally. *McCallagh's Pirate Pub.*

For how much people feared his name as captain of The Siren Song, that same name on this pub—one of only two in the entire village—hadn't seemed to curb their desire for strong drink. Even a hundred feet away he could hear the chatter and merriment that streamed out whenever the door opened to let someone enter.

He kept his gaze locked on that pub sign as he approached, refusing to risk even a glance at the cobblestones out front. There wasn't likely to be any remaining evidence of what had happened all those years ago, but he couldn't bear it nonetheless. Couldn't bear the possibility that all sign of what had happened had been so easily washed away with the rains of ten years.

He should walk straight in, but he needed a moment, so he paused to peer through the square window panes. Despite the years of grime lining the edges of the muntin, the center of the panes were clean, providing a clear view inside, but he couldn't see through the mass of bodies within, milling about, crowding the tables and bar.

Pulling his arm back he laid his hand at his hip, tapping his fingers against the hilt of the dagger concealed under his coat and shirt. No one had seen him take it that night, too busy restraining the man who had used it. He'd pulled it from the body, mesmerized by the way the blood clung to its blade.

He'd only been a kid. Inconsequential. Invisible. And in that moment he'd felt the first threads of his youth pull thin, fraying. The first steps to becoming the man others avoided in the street.

The blade had been with him since, getting him out of—and into—plenty of trouble since. He hoped he wouldn't need it here, couldn't risk pulling it on someone in this port where violence was outlawed and peace mandated, weapons restricted only to the crews of the lords' ships. Yet few of the pirates adhered to the rule, coming into port with blades hidden on their bodies.

Not that the guards at the docks seemed to care much. The past ten years had gone on with so little incidence they'd grown lax. *Careless, Declan thought. But it was to his advantage.*

Still, while he hoped he didn't need the dagger in here—he couldn't bear to cause her any trouble with his return—it gave him the courage he needed to face her again. As silly as it was, it brought comfort.

Confidence.

How would she react? Would she understand why he hadn't been back in this handful of years? Would she have heard the same rumors and stories about his actions and misdeeds?

A pang of regret and guilt threatened to rise into his throat, but he forced it down. He had no use for remorse. Weakness had no place here. Roughing his hand over his scruffy chin, he pulled in a breath. *Time to face the music.*

He pushed the door open and shoved aside the onslaught of memories that rushed him, as easily as he'd shoved the drunkard into the gutter. Confident steps carried him to the bar, his eyes narrowed on the spot where he'd likely find her. Men—pirates, mostly—crowded the room, but they all dispersed as he walked, as if the mere sound of his boots against the wood floor sent them fleeing from his presence. Looks averted. Gazes darted away from his face.

He'd learned long ago the effect confident steps alone could have on others, even before they saw him or his face. But being back here, in the pub where he'd grown up, he didn't feel like the feared man he'd become. Rather he was that scared kid, watching his mother disappear into the mist, seeing his father chase after her, finding them both…

He cursed silently at the memories that dared to defy him, swimming to the surface without permission. But memories weren't so easily intimidated.

Not like men.

He stepped to the bar and moved a newly vacated stool out of his way. He looked straight ahead, despite the urge to seek her out, and tapped his fingers against the bar, waiting.

She'd show soon enough. He could be patient—as patient as she'd been these past years.

"What the hell are you doing here?" Her question came at him as sharp as the dagger at his hip, but he wouldn't let the wince show on his face. Even knowing this was a ruse, a lie meant for the other patrons, so they wouldn't know she'd summoned this meeting, it still stung. She leaned against the bar opposite him, a rag pressed between her hand and the smooth wood.

"Nice to see you, too, sis." He angled his head at her and pulled his mouth into a smirk. Like the town, she hadn't changed much since the last time. Her dark hair still fell like a heavy curtain around her face which was just as pretty, despite the exhaustion and weariness that plagued her features.

Her eyes narrowed, and he could have sworn their green had faded to gray, no longer the bright emeralds he'd remembered from his youth. Or perhaps he'd merely been gone so long her memory had taken on an other worldly quality, etched into his mind with heightened intensity—one of the few memories he hadn't suppressed.

"You shouldn't be here, Captain." She backed away from the bar and tossed the rag over her shoulder as she reached for the near empty mug of a patron to his left, refilling it with ale as she spoke. "We don't want any trouble."

"Ah, but trouble isn't allowed in this port." He flashed her a smirk, but her expression remained cold.

"Not all trouble comes at the tip of a blade."

"Fair enough, but who says I'm bringing trouble your way?"

"It's what you do, isn't it? Wreaking havoc wherever you go. We all know the stories."

"Do you now?"

"Aye. Though I'm not sure I believe them." A playfulness warmed her gaze for a brief moment before the icy stare returned.

"You should," he said, fighting the urge to look down and avoid her judgment, and the face that looked so much like their mother's. That damn guilt struck from somewhere in his gut. He bit it back down.

"Well." She paused to clear her throat. "In that case, you really shouldn't be here."

"Perhaps. But I hear it's the best place to get a drink—and a bit of news." He swallowed hard.

Her laugh surprised him, filling the space between them, taking him back to easier times. "Oh ho ho, is that all you want? A bit of gossip while you sip a whisky?"

"I prefer rum." He snuck a glance at the other bodies inching away from him, careful to keep their faces hidden and backs turned.

"Sorry, I'm fresh out. This lot shares your taste, it seems." She lifted two empty brown bottles from behind the bar and gestured with them at the crowd.

A hush settled through the pub as if all ears waited for Declan's response and all muscles itched, ready to launch their owners out the door if his renowned temper erupted. He clicked his tongue, eying his fellow pirates over his shoulder before turning back to his sister.

"That's too bad, Cait." He pulled the stool behind him and settled onto it. "A glass of whisky it is."

The din of voices rose once again as Cait poured the warm tawny liquid into a relatively clean glass. Pushing it across the wood of the bar she leaned in, not much, but just enough to keep the words between them.

"I'm surprised to see you."

"Why? You summoned. I obliged. You act as though I never come around."

"Seldom enough."

"If I recall, I was just in here—"

She cut him off. "Seven."

"What?"

"Seven years. The last time you were here. Or have all your adventures and escapades clouded that memory of yours?" He'd known it had been a while since he'd been back, but had it really been that long?

"Not clouded, sister. I remember it well. You refusing to help. Denying me aid. Sending me off on my own. Can you blame me for not returning?"

"Sending you off? You left of your own accord. You were a fool, Declan." Her tone had shifted from irritated barkeep to chiding elder sister, and the sound of his name on her tongue threatened to plunge him back into those memories once again.

She lowered her voice and leaned in closer, as if remembering the audience around them. "I needed you here, to help with the pub and the…" She winced, hiding something, but he shooed away his questions. Whatever it was she kept from him, it could wait. She wasn't likely to talk about it in shared company anyway.

"And I needed a sister. I was only ten when it happened. Where were you?" His jaw tightened with the resentment he'd thought had disappeared.

Cait pursed her lips, as a tenderness he hadn't seen in ages softened her gaze. The closest thing he might get to an apology.

He downed the last of his drink and set the glass to the bar with a whisper of a sound. Brushing his hands together he straightened his back and pulled a smile to his lips. "All is forgiven, Cait. You know, though, you could have come with me. You would have made an excellent pirate."

Cait straightened as well, ignoring his words as she leaned her hips into the bar's edge and rested her hands beside his used glass. "Can I get you anything else?"

"Perhaps another time?"

The door opened and new revelers entered, sauntering up to the bar on either side of him, unaware of who he was or why all had given him space. With a glance over to the new patrons, she told them she'd be right with them as she tapped a finger on the bar three times.

She would have made a good pirate indeed.

With a nod of understanding he turned and made his way out the door, offering her a quick thanks over his shoulder.

He'd be back, and hopefully her information would prove worth it.

Aoife pulled her legs up under her and settled into the large velvet armchair, her favorite spot in the library—in the entire building, if she were honest. Dinner had been uncomfortable, to say the least. While no one had remarked on the unusual lack of chatter between her and Lani as they ate, she had no doubt everyone had noticed, and she had no idea how she'd explain it if confronted.

She took a settling breath and opened the novel she'd been reading for the past few weeks, wishing it would get more exciting but knowing it wouldn't. Her mother had confiscated all the interesting books she'd scrounged up on outings into Morshan.

Not that she could pay attention to the book. Her mind continued to whir with everything Lani had told her, making dinner awkward and now causing the words before her to blur into a sea of gray against the cream pages.

No matter how many times she replayed their conversation, she didn't understand it any better. And she had found no solution for her sister to avoid stealing away in the night like a criminal.

Now that would make for a good novel.

But this was real life with her real sister. And she didn't know if she was ready for drama outside the covers of books.

Lost in her mind as she was, she didn't hear the footsteps approaching until someone stood directly in front of her, clearing her throat.

Aoife startled, her eyes flashing up to the face of one of the servants. "Yes?"

"Your mother would like to see you in her office, Miss Aoife." With a quick curtsy, the girl turned and left, not bothering to wait for a response.

Aoife debated leaving the book behind, but her hands needed something other than her skirts to hold them steady. The councilwomen's offices lay just off the main meeting room, where their people brought forth concerns and grievances to the council, a short walk from where she had taken solace in the library.

Aoife rapped lightly on the door, her heart fluttering as fast as her knuckles against the wood.

"Come in." The command came muffled but still stern.

As Aoife nudged the door open, she tried to ignore the panic that rose within. It was unusual to get a summons outside normal council business or lessons. Did her mother know something? Had there in fact been spies along that wooded trail?

Sweat caused the book in her hands to nearly slip to the floor, but she righted it, clutching it tightly with her fingers.

What would she do if her mother knew? Could she lie to her face?

This was far from hiding an extra dinner roll or keeping a pretend pet spider. She might have laughed at the ridiculous spider story she'd conjured up for Lani had she been anywhere else.

"Don't just stand there in the doorway, Aoife." Her mother's words cut through her thoughts, her stare iced over with annoyance, as if Aoife had been the one to initiate this meeting.

"Apologies, Mother," Aoife said with a bow of her chin, and she took a step forward. The room—large and dark despite the blazing fire in the stone hearth—might have been cozy and inviting with its comfortable armchairs and numerous bookcases had it not been for the imposing woman who occupied it.

Melina Cascade's head turned as she took in her daughter, and with a release of breath, some warmth crept over her features, a smile pulling ever so slightly at her lips. "It's all right. I shouldn't have snapped. I did call for you, after all."

She set her book on the end table beside her armchair, uncrossed her legs, and motioned for Aoife to join her in the seat facing hers.

Aoife hoped her brief moment of hesitation wasn't noticeable as she moved to sit. She kept her eyes on the flames, marveling at the colors that danced and glowed as the wood was consumed.

I wonder if that's what being in love is like.

The thought startled her. Love must be similar. The same fiery glow had been in Lani's eyes as she spoke of the pirate and their future together. She'd been excited, burning, yearning for more, craving that companionship.

"How was your walk to Morshan this afternoon?" Her mother's tone held none of the earlier iciness. Melina lowered her head into Aoife's line of sight, pulling her attention away from the flames and her thoughts.

Such an easy question, and yet Aoife had to be careful. She'd need to keep her tongue on a short leash here, lest it get away from her.

She tried to play it cool, lifting a shoulder and offering a bored-sounding, "Uneventful really."

A short laugh sounded from her mother, not quite pleasant but more amused than irritated. "I should hope so, dear." Her mother's eyes dropped to the book Aoife held, and her lips tightened. "Find a new book?"

Blinking quickly, Aoife fumbled to lift the book. "No, Mother. This is from our own library."

Melina's shoulders relaxed as her not quite warm smile returned. "Ah, very good then. It is so hard to keep up with the books that make their way into our bookshops from the ships."

Silence settled between them, tense and prickly. Aoife itched to fidget or move but managed to keep her body under control as her gaze floated back to the dancing flames.

"Preparations are almost complete for your ceremony next month."

Aoife forced a smile to her lips. Would Lani be here for that? Or would Adler be returning before then? She should have probably memorized the visitation schedule instead of wasting time in the library, but she couldn't let her mother see any of these questions play across her face.

"Are you excited?" her mother asked.

"Of course. A little nervous too." At least that wasn't a lie.

"Ah, yes, that's normal. I was so nervous on my matching day. Brigeh and I stayed up all night before discussing which of the lords I might choose. Have you any thoughts about your own choice?"

Sucking in a deep breath, Aoife tried to conjure up the faces of the three lords she had to pick from, but she'd had little contact with any of them. She could only offer an awkward shake of her head as an answer.

Another laugh filled the room, this one warmer than the last. "Again, normal. Perhaps Lani could help you decide?"

"Perhaps." The word came out strained. The corners of her mother's eyes flinched slightly, as if she'd noted the hint of something lingering behind Aoife's answer.

Her mother leaned forward and rested her hand on Aoife's knee in a gesture that might have been comforting had it not felt so foreign. An image flashed in her mind of the women in Morshan hugging their children, smiling and laughing with them as they played games in their small front yards. It had seemed so odd to her the first time she'd witnessed it.

"Did something happen between you two?" Her mother's eyes probed hers, hunting, and Aoife couldn't stop herself from physically recoiling from her stare.

Forcing a smile to her lips, she shook her heard again. "No, Mother. Just nerves is all."

"Be glad you're the oldest, Aoife. You get to have your pick. Poor Darienn will be left with whichever lord remains after Lani's matching this fall. You know, it's also normal for there to be some tension between sisters before a matching. But try not to let it come between you. You have many years of ruling together ahead of you. It's best to keep that bond strong."

"Of course." Aoife couldn't stop her mind from focusing on the future she should have had with her sister, the future Lani was tossing away for a man. For love.

Her unease must have been written all over her face, because Melina leaned in once again. "Is something else troubling you?"

Aoife turned to face her mother. This wasn't a woman to be feared. She was stern, yes. Hard, of course, but that was for Aoife's good, and that of the country. Everything Melina did was for the people and their land, to keep war at bay and away from their shores.

If I speak in hypotheticals alone, merely ask the question without giving specifics, perhaps I can find the answer Lani needs.

Something in her gut twinged at the thought, but she ignored it as her mother nudged her to speak with another dip of her head and a tug of a smile. Her eyes shone with warmth and concern.

"What would happen to a lady of the council if she"—Aoife hesitated, but her mother hummed in encouragement for her to continue—"were to fall in love?"

Aoife forced her gaze to meet her mother's, but Melina had already turned away to stare into the flames.

If Aoife had thought this was an easy question with an easy answer, she'd been wrong. She'd expected—well, she didn't know what she'd expected, but this wasn't it. Her curiosity was sparked, her mind spinning as she watched her mother.

Had Melina fallen in love before?

Had she been forced to let a lover go?

Before Aoife could open her mouth to ask what was wrong, her mother spoke.

"It doesn't happen often." Melina sounded distant, as if she were speaking to the flames, and Aoife had to lean forward to hear. "I only know of once before. My mother's sister."

"Brigeh's mother?"

"No. Nor Fiona's. She never had an heir, and you've never heard her name. Even I don't know it." Her mother seemed to be traipsing down some long-lost path through her memories. "I only heard about her from my mother. As a warning. To not let it happen to us."

"What happened to her?"

"She left, all mention of her stricken from the council records, removed from our history. Forgotten. She was exiled, basically, unable to ever return, forced to leave and never come back. Not allowed to see her mother or sisters again, or to ever wander the streets of Port Morshan or stick her toes in the black sand."

Aoife eyed her mother, whose gaze remained on the flames, glassy and unseeing. She'd never witnessed such melancholy before in this woman, who was usually nothing but strong, determined, brave. She was their leader. Head lady of the council. Yet here she looked…scared.

Or worried.

Certainly this fate didn't sound so bad. There were worse things than being exiled. Especially for someone already planning to leave and never return. Right?

She would go to Lani. Tell her what she'd learned. Encourage her to come clean, to request to be released from her duty, to choose exile. While not an honorable departure, at least it wouldn't require secrecy.

And Aoife wouldn't have to lie.

She shifted in her chair, eager to find Lani to share this good news. But she couldn't simply slip out without a dismissal from her mother, who remained lost in the past. Why was she so distraught over a woman she'd never even met?

Aoife cleared her throat, and her mother turned with a slight shake of her head, as if she were shooing away a fly. Her stare was no longer misty and past-centered but determined, curious, and growing harder with each passing second.

"Why, exactly, do you ask, Aoife?"

She hesitated, her mind nudging her tongue to play the "hypothetical" card. *Oh, no reason. Just curious.* Surely her mother would understand, given Aoife's curiosity was always getting her into trouble. But she got lost once again in the image of Lani on that distant shore, making a home and being genuinely happy. She wanted that for her sister. Even if she couldn't understand it, she understood happiness and the desire for it.

She could answer honestly, secure that happiness for her sister legitimately. But the look on her mother's face seemed to be a dire warning to keep her trap shut. Even if the council would grant exile, it was Lani's to request, not hers.

"Have you met someone?"

Aoife choked on the laugh that burst from her—a nervous tick she had. She could never contain her giggles when the nerves rose. It was only logical her mother would jump to that conclusion, right?

"No." She took a breath to compose herself. "No. Not me."

When would she ever have met someone? Honestly. She'd barely spoken two words to any man, and even then it had only been to the older men in the village or the port.

"Who then?"

Aoife realized her mistake—too late—and cringed. A simple "no." That was all she'd needed. Why had her tongue slipped? The icy stare had returned and now bored into her, as if it could uncover the truth she was doing a piss-poor job of hiding. Aoife looked down at her hands, unable to think clearly while looking into those cold eyes.

She willed herself to stay silent this time. She couldn't lie, but she also couldn't rat out her sister.

"Lani."

Aoife clasped a hand over her mouth before she realized it hadn't been her tongue that uttered her sister's name. Her mother had guessed. And it wasn't a question.

Aoife sat still, not giving Melina so much as a nod, as fear and worry coursed through her. There was no good outcome for her. If she lied and her mother found out, she'd lose any semblance of freedom. But if she confirmed her mother's suspicions, she'd be betraying Lani.

Too long had passed without a response, and she realized her silence alone had been confirmation enough.

This was all going dreadfully wrong. She hadn't planned to broach this topic. She'd meant to keep it hypothetical, to put her mind at ease that if Lani were caught she wouldn't pay too great a price, and now she'd gotten Lani caught in the process.

Her throat tightened, and she swallowed hard around the dread that lodged itself there. What would Lani say to her when she found out?

Her mother spoke again. "And what does she plan to do? Do you know?"

Another breath. Another hesitation. *Say no!* her mind screamed at her.

When she looked up, her mother's cold stare had turned back into to an expression of care, concern, and love. Love for her and for Lani. And before Aoife could stop herself, she broke down, her shoulders slumping from the weight of the secret she'd promised to keep. Her words rushed out before she could stop them, as if propelled by some magic or force she couldn't see and couldn't resist.

"She dreams of running away with him to Daorna and starting a family. It's preposterous. I don't know why she'd want to give this all up, but Mother, she looked so hopeful and happy. Can't she be allowed to leave and have that? Even if it means exile?"

Surely her mother could and would help. Maybe Lani wouldn't be publicly shamed but would be allowed to leave. Quietly. Peacefully.

Melina turned back to the fire. And though Aoife couldn't see her face fully, it looked as if her mother might cry.

"I-I…" Aoife stammered. "I promised her I wouldn't tell, and I didn't mean to tell you. I didn't mean to betray her. But surely being allowed to leave knowingly is better than sneaking away?"

Her mother didn't answer. She continued to stare into the flames, her jaw tightening with each passing second. But not from anger. Rather, it looked as though she were biting back a mournful wail. But it only lasted a moment, a few breaths, and then her face relaxed as she composed herself. She turned to Aoife once more.

"You did the right thing, Aoife. It is always best to be honest, open. And you know you can always tell me anything."

If she had intended comfort in those words, she'd failed, because Aoife felt far from relieved. Something in her mother's words felt like a warning rather than an invitation, making the weight of her guilt even greater. She should not have asked the question. She should not have sought her own comfort. She should have kept her damned mouth shut!

Too late now.

Lani might never forgive her for this broken promise, but maybe she'd get her chance at happiness.

6

Declan

The bell in the clock tower in the village square chimed three. Declan straightened against the stone wall, careful to stay hidden in the shadows as he watched the pub from the alley across the street.

A minute passed. And then another. His confidence wavered with each breath.

With gritted teeth he swallowed the last bit of hope he'd been holding onto that his sister had forgiven him, not that he'd ever admit to anyone how much he wanted to mend the family ties he'd severed when he'd left the island.

He'd stayed away too long, abandoned her, and now—despite being the one to initiate this meeting—she appeared to be doing the same to him.

He checked his pocket watch. Three minutes late. He had waited longer than he normally would, and now it was time to go. He turned on his heel, his shoulder slamming into someone's face.

"Watch it!" the voice hissed in a whisper, a hand rubbing the nose he'd smashed.

"Cait."

"You're not the only one in the family able to sneak around in the shadows, you know."

"You're late."

She didn't offer any words, but gave a smirk half hidden in the darkness.

"How'd you know I was here? I could have been waiting in any of these alleys or shadows."

She wiggled an eyebrow at him. "Sisterly intuition."

He waited for the real answer, but when she didn't say anything more, he groaned. "Fine, don't tell me. I assume we have more important things to chat about?"

"Yes, but not here." With that, she turned around and headed back through the alley, without so much as a gesture for him to follow.

Biting back the urge to stamp his foot as he used to as a kid, he instead followed after his older sister, wondering where she was leading him.

His long legs had him catching up with her as she rounded the corner onto the next street, but he almost ran her over when she stopped to open a door he hadn't noticed in the wall. He let out a huff of annoyance, and she shushed him while motioning for him to follow her inside.

He closed the door behind them, shutting out all light from the street outside, plunging them into pitch black. For a moment he wondered if his sister was betraying him, turning him over to the council's lackeys, the ones who made people disappear under the guise of justice. But what did she have on him? Nothing. He always ensured his men behaved, and he'd been sure to always do as the council demanded, required.

An ache in his chest responded to the images that flashed in his mind. The faces. The bodies. He shook them away.

He hadn't fully recovered from the memories when his sister whispered, "This way."

Cait's footsteps were barely audible. She'd always been adept at stealth as a kid, sneaking out in the wee hours of the morning to do what, he never knew. Not that their parents would have minded. Cait could do no wrong. She was the heir to the family's estate, destined to take over the pub when their parents grew too old or passed on. And that's exactly what had happened, albeit many years earlier than expected.

Declan tried to follow her, worried he might step on her in this darkness. He hoped his eyes would eventually adjust, but there was no adjustment that would help here. The air was cold and odorless. Stone walls lined the corridor, and he counted his steps as he followed in an attempt to determine where exactly they might be.

"Stairs here. Going down. Ten of them. Don't fall," Cait said.

He didn't say anything as he followed.

Ten stairs down. And then he ran into his sister once again. She had stopped. She could have at least told him she was stopping.

Cait didn't say anything, but he heard her unlocking a door and shoving it open. The light blinded him for a moment, a shock after being in such darkness even for the short time it'd taken them. He stepped inside and waited while she locked the door behind them.

Though he'd half expected to find the room filled with other people, it was empty. Just the two of them. And it wasn't cold like the hallway. A fire burned in a small hearth to the left, with a simple mantel above it lying empty. In fact, no decorations adorned the wall other than a single map of the Aisling Sea on the far wall behind a modest desk and a beat-up chair. A rug had been brought down; Declan recognized it from their old living room, the pattern of leaves and trees now faded and threadbare. A simple cot lay in the corner to his right, with a pillow and blanket tossed about as if the owner had risen in a hurry.

Cait walked past the old sofa that sat in front of the fire and motioned for him to sit in one of the two old, mismatched armchairs in front of the desk.

"Welcome to my home," Cait said, easing herself into the chair closest to her. "I'd offer you a drink, but I'm not on duty and I've been pouring drinks all damn day."

"You live here? What is this place? What about our…" He stopped himself at that word. Nothing on this island was his. He had abandoned all connection when he'd stepped onto that ship all those years ago.

"The rooms are still there, of course. I keep them looking lived-in. Helps to keep the council unawares." Settling into her seat, she stretched out her legs, crossing them at the ankles before putting her hands behind her head. She didn't look like someone who had urgent news to tell him.

He eyed her, as the questions churned in his mind. What was she hiding about this place? How did she keep the council from finding it? And how did she keep their residence above the pub looking lived-in without actually living there?

"Ah, yes, brother, you've been away too long, always hiding there on your ship, too scared to come home."

"I'm not scared. And this isn't my home. Not anymore." He cringed at how childish his words sounded, and his chest puffed up against his will, as if it intended to remedy the betrayal his words had committed against his reputation.

"Apologies, Declan. I should choose my words more carefully. I'd hate to be the next victim of your famed wrath." She raised an eyebrow at him. He searched for any sign of mockery in her features, but all he saw was admiration and interest.

"What do you need, Cait?"

"Can't a sister merely miss her baby brother?"

"No one ever misses a pirate. But you're the one who sought me out. I doubt it's for some warm family reunion. So what do you need? Same thing everyone else needs from us? To do your dirty work?"

She bristled and then sat up, leaning forward. "We are not the council, and we do not have any need of your—protection." Even here she wouldn't voice the tasks the council demanded of him and the other captains.

He pressed again. "What is it?"

Cait narrowed her eyes at him, resting her face against her hand and pressing her fingers across her mouth as if protecting the words she, even now, wasn't sure she should utter. A breath. Another. She was certainly testing his patience. Why send him that note if she wasn't going to speak to him now?

Another breath raised her chest, and she dropped her hand as the air rushed from her lungs in a sigh.

"We need what you seek."

His heart raced, but he willed his apprehension not to show on his face despite feeling the corner of his eye twitch. He tried to play it cool, as cool as he could with this woman who had known him since birth.

"Who said I was seeking something?"

"Oh, come now. You don't think you can make inquiries into its whereabouts without us finding out, do you? You really should be careful when seeking information."

He had been careful. He had never used his name. He had never inquired in person. He had always sent anonymous notes via routes that couldn't be traced back to him. The Rogues had improved their methods, it seemed.

"Let's say I am seeking this…this item. It won't do you any good." He relaxed back into his seat, his arms crossing behind his head, mimicking his sister's previous position.

"And why is that?"

He gave a bored shrug. "No one has been able to tell me where it is or how to locate it. I've spent the past two years searching, and—"

"And you have come up empty-handed." He always hated when she did that—finishing his sentences as if she were in his head. Maybe she was.

"Every clue I get leads to another clue," Declan said. "I'm starting to wonder if it even exists at all."

Cait's eyes narrowed a touch, a move so slight he wasn't sure he hadn't imagined it until she said, "Oh, it exists. Rest assured."

What did she know? How had they found it? He'd used every resource, every trick, every bit of power he'd acquired and had nothing to show for it. At least nothing that would get him any closer to retrieving it. And here his sister, who never left the port, who ran a blasted pub, had found it.

He couldn't show his eagerness. Even with his sister he had to be smart. She had strong ties to the Rogues. Hell, she was probably leading them by now. Ambition ran through her veins as much as it did his, after all. He should have known she'd never be content behind that counter pouring drinks.

"And what does your…organization…need with this item?"

"That's none of your concern." That icy, detached attitude snapped into place.

"Ah, sister, but it is. It is my concern. Because if I go retrieve it, risking my neck and my ship to do so, I intend to use it for my own purposes. What possible reason would I have to be selfless and hand it over?"

She laughed. Short and quiet, but a laugh nonetheless. He clenched his jaw at the sound, fighting back the childish impulse to yell at her.

"Declan, Declan, Declan. I don't expect you to be selfless. None of us do. You see, it's in your best interest for us to acquire it. And use it."

"To what end?"

"The council's."

"And why would I want the council's demise exactly? They give us safe harbor, a place for my crew to rest, a chance to—"

"A chance to what? Be their slaves? Their grunts? Do you really fancy yourself free?" She raised a brow at him, but her eyes remained clear, questioning, with no sign of the mocking humor he'd become accustomed to with her.

He didn't answer. He had no answer to that.

She sat back in her chair, steepling her fingers under her nose. "And why *do* you seek it exactly?"

"Because I can." He shot her a wink, but she wasn't amused. With another half shrug he added, "And the usual, I suppose. Victory over my adversaries."

"Ah, yes, the pirate lords. They are a bunch of—"

"—cocky assholes." It was his turn to finish her sentences.

"Well, I was going to say handsome rogues, but I suppose that works as well."

She looked at him as if waiting for him to offer the truth, but he wouldn't fall for it.

"You see, brother, we essentially want the same thing. Freedom."

He could have argued over that word, claimed it wasn't what he sought, but her words had awakened the desire he'd been avoiding, the need to loosen the bonds around his wrists and neck, the ones that kept him in service to the ladies of the council.

Was he really going to do this for Cait, for the Rogues? He would at least consider it, especially if it meant taking down the pirate lords.

"So where is it?"

"North. The Black Sound."

His heart tripped over its next beat as he struggled to swallow his dread and keep his face free of any emotion. He should have known it'd be there. Of course it'd be there, the one place no ship could enter.

She let out a small chuckle, as if she could read the hesitation—no, the fear—behind his blank face. "Don't be so nervous, Declan. We wouldn't be sending you unprepared. Or at least, not without information that could help you prepare."

"How—" He didn't have time to finish the question before she was answering it. Another joy of sibling connection.

"Yes, the sirens guard the sound, and yes they like to, well, you know."

Indeed, he knew. Everyone knew.

"There is a way around them, a way to get in undetected." She was smiling now, apparently enjoying the discomfort he felt building.

He leaned back, roughing a hand over his stubbled chin. "The only way to do that would be—"

"—with fae magic." She finished his sentence again, and he bit back his frustration, trying not to let it seep into his next words.

"If you hadn't noticed, all the fae died in the war."

"Not died. Fled. For Larcsporough."

"That still doesn't help me."

"Aye, but not all of them left. Three sisters remained behind."

"Why would they stay? When the rest of their kin left?"

"They've been deceived, lied to, tricked into staying in the area, since the treaty was signed and the council was formed. Free them—convince them to help you—and you'll be able to get past the sirens to the dagger."

"And how do I convince them? I can't merely claim they've been deceived. They'd never believe me."

At this, his sister stood, walked to the desk, and unlocked the top drawer using a key she produced from around her neck. She reached in and held up a letter. "This, Declan, will get them to follow you. A letter from their kin."

It could work. They'd surely trust the fae insignia pushed into the wax seal, trust the words written in their own ancient tongue.

"Where are they?" The whisper of dread that had been building in his chest seeped into his bones before he'd even finished speaking. The only place less desirable than the Black Sound was probably where he now needed to go.

"The council hall."

"Well, shit."

The night had brought nothing but restless hours spent tossing about until Aoife had completely given up, dressed for the day in her favorite outfit, and settled into her reading chair beside the cold fireplace in her room.

That had been four hours ago, and she had only managed to read all of two pages. If that.

The words had long since blurred in front of her. Her fingers no longer felt the book.

All night her mind had spun, thoughts slamming from one side to the other. The pit in her stomach had only deepened, while the fear and dread and guilt had eaten a hole in her chest.

Lani would be exiled. Removed from the council—and from her

life. But when? Would she get a proper farewell? Get a chance to explain what had happened? Her mother had given her no indication as to what actions the council might take.

But she had an idea of how Lani would. And that's what left her insides feeling like the muck that lined the streets of Morshan.

Aoife was an awful sister. A horrible friend. A traitor.

But she couldn't undo it. Couldn't go back in time and fix it and make it right.

Even if she had the power to do that, possessed the magic she'd heard about in history lessons, would it even help? Would it fix anything?

A nervous laugh shook her chest. Magic hadn't made life easier for her ancestors or all the people of the Aisling who'd fought and died in the war. War brought death, whether one had magic or not. War showed no mercy, paid no heed to the powers one wielded.

Any who survived were left to pick up the pieces, to put it all back together, to mourn those lost—like the fae who remained at the council hall, the last of their kind, offered refuge here if they would use their magic to serve rather than harm.

Aoife had seen the fae only once, when, at the age of eight, she'd wandered into an area of the hall forbidden to the heirs. She hated to disobey, but her curiosity had spurred her on to discover what they looked like and how their magic worked.

But she hadn't made it far.

Though she'd marveled at their pointed ears and lithe bodies, the sound of their voices—inviting yet haunting—had sent her running back to her room. She'd never gone back, had told herself there was a good reason those hallways were off limits. She'd meet them again when necessary. And not a moment sooner.

A scream pierced the air, snapping Aoife from where her thoughts had wandered. It was loud enough that for a moment she thought it had come from within her room and not from the hallway beyond her closed door.

She leapt to her feet, letting the book fall to the floor as she rushed into the hallway. She'd never heard such a scream, but she knew whose voice had made it.

Lani.

She forced her posture to remain as straight as she could manage despite the fear settling in her gut. The hallway was empty, but there. Lani's red curls disappeared around the corner. Aoife raced to follow. She had to help.

"Wait!" she cried after them, but her voice didn't sound like her own. In the next corridor she found two women—women who had helped raise Aoife and her sisters from infancy—dragging Lani forward as she flailed between them. She called out again, but they didn't heed. Didn't even pretend to hear her.

Around another corner and down the main stairs Aoife rushed after them, but her feet slipped, and she stumbled, keeping her from shortening the distance.

"What are you doing?" She shouted the question, though she already knew the answer.

They were exiling Lani now. They hadn't planned to tell Aoife. Hadn't planned to give her a chance for one last hug and one final goodbye.

They were at the council hall entrance then, and Aoife stopped at the sight of her mother and aunts standing at the door. She half expected to see the fae there with them, as if this occasion warranted their magical presence. Surely exiling someone required some kind of enchantment or spell to keep them from returning, since the threat of violence was not an option.

No fae stood there though. Only the ladies of the council kept watch, their faces hard and unmoved. Even Fiona, Lani's own mother, showed no emotion as she watched the maids restrain her daughter, now trembling. It was as if she'd already forgotten her daughter existed, had already written her out of her life and her memories.

No words were spoken. The ladies only glared at the young girl before them, the girl who had once been one of their own. The nod from Melina was so slight, Aoife wasn't sure she hadn't imagined it, but the maids were then pulling Lani toward the exit and down the front steps, where a black carriage waited with a single horse at the lead.

Lani's feet dragged against the stones of the stairs, the sound of her scrambling shoes torturing Aoife as she stood there. She couldn't move. She should run to her, pull those hands off her sister's arms and help her, but fear held her in place, and she could only watch.

When they reached the carriage, a maid loosed one hand to reach for the door, and Lani took the opportunity. Twisting away, she caught the other woman off guard and got her arms free as she turned back toward the house with a growl.

Her eyes met Aoife's before she'd even managed to take one step.

Aoife had never seen an emotion such as what now simmered in her sister's eyes. A mix of despair, anger, betrayal, and fear. Yes, it was fear in those seas of green Aoife had grown up with. Before she could think better of it, she was moving toward her sister. But she hadn't made it over the threshold before hands like iron were on her, gripping her arms with such force she almost cried out.

The maids had used Lani's hesitation to regain their control. They pulled her back toward the carriage, the door now open so all they had to do was shove her inside. They didn't seem to even try to be gentle, using all their might to lift her up and in. The door slammed closed.

Lani's eyes appeared at the window between her hands pressed to the glass. The coachman lifted the reins to spur the horse forward, and her sister's gaze burned into hers. Aoife opened her mouth to offer a silent apology, but the carriage was already leaving. And all Aoife could do was stand and watch her sister being driven away from home, disowned, exiled.

Her mother's grip loosened, but Aoife couldn't relax, even when her mother whispered beside her that it was for the best, that Aoife had been right to tell.

But Aoife had noticed two things.

First, Lani hadn't had any belongings with her. No luggage. Though, that could easily be explained as part of the exile and punishment, being sent away with only the clothes on her back.

The second observation wasn't as easily shaken though. Not once had her mother assured her of Lani's safety, never noted that it would be okay, that Lani would be all right.

And somewhere in Aoife's gut, fear began to brew.

Fear for Lani, but also for herself.

Aoife ran as hard and as fast as she could after the carriage. She half expected her mother to send the staff after her. Perhaps she'd be exiled too. It was what she deserved after her betrayal.

But they didn't. They let her go on her fool's errand, her short legs no match for the horse that carried her sister away.

She lost sight of them around a bend. They were likely taking her to the docks, but with the stitch in her side sharpening with each breath, she stopped, doubled over, gasping for air, hating herself for giving her sister up. And now giving up on saving her.

As if she had any chance of convincing them to change their minds. She had no idea what she would have said or done if she'd caught up with them.

Her mind jumped from option to option. She and Lani could have escaped together on a ship. They could have sneaked aboard, gotten word to Adler, met him in Daorna. Aoife would have been a third wheel, but at least she'd be with her sister.

But she'd failed. Failed to keep up. Failed to stop them. Failed to free her.

And now she sat on the black sands of Calypso Cove, where the teal water of the Aisling was so vast it seemed to drown her despite that the tide would likely not reach her toes for another hour. She ignored the sharpness of the rock digging into her back. She'd long lost feeling in her backside, but she didn't care.

For years this had been her place to clear her mind. Here she could let the worries and pressures of life at the council hall get washed away with the sound of the water over the dark shore. The sharp edges of the cliffs rose behind her, as if sheltering her from the world and the life she had come to find respite from.

Respite.

So many people came to these shores to find such rest, a rest made possible by the treaty signed centuries ago between the council and the pirate lords to keep the waters around Cregah safe for everyone—pirates, merchants, and travelers alike. Beyond these shores, all bets were off.

Aoife had heard the stories over the years during her outings in town. Harrowing tales of travelers narrowly outrunning a pirate vessel and escaping into the dock at Morshan, while others hadn't been so lucky, having their hulls emptied before being sunk to the depths, any survivors left to float on the sea in a simple rowboat. And then there were the scuffles among the pirates themselves, which ranged from mere pranks to ruthless encounters designed to take out the competition.

Life on the sea seemed to bring nothing but danger and death. No wonder so many people sought refuge here. But Aoife didn't seek rest in town like everyone else. She had enough people around her all day back at the hall; the maids and servants constantly hovered over her. All the noise. So much noise. All the time.

These were the moments she needed, here in this cove, on these sands, shielded by the cliffs and boulders, where she could just be. Alone. In silence. Where she could sort through her thoughts and calm her worries and concerns.

But her thoughts wouldn't be calmed today, and she cursed the waves for not being able to do what she needed—to wash away the voice inside her that chided and lectured and screamed at her for what she'd done.

She'd betrayed Lani, and the veil of regret wouldn't be lifted, not even in this place of peace and quiet. She swallowed hard, but the guilt remained. It seemed to coat her tongue, line her throat, until it settled into the pit of her stomach, sitting like sour milk, curdling and making her want to retch.

Her eyes glazed over, no longer seeing the beauty of the sea through the tears welling up. She never should have made Lani confide in her on that path, never should have forced the secret out of her. She'd promised to keep quiet, and then she'd been dumb enough to start that conversation with her mother, and now there was no going back.

Would Lani ever forgive her? Would Aoife forgive if the tables had been turned?

Not that she'd ever get the chance to beg for that forgiveness now. At this very moment Lani was probably being shoved onto a boat, forced to leave and never return. The scribes were likely already in the archives removing her name from all council records. She'd soon exist only in memories and thoughts, the only place the council's reach couldn't venture.

Or can it? Aoife trembled at the rogue thought, but she bit it back.

Wiping away her tears, she drew in a deep breath. No. Her mother and her aunts weren't the enemies. They were the protectors of this island and its people, and the peace they kept was worth all the sacrifices required of Aoife and her sisters. This she had to believe and hold onto, for she feared to lose that reality, to lose that truth, would be to lose herself completely.

Would that really be so bad?

She fumed as her mind betrayed her once again. What was that piece of her that kept pulling her away from home, urging her to—what—leave? She couldn't. This was her home and her duty, and now with Lani gone—Lani, who had let her heart get stirred by a handsome face and a sweet smile—Aoife couldn't chase that dream, couldn't follow suit. The council needed her. Her people needed her.

Yet she couldn't deny the pang that hit her. Was this envy? Had she been jealous of Lani for getting a chance at love? She had to admit, even if only to herself, there was a small part of her that silently and secretly wanted what Lani was getting, a life with Adler across the sea. A life like those in their favorite books.

But it was a life she couldn't have.

At least one of them could though.

In her mind she saw Lani at the docks, her red curls being tossed about by the sea breeze as Adler approached, taking her hand as he led her off the ship that had brought her to their new life on Daorna. She could see her sister's smile, the joy in her eyes, the love wrapping around the two of them. Yes, they would be all right. They would thrive.

Aoife had to believe all she envisioned would come true, or the guilt and that last burning stare from her sister might consume her entirely.

Something moved in her periphery, snapping her out of her spiraling thoughts.

She leaned forward, her ear to her shoulder and her eyes squinting. There, gliding through the water toward the beach, something—someone—swam toward her.

Her heart gave a start, and her limbs tensed from the inexplicable panic that struck. There was nothing to fear on this island, thanks to the council. Yet she couldn't bite back the prickling unease at the sight of someone coming from the sea—and without a boat, no less.

Using the path, though it was overgrown and difficult to find, would have made more sense. But during the past ten years she'd never heard of anyone coming here, had never seen another soul. Especially not one swimming in these forbidden waters, where recreation had been outlawed since long before Aoife's time. Everyone knew the stories of the poor souls who'd been caught in the riptide in this cove, carried out to sea, and never heard from again.

Yet this figure swam with seemingly little effort, comfortable and at home in the water.

Then the person stood with ease as the foaming edge of the tide swirled around his calves.

Aoife's mouth fell open. Indeed. It was a man.

She blinked and shifted her head to the other side as she peered at him.

Men were not a frequent sighting at the council hall. While the pirate lords and their crews visited monthly, villagers only made an appearance at the harvest offering once per year. Occasionally they came to report a grievance, but even then these reports were rarely handled by men.

This man looked like no villager, but neither did he look like any pirate she'd ever seen. His dark hair, cut close around his ears, lengthened gradually toward the top of his head, where it ended in a wave that fell into his eyes. His gaze remained cast down at his feet, and he hadn't yet noticed her sitting against the boulder.

His trousers were made of a simple linen, dyed a dark color that nearly matched the black of the sand now clinging to the hems and to his boots, and contrasted starkly with the white of his shirt, which no longer hung loose as intended but hugged his body, the light fabric curving around the sharp edges of muscles she could never have imagined on a human form. Her hand fell to her own stomach as she wondered if she, too, might have cords of muscles hiding somewhere beneath the softness.

At his waist a dark teal sash hung.

So he was a pirate, yes, but no lord's ship bore those colors.

His chin lifted and turned as he took in his surroundings. Even from twenty feet away Aoife could see a seriousness in his expression that felt…familiar. Almost like an echoing of the emotions she'd been wrestling with all morning. What had happened out there? Had he narrowly escaped the current? What had caused that pain in his eyes?

She waited, holding her breath, as if she weren't conspicuously perched in the center of the cove and could simply hide by not breathing.

With deliberate care he turned his head, his gaze passing over her, past her, before pulling back when he realized more than rocks and sand lay before him. His expression softened, eyes alight with the same curiosity she felt within herself, and his lips abandoned their previous remorseful look for a mischievous smirk.

He took a step forward. Then another.

And then he spoke.

"G'morning, Miss…" He lingered on the word, inviting her to finish his sentence by offering her name.

Her mind wobbled, darting around in search of her own voice, which remained elusive, not from nerves or fear, but from confusion mixed with a familiar flutter of curiosity. At the council hall the men never spoke to her, and she never spoke to them. There'd been no need. On her trips to the villages, she always dealt with the women who owned the shops and eateries, only ever nodding and offering a polite smile to the men she encountered.

Raising his brow and nudging his chin further, he pushed her to answer.

"Aoife Cascade," she said. This couldn't be proper. What was she thinking? She brushed her hands against the folds of her skirts to wipe away the clammy sweat that had begun pooling in her palms.

What would Mother say if she found out Aoife had given her name to a man? And a pirate, at that. There were rules about this. The ladies of the council were only to engage with the pirate lords they were matched with, never with the crew. And here she was, not only talking to a crew member, but giving him her name. She had obviously lost her mind.

"Ah, so you do have a name." The smirk transformed into a smile, kind but with a hint of laughter, like he was telling himself a silent joke. She liked it, though she shouldn't.

"I do indeed. What kind of person doesn't have a name?" She jutted her chin up at him. He seemed so tall, but then again, she was still sitting in the sand. The rock seemed to dig more pointedly into her back, as if chiding her for being such an idiot.

"Fair point, miss."

She waited, expecting him to offer his own name in return, but he didn't. He simply eyed her, that obnoxious smile remaining.

"And are you the kind of person without one?" she asked, then clarified for his possibly simple mind. "Without a name, that is."

He laughed in return, a pleasant sound, hearty and full, not at all similar to the tinkling bell-like laughs she'd heard all her life. "I am the kind of person—" He paused to clear his throat or to stall long enough to devise a cover.

Like you should have done.

"—who doesn't give his name to just any stranger he meets."

She huffed. "That isn't exactly polite, is it?"

"Who said I was one for politeness?"

She studied him, her gaze trailing across his face, wishing she hadn't given her real name to this stranger. When his eyes fell, resting lower than her face, she opened her mouth to chide him but then realized her arms were bare, visible. She flashed a hand up to pull the length of her sleeves down, covering the designs etched onto her forearms. She kept her face down as her cheeks warmed with embarrassment, kicking herself for feeling any shame about her status.

He moved toward her, each step sending a twinge of dread through her bones. Here she was, a council heir, alone and unprotected in a secret, long-forgotten cove. He could do whatever he wanted to her, and no one would know. No one would find her body or hear her screams over the surf. The commanded peace on these shores seemed distant and inconsequential in these moments as she listened to his feet in the sand.

She held her breath and waited. With eyes clenched tight she imagined the hands that would soon grab her.

But no hands came.

Instead she heard a thud and a sigh as he settled onto the ground beside another boulder nearby. She stole a glance at him, keeping her head lowered.

The stranger ran his hands through his hair, shaking out the last of the seawater, before running them along his neck, his head turning and rolling to stretch out any kinks. With a steady exhale he settled back against the rock, his face turned toward the sea, the muscles in his jaw tensing before settling into a content expression.

Had he recognized the markings on her arm? Everyone on the island should know. Would know. So why didn't he note it? Why did he ignore it?

She could demand his reverence, insist he show her the proper respect her station deserved, but her bones became heavy as she remembered why she'd sought refuge here today. She tried to relax, but her nerves were frayed, cut through with worry and guilt over Lani. She envied this stranger's ease. He seemed as calm and gentle as the sea that swept toward them and then away. Back and forth.

Just like her heart. Back and forth between whether she'd made the right decision or a dire mistake.

"So…" The word cut through the sound of the receding waves.

"Yes?" She tried to sound confident, regal, but her voice cracked under the stress.

"What's a council heir doing here on this beach?" He didn't look at her, but kept staring out at the sea before them.

So he had recognized the mark. She hated lying to anyone, even to a stranger. It didn't sit well with her heart, and perhaps that was why she'd broken so easily under Mother's questions. But this wasn't her mother. She owed no loyalty to this pirate.

Before she could answer, he gave a short laugh. "That hard to come up with a cover? You really should have those planned ahead of time. You know, just in case."

"I don't need a cover. I'm not doing anything wrong." He spoke with such audacity. She'd never heard a man speak to a council member in that way before, as if he were an equal or even superior.

"Of course not, Miss Cascade." He bowed his chin in reverence, but she detected a hint of mockery. "I was merely making a joke."

"Oh, yes, of course." She cringed at how ridiculous she sounded, stumbling over her words. This wasn't how an heir should act.

"You do know what a joke is, yes? Or has the council outlawed humor as well?"

Now he'd certainly gone too far. What nerve he showed! Straightening and turning away from the boulder, she mustered up every bit of regal decorum she had been taught and faced him.

"Excuse me?"

He held up his hands, palms toward her in retreat. "No harm meant. Merely another joke." And with a chuckle he settled his gaze back on the water, that dreadful smirk once again plastered on his face.

She had no retort though. Her mind went completely blank aside from a desire to stick her tongue out at him as she often did with her sisters. That would certainly not be regal in the slightest. Here this man had the nerve to disrespect her, and she couldn't come up with any words to put him rightly in his place. What would Mother have said to him? What harshness would she have laid out to correct him? How many times had Aoife received her mother's stern reprimands when she'd screwed up?

For a long moment they sat in silence, both staring out at the waters. She wondered if she could simply get up and leave him sitting there alone. Or would that be as rude as his so-called jokes? She couldn't repay rudeness with rudeness. That was uncouth and not becoming of a council lady.

"Do you swim these waters often?" It was a stupid question, she knew, but she couldn't handle the silence any longer.

"Oh, have you deemed me worthy of conversation?" That damn attitude again. She cringed at the names she wanted to call him. Definitely not ladylike.

"I wouldn't say worthy, but you're the only one here."

"So you do have a sense of humor." That smile flashed again, and she wanted to smack it off of him.

"You're exhausting, you know that?"

"I've been told that. Last night actually. But that young lady seemed much more pleased by that fact."

"You're disgusting."

"Hey"—he raised his palms again—"you're the one ruling over a land that aims to please everyone, including men of the sea. And we have needs."

"So I've heard." She had indeed heard of those particular establishments that were placed inconspicuously around town. Though she'd heard they were more for the pleasure of the village women and not truly for the pirates and merchant sailors.

"You can leave if you want to. I have no need of you or your company. I'm sure the council is wondering where you've wandered off to." His voice no longer held that tinge of humor, the former amusement replaced now with annoyance and frustration.

She crossed her arms over her chest and shoved herself back against the boulder, ignoring the sharp pain that resulted from hitting that stupid edge she'd forgotten about. "I leave when I want to, and I am not quite done enjoying the view."

"I am pretty nice to look at, it's true." He said it matter-of-factly, and each word poked at her further, like a thorn in her side being twisted.

"I was here first anyway. Perhaps you should find a different spot to relax in."

"Fight me for it?"

"What? No! Never."

"Oh, right. Land of peace and tranquility." His tone was so mocking she couldn't ignore it, and the need to defend her home and her mother and the council bubbled up and out before she could stop it.

"Yes! This is a land of peace. No fighting. No violence. We value peace above all else."

"And would you fight for that peace?" He raised his brow, his face showing no sign of this being another of his asinine jokes.

"Don't be ridiculous."

"I'm not. Sometimes peace must be fought for. Ask the king of Caprothe. He certainly fought for the peace you now enjoy."

"I'll be sure to do that the next time I see him." Not that that was possible. The Caprothen king who had fought for and signed that peace treaty was long since dead.

"Funny that you speak of peace, Miss Cascade, when your council—"

"When my council what? Keeps order? Provides rest to everyone who comes here, including your kind?"

"My kind." His eyes narrowed as he clenched his jaw. She'd struck a nerve. Good.

"Yes, pirate. Does your captain know you've wandered off?" She was pushing him now, goading him, and it felt good.

"Aye. He does. But I should be getting back. To *my kind* and all."

Aoife didn't offer a response but glanced toward the path behind them that led between the cliffs. He rose and, not bothering to brush the sand off his pants, turned to leave, his eyes blazing as he met her gaze.

The look from him snapped something inside her, pulling her back to why she'd come here in the first place. Forcing herself not to watch him as he walked away, she pushed her gaze back out to the encroaching tide. She shouldn't have let him get to her, shouldn't have stooped to his level. She'd insulted him, and though she shouldn't feel bad for it—not after he'd attacked the council and all they stood for—she did all the same.

She didn't want to think of him anymore, but every time she pushed him from her mind, Lani's face surfaced, haunting her.

Would she ever stop screwing up? Would she ever find the grace she was supposed to embody as a councilwoman? Or would she forever be stumbling over herself, hurting people, insulting them? If only she could go back in time, change everything she'd done, keep her mouth shut... both at the council hall and here on this beach.

Aoife stepped through the trees, carefully watching the path before her so as not to trip over the roots and stones that made it nearly invisible. A shiver of an inkling crept over her chest, a feeling that eyes were upon her. She ignored it, summoning whatever shred of bravery and pride she had remaining after putting that pirate in his place.

Had she hurt him? Impossible.

And even if she had, why should she care? She was an heir to the council, soon to be made a full lady. He couldn't do anything to her, and he'd be stupid if he even thought to. She had the power. He didn't. This island was theirs.

As she stepped over branch after branch, she kept her steps as light as possible—staying quiet from what, she didn't know—except she did know.

If the pirate had lingered, she didn't need him coming back to stop her. She didn't trust what he might want from her when there were no witnesses. She'd learned about the true nature of men in her courses; they only wanted power, riches, and flesh, no matter what they had to do to get it. Even if Lani had found one good man among them, he was the anomaly, the exception.

And Aoife had been stupid to talk to that pirate, to tell him her name. Her mother might slap her if she knew she'd done that. Sands, she should slap herself.

It wasn't that she couldn't talk to men, but she should have paid more attention to the prickles on her skin warning her he was dangerous, different than the men she encountered in the villages and at the markets. He had a drive. A mission. Something nagging at his heart and brewing in his mind. She'd seen the same tension in her mother, that same lost stare of worry mixed with dread and determination.

She shook her head.

Not her problem.

She had no use for a pirate.

She had bigger problems back home.

And just like that, the image of Lani's face—twisted with anger and pain and betrayal—slammed back to the forefront of her mind. The regret and guilt rent her heart once again.

At least that pirate had provided a bit of a distraction.

And now she had to face that guilt head-on as she made the long walk back. She welcomed it though, open arms wrapping around it, cradling it like a baby she didn't want but needed to nurse nonetheless. She owed Lani that much, forcing herself to feel this pain.

For the whole trek along the same path she and Lani had strolled down yesterday—had it really only been yesterday?—she stroked the guilt in her heart, letting the tears fall freely when she no longer felt the phantom eyes on her back and was sure no one was watching.

But she wiped them away and took a cleansing breath to force clarity into her eyes well before nearing the council hall gate.

Her mother might understand the tears, if her reaction last night was any indication. But that coldness of her stare this morning when they'd sent Lani away…

Now Aoife wasn't sure what to think.

As she walked through the front door, she kept her gaze forward and chin lifted. The staff bustled around as usual, as if nothing had changed that morning with Lani's departure, as if she really had been erased from their lives. There was no sign of the emotional departure that had taken place.

She'd nearly made it back to her room when her stomach rumbled in protest, a painful reminder of the meals she'd missed. Still too many hours until dinner. Maybe she could scrounge up a snack from the kitchen or pantry.

Without another thought, she let her feet carry her away from the quarters down to the servants' area, her eyes not noticing any of the cold stone walls as she walked, her ears not registering anything save her slow steps.

Until she neared the kitchen and the sound of hushed yet excited voices forced her to focus.

As a council heir she could have simply walked in, but something within her—something she couldn't quite name—had her pushing her back against the wall and angling her head toward the door to listen.

The coldness of the stones permeated her tunic, but she ignored it as she strained to hear their words, not sure what she hoped they'd be discussing. Maybe she wanted some reassurance that Lani wasn't completely forgotten, that these people—the people who had raised them and fed them and cared for them—wouldn't cast her sister aside so easily.

"My hands are so tired," one voice uttered.

"Tell me about it. So much bread to knead and bake," another voice said.

Aoife didn't recognize them, but then she'd never been great at placing names to faces and voices. It was one of many areas of frustration for her mother, who had spent the last two years impressing it upon Aoife that she must remedy this if she was ever going to be an effective leader. If she were ever to serve their people well, she'd need to be able to remember them—their names, their families, their circumstances.

"You'd think with one less mouth to feed we'd get a bit of a reprieve."

"And with that coming-of-age ceremony being canceled."

A scoff and a sigh sounded before the response.

"Yes, but now they're insisting on making Miss Cascade's ceremony even bigger. Grander."

"As if that could cover up the fact that they've lost an heir?"

"They're going to have a hell of a time covering this up with the people. People talk."

"Not if they're smart."

"True. But how many of them are really that smart? They're as dumb as that brat."

The word, spat with such disdain, struck Aoife in the gut. They had to be talking about Lani.

"Can you believe she actually ran after them?"

Her breath hitched. Not Lani. Her. They were talking about *her.*

"They should have dealt with both of them, to be honest."

"Definitely. Do we really want someone like her on the council? Someone who holds more loyalty to her sister than to the people?"

"Even that's questionable. She's the one who turned the girl in!"

Aoife squeezed her eyes shut. Their words shouldn't sting, and yet they did. She should turn, leave. She already had enough guilt pressing down on her. She didn't need to listen, but her feet wouldn't budge.

"Not even on purpose though. And certainly she had to know what would happen."

"Not too bright, is she?"

"Naive, perhaps. I mean, even the younger one has figured it out."

Aoife's eyes scanned the hallway without seeing anything. Darienn knew. But knew what? What had Aoife not figured out? What in the sands were these women talking about?

"Yes, but what were they to do? They're now short one heir. They can't be short two. Can they?"

"Did you hear who they had take care of it?"

"A young pirate, I heard."

"And a handsome one at that."

"Most of them are, aren't they?"

"I certainly wouldn't complain if I had to die by his hand. Those eyes being the last I saw before it went black?"

"Aye, she could have chosen a worse way to die."

All the oxygen got sucked out of the room with that single word.

Die.

They'd both said it.

The carriage hadn't taken Lani to the docks. She wouldn't be sent off to meet Adler.

Aoife's knees started to give, all her strength seeping from her bones down into the floor. But she couldn't collapse here. She needed to move before they found her.

The laughter and chatter continued, but she didn't hear another word.

And her limbs didn't listen to her desperate urging to get going.

Die.

Dead.

Lani hadn't been exiled. She hadn't been safe.

Everything began to spin, and when her feet finally moved to carry her back to her room—all thoughts of food now forgotten—it was a marvel she remained upright.

Everything she knew. Everything she believed. Everyone she trusted.

Was it all a lie?

Could she trust the gossip of a few servants?

Her chest caved under the weight of her confusion.

She clicked the door to her room shut behind her and froze. Nothing made sense. None of it.

Peace. This was a land of peace. No weapons. No violence.

But a nagging curiosity began to gnaw in her chest.

This would explain the stark fear she'd seen on Lani's face—not the sadness from merely having to say goodbye to her sister and home, but outright terror. It was that look that had pushed Aoife's feet down the council hall driveway after the carriage without a second thought.

Had Lani known what the cost would be? Is that why she'd planned to sneak away? Was Aoife truly that naive and trusting to not know what the council was capable of?

Her room was spinning as badly as the hallway had, and she couldn't find any firm footing for her mind to settle on.

She moved to sit down on the bed, hoping it would help, but before she even made it a half step, a knock came at the door, and she jumped.

"Yes?" Her voice sounded and felt distant, as if it came from someone else.

The door opened, and a head peeked around the edge. Darienn's blue eyes stared at her with curiosity and concern.

"Aoife?" She sounded as timid as the mice that skittered around the gardens outside, younger than her seventeen years.

Aoife gritted her teeth, fighting back the annoyance that always began to simmer whenever Darienn spoke. Or breathed. Why had it been Lani who wanted to run away? Why couldn't it have been this sister who fell in love and wanted to run off with some man?

But looking at Darienn and seeing fear in her eyes, Aoife bit back the sharpness that had been ready to pop out.

"Come on in, Dare." She hoped the words sounded inviting enough, and she motioned with a hand for her sister to join her on the edge of the bed.

Darienn entered, albeit timidly, as if unsure Aoife truly meant the invitation. She kept her head down as she sat beside her sister. Her hands worked the folds in her skirt, as though a slew of thoughts and questions were fighting to be voiced.

For a moment Aoife forgot how much younger Darienn was than she and Lani. A full three years separated them, yet Darienn had physically matured far more quickly than Aoife had, her curves already generously feminine compared to Aoife's modest frame.

Not exactly the time or place to be worried about such things, don't you think?

She shooed the thought away, instead moving to look her sister in the eye.

"What's bothering you, Darienn?" She cringed at the stupidity of the question.

"When you disappeared right after Lani..." Darienn's breath hitched with a suppressed sob. "I worried you'd both left me. Alone."

Another punch of guilt hit her as the tears spilled over and glided down her sister's cheek. All those times she and Lani had excluded Darienn from their sisterly outings and chats; she'd always assumed Darienn had resented them, but now it seemed to be the opposite.

She tried to smile and make a joke, maybe help lighten the mood a little. "Without us, though, you could have all three pirate lords to yourself in a few years."

"I don't want three pirate lords."

"Certainly three is better than one. Three times the man to please you and dote on you and keep you company."

"One is enough for that. And they're not the same as sisters."

"We are better looking in a dress, I suppose."

"You smell better too." Darienn snorted at her own joke, and Aoife couldn't help but let out a small chuckle.

Silence settled between them, but at least Darienn's tears had dried.

But something was still nagging at her sister. Aoife could see it in the little fidgets and twitches in Darienn's fingers and legs as she sat.

"What else is bothering you, Darienn?"

"Do you think they really let her leave?"

Aoife froze. She didn't even know if she was breathing as she chewed on the question, felt it swirl around with the words the servants had spoken earlier. They'd said Darienn knew. Was her sister playing dumb now? If she didn't know, Aoife didn't plan to be the one to spill another secret unnecessarily.

"Of course I do. Mother wouldn't lie. Why—"

"I heard the ladies talking after she was sent away."

"You can't trust the gossip of the servants, Darienn." This she said as much to herself as she did to her sister, hoping to the sands it was true.

Darienn fidgeted more, her eyes skittering over her lap and her feet and the floor, refusing to meet Aoife's gaze.

"Not the servants. Our mothers."

Aoife froze and forced a dry swallow down before she asked, "What did you hear them saying?"

"It made no sense. I couldn't put it together."

"What did they say?" She struggled to keep the impatience out of her tone.

"Something about the pirate they'd commissioned for the job."

"That could have been about anything. You know the pirates help with—"

"They said her name, Aoife! There was no way they were talking about anything but our sister. Doesn't it worry you at all?" Now Darienn's eyes rose to meet hers. A fire within them had burned away all the tears. "Or were you hoping for more than one lord for yourself?"

"Get out." The words came out with a snarl, low, guttural, menacing.

But Darienn didn't rise. Tension, resolve, settled into her previously timid bones. She was going to push, hard.

"Is that why you ratted her out, Aoife? You wanted her out of the way? Wanted her—"

"How dare you! The last thing I wanted was for her to leave me here with you." Although Aoife meant it, she still regretted her outburst. She didn't like being nasty, and even hated that she disliked this sister so much. She wanted to be kind and nice and loving, but Darienn was like that obnoxious rock in her shoe that could never be removed no matter how much she shook.

But Darienn appeared unfazed by her words. She'd expected them, perhaps, after all these years of being ignored and brushed aside.

"Then why?"

"I don't know." She could have denied that she'd ratted Lani out, but that was what had happened, regardless of her intention. Intentions meant little.

"I think you do, Aoife." Her sister's voice was now gentle, no hint of the earlier accusations. "You're not vindictive or mean. Even when you are to me, I know you don't like to be. I can see the guilt and regret in you. Like a warm blanket you're keeping wrapped around your shoulders, as if it's a comfort to let you know you're not as cold as the words you utter."

She had no words for her sister now. Her sister who had perceived so much. And so accurately.

"Aoife. I don't think you meant to tell Melina."

"Wait. What do you know about Lani's plans? Did she talk to you?"

"Not willingly. I told you people don't notice me. I saw her go into your room with a set of clothes, men's clothes it looked like. When she came out again, her arms were empty. I stopped her. Asked her what they were."

"And she told you?"

"It wasn't easy to get it out of her. You know how secretive she is. Though that didn't make her good at sneaking about." It might have been funny had Lani not been carted off that morning.

"What did she tell you?" Aoife wasn't going to risk spilling more secrets if Darienn didn't know them.

"She had stashed the clothes in your room with plans to don them before leaving to meet Adler."

"But why my room? Why not keep them in hers?" The questions were more for herself. She didn't expect Lani had provided any explanation to their sister.

"She'd raised suspicions. At least she thought she had. She couldn't risk having them in her room. She was afraid they knew she was planning something."

"They who?"

"Our mothers, as if they deserve such titles." Darienn now spoke with air of maturity Aoife had never heard from her before. What had happened to the young girl who believed in the court and the ladies and the mission of Cregah so wholeheartedly?

"What do you mean?" The doubt sparked again before she could douse it.

"How can you be so naive? You're older than me. You've seen more than me. Or have you been willingly remaining blind?"

"What are you talking about, Darienn?"

"The disappearances."

"Exiles."

"Call them whatever you want. They happen."

"For a reason." Even as she said the words, the doubt kept poking at her insides.

Darienn only shook her head.

"Wait, Darienn, did our mothers catch you listening? Do they know you heard?"

Darienn toed the floor a bit, not in a timid fashion, but more like she was trying to find the right words to answer. "They don't know what I heard, I don't think. But I knocked on the door then."

"Why? You know interrupting them never goes over well."

"They didn't seem to mind. I had every intention of confronting them, actually. Asking them what they had meant, what they had hired the pirate to do to our sister. But standing before them, I clammed up. Couldn't ask. So I told them I was worried about you."

Aoife blinked, trying to figure out what Melina might have thought of such a claim. "And?"

"She told me this would help." And with that, Darienn pulled something from the pocket of her dress.

A silver chain with a glass vial. It dangled between them as Aoife stared at it and at the black sand it held.

She didn't reach for it, but she couldn't pull her gaze from it as she asked, "What…"

"Your mother said Lani wanted you to have this before she left."

Aoife squeezed her eyes shut. She would not cry in front of Darienn, wouldn't let Darienn see her tremble with the fear that erupted within her.

If she'd doubted what the servants had said or what Darienn had claimed to overhear, all uncertainty vanished now. They'd killed her.

And Darienn knew. Didn't she?

Darienn had suspected the exiles were a ruse, that people were being killed. But what was she going to do about it? Lani must have also figured it out and had chosen to escape. Would Darienn do the same?

Aoife reached for the necklace and gripped it tightly in her fist. "What will you do, Darienn?"

"I think the bigger question is, what will you do?"

"What do you mean?"

"That stunt you pulled today, running after Lani as you did. It didn't go unnoticed."

Her panic now burned bright. Would she be next? Would she be the one thrown into a carriage and dealt with by some pirate?

"But no. I'm loyal to the council, to peace!"

Darienn angled toward her sister, placing a hand on Aoife's knee. "It's your word against your actions though."

Aoife searched Darienn's eyes for any sign of malice or mischief, something to tell her whether this little sister, the sister she and Lani had ignored for her whole life, could be trusted. But after so many years of avoiding her, it was impossible to read her expression.

"I could stay. Prove myself."

"But could you stomach ordering exiles as needed? Calling for the deaths of your people in order to keep the peace?"

None of this made any sense. The room began to whirl again. Her sister had to be crazy. But the staff. The necklace. The necklace her sister *never* would have parted with.

No. She couldn't have any part of that. But what were the options?

She'd nearly forgotten Darienn was still with her until the girl stood and spoke again. "You have the clothes she left behind. If it were me? I'd see those as a gift. Take them. Use them to run. Get the freedom our sister almost found."

Aoife looked up again, the threat of tears stinging her eyes. "Is this your way of getting all the pirate lords to yourself?"

She repeated her earlier joke, but Darienn's expression shifted into something Aoife couldn't quite place. "We all must make sacrifices, sister. Mine is to stay behind."

Before Aoife could ask any more questions, Darienn had turned and was out the door, leaving her alone with her thoughts. And a choice.

The girl had certainly caught Declan by surprise at the cove. And gotten under his skin in the process.

That look of disdain she'd given, dripping with thick condescension, still irked him. He shouldn't have let it get to him, but something about the way she talked down to him kept him from brushing it aside. It had been years since anyone had dared speak to him in such a tone. Among the pirates there was an air of respect, even as they fought and battled for power, influence, and goods.

She'd had none for him. And it stung. More than it should have. But he shouldn't have expected anything else from a council heir, especially given his status as a lesser pirate captain and not a lord.

He huffed as he kicked a stone out of his way. He'd needed that time to think at the cove, to gather his thoughts before he discussed plans with Gavin and Tommy. And now here he was, trudging back to the village and the pub with his mind still a jumbled mess. The walk back would have to suffice.

He had intended to return to the ship immediately following his meeting with Cait, but it had been impossible to turn down her invitation to rest and sleep in her cozy hole of a room. His body had melted with appreciation onto that sofa. Not that it was any more comfortable than the feather mattress he had back on the ship, but the simple act of relaxing—as much as he could expect to on this island—had been welcomed by his stressed and aching muscles.

Cait had let him sleep longer than he'd intended, waking him in late morning with the smell of bacon and eggs on toast. He'd scarfed down the food with a quick word of thanks, not bothering to ask her where she'd cooked it when this *home* had no kitchen. Not that it mattered anyway. It was hot food. A taste of home.

Home. The word plagued him as he ate, but he managed to shove it aside as he stood to leave. Before he could step out into the hallway, she'd stopped him and uttered two words to him.

Not a farewell or a thank you. A deadline.

Thirty days.

What happened in thirty days, he wasn't sure, and he hadn't bothered to ask, knowing she wouldn't explain why the Rogues needed the dagger on such short notice. He'd left his sister and her hideaway, hoping to make it back to the ship before the council found him to collect the debt he owed for docking his ship in the port.

But he hadn't made it.

Not that he'd expected to, despite all his hope to the contrary.

He had known the port guards would have reported his ship's failure to pay the fees, and they'd track him down one way or another. Such was life in Morshan. At least for the pirates. It was enough to keep him from sailing into this port year after year. Even if he hadn't been plagued by the memories of his childhood here, he would have made the same call to avoid these shores.

And he had for seven years.

So he hadn't resisted when they caught up with him at the docks, even as his ship—and his solace—had been in view. He hadn't bothered to apologize for not paying the fee, hadn't tried to draw his concealed blade. He'd simply gone with them and done as directed.

If he'd known how much of his life as a pirate would consist of taking orders from people, he might have opted to stay home all those years ago.

Or not so much.

A huff of a laugh escaped at that thought. No way would he have stayed behind with Cait to run the pub, to be a lesser citizen as all men were on Cregah. Even if he wasn't completely free on these shores as a pirate, even if he found conflict out on the sea, at least out there he was in charge of his life and his ship, was more than a tool to be wielded.

Isn't that what you are anyway though?

No. He could choose not to bring the dagger back to his sister. He could do what he pleased. He could make his own decisions, take the dagger for himself, flee to other seas and lands beyond this wretched place.

The sounds of Morshan crept toward him as he neared the town. He needed a plan. If he were going to infiltrate the council and beg some ancient fae to help him, he'd need his head clear. But every attempt he made to focus his thoughts on the matter at hand got derailed by visions of that stupid girl—that heir—moping about in his cove.

He suppressed the growl he wanted to unleash. He should have taken the path to that forgotten beach, should have traipsed through the trees and undergrowth instead of swimming in. Had he done the smart thing, he could have noticed her sitting there before she spotted him, could have avoided being seen. Could have avoided her incessant blathering.

How had she even known about that spot? He'd assumed everyone had forgotten of its existence after the little girl had drowned all those years ago and its waters had been banned for the safety of the people.

But he'd chosen to swim to the beach instead, not because he liked to taunt death—though that was perhaps akin to his profession—but because he had needed that dive off the high cliffs into the deep teal waters. Needed the swim and the challenge to clear his mind from all he'd done and all he would yet need to do.

He knew it was risky, with the current being as strong as it was around that cove, but in the end he'd been unable to resist the call of the water, the inner pull it had on his bones, like a beacon urging him to return home.

Home.

His home—the one he'd once had above the pub—was now no more than a shell, a front, a facade to keep the council unawares.

His sister was smart; he had to give her that. But how exactly did she think he could sneak inside the council hall? He'd need help, but who could help him? The pirates rarely worked together, and when they did it was usually only the lesser captains. There'd be no hope of getting a lord to aid him. His crew was exhausted. They were short on supplies, even with what little they could trade here in Cregah.

They'd managed to keep from being breached, sunk, or pillaged, but his enemies had won all the same, even if not physically. They knew he was defeated. He bit back the anger and fisted his hands at his sides. It wasn't about revenge. He didn't want to destroy them. He simply wanted to be free of them.

And now Cait had given him a way to achieve that freedom.

An impossible way, but a way nonetheless.

Again his mind turned to the heir. Aoife. She'd be heading home soon to the council hall. He stole a glance behind him, half expecting to see her trudging up the path, but it was empty and silent. He could have pressed her for information, and in fact, that had been his plan after he'd noticed the tattoos betraying her status. But her tongue had stayed him, put him firmly in his place, and his bitterness and stung pride had kept him from seeking out the knowledge she possessed.

She could still be his way in, perhaps, but not without proper planning. With a job this big he needed to avoid rash decisions and take his time. Some time at least. As the Black Sound was a good ten-days' journey—with an abiding wind and no storms or confrontations—he'd need most of the thirty days simply to make the trip there and back.

He bit back a curse as he cleared the last of the trees and ventured into town. He needed a drink to calm his nerves before his men arrived to plan.

11
Aoife

Darienn's words echoed in the quiet room long after she'd left. Aoife didn't know how long she'd remained sitting there on the bed, staring at nothing, seeing nothing. Only hearing those words.

What will you do?

Could you stomach calling for deaths?

No.

She couldn't. Couldn't stay. But the thought of leaving everything behind scared her almost as much as staying and having to do the unthinkable.

It's not like you'd be killing them with your own hand though.

She shook the thought away, but it was quickly replaced with an image of Lani's terrified expression. No. Her hand or not, she could not be the cause of such terror.

But if she stayed, maybe she could stop the killings. Maybe she could call for change and make them see it was wrong.

A laugh echoed in her head.

What could she do really? She'd ratted out her sister by accident. She never did anything but stumble over her words and screw everything up. More than likely, her mistakes would hurt people more than her successes would help them. Her people were better off without her. Maybe if she left she could find someone who had the ability to truly help them. Rescue them.

Rescue.

Such an odd word. Her thoughts drifted back to all the times she'd gone to Morshan, searching the faces in her memories for any sign they needed rescuing. Even if she couldn't remember names, she could see faces clearly. How many of the people she'd met had later been exiled? Surely not that many, but did she even know the real numbers? If the council had lied about what "exile" truly meant, perhaps they had also hidden how many they called for.

Still, the people in her memories seemed happy enough. Perhaps they would be fine.

But what about outside of Morshan? How do the other people fare?

She didn't know. She'd never given them much thought. The guilt twisted her stomach tighter. What kind of ruler would she be if she hadn't even thought of the people beyond those she'd met personally?

Running felt wrong.

But staying and failing her people felt worse.

She needed to leave. It was better for everyone if she did.

A gift. That's what Darienn had said, right? She had the clothes Lani had left behind.

Aoife stood and spun around the room, her eyes searching for something that looked out of place. But everything was right where she'd left it. The books on the desk. The clothes on the bed. The half-drunk cup of tea, now cold, on the end table. The pile of blankets on her reading chair. The chest by the wall.

She stopped.

The chest had been latched closed. She always put the latch down, an open latch being a silly pet peeve of hers, like a cabinet left open or a drawer not pushed all the way in.

She rushed to the chest, slipping Lani's necklace over her head before lifting the lid. Nothing was out of place, but certainly Lani wouldn't have placed them on top for anyone to easily discover. Her hands dug through the contents, pushing aside blankets and cloaks and papers and letters until they brushed against a fabric foreign and new to her.

Coarse. Rough.

Not at all like the linen and silk and velvet she was used to.

Her fingers gripped the fabric and pulled it out. Pants. Shirt. Vest. Jacket. Boots. And a small brown hat. So much more complicated than the simple dresses she usually wore in the council hall. Would she even know how to put the unfamiliar items on?

I'm not as stupid as they all think I am. How hard can it be?

It took her longer than she would ever admit to anyone to put on the new clothes. The feel of pants against her legs felt constrictive yet oddly freeing. She'd be able to move more quickly and quietly in these than she would in the skirts she normally wore.

After lacing up the boots, she let a word of thanks echo in her mind that she and Lani were so close in size. At least in the shoes. While the clothes were in the masculine fashion, they were notably cut for a woman's figure, intended to gently hug the curves while simultaneously hiding them. Though Aoife's curves, or lack thereof, were more swallowed than hugged by the garments, they were effectively hidden, and that was all that mattered.

When Aoife stood, her hair fell over her chest and caught on one of the buttons. She had to do something about her locks. The clothes helped, but her hair would be a dead giveaway. Even with pins there'd be no way she could hide all of it under the hat Lani had stashed.

She ran to the desk, ripped the drawer open, and found the old pair of scissors. Not as sharp as they once had been, but they would do. It wasn't like she had a knife. A knife would have come in handy for the journey she was about to take, but she doubted anyone sold knives on the island. And she couldn't risk a stop in the kitchens to snag one.

Taking an old cloak from the chest, she spread it across the bed. Without bothering to check the mirror, she held out large sections of hair and cut, careful not to let any fall to the floor, but dropping them onto the cloak instead. She couldn't simply toss the hair into the waste bin where someone would certainly spot it and report her.

A nervous chuckle escaped at the thought of what words they'd utter. *Miss Aoife has cut off all her hair.* As if they would punish her for a haircut. But her stomach tangled again with the understanding of what these people, her people, were capable of.

After chopping her hair to chin length—similar to how the younger, newer pirates wore theirs—she wrapped the clippings up in the cloak, which she then placed back into the chest, and stashed the scissors back in the desk. She ran her hands through her hair before slapping the hat on her head. Only then did she allow herself a glance in the mirror, pleased when she saw how little she resembled the heir she'd been before, even with the clearly feminine softness of her face.

Her eyes fell to the vial of black sand that dangled against her chest, and she carefully tucked it under her shirt. Drawing in a deep breath, she turned for the door, and without another look around the room, she walked out.

She kept to the shadows in the hallway—not hard to do given the utter lack of windows in this place. For the first time in her nineteen years she saw the cold and harsh reality around her. The council hall was unlike the warm and inviting cottages and homes she passed in Morshan. This was nothing but cold stone to surround the cold hearts she had previously assumed were part of their noble roles.

But what she'd learned about their actions went beyond any formality required by their station. Her mind flitted as she walked, with quick and quiet steps, recalling all the times she'd yearned for a hug that never came or a warm word of encouragement where there had only been admonishment and lessons.

She was an heir. But to what? Not a family. A tyranny? She still struggled against that thought, that she had been born and raised to wield fear over her own people. But she couldn't deny the truth in the necklace her mother had given her, the piece of her sister now pressed against her heart.

Voices sounded nearby. Her breath hitched as she stepped into a doorway, hoping with all her might that no one might be in the room and open the door to find her there.

She waited and listened, holding the air in as tightly as she could so she could determine if the voices were getting closer or moving away. When she was certain they were not coming toward her, she released her breath slowly, silently. Couldn't take any chances in case they were approaching her on soundless feet.

Risking a glance around the corner of the stone wall, she found the hallway empty and breathed a sigh of relief. The front door would be too conspicuous, and with no pirate crews scheduled to visit for another week, she couldn't risk being caught at the hall, even if they thought she was a pirate.

Instead she turned back toward the servants' entrance on the east side of the residence. It would allow her to use the cover of the bushes that lined the path out to the side gate, and then down a lesser-used road through the forest that surrounded the grounds.

There shouldn't be any staff out there, or any deliveries being made. She'd heard her mother and aunts talking about the last of the provisions arriving the day before for her matching. Not that it mattered now. But she couldn't worry herself over that. All that mattered was that the path would be deserted, the staff busy elsewhere.

She hoped she hadn't miscalculated any of this as she rounded the last corner and hurried down the steps to the door that would lead to her freedom. The door was made of heavy wood, with a single window placed slightly above her head. If she reached up on her toes she could just barely see out.

A glance to the left and then to the right assured her the way was clear.

The hinges creaked, as if announcing her presence to everyone in the servants' residence and the kitchen and the laundry and probably one hundred yards in every direction. She cringed at the sound, but she couldn't risk waiting to see if anyone noticed.

Thankful once again for the clothing that allowed her to slip through the small opening, she squeezed through and inched the door closed, this time the hinges obliging her by remaining silent.

Once the latch clicked shut, she turned and darted down the walkway, hoping no one would notice the man fleeing the council hall toward the gate and the forest beyond.

Freedom waited beyond that gate, and she was on her way to greet it.

The sun had just started to slide behind the rooftops as Declan strode back through the streets of Morshan toward the pub. He glanced around as he walked the same stretch of cobbled stones he had the night before, watching the villagers who milled about in front of their homes. They paid him no mind as they chatted. One woman rattled off a story of a new stew she'd made for her family, and how no one but her youngest child had enjoyed it. Another pair of ladies discussed how best to get blood stains out of clothing. Declan tried not to think of why they'd need to be worried about that. Not his concern. Amid the chatter and conversations of the neighbors doing life together, he heard the tinkling of children's laughter on the breeze, the sounds of games being played on the lawns behind the fences.

Had it really been only last night that he'd pushed the drunk to the side and said hello to his sister for the first time in seven years? Today the golden sunlight seemed to be attempting to wash away any of the dread he felt about the mission he'd agreed to take on. And he could have let it, perhaps. He could have taken in these sounds and smells of a simple village living its life and be grateful these people had some semblance of normalcy. But at his core he knew it wasn't true. Yes, the laughter and the friendship seemed genuine, and it probably was, but he knew—better than most—that it lay atop a foundation of loss, fear, and hardship.

Not my problem.

All he had was what lay before him, and that was the dagger and success and eventually freedom. He could almost taste it, almost imagine how sweet that feeling would be when he could finally step upon his own property of solid land, away from pirates and lords and councils and all their demands and threats. But it was still far off, like looking inside a bakery window and seeing the treats while finding only lint in your pockets.

He rounded the last corner and spotted the weathered pub sign swaying in the breeze up ahead. He opened the door and kicked the last bit of black sand off his boots before stepping inside, unable to push away the memory of his mom chiding him for having dirty feet in her establishment. *"People eat in here, Declan, and we will not have them eat among the muck and filth on your boots!"* The words themselves may have been harsh, but her tone rarely was. She'd had a smile as warm as the sunshine at his back, and a will as hard as the stones beneath his feet. And now…

Inside he found the pub less crowded than it had been the night before, but still far from empty. Three men sat at the far end of the bar, huddled over a pair of nearly empty glasses. Judging by the stoop in their shoulders and the tilts of their heads, it was not their first pour. A group of sailors sat at the table to Declan's right. He recognized them as members of Captain Thorne's crew of the *Falling Star*, another new ship vying for power in an overcrowded sea. He gave them a nod, as if to say,

"Sorry for the run-in a month back. No hard feelings. Let me buy you a drink."

The forced peace on the shores of Cregah seemed silly to him, but he understood the pull of rest, even if it meant setting aside past grievances, no matter how recent.

One of the men dipped his chin in greeting. Another raised his glass a fraction of an inch. The others stared at their hands. It wasn't a surprising response, especially considering how the noses and cheeks of those with lowered eyes had gotten quite acquainted with his fists during their last meeting.

He could barely stifle the smirk that threatened to creep up at the corners of his mouth.

To his left, at a table tucked into a dark corner at the end of the bar, he spotted his own men, both with glasses near full. Cait had likely insisted they couldn't stay unless they spent money, and they'd obliged but didn't want to be lost too far in their drinks before he showed.

He approached as those at the bar and other tables glanced over their drinks and kept their whispers low.

"Glad to see you made it," Declan said, pulling the chair around beside Tommy so his back would be to the wall and not to the door or the bar. One could never be too careful, even here.

"Of course. Though Miss Cait sure has a tongue on her." It was Gavin who spoke, pulling his own chair around to give Tommy room to do likewise. No pirate liked having his back unprotected or his eyes off his surroundings, but the captain's back took precedence. Always.

"Well it's no surprise, given that she's related to our dear captain, you know," Tommy said with a nod.

"Your mother?" Gavin eyed Declan, eyebrows raised and jaw hanging open.

"What? No, you dolt." Tommy kicked Gavin under the table. "Do you think she birthed him when she was ten? If that?"

"No, no. She just has that sternness one expects from…" Gavin stumbled over his words.

"She's his sister," Tommy said.

Gavin studied Declan.

"See the resemblance?" Declan asked. "I know I'm the better-looking, but she at least got a small portion of the McCallagh good looks."

A towel flew in his face, and he glanced up to see Cait standing before them with a full glass in her hand.

"What?" he asked. "I think I'm adorable."

"Of course you do." There was a bit of a twinkle in her eye as she spoke. "Seems I got all the brains though."

Tommy and Gavin let out a guffaw in unison and then quickly choked it back and stole a glance at their captain. Declan waited, keeping his gaze on his sister. The laughter didn't bother him in the slightest, and had he been in a room other than one teeming with those ready to kill him the second they left the safety of the port, he would have joined in. But one did not keep such a reputation as his by being lighthearted and soft.

"It's a shame though," Cait said. "All those good looks and you waste them by spending all your time with a hundred sweaty men aboard a ship. You could certainly find a nice lady to share your life with instead."

In his periphery, Declan could see his men trying to hold in their laughter, but his eyes never strayed from his sister's as his pulse accelerated and his cheeks warmed against his will. At one time, long ago, he had hoped for just that—the love and companionship he'd seen his parents share. But those dreams and plans had shattered as quickly as the glass he'd dropped that night. No, love got no one anywhere good.

"Perhaps, Miss Cait. Perhaps." He tossed the towel back to her, his gaze never straying. Neither did hers. She lifted the glass, held it to her lips, and took a long swig of the deep amber liquid before placing it down half empty before him.

"Aye, that's some good rum," she said with a nod before turning on her heel and heading back to the bar.

Declan watched her walk away, conjuring up an eerie image in his mind of their mother all those years ago running this same pub, towel over her shoulder, a lightness in her steps borne not from a carefree life but from the necessity to be ready to move quickly should trouble arise. Hers had been a life lived on her toes, a life lived waiting for the other shoe to drop, for the veil to come crashing down around her. For the mask to be lifted and the truth revealed.

"Sir?" Tommy's voice pulled him back to his own table and the matter at hand. "Why did you want to meet here?"

He felt the stares of both his men weighing heavily on him. "Can't a captain have a simple drink with his best men?"

He raised his glass to them. They didn't do the same.

"Aye, he can." Gavin dipped his chin lower to show his respect. "But this is a tad out of the ordinary for you."

Tommy added, "To come ashore. Then to stay longer than planned. It's curious." At least Tommy knew better than to mention the note, trusting that Declan would share about it if it were necessary.

Which it wasn't.

"I know. It'll all make sense eventually. We have a lot to plan and little time to do it." The men leaned in an inch, not daring to come too close lest it raise suspicion among the other pub patrons. The remoteness of their table offered them some protection from their words being overheard, and though no one in the room appeared to be interested, the three pirates of the *Siren's Song* knew better.

"But not here and not yet." He looked at each of his men. "This really is merely a simple drink among friends."

The men still didn't lift their glasses. Suspicion and questions burned in their eyes as they looked at each other and then back to him.

"Fine, fine. If you won't relax, I can at least say the obvious. We need to recruit a few more hands."

"We aren't allowed to—" Tommy began, but Declan raised his hand.

"I know. We aren't recruiting them here. We need to get to Foxhaven. By tomorrow evening. Time is short, and we can't wait."

"By tomorrow?" The surprise was evident in his helmsman's tone. "But that's normally a two-day journey. A day and a half with a miracle, maybe. There's no way."

"If anyone can make it happen, it's you, Gavin," Declan said, his eyes stern.

He didn't hear Gavin as he protested to Tommy, as movement in his periphery pulled his attention away from the table.

A man shifted on a stool at the bar. Declan had noticed the man arrive shortly after him. He'd looked so uncomfortable and hesitant ever since that Declan had taken special notice of him. The man risked a glance in Declan's direction. A mistake. Their eyes met for a split second, and Declan recognized them at once.

Not a man. The girl. The heir.

His jaw tightened as her eyes darted away and her fingers fidgeted with the glass before her. He bit back a laugh. What was she wearing? Gone was the prim and proper attire of the council. Her long hair was now cut short—and not cleanly, as if she'd done it herself. In haste. With no mirror.

But the desire to laugh was at war with bitterness as he began to suspect she was there to get in his way. Had the council sent her to spy? It was a ridiculous notion, to be sure. They wouldn't send one of their heirs to do such a thing, not when they had so many pirates on the island to do their bidding.

As much as he wanted to assume it was mere coincidence, he had the sinking suspicion it was no accident she was here, in his family's pub, watching him. He needed answers, and quickly. He couldn't risk any possibility she'd ruin his plans. Even by accident.

He turned back to his men, being careful with his words in case the lady could hear him from her perch. "Let's get back to the ship."

The men stood, the glasses before them still mostly untouched, though Declan raised his and downed it, wondering if his sister had lied the night before about being out of rum, or if she'd gotten a fresh supply in this morning. It didn't matter. He had a bit of rum in his belly now, and that was enough.

Tommy and Gavin seemed to be waiting for him to make the first move toward the door, but he had to take care of the girl first.

"You both go on ahead. I'll be right behind you." He nodded toward the back of the pub. "A bit too much drink in me."

A curious look passed between his men, who were no doubt wondering how half a glass of rum could qualify as *too much drink*, but with a shared shrug and a huff of laughter between them, they nodded and strode out ahead of him.

When they'd gone, he began his walk through the pub to the door at the other end of the bar, the one leading to the alley where patrons went to do whatever one did behind a pub. He shuffled his feet—not too much, but enough to make it appear that his wits were dulled a bit by drink. He stumbled as he passed Aoife, knocking his shoulder into her lightly. He muttered an apology before continuing on toward the door, ignoring Cait's mocking stare from behind the bar. Upon reaching the door, he forced himself to fall out into the alley.

A quick glance around proved he was alone, as he needed. He stood straight. He thought of pulling the smaller knife from his boot, but he could get to it easily enough if it were needed.

He plastered his back against the wall just to the side of the door. It would hide him from view when it opened again in three…two…one…

The door eased open. He waited and listened to the steps coming out into the alley. Light. Soft. When he was sure she'd cleared the doorway, he pushed it closed, wrapped his right arm around her waist, and spun her toward the wall, turning her until her back was against the stones, pinning her wrist behind her. He pressed his body firmly against hers as his left hand covered her mouth, stifling her yelp.

From this proximity he could see the flecks of gold in her green eyes—eyes wide with surprise and terror and perhaps a bit of annoyance that made him want to laugh again.

She pushed against him, struggling to free her right arm, which was trapped between her back and the wall. He only shook his head and clicked his tongue at her.

He bent closer, trying to ignore the soft scent of vanilla, sugar, and cedarwood that clung to her and sent a wave of unwelcome warmth through him.

"You know, you didn't have to don such a disguise to get more time alone with me."

He pushed his hips into hers to emphasize the suggestiveness, but the movement had as much of an undesired effect on him as it did on her, and he pulled away slightly before she could sense his body's betrayal, but not enough to allow her to escape his grasp. She pulled her face away, and he allowed her to free her mouth for the sheer curiosity of what reply she might have for him.

"How dare you suggest such a thing?" Aoife spat through clenched teeth, yet she kept her voice low. Too low for a lady who might want help and rescue. No, while she might not want to be held by him, she certainly was in no rush to be discovered by anyone either.

"And yet here we are. What am I to think, Miss—what was your name again?"

"Aoife." Again through her teeth. She continued to struggle fruitlessly.

"Right. Aoife. What am I to assume when you follow me into a pub and stare at me while I try to enjoy a drink with friends?" He loosened his grip a touch, ready to tighten it again if she tried anything stupid. He angled his hips, digging one side into hers and maneuvering a leg to keep her from jamming a knee into a particularly sensitive part of his body. "What is it that you want, then, if not the *pleasure* of my company?"

"Others may find you roguishly handsome, Mister—I'm sorry, I don't believe I have the pleasure of your name." She angled her head in a challenge, her eyes taunting him.

"No, you don't have the pleasure."

"...but I, sir, am not in the least bit swayed by your charms." Her eyes narrowed, and he could have sworn he caught a hint of a lie in her words. Perhaps he'd had just as much an effect on her earlier in the cove as she'd had on him.

"So you admit I have charm." He flashed her a smirk. "A shame it has no effect though, miss. We could have had some fun." He pulled away now, certain he'd made his point that he was in control here, but only took half a step back.

She stretched her shoulders and wrists out from where they'd been pressed too tightly into the stone.

He asked again, "What is it you want, if not—"

"Take me with you."

His eyes narrowed, and he hoped she didn't notice the catch in his breath. That was certainly not what he had expected from her. The council usually demanded other services, though usually the council didn't ask for his help themselves but through staff and couriers and messengers. Never through the ladies and their heirs.

"No." But even as he uttered the words he felt the two sides of him battling it out within. She could help him. She knew the council hall. She knew her way around. She might even know about the fae—where they were kept, what they were like. And yet, there was a part of him—the part that had blurted out his response—that didn't want to risk having her aboard a ship full of pirates.

It was a part he'd thought he had buried years ago, a desire to protect and defend those he cared about. But he didn't care about her. She was a nuisance. Annoying.

"I heard you in there," she protested. "Your ship is short of men. Your captain needs more crew."

"And what do you know of sailing and piracy? You're so ready to be the sole woman on board a ship of miscreants and thieves and murderers? And away from the safe and *peaceful* shores of your beloved Cregah?" His words were filled with more rage than he intended, that protective side of him refusing to back down despite his urging.

She didn't answer but merely looked down at her feet, shame crossing over her features, and he almost felt pity for her and her plight.

"That's what I thought." He backed up further, sure she was no risk to him now that he'd seen the desperation in her features, her need to escape the island—a need that mirrored his own.

"Please." It came out barely a whisper.

"What?" He pretended not to have heard her.

As she raised her eyes to his, it was clear her pride had returned and she was bitter to have to resort to begging. "Please. Take me with you. I cannot stay here."

"Ah, but I cannot take you either. What would my captain think?" He exaggerated his sigh, forcing the impatience growing within to come out as boredom. "I really have to get back though. I'd hate for them to leave without me."

He moved to the side, away from her, but she placed herself in front of him once again, blocking his way.

"I don't care what your captain thinks. I *need* off this rock." There was a fire in her eyes that both excited and infuriated him. She was wasting his time, even if she had inside knowledge that could potentially help him. "I must leave. The council—"

He couldn't let her finish that sentence. He slammed his lips against hers, pressing hard. He could feel her resistance. This was almost certainly the first time she, as an unmatched council heir, had been touched by any man, and she didn't seem to like it, not that he was trying to be gentle or affectionate in the slightest. She pressed back against him, her lips as rigid as the rest of her body, and slammed him back with her hands before slapping him across the face.

He'd expected that response.

"What—" she started.

He leaned back in, pushing her back against the wall, though not as forcefully as before, his face close enough that he could have kissed her again had he wanted to. "I needed to shut you up. You, of all people, should know the council has eyes and ears everywhere. You'd do good not to speak so loudly in such a quiet alley where they're sure to notice."

She blinked. "But I'm dressed as a man…"

"And your point being?"

"Wouldn't that look…" Her thought trailed off, and she seemed to be fighting the urge to look around for the council spies. Her jaw and gaze hardened as she lowered her voice once more. "Please."

A single word heavy with desperation.

"My answer stands. Find another ship to carry you. I—my captain—would not be keen on me bringing a stray aboard."

"I have no money. I can't buy passage. What do you expect me to do?"

Declan could see her trying to keep the confidence in her eyes, but they'd begun to betray her.

The sun had completely set. He had to get back to the ship soon. Time was against him here, and she was holding him up. He needed to be rid of her.

He placed a hand on her hip, giving it a squeeze and pressing his body against hers. She tried to step back, but she was already pinned tightly against the pub wall. He ran his hand over her hip before tracing it back up along the curve of her waist and settling it against her ribs. He leaned in—ignoring the way heat spread through his core—and heard her breath catch. His lips hovered over hers, close enough to feel the warmth radiating off of them, but instead of kissing her again, he moved to her ear and whispered.

"You have more than money to offer. I know many a pirate who would accept such…payment."

Before he'd even finished the sentence, she put her full weight into shoving him back. He didn't stop her, let himself be pushed a few feet away, his hands up in retreat. If any council spies were watching, he wasn't going to let them accuse him of forcing himself on another person.

Aoife huffed a breath as she turned away. He let out a hearty laugh at her as she opened the pub door and headed back inside, hoping it was enough to keep her from demanding his help again.

As he strode down the alley back toward his ship, he couldn't help but wonder if he'd made the right decision by turning her down. She was obviously in trouble. The council would be on the search for her. What would they do when they caught up with her?

No. Not his problem. Not his concern. Even if he could have used her knowledge of the council, could have benefited from her help, he couldn't risk having her on board. She couldn't protect herself, no matter how feisty she was, and he couldn't be hindered by the need to protect anyone other than himself.

The night was so dark Aoife could barely see the pirate as he walked ahead of her down the cobbled streets. She wasn't sure what she had expected when she'd confronted him in that alley. Had she really expected he would take her with him, that he would risk his captain's wrath to bring her on board, that she could even pass for a man at all with a simple haircut and wardrobe change?

He had not been fooled. How could she hope to fool anyone else?

But the goal wasn't to fool people indefinitely, just long enough to get off the island.

He'd told her to go find someone else to take her, but she couldn't waste any more time looking for another option. She needed transport now, and there was something about him that told her—even as he angered and annoyed her—she could trust him. He could have taken advantage of her in that alley. Even with council spies everywhere, he could have done more in those shadows.

Her heart beat wildly in her chest as she approached the docks. Despite the late hour, there was enough foot traffic she was able to stay hidden as she followed, weaving in and out among the men who carried crates on and off the various ships. She kept her head low, the hat shielding her eyes as she watched him walk on with confidence. How strange that all the men seemed to give him clearance, as if they were performing some kind of choreographed dance to the music of boots on the dock and water lapping at the posts below their feet.

A beautiful and curious dance. Was she imagining it? No, there. Two men skirted out of his way, keeping their heads down.

Who was he?

She'd tried to catch some of the conversation back at the pub, if only to get his name. Not having his name annoyed her more than she would have liked. Why did it matter if he was more private than she was? Though maybe it was more that she was mad at herself for being stupid enough to give him her name and he'd shown his smarts by refusing to reciprocate. She huffed a breath at the memory. She'd need to be smarter. He'd outsmarted her again tonight when he'd anticipated her in the alley. He'd appeared inebriated, bumping into her as he stumbled toward the door. It had all been a ruse, and she had fallen for it. Completely. Stupidly.

All those years of training at the council hall, and she had no practical knowledge. Sure, she knew the history of the Aisling War, the beliefs that had formed her country and led to the establishment of the council. She knew how to paint and how to write and how to read. But she didn't know how to lie. She didn't know how to sneak about. She'd need to learn.

As they passed ship after ship, gangway after gangway, she wondered which vessel he'd board. Which she would need to sneak onto.

They were nearing the end of the docks, and she half expected to see him simply jump off into the water to throw her off course. Even with all the care she was taking, she would not be surprised to learn he knew she was there, his shadow in the night, following him.

But he didn't go into the water. At the last ship, at the end of the dock, he turned. Men were scattered along the dock getting the final crates on board. He stopped to have a word with one of the men, but from her position leaning against a post—doing her best to pretend she was tired, sick, or had had too much rum at the pub—she was still too far away to hear any of their conversation above the shuffle and bustle of all the sailors and pirates.

From under her hat she watched their exchange. Whatever they were discussing, he did not seem happy. Far from it. He seemed to be in a hurry, and while he was frustrated with the man holding the crate of supplies, he also seemed to be showing a hint of softness. Or maybe she only hoped he was.

With a growl of a sigh, the pirate turned and stomped up the gangway to the ship. She looked up at the prow in search of the ship's name. The figurehead was a carved siren. But not one of those she'd heard so many tales of as a kid—tales of monstrous women, evil and darkness incarnate, with black souls that preyed on the lives and hearts and breaths of men and sailors and anyone who made the mistake of venturing into their waters.

No, this siren carved from wood was beautiful and seemed peaceful. And yet there was a smirk on her face as if she held a great secret.

Aoife pulled her attention away from the figure and focused on the name painted on the hull.

The *Siren's Song.*

She'd heard of this ship, but only bits and pieces. Not much at all.

Last year when she'd been attending the dinner with the visiting crew of Lord Saarin she'd heard them mention the *Siren's Song.* They'd all laughed while discussing the young captain who ran it, but she remembered how there'd been a hint of respect in their tone. And consternation. The captain of this ship was making a name for himself, though no one at that table had bothered to mention his name outright. Apparently they'd all known who he was, and there was no need to utter it among the council ladies.

The pirate lords were working to knock him down a peg or two. She remembered that much. She'd wanted to ask them why the pirates weren't more united. Her tutors had thoroughly covered the alliance of the pirate guild in their lessons, the way ships would often come to one another's aid when there was a large shipment of goods to be looted or if they had a run-in with one of the policing ships from Caprothe.

But from what she'd overheard at that meal, the alliances were waning. Particularly with the pirate lords, who seemed to enjoy the perks they received by being in full partnership with the council. They seemed to be holding onto those with as much might as they could, and each pirate lord was working to keep the newer, lesser pirates and their crews from gaining any foothold.

These other ships did much of the work of looting the merchants that crossed the Aisling Sea every year, and the pirate lords would then attack them and take a portion of the bounty, saying it was needed for the council. And indeed, the lords did need more riches than they could possibly gather on their own each year. Such was the price of the seats at the table in the council hall—and the privilege of warming the councilwomen's beds.

Aoife cringed inwardly. She had all but accepted her fate as a council heir. She'd been prepared to be matched to one of the three remaining pirate lords—there were six total, and she was supposed to know all of their names and the names of their ships, but she always had such a dastardly time with her memory. It seemed pointless to remember all six when there were only three potential matches for her, each of whom would be matched with one of the council heirs—Aoife, Lani, or Darienn—when she turned twenty.

Aoife's matching was looming, only a month out, and she'd spent the last year readying herself to take her place as required. But now, after what had happened to Lani, she couldn't stomach the thought of going through with it.

No, she couldn't stay, and her only chance off Cregah was preparing to weigh anchor. She'd have one opportunity, and she had little idea how she was going to pull this off, but it was a risk she needed to take.

With a deep breath, she forced her feet forward, pushing away from the post and making her way toward the man the pirate had spoken to.

Grabbing one of the last remaining crates from the docks, the man headed toward the ship. Without another thought, Aoife picked up the final crate and kept her head down as she followed the man up the gangway, keeping her feet light so he would hopefully not hear her behind him.

Though the ship was docked, the wood beneath her feet swayed enough to surprise her. She'd never left solid ground before, and somehow, in all her planning, she hadn't stopped to think of what walking while floating might feel like.

Still, it wasn't so bad. At least she didn't fall or trip as she followed the man down the stairs and into the hold, careful not to make eye contact with any of the other crew who were rushing about to get the ship ready to leave. No one seemed to notice her. Though, in truth, she wouldn't have known if they had, and she dared not lift her eyes to check.

The man in front of her went down another set of stairs and then into the darkness of the hull. He set the crate down beside the others he'd already loaded and then turned to find her standing there with the one he'd left outside.

She braced herself for his reprimand or an interrogation, but it didn't come.

"Oh!" the man said, surprise written clearly on his face even in the dimness of the hull. The few lanterns cast little light around the room, keeping everything, including their faces, in shadows. "Thanks for grabbing that for me, boy. Captain was likely to have my head for being behind on getting it all loaded. Set it down over there." He pointed down to his left, and Aoife moved to do as told. "I appreciate the help."

She almost sighed with relief, thankful the ruse had gotten her on board. Her disguise had worked. But the man didn't head back up the stairs just yet. Though she kept her chin down, she sensed him staring. She waited, holding her breath, nervous that perhaps he'd see her feminine features despite the dim lighting, or—more likely—he would catch the scent of cleanliness on her clothes and skin. She certainly didn't fit in here, and even she could smell the sweetness of the perfumed soap she'd used that morning.

"Hold on." The man stepped forward, bending down to look under her hat. The stench of sweat and grime and salt permeated her nose, and she had to fight the urge to back away from him. She held her ground, her feet firmly in place. "Who—"

He reached a hand up to rip the hat off her head, but she ducked out of the way, her hat slipping and falling to her feet. She wasn't sure what she was thinking. But in the next second, she realized, as her heart fell into her stomach, that she was no longer on the safe shores of Cregah. She was on this man's ship, a pirate ship no less, and he could do as he pleased.

She froze again and dared to look up. Squaring her shoulders, she clenched her jaw and steeled herself against whatever he was going to do to her.

But he didn't say anything. Instead he stumbled back a step as if he'd seen a ghost. And maybe he thought he had. A chuckle might have escaped her throat under normal circumstances—if she weren't having a confrontation with a pirate and facing almost certain death. She swallowed and waited, but he merely stared. He opened his mouth as if to speak, but when no words came, it snapped shut again.

"Look," she started, and the man took another half step back. "I'm no ghost."

"Well, I know that, girl." His features scrunched with annoyance. "I may be a pirate, but I'm not stupid."

Confusion wrapped around her insides. This wasn't going at all as she had expected. Why hadn't he grabbed her yet? Weren't pirates fearsome? Terrible? Ruthless? Yet here he stood, staring at her as if he couldn't decide whether to gut her or kiss her or drag her above deck to parade her in front of the crew.

"Apologies, Mr.—" She didn't know why she thought he might give up his name when the last pirate she'd met had refused. Perhaps it was a remnant of her life back at the council hall, the polite decorum not easily discarded. *Like your hair and clothes.* She smirked to herself before aiming to speak again, but the man interrupted.

"Collins. And no mister for me, miss. I'm no officer."

She wasn't sure what to say to any of this. Though she hadn't quite known what to expect when she sneaked on board behind him, she hadn't expected to have such a civil discussion once she'd been found. And she'd certainly expected to be caught. That was a given. The pirate in the pub had been right. Certainly her disguise was abysmal, but she had hoped to at least not get caught until they were out to sea.

So they could throw you overboard instead?

She admitted to herself that none of this had been the best idea. But her council lessons hadn't exactly covered the topics of strategy and deception. An heir to the council—a council lady—had no need for such skills.

"Well, Collins. I should be going." She said the words despite having no real plan in mind.

And he must have noted the ridiculousness in her words as well. "Going where exactly?"

"I need to see…a man."

"Well, we have plenty of those on board, though not as many as we had before."

"What do you mean?"

"Sadly we lost several in the latest skirmishes with the lords, and another quarter of our crew is out there, laid up in the hospital, badly wounded from the shot fired upon us. We were lucky to have been close enough to Morshan—and lucky, too, that the captain agreed to finally come here—or I bet we would have had to send a good lot of them to their final resting in the depths." He glanced down at his feet as he spoke but then looked around, his nerves getting the best of him, as if he'd only realized now that he was talking to her and not to himself.

"What do you mean, 'finally come here'?"

He looked at her again. There was no malice in his eyes, only concern, but whether it was for her well-being or for his own hide, she wasn't sure. A war seemed to be raging behind his dark eyes, and she could only imagine what options he was weighing as he stared.

She spoke before he could answer her question. "Look, I don't want to get you in trouble…"

"Why would I be in trouble? I'm not the one who boarded someone else's ship without permission."

"Yes, but you are a crew member who allowed someone you didn't know to sneak aboard behind you. And thanked them for their help."

"Ah, indeed. But that is my price to pay, and my punishment to face, I suppose. I'm not worried. But you should be. Captain McCallagh is in a right mood these days. He's normally a…" He trailed off, perhaps realizing he was about to divulge more information than he should.

McCallagh. The name sounded familiar, but she couldn't place where she'd heard it.

"Regardless," Collins continued, "I'll need to take you to him, and I didn't get quite the amount of rest I would have liked, being in port for so short a time, so I'd much rather you go along peacefully."

"Of course."

Peaceful is all I've known my whole life.

And it was a lie.

"This way." He turned and waved a hand back toward the stairs. "Ladies first."

Aoife's confusion grew. Had everything she'd assumed about pirates been a lie? Like everything else in her life? Had she really been misled about the entire world beyond the walls of the council hall and the Cregahn shores?

And yet he'd talked of violence out on the seas. Open violence. Real wounds. People dying. But people died on Cregah too. Aoife was starting to wonder which was worse—a death people acknowledged outright and mourned even as they doled it out to others, or a death covered up and ignored and dressed up as something else entirely.

Collins gripped her elbow lightly as they headed up the stairs. A great number of boots thumped on the old wood above her head, and she wondered if the echo made it sound like there were more men than there actually were. When the lords and their crews came to dine at the council hall, she'd always marveled at the great number they brought with them—twenty men sitting around the table with the ladies, enjoying food and drink and laughter. But none of those dinners had prepared Aoife for the sheer multitude of crewmen she saw on deck as she and her escort reached the last of the steps.

Thirty to forty men hurried about. She had no idea what they were all doing. The pirate at the pub had been right; she knew nothing of sailing. She would be a liability and no asset on a ship. There didn't appear to be enough work for all the men, and some lounged against the railings, waiting. She briefly recalled the reason for this from a conversation she'd heard at the dining table years ago.

"*Aye, we do employ more men than are actually needed to sail a ship, even one as impressive as ours. But the key to being a pirate—and how we have become one of the most esteemed among our lot—is our ability to intimidate. And we do that with numbers.*" The pirate lord—she couldn't recall which it had been, as she usually daydreamed during those meals—had been quite proud of his ability to not only take down merchant vessels, but also keep lesser pirates in check.

Lesser pirates like the ones she was hoping to sail with now. Not like she'd had any other choice though. It wasn't as if a pirate lord would have given her passage. Not when they enjoyed such close companionship with the ladies of the council. Lord Madigen had been visiting her mother twice a year for the last however many years. It was a relationship Aoife had never quite understood, not even after all the history lessons and instruction on council life. It was something she'd assumed she would come to understand when the time came for her own matching.

Collins nudged her forward. When had she stopped walking?

She felt all eyes shift to her as she and Collins made their way across the deck, around the main mast, and toward a door under the quarterdeck just below the helm. This had to be the captain's quarters. She swallowed hard, but her mouth had gone dry, and her throat chafed. Collins positioned her directly in front of the wooden door. It was more ornate than anything else on the ship, but the wood was weathered and worn by the years of sea air and perhaps the same battles that had diminished the crew's numbers.

He leaned around her and knocked lightly on the wood and waited. One second. Two seconds.

Behind her all had gone silent, and she knew, even without turning around for verification, that everyone had frozen. She could still feel their stares on her and wondered if the pirate from the cove was among them, waiting to see how his captain would deal with her. If she heard him laugh at her, she might die from humiliation.

"Enter." The command sounded from behind the door. The voice held a hint of familiarity, but she shook the thought aside, telling herself all pirate captains sounded the same.

Confident. Intimidating. Harsh.

But this command hadn't sounded as harsh as she'd expected. Then again, he didn't yet know that someone had tried to stow away on his ship. She pulled her shoulders back and pushed her chin up as Collins pushed the door open and led her inside with a gentle hold of her elbow.

It took a moment for her eyes to adjust to the dimness of the quarters, the only light being from a few lanterns, as the moon was not yet high enough to provide any light through the windows that sat behind the figure she now faced.

The man was bent over his desk, a hand worrying a spot in his forehead as he looked over what seemed to be a map of the area. Even in the low light she could see him well enough that a sense of familiarity began to tingle in her gut. Something about the movement in his fingers as he moved them over his temples and then through his dark hair. His hand rubbed the back of his neck, but he still didn't look up.

"What is it?" he asked.

The voice was indeed unmistakable.

"You!"

For a moment Aoife didn't realize she had spoken, but she quickly snapped her lips shut.

Collins gave her arm a squeeze in warning. His whole body had tensed beside her, but she only noticed for a second because all her focus was drawn to the man before her, who was in fact the pirate from the cove.

And he now looked up at her, his head angling slightly toward his left shoulder as he eyed her. Was that a laugh that escaped him? He clicked his tongue, and his shoulders slumped, though Aoife didn't know whether it was from exhaustion or exasperation.

"I should have known you'd do something stupid." That damn smirk she'd seen on him back in the cove pulled at his lips once more. "Again."

"You're the *captain?"* This was probably not how she was supposed to speak to a pirate captain, but she couldn't help it.

"Aye, and you'd be good to remember that when you speak to me." Though his words had a bite to them, his eyes still shone with a hint of mischievous humor, as if he found this whole scenario to be hilarious. And perhaps she would have agreed if she weren't the one standing before him waiting for his judgment. "Release her, Collins. She won't be going anywhere."

Aoife balked at this, but only internally. She wasn't about to let him see that he'd affected her in any way.

The captain narrowed his eyes at her. "Leave us."

The words were not for her, and for the first time since she'd stepped into his quarters, a spark of fear lit inside her chest.

She swallowed hard and gave Collins a dip of her chin in thanks for his gentle handling. In return the man raised a brow at her. Was that his way of wishing her good luck?

"Aye, Captain." Collins turned and made the three steps to the door in short time. Aoife held the captain's gaze, refusing to let the growing fear get the best of her—or at least keep him from seeing it. She didn't hear the door creak open. Instead, Collins spoke again. "All supplies are aboard, sir. We're set to leave when you are."

The captain didn't give his man another word; a slow nod was all the acknowledgment he offered. With that, Collins slipped out of the room, leaving Aoife to face this man who had intimidated and humiliated her in the alley. But hadn't she chosen to follow him? If she hadn't wanted to face him again, she probably should have picked a different pirate to shadow and sneak behind.

Yet here she was, and she had no idea what to expect.

Story of my life these days.

Declan had certainly expected the girl to be a problem, but he'd assumed it would be later, when he'd returned from Foxhaven with more crew. He should have known she wasn't going to leave it when he'd insulted her back in that alley. She might not be the brightest, but she had spunk.

That makes her a liability.

He'd been captain all these years, and still some decisions didn't come as easily as others. He could command the crew with ease in battle, but in these slower moments when he didn't have adrenaline pushing him to act on instinct, his thoughts too often disrupted his focus. It was certainly difficult now to focus on the task at hand with Aoife staring wide-eyed at him. The lantern's flame flickered, its reflection bringing out hints of gold in her green eyes, making them appear… He couldn't describe the effect, exactly, but the word *magical* seemed fitting.

"What am I going to do with you?" He leaned back in his chair and pursed his lips. He made a point of looking her up and down. Intimidation was the name of the game when it came to piracy. He'd learned that lesson early enough during his first days as a cabin boy on the *Reckoning*.

"Take me with you." Her voice held no sign of the fear he saw playing at the corners of her eyes. Those damn eyes.

He shifted his own gaze down to his desk and the map laid out before him as he steepled his fingers below his chin. "Ah, don't you want to know my name?"

"I've given up hope of you telling me. You're the captain. What more do I need?"

"And did you know which ship you were boarding?"

"The *Siren's Song*. Am I supposed to be impressed?"

"Ah, I see pirate news doesn't reach the ears of the council then?"

"Is there something special about you and your ship?" Her eyes danced as she spoke. Spunky indeed. And also irritating.

He picked a piece of invisible lint from his shoulder. "Simply noting how the pirate lords don't bother to mention the *lesser* ships when they're warming the seats around your table. Among other things." The girl's cheeks blushed at his words, and he had to stifle a chuckle at the sight.

"Oh, they mention the *lesser* ships, but never by name. I suppose they don't deem you worthy of specific mention."

"Yet we are deemed worthy of being attacked on the regular."

"Why is that exactly? Isn't there an alliance among the pirates?" Aoife leaned closer, and any hint of the fear that had been tugging at her features was replaced with a curiosity he would have found endearing—maybe even charming—on anyone other than this girl who was ruining his plans yet again.

Plans. A curse ran through his mind. He needed to get back on track and take care of this girl so he could focus on the important matter at hand.

He didn't answer her question but repeated his own. "What am I to do with you exactly?"

While the question was rhetorical, uttered more for himself than for her, he wasn't surprised when she opened her mouth to answer. He held up a hand to cut her off and shook his head slowly as he pondered his options.

"If I take you with us, I can't guarantee your safety. And even if I can protect you from the men, I don't have time to deal with a distracted crew. Even with you dressed like that, a woman on board doesn't help matters."

She moved to speak, but he again stopped her, this time with the sharpest of glares. If he was going to allow her to remain on his ship, she needed to learn some damn respect.

"But it is obvious you are desperate to leave." He could imagine the snarky response she wanted to utter. *I told you as much, you idiot.* And he nearly laughed at the thought. But she stood before him, silent, her gaze like cold steel. "I fear if I were to send you away, you would get yourself in a much worse situation than you find yourself in now. And while I shouldn't care—and in fact, I don't—there's no harm in granting you passage. And so I'll allow you to stay. But only until we reach Foxhaven. There you'll leave us and do so peacefully."

He waited for her reply, but she still stood staring at him. They studied each other for what seemed like hours but was likely only a few seconds. But a few seconds of this silence was enough to drive him mad. He refused to be the next to speak though. He wouldn't yield any of his power on his ship, especially to her.

Aoife dipped her chin. "Thank you."

"So it is agreed. We'll provide you passage to our next stop, and then we will part ways."

But even as he said the words, he felt the niggling voice in the far corner of his mind pointing out that she could help in his plans. He had refused to entertain that idea before, but now she was here on his ship, in his care already, so what did it matter if he chose to keep her on for the remainder of the job? Still, that decision could be made later.

"There are some logistics to work out, of course," he said. "We are not set up to have women aboard our ship. We are but a crew of crude men with thoughts and drives as dirty as our bodies. And I certainly can't have my crew distracted by your presence in their quarters."

Aoife squirmed, but only slightly. So slightly Declan could only assume she was using all her might to not let him see how uncomfortable she was. And how little planning she'd actually done when deciding to sneak onto his ship. Or any ship for that matter. What had she been thinking?

He leaned forward against his desk, once again steepling his fingers, this time in front of his lips. He kept his focus on her as he released an exaggerated sigh, his shoulders drooping as if the weight of the breath leaving him would force him to collapse onto the desk in front of him. *I should have been an actor, not a pirate.*

There was something about watching this girl's face as both of them waited for the other to speak. Such pride, conviction, need. Mixed with a youthful innocence he had only ever seen on this island. He pushed that thought aside. No, he needed to focus and make a decision. Yet he couldn't deny how fun it was to watch her battle the desire to stand her ground and flee from his sight and give up on this notion of running.

"So where will I stay then?" Aoife jutted out her chin as she spoke, and though she hardened her expression and set her jaw, he could see the fear return. No, perhaps not fear. It was more like worry that tugged at her, betraying her brave front.

"Now, I could displace my officers and let you have their quarters, but they don't deserve to be pushed below decks with the rest of the crew."

"What about your…" Declan raised his brows at her as a smirk crept across his lips again, and she trailed off.

"And here I thought you said my charms had no effect on you."

"Oh, I didn't mean it like that. Why can't I stay in here? Without you?" She held his gaze, almost daring him to make another joke that would be his last. Sands, he wanted to laugh at her again, but he managed to shut it down. As much as she annoyed him—and screwed up his plans—he had to admit it was fun to mess with her. He shook his head slowly.

"That wouldn't do at all, I'm afraid. I've grown rather attached to my accommodations. I've worked hard, done some things— No, this space is mine."

Aoife took a half step forward and opened her mouth, likely to protest, but he held up his hand to stop her.

"I wasn't finished." He spat the words as his annoyance crept back up. She might be cute, but her inability to listen was beginning to really grate on him. "You will stay in here—"

"Thank you," she muttered as her shoulders relaxed and a breath escaped her, as if she'd been holding it this whole time.

"—with me."

"What? No!" Her eyes grew wide, and her head began to shake quickly in protest.

Declan leaned back in his chair and propped his boots up on his desk, his arms sliding back behind his head. "Trust me, princess…"

"I'm not a princess."

"Excuse me. Heir." She winced and glared at him. "Fine. Aoife. Trust me when I say this isn't my ideal either, but between sharing quarters with you and having to share a cramped space with my officers, I'll take the former."

"I guess I do smell better."

Such an odd time for an attempt at humor. What an odd, perplexing creature she was. So different from Cait and the other women he'd met over the years. But maybe this was simply how all heirs were, all women who were raised in the council hall.

"Aye, but that won't last long, I fear. Life aboard a ship tends to force us to forget the luxuries we knew when we had a home on land."

"But where do I sleep?" Aoife glanced around the quarters, and he realized she likely wasn't familiar with the layout of a ship, particularly a captain's quarters.

"Would you like a tour of your accommodations then?" He flashed her a smile—not a smirk—but quickly smoothed it away as he chided himself. *What are you doing? You don't have time to play around like this.* "It won't take long," he said, as much to himself as to her.

Declan rose from his seat and waved an arm as he said, "This would be the main office, of course. It's not much, but it allows me a space to meet with my officers, to plan, to strategize, to gossip about the crew and those we meet in ports." She didn't laugh.

He pointed to a doorway off to his left. "There's a small dining room in there."

"You don't eat with the crew then?" He grimaced at her, and she huffed. "Of course not. How silly of me."

He turned and stepped to the door nestled between his bookcases on the opposite wall. He motioned for her to follow and bit back his annoyance when she took her steps with hesitation. Maybe this would take longer than planned if she kept moving like a snail through honey. When she finally moved to stand beside him, glancing up at him without turning her head fully, he continued. "And these are the sleeping quarters."

She peered in through the open door before looking back at him.

"It's so small," she said.

"Not something any man likes to hear from a lady, miss." He let out a sigh to cover up yet another laugh that threatened to escape. "Alas, we can't all live in the grand council hall, but these are the most comfortable quarters on the ship. And they are now yours." He dipped his head toward her.

"And where will you be sleeping?" Again she eyed him from the side, not fully turning toward him.

"Despite your quick judgment of this bed, it is large enough for both of us." As expected, she turned to him, her eyes widening again and her mouth opening to speak. He shut her down with another silent reprimand. "Don't worry, Aoife. I vow to be the most upstanding and respectable of men."

"You're a pirate."

"Even pirates have manners. We simply decide who is worthy of receiving them from us."

"And I am? Worthy?" Her brow scrunched up, sending creases across her forehead, barely visible behind her poorly chopped chestnut hair.

"Worthy enough, I suppose. But if you'd prefer to take your chances with the crew below deck, or even in my officers' quarters, by all means."

She took a step toward the door to study the small bedroom, and he wondered what she thought of his simple space.

Why should you care what she thinks?

Yet still, these were his private quarters, and while it was just a room aboard a ship, he still felt as if he were having his soul laid bare before her. Tommy and Gavin and the cabin boys had been in here a million times, but those men already knew him and many of his secrets. And he had never had the same urge to impress them as he did with her, an urge that only grew as he watched her inspect his space.

The bed was indeed large enough for the two of them, and he tried to ignore the tension that started in his chest and sank to his gut—and then lower—at the thought of lying beside her. He shoved the image aside and turned away before she could have a chance to sense how the thought affected him.

From behind him she spoke again. "Why can't you sleep on the floor?"

He started to walk toward the door. He didn't have time to discuss this further. Reaching for the door handle, he looked back over his shoulder at her. "The floor would be bad for my back. And it is only for two days, miss. You have my word I will not touch you. You're safe in here—from me and from my crew—for the short time you are here. Now, feel free to get acquainted with your temporary home, freshen up, rest, relax. You've had a long day, I'm sure. And I need to attend to things so we can keep to our schedule."

He didn't wait for a response or a glare, but instead turned and exited the room as quickly as possible. He'd wasted more than enough time trying to make a stowaway comfortable on his ship.

Had he gone soft? *Some pirate you are. A lass comes aboard your ship and you give her your bed?*

A true gentleman would have agreed to sleep on the floor or bunk with his officers, perhaps.

But he was no gentleman. He was a pirate, manners or no.

As soon as the captain had left, Aoife made her way across his quarters toward the door. She wasn't sure why she did it. Perhaps to ensure he was really gone and she was truly alone. Especially before she undressed for bed.

He was right. She was tired.

She laid a hand on the rough wood of the door, its texture a stark contrast to the pampered softness of her pale skin. So much set her apart from the crowd she was trying to hide among. Her cleanliness. Her feminine features. Her softness. Everything about her screamed non-pirate. And normally she would have been proud of that, but it wouldn't help her here.

Perhaps she should rethink this plan, but the distant shouting outside the door kept her from focusing on the task at hand. A yawn escaped her, reminding her of the exhaustion. It had been a long day. Had Lani truly been—exiled—this morning? A sharp pain hit her sternum at the thought of Lani dead. Not exiled. How could she survive a world without her sister's smile, her quiet humor, her silliness, the way she'd always teased Aoife for her absentminded, awkward nature? She'd never see Lani's face again or hear her laughter. She'd managed to avoid this pain all afternoon and evening, preoccupied with the simple need to escape and get away. But now she had nothing to do but wait, so the pain and torment—and the knowledge that it was all her fault—came flooding in against her will.

The weight of it all threatened to push her to the floor, the sharpness in her chest seeming to crush her, and her shoulders bent as she curved around it, as if she might fold up and disappear into the grief. She'd expected to cry and sob, but she must have been too tired to do so.

Or you're such an awful person you can't cry for your dead sister.

That thought intensified the pain, causing slight tremors to course through her, but still no tears came. She leaned against the door, forcing herself to remain upright. She couldn't bear the thought of him coming back in here and finding her curled up on the floor like a baby. Of course, if he came in at this moment, he'd have to push her off the door.

Still, she didn't move. She remained there, head pressed against the wood, warm from the moist sea air.

The voice inside her became a jumbled mess of self-loathing, reminding her how she'd betrayed the person closest to her and now she was utterly alone in the world. Except for the man she'd have to share a bed with for two nights. She steeled herself. She could do that. Sure, it was improper. And unnerving. But this wasn't a holiday. It was about survival. And if survival meant sleeping next to a man who annoyed the living daylights out of her, she'd do it.

Who was this man exactly? She finally had gotten his name, from Collins, but that didn't help her much. She kicked herself for not listening to all the tales told by the pirate lords' crews. She recalled the number of times she had heard—from all three pirate lords—that the young captain of the *Siren's Song* was getting too big for his ship and needed to be put in his place. When they'd started to boast of how they'd kept him from scoring some bounty, stopping him from reaching a port here or an island there, she had tuned them out. Pirate strategy and conquests were far from her areas of interest.

And yet she had a vague recollection of the stories she'd heard about this young captain. A captain so brutal he rivaled the first pirates who had sailed the seas immediately following the signing of the treaty. While the lords hadn't described his actions in detail—being in the company of the council ladies, after all—it had not been hard to envision all manner of heinous actions, the very kind the council and the people of Cregah had vowed to keep from their shores.

She found it hard to believe this was the same man from those stories. He'd been so polite, so cordial. Or at least more than she'd ever expected. And his quarters seemed far from those of a ruthless barbarian.

Straightening, she pushed away from the door, glancing around at the rich wood and sparse furnishings. It certainly wasn't like her lavish home at the council hall. There was little, if anything, here that didn't serve a purpose, didn't have a use. While her life had been one of leisure and simple enjoyments—music, art, books—the state of his quarters indicated a life focused on work. Except for the bookshelves along the wall. Far from empty. What need did a pirate have for books? Did they describe pirate strategy? Maybe they were merely ship logs or journals in which he took note of all his victories. And losses. She felt a pull toward those shelves, a need to feel the rich leather and softness of the pages against her fingers, to see what this man kept and stored. What he valued.

But voices outside the door pulled her attention away from the shelves and the books. They must have been just on the opposite side, because she could hear them more clearly than any of the other noises from the crew readying to sail.

"Captain, it's not right."

Aoife didn't recognize the voice, but it had a youthful yet experienced tone to it.

"I strongly advise against this." The man must have had some influence with the captain to be allowed to offer such an opinion and counsel. An officer perhaps.

"Aye, Tommy, I know," the captain said.

She waited to hear more from him, but it was the other man, Tommy, who spoke again. "The crew doesn't like it. You know it's bad luck. It will not bode well, especially if we're trying to get to the sound and back within such a short time frame."

"Mere superstition." The captain huffed in frustration.

"Perhaps, but superstition has a mighty effect on the ability of men to focus on their duties."

"Self-fulfilling prophecy that is. She's only here until we reach Foxhaven."

"You mean to leave her there?" Tommy's shock was evident in his words, even through the thick wood of the cabin door. And though Aoife didn't know what the man looked like, she could still picture the expression he must have had on his face as he asked the question.

"I can't risk taking her further. It's not ideal, but she's not my concern."

"You sure about that?" Tommy seemed to be toeing a fine line with that, and Aoife braced herself for the reprimand that was sure to come.

"Watch yourself, Tommy." The captain's words didn't carry the harshness she'd expected. The men must have been close friends.

"Excuse my boldness, Declan." Aoife started at the captain's first name being uttered. Close friends indeed. She pressed her ear closer to the door, not wanting to miss anything as their voices became softer.

"She remains. Until port. And while she's with us, she is under my protection. No one is to touch her or bother her. I have promised her that much. Once she's off the ship though..." Declan's voice trailed off, and Aoife felt a sudden pang of fear.

What should she expect in that port? What should she be preparing for? She had only aimed to get off Cregah. She hadn't thought about where she might be heading and how it might be far worse than the land from which she'd fled.

"Aye, sir. Understood."

Footsteps neared them, and someone else joined the conversation, but too quiet for her to hear.

Declan answered. "Very well, Gavin. As my quarters are currently occupied, we'll meet in the officers' quarters. Fetch Mikkel and meet us there."

There must have been a nod in response, but Aoife didn't hear anything more than footsteps walking away from the door.

Her body felt heavy under the grief and uncertainty. What she wouldn't give for a hot bath like only the staff at the hall could draw, with dried flowers from the gardens and soothing milk. She doubted she'd ever have such luxury again. And here she was on an old, smelly ship with nothing but the clothes on her back, sharing quarters with a man she only knew from bits and pieces of stories she'd overheard.

Another yawn reminded her once again of the weariness she'd managed to ignore while eavesdropping, and now she didn't care who might lie beside her in the bed. She simply needed to sleep.

She took a step away from the door, but at the same moment the ship lurched forward, and she stumbled to the left, slamming into the wall and smarting her shoulder. This was going to be difficult to get used to. The ship swayed, gently rocking as it began its journey away from port. At least the captain wasn't here to watch her wobble across the small quarters. To steady herself she used the desk on the right and the bookshelves on the left, too tired and too focused on not falling to bother perusing them as she'd wanted to. She'd have the next two days to do so.

She turned into the room and lowered herself onto the edge of the bed, surprised by the softness of the mattress. She'd expected something coarser, like straw. But this reminded her of the feather beds she'd grown up with.

Probably looted from some poor merchants.

She should have been more disgusted by the thought, but in this moment, with her limbs and joints screaming for rest, she was thankful for such accommodations. Without bothering to kick off her boots or remove any of the unfamiliar clothing, she lay down, closed her eyes, and let herself be lulled to sleep by the rocking of the ship.

ꟹ

The sun streamed in through the windows, its light bending with the waves in the glass as it warmed Aoife's face. Keeping her eyes closed, she stretched her legs, perplexed by the heavy weight of her feet. And for the briefest moment, with the softness of the feather mattress cradling her, she forgot where she was and what she'd done.

And then it hit her.

The roll of the ship beneath her bones. The weight of reality crushing her chest, sending the feeling of a million creeping legs over her skin. Her breaths quickened, and she clenched her eyes shut, but it only made it all worse.

Slow it down. Breathe.

She repeated the words to herself, trying to remember all the things the doctor had recommended for these attacks.

What had the doctor suggested? What was the phrase she was supposed to use?

Something about fear and safety.

Even though I'm afraid, I'm safe.

The mantra helped little when she remembered where she was. In the middle of the Aisling. On a ship full of pirates. Well-mannered pirates or no, she felt far from safe.

Her stomach growled a mantra of its own, which only intensified her longing to be back on land, in the council hall, with the staff bringing breakfast. She couldn't remember the last time she'd eaten, but it must have been a while ago given how earnestly her stomach complained.

She needed to get herself under control if she was going to dare walk anywhere in search of food.

Breathe. I am safe. I am safe.

She willed herself to believe it, and as her hunger mixed with the nausea from the ship's movement, she forced her eyes to remain open—which seemed to soothe the rolling of her stomach.

She'd nearly gotten her breathing slowed and the tingling in her chest eased when a movement beside her had her freezing in place.

Holding her breath, she inched her head toward the movement.

Captain McCallagh—Declan—lay on his side, facing her. His eyes were closed, so she dared let herself take in his full form. He lay atop the blankets, as she did. Whether it was because he hadn't wanted to disturb her or because of the heat in the cabin, she couldn't be sure. Not that it mattered, she supposed.

His white undershirt and loose bottoms left much to the imagination, and she was more than okay with that. If it weren't for his attitude, she might have found his face pleasant enough. But even in sleep he looked troubled, as if his dreams were stressful and tiring. While she'd managed a dreamless sleep that left her more rested than she'd expected—even with the panic she'd woken to—she could see the muscles in his forehead and jaw tensing from thoughts or images she wasn't privy to.

What do I care what's bothering him?

Care? No, she didn't care. It was curiosity. Nothing more.

She merely wanted to know who he was—this man who had taken her into his care and kept her under his protection. The way he'd said it yesterday, when he'd told her he would watch out for her, even for the two days, seemed like it had pained him. Likely he was annoyed having her aboard, and she couldn't blame him, could she? He'd had plans, an agenda to follow, and she'd mucked it up by trespassing on his ship.

Had there been a better option? She doubted she would have received better treatment from any of the other captains in port. Not even the lords she'd met at the council hall, even those who were potential matches for her. There was no wooing or courting with the matching process. They were matched by lottery, completely by chance, drawing a name from a bowl. It had seemed so odd to her, like a game—a somewhat unfair game, as the oldest heir would get first pick, though Aoife's situation would have been better than Darienn's, who would have been stuck with whomever was left after Lani and Aoife had selected. And now, Darienn would get her pick of the three—or maybe all three. Aoife wasn't sure how that was all going to work out now that there was only one heir remaining.

Not your problem anymore.

She shoved all thoughts of her old life aside, trying instead to focus on her current situation and wondering how she was going to possibly prepare for wherever they were heading.

She hoped to drive all the unnerving questions from her mind by studying his face again, as if she could deduce exactly who he was behind that stupid smirk.

There was something roguishly handsome about the stubble covering his jaw. And his hair. Most pirates Aoife had met wore theirs long, but not this captain. She wondered how he kept it so nicely cut while at sea, thinking of the shoddy job she'd done on her own hair the day before. And why didn't he keep his hair all one length? She would have thought it easier to manage without the longer pieces falling into his eyes, as they were doing now.

Without thinking, she lifted a hand to move the hair away from his eyes, but before she touched it, his lips moved and she froze.

"Morning, miss." His eyes remained closed, and she held her breath. Maybe she could pretend to be sleeping, though not with her eyes wide and staring at him. She should clamp them shut, but everything had frozen, and her body refused to listen or move.

"It's not nice to stare."

How did he know?

Slowly his eyes crept open, and he peered at her through the lock of hair she'd wanted to touch. He raised a brow, and she blinked, unsure of what to say or do.

"Ah, I've rendered you speechless. With my good looks, no doubt." He stretched a kink out of his neck before propping himself up on an elbow, his hand unnervingly close to her breast. She pulled back from him, desperate to put additional space between them.

She ignored his comments. "What is Foxhaven like exactly? Should I be nervous?" She kicked herself for not showing more confidence, but—rested or not—she didn't have the energy to drum up any, even for show.

"Perhaps. Probably should have thought of that before you trespassed and forced me to give you passage." He rolled over onto his back, his eyes turning to the wooden beams overhead. His linen shirt pulled tight across his chest, which was still as impressive as when she'd first seen him in the cove. She cleared her throat, as if that would also clear away the unfamiliar—and unwanted—warmth growing within, and she forced her eyes away from him, focusing on the wall beyond.

"I didn't have much choice." Her voice came out a near whisper, so low she wondered if he'd hear.

"There's always a choice. Good outcomes? That's another story. But a choice always remains."

She pondered his words and chewed on that basic truth.

She'd had a choice. That was true. Stay in the council, be matched to one of the pirate lords, rule over Cregah and administer justice with brutality under the guise of peace and care. Or run.

Had she taken the coward's way out? Even heading toward unknown hardship on the sea and in distant lands, she had run. She could have stayed and served. Maybe she could have changed things, worked from the inside out to right the wrongs. But no. That seemed impossible.

Her stomach rumbled again, loud in the silence hovering in the bedchamber.

She glanced at him. "Is there food?"

He turned his head toward her, his brow furrowed.

"What?" she asked, as if this was a natural and obvious question. To her it was, and her stomach grumbled again to make that point clear to him.

"Nothing. Simply seemed out of place for the deep conversation we were having."

"You thought that was deep? You merely pointed out the obvious."

He scoffed. "So obvious you hadn't thought of it until I mentioned it, eh?"

She glared at him. Why couldn't she hide things better? Had she looked so surprised to be told she'd had a choice?

"Food?" she noted again, and he grumbled out a sigh.

"Yes, we do have food, though nothing quite as nice as what I'm sure you're used to getting."

"At this point, I'll take whatever I can get." She lifted herself up onto her elbows and made to get up from the bed.

"Careful what you say. You might get your wish."

"All I really wish for right now is food. So if you could just tell me where to go to get some, I'll take my leave." She stood, or rather wobbled, on her feet as the ship kept up its bobbing. Steady or not, she managed to face him, well aware that her hair likely looked as disheveled as her clothes.

He cocked his head and sat up. "You won't be going anywhere."

She moved to protest, but he continued. "The food has come to you." And with that, he pointed out the door, and she took several uneven steps backward until she was in the main room of his quarters. A glance around showed nothing but his jacket flung over his desk chair, the map rolled up and set aside.

His annoyance came out on a breath. "There. In the dining room."

Right. His cabin was larger than she'd remembered. Her stomach grumbled again, urging her across the worn carpet, the reds and golds of which had become faded from the sea air and boots scuffing across it.

The dining room was scarcely bigger than her closet back at the council hall, but then, on a ship one couldn't have lavish ballrooms and seating for thirty. Atop the table she spied a modest yet fresh-enough-looking spread. She didn't bother to pull out one of the four chairs before reaching to pick up some hard cheese with her left hand and a handful of grapes with her right. Declan came up beside her just in time to witness her stuffing her mouth full of food.

"You shouldn't eat so quickly. Or so much," he warned.

She grumbled at him and turned back to the food to grab a roll. He kicked the chair out away from the table. "Sit. Before you get sick."

His words seemed to bring her back to reality—she was on a ship, rolling and tossing across the water—and her stomach turned. She plopped into the seat and braced herself against the table with her forearms. She refused to look at him, refused to see that know-it-all smirk on his face.

"You're welcome," he said and settled into the chair to her right, leaning back. But he didn't touch any of the food.

She swallowed. "Not hungry?"

"Oh, I am, but I prefer to give myself a bit of time to wake up before I gorge myself."

"Sleep well?"

His eyes narrowed at her. "What next? Will we chat about the weather?"

Aoife ground her teeth until they ached. Why couldn't he just be civil and act like a regular human being?

Because he's a pirate. There's nothing regular about him.

"Fine. We don't have to talk." She gave him a shrug and turned her attention back to the roll in her hand, picking it apart and placing small pieces on her tongue. She hoped he wouldn't notice her heeding his advice to slow down.

"We can talk. I simply prefer not to talk about trivialities."

"Ah, so you're a deep thinker then, Captain McCallagh?" He ignored her baiting, and that irked her more than any retort he could have uttered. "There is nothing trivial about inquiring about one's health, you know."

"Only when one genuinely cares about the answer, and I doubt wholeheartedly that you care one bit about how I am faring or how I slept."

He was right. Or rather, he should have been right. She shouldn't care about how he was feeling, not after he'd been so brazen with her in that alley. Not after he'd insisted on her sharing his bed. She shouldn't care. Yet, the way his brow had furrowed in his sleep and his jaw had been so tightly clenched concerned her for some reason. Something was bothering him, and she wanted to know why and what. But could she dare to simply ask him?

"What had you so upset?" Aoife kept her voice and her gaze low.

"When?" The bite in his tone had disappeared, and he seemed more…normal.

"While you were sleeping." She risked a glance at him through her lashes, only to find him watching her, his thumb rubbing against his lower lip. She waited, wondering if he was going to answer or if he was going to retreat and evade. Would he make a joke, or would he trust her with the truth?

His shoulders slumped under an invisible weight, and she held her breath, not wanting to risk scaring him away from telling her what that weight might be.

"Well, if you must know, I am dealing with an unexpected guest on my ship, and tending to her is keeping me from tending to the rather important business I have at hand elsewhere. And now, instead of planning and meeting with my men, I'm having to babysit."

She ground her teeth again as bitterness coated her tongue, but she forced herself to toss him a nonchalant shrug before reaching for a piece of salted pork.

"Fine, don't tell me."

"Aye, yes, in fact, my troubles do go beyond you and the little wrench you've thrown into my life." He sat up and leaned toward her. "But if you think I'm going to confide in you simply because we're sleeping beside each other for a couple nights, or because I offered to ensure your safety whilst aboard this ship, then you're as crazy as I am for not taking you back to the council myself."

And with those words, he shoved his chair back, the noise of old wood scraping so loud it made her cringe. He was out of the dining room in two steps, and she turned to see him grab his jacket and shove his feet into his boots before heading out the door, letting it close with a bang.

Although she hadn't learned what had been bothering him, she still turned smugly back to the food. She'd gotten to him, and that was fun in itself, perhaps better than actually learning the truth.

Declan stomped out of his quarters and at once scolded himself for acting like a moody child. His hands fisted, nails stinging his palms, but it only made him feel more irritated with himself for not remaining calm.

The sea air rushed past him, pushing his hair into his eyes. He pushed it back with his hand before stepping out onto the deck of his ship. His men were scattered about, some tending to the rigging while others eyed the horizon. One younger crew member noticed Declan from where he was cleaning part of the deck, which was likely still bloody from the previous skirmish, and dipped his chin in greeting. Declan returned the gesture before striding over to the stairs and up to the quarterdeck, where he found his officers chatting at the helm.

"Slept well, I see," Tommy offered, straightening the gray wool cap on his head. Why the man insisted on wearing the damn hat in this heat, sweltering and sticky even in these early morning hours, Declan could never understand. Normally he might tease about it, give him grief for having such an attachment to an article of clothing, but he was in no mood this morning.

"Well enough," Declan answered and leaned against the deck railing, looking out over his ship and his crew.

He couldn't stop his mind from playing through a number of irksome retorts the girl might have uttered had she been here. He should have left her on that dock or taken her back to the council. What would they have paid him for her return? What would they have granted? What might they have asked him to do for them?

A shiver rose up his spine, but he ignored it. No point in thinking about the what-ifs. He'd done what he'd done, and now he'd have to figure out the next step forward.

"If I may, Captain." It was Tommy again, but he'd inched closer, his head now near Declan's shoulder as he said in a whisper, "Did you get what you needed?"

Declan's brow rose, and he nearly laughed when a shocked expression spread across Gavin's face. Tommy apparently was incapable of speaking quietly.

"Not even close," he said.

"That's a shame." Tommy took up the spot beside Declan, mimicking his stance against the railing, both men ignoring Gavin's confusion over their conversation.

"Aye. It is."

"You have time though."

"Not much. With these favorable winds and Gavin's skill"—he threw a nod in the helmsman's direction—"we'll be in Foxhaven on schedule."

"More than enough time, I should think. Especially for a man such as yourself."

"No one likes a kiss-ass, Tommy, especially me. You've been with me long enough to know that."

"And yet, here we are."

Declan groaned and dropped his head into his hands, hoping his crew would merely assume he was tired. Though he didn't care too much if they knew how frustrated he was. They'd seen him—and stood by him—in similar enough situations and had continued to support him as their captain. Perhaps it was the honesty with which he ran his ship that earned such loyalty.

"I simply don't think I can stand to be in the same room with her. You know, when she's conscious. And talking. Always pestering me. Her voice. It's like the grating sound of iron against iron."

"And yet that noise always leads to something good, yes? Sharpened iron?" Tommy gave him an elbow to the arm. "Let her sharpen your iron, as it were. Use her. Or do you have another idea for how to gain the information we need to complete this job?"

Declan straightened away from the railing, turned, and leaned back against it, noticing how Gavin whistled and glanced off to the side to show he wasn't eavesdropping or butting in on their conversation. "What do you think, Gavin?"

Gavin feigned surprise as he turned to him. "About what, Captain?"

"Oh, come off it. We both know you're listening." He gestured to Tommy, who was still looking out over the deck.

Tommy didn't turn but called over his shoulder, "Speak, Gavin."

But before Gavin could utter his own opinion on the matter, heavy steps approached, coming up the stairs. The three men turned to see Mikkel trudging up the steps awkwardly. Declan often wondered how the man had survived so long without the sea tossing him overboard.

"Captain," Mikkel started, only offering the slightest of nods to the other officers present.

"What is it?" Declan's words came out not harsh but to the point, the way Mikkel preferred. He hated mindless chitchat. Quite unlike

Tommy and Gavin, who had to be nudged through conversations and guided past all the rabbit holes they found as they spoke.

"The men are restless, sir."

Declan looked around, searching for any sign of the restlessness.

"They hide it well enough, but there are murmurings, " Mikkel said.

"Murmurings?"

"Aye, they're nervous. About—"

"Her," Declan offered.

"Yessir. The girl."

"Woman," Tommy interjected over Declan's shoulder, and Declan elbowed him in the gut.

Mikkel shot Tommy a glare. "Either way. They're nervous all the same."

"What is there to be nervous about exactly?" Declan asked, raising his arms as he spoke. "We have good wind. We're making good time. We have food in our bellies, and we got at least an ounce of rest at Morshan. Yes?"

Mikkel shuffled his long legs, marking an invisible line in the wood of the deck. "It's true enough, I suppose, but it's not the present that has them uneasy. It's what's coming. Even if we're rid of her in Foxhaven, they worry it will not bode well for us later on."

"So what you're saying is, even if we leave her in two days' time, they worry having her here now will bring us ill fortune later."

Mikkel nodded before tucking his dull brown hair back behind his ear, his eyes as stern and serious as the weathered lines in his face. The bo'sun was older than Declan and his officers, but not by much. Still, they'd been grateful for his years of experience and the respect he garnered from the crew.

Declan kept leaning against the railing, trying to keep his expression casual. "So there's nothing that can actually be done now to stop that ill fate." It wasn't a question.

Mikkel again fidgeted uneasily. Declan waited, knowing what his bo'sun was going to suggest. What the men wanted.

"They'd like to be rid of her now, sir," Mikkel said.

"Ah, yes," Declan started.

He turned back to look over his crew. They'd gotten some rest in Morshan; that was sure. Those who hadn't been left back at the hospital on that rock were strong, rested, and bitter, and they now craved something he couldn't readily give them. Retribution. Revenge. The desire to deal a mighty blow—or maybe execute a covert attack—against those who had killed their brethren and lightened their pockets, keeping them from bounties they would have surely snatched. And now, unable to exact revenge outright, they looked for some way to quell that need.

And throwing the girl overboard? He could understand the impulse. Especially after spending time with her.

"But no, Mikkel. That won't be an option. You see, I've promised to protect her while she's aboard the ship. She has my word. I will not go ba—"

"You are a pirate, are you not?" Mikkel dared to interrupt, and Declan's body tensed, from the toes in his boots to the muscles in his jaw.

Perhaps he should have chosen to run his ship like the other captains, drive his crew more ruthlessly, doling out harsh punishments for any sign of insolence and disrespect. But he'd chosen to be different, chosen to treat his crew with respect, expecting the same in return. He saved his ruthlessness for those who needed it and deserved it, and he earned his crew's loyalty by showing he could lead them to glory and riches without beating them down.

But this affront from Mikkel could not stand. His heart pounded against his sternum, and all his options swirled in his mind. He needed to grasp one and act quickly.

He stepped in close to Mikkel until their faces were mere inches apart. He kept his words low enough that the others couldn't hear.

"Aye, Mikkel. I am a pirate. And a captain. Your captain. If you don't like how things are run on this ship, or how I handle my own personal word and code of honor, you are free to leave. Now. But if you would like to remain my bo'sun, would like your share of the bounty we're after, then I advise you watch your damn mouth and don't interrupt me again, or I'll have Tommy here place you in the brig until you can learn your own bit of respect and courtesy."

Mikkel inched back, his features a mix of frustration and concentration as the muscles along his jaw tensed. He dipped his chin in a slow nod, never shifting his gaze away from his captain's. "Of course, Captain. My apologies. I spoke rashly. The crew's unease must be grating on me."

"All is forgiven." Declan stepped back. "But do ensure the men know. The girl is off-limits. I find out someone has laid a hand on her, and they won't have a hand to lay on any other woman or themselves. Understand?"

Another nod.

Declan continued. "As for the restlessness and the superstitious bullshit, remind them they are the crew of the *Siren's Song*. Superstition holds no power here. We'll pick up new men, be rid of the lass, and be on our way to retrieve the greatest of treasures they could imagine."

"I'll tell them, but I don't know that they'll listen."

"They trust you, Mikkel. As I do," he said, clapping the man's shoulder before gesturing back to the deck. "Now go. Do your job."

Without another word, Mikkel turned and scurried down the stairs. Had Declan been too lenient, too soft?

He knew he didn't sound like other pirates. He knew his words and his actions and his values put him at odds with others in this line of work. Unlike most of the men who sailed the seas, he'd come from an educated background. His father had been his teacher while his mother and sister had run the pub. He and his father had pored over books, any books they could get their hands on, discussing the ins and outs of various figures and characters, discussing the war strategies they saw displayed in the history texts—why some had failed and others had succeeded. His father had instilled in him this love for learning, a love for the written word and the benefit of studying—especially history.

It was during that studying that he'd learned about the dagger. The dagger was all but lost to myth and legend. No one spoke of it anymore, except perhaps in children's tales. But in an old text, which he still kept in his quarters, he and his father had read about the rise and fall of the King of Tyshaly.

It was this knowledge that had sent them on this quest, and while he didn't owe it to his father to find it, he did hope finding the dagger would be the way to earn his freedom from the pirate lords, to finally gain victory over their larger ships and crews, to be able to—after enough wealth was acquired and enough loot was taken—set up a home where he could rest and read and forget all about the pain of the past.

Ah, to rest. So much standing in his way before he could do that.

Not the least of which was his sister's need for the dagger first.

He needed a plan, but so far he—with the help of Tommy, his master gunner, and Gavin—had not yet devised the best way to get into the council hall and retrieve the fae sisters. He needed intel. He needed an in. And his in was currently in his quarters, likely now sick from all the food she'd been engulfing. Never mind that he wasn't helping the situation by denying her the freedom to leave the cabin for some fresh air. He might need to ease up on that, but he couldn't trust her to not do something stupid, cross the wrong man, slip and fall overboard. Who knew what trouble she was capable of getting into?

A throat cleared behind him, and he turned. Tommy's brows were raised, eyes aglow with his usual brand of curiosity and humor.

"What is it?" Declan asked. He probably should have hired someone other than his childhood friend to be his quartermaster, and he often wondered if the crew distrusted Tommy because the two were so close. But it had never seemed an issue. Not to say it couldn't quickly become one. Especially if this job went sour.

"You know, I think Mikkel half expected you to stick a dagger in him."

"I think he would have actually preferred it," Declan said, releasing a sigh. He did try to keep his exasperation and doubt from showing when he was out in the open, visible to his whole crew, who could always be looking for a reason, a weakness, to exploit and overthrow him as captain.

"What man wants to be gutted though?" Tommy gave a shrug and then scratched at his forehead. "Plus, we're already short crew. Losing a bo'sun wouldn't help us."

"And if I lose the entire crew to mutiny? What then?"

Tommy scoffed. "That's unlikely. For now."

Declan straightened at the words. "What do you mean, 'for now'?"

"I'm only saying I don't know if the crew can survive many more run-ins with the lords. They need some victories, Captain. And they need them soon. Or they very well may look for a captain who can deliver—either on this ship or another that would have them."

Declan ran a hand through his hair and breathed the sea air deep into his lungs, as if the brine could preserve his place as captain, preserve the honor and respect he'd worked so hard to earn. If only it were that easy. But he knew Tommy was right. They needed a victory. They needed information.

As if Tommy could read his mind, he spoke again, leaning close and keeping his voice down. "Like I said last night, we need the girl, Declan. And what she knows. No one else here has stepped a foot inside that hall, and we can't risk everything on rumors heard and passed on by drunken men."

"Aye. I know. Don't like it, but you're right." He pushed himself away from the railing and started down the stairs. "Gavin, keep us on track."

"And where are you going?" Tommy asked.

"To find out what she knows."

"Good luck!" Tommy called, and Declan bit back a swear. He was going to need more than luck to get her to cooperate.

Cait moved the rag across the bar, wiping up the last of the spills from the previous night's patrons. Even after so many years spent running this place, taking up where her mother had left off, somehow she still loved it. Sure, the patrons could smell better, could act more like gentlemen instead of the pirates they were, but all in all, she was content. Happy.

Until she remembered where her pub was located and the heavy hand that wielded its power over this port and all the villages and people on the island.

She settled against the bar, hips digging into the old wood, shoulders caving under the pressure, hand gripping the towel as if it were a lifeline to her sanity or a dream she'd had long ago as a child and feared would fade the older she got. Declan had left the night before, and no doubt he'd noticed the poorly disguised woman who had trailed after him. Cait didn't need to worry about her brother. He had a good head on his shoulders. He could handle one silly woman. How she'd thought a set of clothes and a poor haircut would work... Cait shook her head at the image in her mind.

Declan could manage, for sure, but would the woman delay him on this job? She couldn't. He needed the dagger as much as the Rogues did. Though, there was a small part of her that wondered if he truly intended to bring it back to her or if he'd take it and run, use it to conquer the lords.

She couldn't worry about that. No point in worrying about stuff she couldn't change.

Declan was their only option, the only one who still believed in the legend of the dagger enough to have already been hunting it down. In reality she hadn't even been sure he, in fact, was searching for it. When a couple drunkards had come into the pub yammering on about a young captain chasing after legends and stories and enchantments, she'd guessed that young captain was her brother.

She'd guessed and been right. Or lucky. Would the luck continue?

There was still so much to do, so much to plan for. So much that could go wrong.

The door banged open, and Cait turned toward it, calling out, "We don't open for another few hours."

Two men stepped in, dragging in muck and filth from the streets and dirtying the floors she'd mopped up that morning. She forced herself to hide her anger over such disrespect. If they were any other patrons she would have put them in their place, but something about these two stayed her tongue. She eyed them, managing to keep her expression as neutral as possible. The years of practice dealing with the men the council sent to her door had paid off. But it had been a while since they'd sent anyone so overtly to her.

They'd undoubtedly been sent by the council, though, as her regulars all knew her hours and respected them. The men stood at about the same height, equally dirty and scruffy. The way one stood ahead of the other indicated some form of rank. *Or perhaps one is merely shy.* The green sashes around their middles and their necks marked them as members of Donovan's crew on the *Harbinger*. Not a good lot. As if any pirates were good, though some were notably better than others.

The one in front lifted his chin and spoke. "You should consider keeping your doors locked, then, miss."

"Thank you for the reminder. I must have forgotten to lock it again after I was done sweeping all the dirt and grime out from last night's customers."

She couldn't prevent her eyes from narrowing ever so slightly, wondering if they were smart enough to take the hint that she was not pleased by the mess they were making on her clean floors. They didn't budge or speak again, only stared down at her. "How can I help you, gentlemen? I can't pour you a drink outside business hours—council rules and all—but if you need help finding the nearest inn or a nice shop to purchase something for the ladies in your lives, I'm happy to oblige."

The second man didn't move a muscle, not even a hint of a smile or a twinkle in his eye to indicate he'd heard her. It was the closer one who spoke again. "Funny you should mention the council. We are here on their business."

Of course you are. Her bitterness rolled around in her mind, but she somehow managed to keep it hidden.

"Oh? You two strapping lads selected by the council. Whatev—"

The man interrupted. "Stop. Now." Cait closed her mouth gently, being careful not to snap it closed. It was dangerous to play up the innocent pub owner act for too long.

"What do you need?" All sweetness had vanished from her tone. "I'm busy, and I have to get the pub ready to open this afternoon. And at some point I'd like to grab some food. It's only me here running this place."

"We're looking for someone."

"Oh?"

"A girl. Older girl." An image of the disguised girl immediately popped into Cait's mind.

"We don't get many girls in here. I think I'd remember seeing one."

"She might have been dressed as a man."

And poorly. Poor girl.

Cait pretended to ponder their words, lifting a hand to her chin. She could have been an actress had her parents… She cut the thought off. "May I ask what she's done? Last I knew, women, even girls, were allowed to do as they pleased on Cregah. Has she done something wrong? Is she in trouble?"

"That's none of your concern, miss."

"Ah, but it is, you see? If there's a dangerous fugitive on the loose, someone who has broken our sacred rules of peace, I need to know! I need to be able to keep my promise to my patrons that they won't have trouble in my pub, that they can rest and drink in peace without worrying about some young maiden stabbing them in the back while they sit unawares." She'd gone too far with that, perhaps, but her patience was wearing thin, and she feared she'd lose any ability to hide her disdain and contempt if they stayed much longer.

"Yes, of course. My apologies." The man behind him remained silent, a statue, his stare boring a hole into her. "Nothing like that, miss. The council merely needs to speak with her."

"Of course. Anything to help the council. You know that." The silent one's eyes twitched at her words, as if he could perceive the mockery and attitude beneath them. She ignored it, though, and continued. "I don't recall anyone in here last night that might have been a girl posing as a man. And unfortunately all the crews who were here last night set sail this morning, I believe. Otherwise I would have recommended you seek them out."

"And which ships were those exactly?"

"Oh," she said, hemming and hawing as if she needed the extra time to recall their names. "The *Curse Bringer* and the *New Moon*...and I think there was another. Song-something, or something-song." At those words, the men looked at each other. As she'd expected. Her brother's ship always got reactions like that.

"The *Siren's Song*?" the second man broke his silence to ask.

"Ah, yes, that's the one! A peculiar name for a ship if you ask me. I always thought pirates and sailors were a superstitious lot, and I don't know anyone who would trust a siren, especially a singing one." She wanted to laugh at their reactions. Though they did a fairly decent job of hiding their unease, she had seen it often enough in the faces of her customers to recognize it plain as day now.

"The crew from the *Siren's Song* was here?" the first man said.

"Yes. But only briefly. They didn't even finish all their drinks. All that booze. Wasted. But at least they paid handsomely, so I suppose not all was a waste. Nice gentlemen though. Not like the others I get in here. I mean, not that they aren't all nice, but some are more grumbly than others. You know? That lot, though, was quite agreeable and pleasant, if I do say so myself." Cait prattled on, and she hoped they'd stop her soon, because she was growing weary from chattering like an idiot.

"But no girl, miss? You didn't see anyone you didn't recognize?"

She pretended to think again, looking up to the rafters as if the answer could be there. "No. I mean, I didn't recognize the *Siren's Song* crew, at first, as they don't come to Cregah much at all, but none of them looked girlish. I mean, the stubble and the deep voices would be rather difficult for a girl to fake, I'd think. Not that I've ever tried to pretend to be a man, so maybe it's not all that hard." She was tempted to attempt this, lowering her tone to say something a man might, but before she could continue, the pirate before her interrupted, his annoyance becoming more and more obvious.

"Thank you for your time, miss." They both seemed rather eager to get away from her and her blathering. "If you do see someone suspicious, or hear of anything from the other residents—"

"The council will be first to hear about it. You can be sure of that." Cait had always hated lying as a kid, and she regretted now that it had become a daily necessity for her, but that wasn't her fault. The council had pushed her to set aside any morals when she'd learned what they were capable of. What they did. And now she'd grown good at deception. She quietly—and only briefly—mourned the loss of her innocence and her honor.

No, she had honor still. It was these men here and the women they served who lacked it. She ground her teeth together, hoping they couldn't see the tension in her jaw or the tightness in her eyes. She needed them to leave before she said something wrong or let the facade slip.

"Now, if you please, gentlemen, I really must get back to work." Giving them as sweet a smile as she could, she lifted her eyes to the door behind them.

"Of course. Sorry to have bothered you, miss." They both turned, and Cait nearly laughed at how quickly they made their escape, as if worried she might bombard them with a flood of words again if they lingered.

Through the windows she watched them walk away, shaking their heads at each other. Yes, she could have been an actress.

But she had little time to congratulate herself on a stellar performance, because the truth remained. That girl hadn't been just any girl. Whether the girl was a threat to Declan's mission—and the Rogues getting what they needed—or not, she was indeed in danger. There was no doubt of that fact, if the council was hunting for her.

Cait reached below the bar and pulled up a glass and a brown bottle. Filling it to the brim, she lifted it up, giving a toast to the empty room. "Here's hoping you're okay, silly girl. Wherever you are."

She downed the liquid, savoring the burn as it glided down her throat and settled into her belly. She hoped the girl had ended up with Declan. Plans or no, his ship was likely the only one she'd be safe on, and Cait didn't need to know the lass to wish for her safety, even if her presence on his ship put their mission at risk.

Possible danger aside, Aoife could not wait to get to Foxhaven, if only to get a break from this blasted rocking and what it was doing to her insides.

She had at least managed to make it back to the bed to lie down, but that offered little help beyond keeping her from falling over as she tried to walk. She had thought maybe sleep would do her some good. After all, she'd slept perfectly fine the night before. But every time she tried to close her eyes, her stomach rolled and churned like the waves outside.

This was going to be the longest two-day voyage of her life. The only voyage of her life actually, but still. She'd often daydreamed back at the council hall—during classes or the pirate dinners—about how exciting and fun life on the seas must be for the men who chose that path. And now she knew better. There was nothing fun about all this.

Nothing fun at all about what was going on back home either. Or what had happened to Lani.

Aoife wondered who had been tasked with "dealing with her." Of killing her. She'd known the council regularly called on the services of pirates, but she'd always thought it was to ensure safety in the villages and towns, confiscating contraband weapons found on the island or something. But knowing now what her mother and the other councilwomen had been doing, she had to assume they'd use pirates for the messy work of execution. Who else was there to do it? If a pirate was caught in the act of carrying out the orders, the council could simply exile them, deny them safe harbor, keeping themselves in the clear from public suspicion.

That very thing had happened a handful of times in Aoife's life. She'd watched her mother sentence pirates and their men to exile. Aoife had never paid much attention to those men who had been caught. They were lesser pirates, none of them a possible match for her, and so she'd had little need to spend energy on remembering their names. But now, after having asked a pirate for safe passage on his ship, having seen and experienced them acting far more civil than she'd imagined, she wished she had seen them as worthy of her time. At least worthy of her memory.

And yet, she couldn't keep the bitterness from burning in her chest, at the knowledge that these men willingly killed her people. Perhaps they didn't like doing it, but how could they not? They were pirates! And as Declan had said, there was always a choice. They could have just as well stayed away from Cregah to avoid having to do such things for the council. Couldn't they? The only ones required to stop in were the lords, per the treaty, but she couldn't fathom the council putting those men at risk of being caught and needing to be exiled, as then they'd lose their ability to secure heirs.

Aoife tried to close her eyes again, but the sound of the door opening and boots walking across the cabin had her opening them again quickly. She considered sitting up, but the thought of moving even an inch turned her stomach. She stared at the wooden beams above her head, tracing the swirls and grooves as the footsteps drew nearer.

"Told you not to eat so fast." The voice came from the doorframe beyond her feet. She tilted her chin down to look at him, careful not to move too much. He stood against the frame, relaxed and casual, with his arms crossed in front of his chest. She expected to see the usual twist in his lips as he mocked her, but instead his face looked almost bored, though there was a hint of stress or worry playing behind the mask he wore so handsomely.

She banished the thought quickly with a shake of her head, and he laughed as she winced at the wave of nausea that followed the slight movement.

"Don't laugh at me." She'd meant for the words to come out menacing, but they were pitiful in her ears. And likely in his as well. "I've never been on a ship, you know. How long does it take to get used to it? How are you all able to move about without losing all the contents of your stomach every other step?"

"Apologies for laughing," he said with a bow of his chin. She shot him a look, trying to determine if there was any mockery in his words. There was none, even as he continued. "It depends, really. Each person adjusts differently. Some never get used to it. They're usually the first to be tossed overboard during a storm, not being able to keep their feet beneath them when the ship starts rocking."

"But it's rocking now. You mean it gets worse?"

Another laugh, but this one he cut short himself. "Aye," he said. "Much worse during a squall. I remember my first one as a cabin boy. I thought I'd never see the break of the sun through the clouds. Certainly thought the sea would take me as its prize. But it hasn't yet."

Aoife moved to sit up, feeling ridiculous to be talking to him while lying flat on her back. Propping herself on her elbows, she waited. When her stomach didn't revolt at the movement, she continued until she was sitting cross-legged, her elbows resting on her knees. She looked up at him again, surprised to see him studying her with a look that almost showed genuine concern.

"Are you quite settled now? Or do you need another half hour to shimmy a few more inches?"

She glared at him.

"So what do you want anyway?" she asked. "Did you just come to sit and laugh at my seasickness?"

"I'm not sitting," he said with a gesture to his upright position. She rolled her eyes, and again she felt like a little kid, remembering all the times she and her sisters had taunted each other when they were younger, pulling each other's hair, singing teasing songs about one another, and playing immature pranks whenever they were sure they wouldn't be caught.

But no, she wasn't a kid anymore, and neither was this captain standing before her. She would not stoop to such a childish level. She was an heir after all—or had been anyway—brought up to be mature and regal.

And a killer.

The thought punched her in the gut, hard enough to make her recoil. Thankfully he would likely assume it was the ship's movement causing such a reaction.

Drawing in a deep breath, she straightened up as much as she could and looked at him with as pleasant an expression as she could muster. "I see that. It was a figure of speech, Captain."

But he didn't take the bait, instead changing the subject. "Actually, Miss Aoife, I came to talk to you and keep you company for a bit."

There was no hiding her reaction to that, as her shock pulled at her features. "Shall we talk about the weather then?"

Not even a hint of perturbation on his face, which would have made her want to stomp her feet, had they been on the floor. Why did he always reduce her to this frustrated, childish state?

"If you like, we can," he said. "It's rather hot today. Not a cloud in the sky. A pretty good breeze filling the sails."

"It would be nice to get a bit of that breeze and sunshine, to be honest," she said.

His eyes turned to the ceiling above her and then to the windows beside her. "I think we could manage that. It might also help your stomach adjust better."

She couldn't keep her eyes from lighting up at his words. She'd expected him to deny her request, insist on keeping her locked up in his cabin, though she only now realized that he likely hadn't locked her in and she could have left at any time. But that might not have gone well, given how unreliable her legs were on this blasted ship.

He took a step away from the doorway, holding out his hand. "Well, come on then. Let's get you some air."

"Why are you being nice to me?" The question came out before she could stop it. She'd only meant to think it, but her tongue had betrayed her.

He lowered his hand and gave a half shrug. "Excuse me for offering. I'll see you out there." And with that, he turned on his heel and strode out, not slowing his pace to wait for her. Before she could even start to move her feet to the floor, he was out the door and clicking it shut behind him. She muttered a curse. He would certainly mock her if it took as long to get out of the cabin as it had to make it from the dining room to the bedroom.

She gritted her teeth, and with a hand on her stomach—as if that could settle it—she forced her feet to the floor and stood. So far so good. The thought of him laughing at her again made her ignore the wave of nausea as she moved. Pushing herself forward, she clenched her teeth when she stumbled and a wave tossed her against the desk. A minute later she had a hand on the door and was pulling it open, beaming with silly pride for having made it without vomiting all over his rug.

He stood there casually once again despite having no doorframe to hold him up this time. His gray eyes laughed at her—if eyes could laugh—and he opened his mouth to speak, but she stopped him.

"Don't. You. Dare." She bit off each word.

"Dare what?" He lifted a hand to his chest in feigned innocence.

She let out a growl and would have thrown her arms up in frustration had they not been the only thing holding her steady and keeping her from falling into him. "Are we going to chat in the doorway? Or is there somewhere else we can go sit?"

"Is the doorway not good enough for you, miss?" His eyes traced the wood around her, admiring it as he spoke. "It's a rather nice doorway, in my opinion. The finest on our ship actually. But if you require somewhere else…" He turned without finishing his sentence.

Before she could reply, he was off again, not bothering to offer her an arm to steady her, though she wasn't sure if she would have taken it anyway; her pride was too thick to allow it. But still, the thought of having to walk and stumble in front of an entire ship's crew made her stomach toss even more.

With a deep breath, Aoife steadied herself, pushing her chin up as she took the first step. Then another. She could do this. Surprisingly it was far easier to walk on the ship when she had the fresh air in her lungs and the breeze on her face. With her confidence building, she picked up the pace. The crew watched her as she walked across the deck to where the captain had stopped at a railing midship. Keeping her eyes on her target, on him, she ignored the stares and the glares, the hushed whispers, and the way the pirates seemed to inch away from her as she passed.

Declan stood with his back to her, his elbows resting on the railing and his gaze settled on the horizon. He didn't turn when she came up alongside him. She steadied herself against the railing, mere inches away from him, careful not to touch him. He didn't say anything. Aoife glanced at him out of the corner of her eye, not wanting to spook him—as if he were some wild animal she was approaching. There was something about him she couldn't quite place, something different, something that sparked curiosity in her. She didn't care about him. Of course not. But that didn't keep her from wondering who he was exactly, why he seemed so different from the other pirates she'd met, and what he was after.

"Feeling better?" Declan asked, though he continued to look ahead, his gaze lost in the depths of the sea around them.

"A bit, yes. Thank you." Aoife ran her fingers along the smooth wood of the railing. She'd expected it to be rough. Then again, she'd expected the pirates to be rougher too.

"Don't get it into your head," he said, this time turning to face her, "that we're all nice and accommodating. I have a reputation to uphold, of course."

A single huff of a laugh escaped her lips. "I won't tell anyone."

"Good. I'd hate for that tongue of yours to get people thinking I've gone soft and all."

"Whatever you say, Captain McCallagh." She'd hoped he would act a bit more perturbed by her poking at him, but his expression darkened. He seemed to see through her as if she weren't there at all. Her own smile faded, and her curiosity peaked again. Why did his face do this? Where had his mind taken him? What was he dwelling on? It annoyed her to not know, and it annoyed her more that it bothered her so much.

Aoife slumped her shoulders and turned back to the sea. She could wait for him to speak first. After all, he'd been the one who had wanted to chat, while she would have been content to lie in bed the rest of the day. Actually, no. The thought of being shut up in that cabin with the stale air made her stomach roll again. This was much better, with the air and the breeze and the sunshine. She could almost understand why men had chosen a life on the seas instead of returning home after the war. Almost.

"How old are you, Aoife?" Declan's question came out gruffly, and he cleared his throat before she could respond. She didn't turn.

"Nineteen. Twenty next month."

"Ah." In her periphery she saw him rough a hand over his chin. "So the matching would have been—"

"Next month," she said, interrupting him before she could think better of it. "What do you know of the matching?"

"Common knowledge. All who dwell in and around the Aisling Sea know of the agreements between the council ladies and the pirate lords. And even if they didn't, the pirates certainly would all know about it. Pirates talk."

"Of course. Like a bunch of gossipy old ladies." Aoife stifled a laugh.

"Pretty much. Perhaps worse."

Why was he being so civil? Was this the real Captain McCallagh before her? Or was he playing a game, toying with her? She couldn't be sure. Was this merely another side to him? He was such a mystery. A mystery needing to be solved.

"You weren't looking forward to the matching."

"What makes you say that?" Aoife couldn't keep the defensiveness from peppering her words.

Declan gestured to her getup. "You ran."

Her stomach twisted against her will as those two simple words reminded her of how she'd betrayed the council and abandoned her duties to Cregah.

"Yes," she whispered.

"Why? Why leave? I'm sure life at the council hall was comfortable, with all the luxuries one could hope for and none of the hardships and challenges."

She had no response, no idea how to explain. Did she even want to? She wasn't even sure she could utter Lani's name. Voicing her betrayal would solidify it, make it real.

"Or did you simply not care for any of the potential matches? I wouldn't blame you if you didn't. They're a miserable lot."

Aoife snatched at the opportunity to avoid all mention of her lost sister. Dead sister. "What do you know of them?"

"Trying to get the scoop on them?"

"Well, you did say pirates were gossips. I'm sure you know more about them than I do."

His face changed in an instant, annoyance flashing across his features, as if there were an hourglass counting down in front of him. Something was urgent. But they were on a ship, at the mercy of the winds, so why was he so frustrated by this conversation?

"I know enough about them to know you wouldn't have been happy with any of them." Before she could question how he could possibly know that, he added, "No one would have been happy with them."

"That ruthless and callous?"

"That stupid and dull." Did he just wink at her? Honestly, his moods seemed to shift as much as the ship beneath her feet, and Aoife found it difficult to keep up with which side of him she was speaking to. Was it the brooding one or the snarky one or the grumpy one?

"Maybe you're jealous?" Aoife said with an exaggerated sigh. "Want to be a pirate lord yourself, Captain?" She knew she was treading in dangerous water here, egging him on, pushing to get information and answers from him. But he didn't give her the reaction she wanted. Nor the answers she sought.

"No. Even if I could become one, I wouldn't. I'd never wish that title on anyone."

"All for the best anyway. The three eligible matches now have to fight over one heir." Aoife clamped her mouth shut too late, realizing her mistake. She'd opened up the conversation to the subject of her sisters, and she started to feel sick again at the thought that he might ask about Lani and Darienn. She held her breath, as if that would keep him from asking.

But he didn't.

"What was life like at the council hall?" Declan asked, his voice calm and casual, as if they were simply making small talk.

Aoife released her breath, thankful to have avoided the more uncomfortable topic, at least for now. "It was life? I guess. Boring, dull, but comfortable."

"Were you happy?" She shot him a look and then gestured to her outfit and the mess she'd made of her hair. He laughed. "Fair point. You know, there is one thing I've heard rumored about the council, but…"

Aoife narrowed her eyes at him, and her heart began to race in her chest. Did he know what the council did to people? Had the council used his crew to carry out the "exiles"—perform the executions? She wasn't sure she could speak to that if he asked. She might be sick all over again, and not from the rolling of the ship.

"What have you heard?" She kept her voice low, scared of what he was going to ask about.

"Oh, never mind. It's nothing. Mere children's stories and legends." He waved a hand toward her as if he were dismissing this conversation that he had started. But now her curiosity was dancing around in her head once again, eager to know what it was people said about her family and the council that could be marked as legend.

"You can't do that. You can't bring it up and then drop it so suddenly."

"Of course I can. I'm the captain."

Two sides fought inside of Aoife: the side that wanted to grab the man and shake him until he asked his question and the side that wanted to walk away and end this pointless conversation. She got the distinct impression he was playing some sort of game here, a game she didn't know the rules to and had no idea if she had any chance of winning.

"Well, if that's the case, I'll just be retiring back to our cabin." She pushed away from the railing and made to turn away from him, hoping he'd stop her so she wouldn't have to make the embarrassing walk back across the deck just yet.

"My cabin," he corrected her.

She waited, hands on her hips, feeling completely ridiculous in these clothes and with her hair shorn as it was, but she maintained the level of pride she'd mastered from her council lessons.

"Fine, I'll ask." He motioned for her to join him again. "But you have to promise you won't laugh."

She obliged but said nothing, letting her raised brows prompt him to get on with it.

"The legend—or I suppose it's more a mere rumor—is that the council ladies have three fae sisters working for them."

Aoife froze. Of all the things he could have asked.

According to her mother, no one knew of the Bron sisters, believing they had fled south to Larcsporough. The council went to great lengths to keep their presence at the hall a secret. It was only by accident that Aoife knew of them herself. At the age of eight she had taken a wrong turn while daydreaming and ended up in a hallway she'd never seen before. That darn curiosity had gotten the better of her, and she'd gone through a door that had mysteriously opened as she'd walked past.

And she'd seen them. Three sisters, as different in appearance from one another as she and her own sisters were, yet their features held an eerie similarity.

She had known in an instant they were fae, the subject of many stories from the Aisling Sea's history. But she hadn't known why they were there in this chamber in a forgotten hallway of her home.

She had intended to run back out and forget what she'd seen, but something about the sisters standing together in the center of the room, talking to one another in hushed tones, had her stepping forward without thinking of what might happen to her or what she was even going to do when they noticed her.

But they'd already noticed her. And when one of them had spoken to her, she'd frozen in place, her breath stilled but her heart racing.

"Ah, sisters, it's Miss Aoife. She's come back to see us all these years later." It was the tallest fae; her back was to Aoife, her red curls spilling around her shoulders. Aoife noticed the points of her ears poking through her hair, and curiosity stirred in her once again, mixed with the fear that came with the fae knowing it was her despite not seeing her. She remained still, waiting, so mesmerized by their appearance she didn't think to ask what she'd meant by come back.

"Renna, what do you think she wants?" said the tinkling voice of the shortest fae, who had an auburn hue to her curls. The color reminded Aoife of the jars of cinnamon and spices she liked to marvel at in the kitchen. This fae turned to the other, Renna, with eyes that showed she looked to her for direction. Even at a young age, Aoife could detect a hierarchy. She'd seen it with her own mother and the council ladies, and it was easy to identify here as well.

"Perhaps she's come to play with us!" The third fae spoke now, her golden eyes flitting to Aoife and back so quickly she wasn't sure it hadn't been her imagination. This fae was the most beautiful of the three—as far as Aoife could tell, with Renna *still not facing her. She was fascinated by those golden eyes, how they contrasted so perfectly with the milk chocolate color of her hair, which seemed to have a red shimmer to it when the light hit it just right. But her words sent panic through Aoife.*

She'd heard all the legends about the fae. Everyone had.

"Shush, Maura." Renna *had spoken again and was now looking over her shoulder to glance at Aoife for the first time. "We don't want to scare her away."*

"It's been so long since anyone's come to visit." Maura's words carried a hint of impatience and longing that increased the unease in Aoife's chest and stomach. "What do you think, Bria?" she asked, turning to her other sister.

"I do miss company, but..." The shorter fae let her words trail off, her eyes still looking to Renna *for guidance.*

"Let's let her decide, shall we?" And with these words, Renna *turned fully, her eyes—a sparkling mix of blues—boring into Aoife with an intensity she'd not even seen when her mother was at her angriest.* Renna *dropped an ear to her shoulder, her expression questioning Aoife, daring her to speak.*

But Aoife couldn't. And she ran. Turned and fled as fast as her legs could carry her.

She vowed to never return.

A cough sounded, cutting through her memory and pulling her back to her present company. She turned to Declan, whose gray eyes searched hers with such precision and sharpness, she thought he might actually be able to witness her memories simply with his gaze.

"Sorry." She cringed at how meek and nervous she sounded.

“So it’s true then?” His chin lifted.

“I didn’t say that.” Fingering the wood of the railing, she kept her eyes away from his.

“Not with words, no. But it’s written plainly all over you.”

“What of it? Why does anyone care if the fae are real and still on Cregah?”

“Not just on Cregah. Imprisoned in the hall. Serving against their will.”

Aoife started to protest, eager to defend her mother, but she snapped her mouth shut. He wasn’t wrong. They had been imprisoned there, and despite her mother’s insistence all those years ago that it had been for their safety, she knew in her gut that was a lie. Like everything else. “You didn’t answer my question.” Now she looked at him, challenging him to respond.

“I want to set them free,” Declan said, giving her a shrug. But he’d said it low enough that the waves drowned the words out so only Aoife could hear.

“Out of the goodness of your pirate heart, no doubt.”

“Of course not. They have something I need.”

Her stomach tightened against her will as she remembered the beauty of those sisters and the magical way their voices danced through the air. Was that jealousy? It couldn’t be. What did she have to be jealous about? It wasn’t as if she wanted to stay here with him. He was incorrigible and rude. And yet the feeling remained, the same sensation that had presented itself when Lani had divulged her secret.

“And why are you telling me this, exactly?” But she’d already guessed why. She was from the council. If he truly sought to free the sisters, he’d need her knowledge of the grounds to do so.

“Surely you’ve already figured that out.” How did he always read her mind like that? She ground her teeth and took a deep breath of the sea air.

“And what do I get in return? For helping you?”

His eyes brightened. He must not have expected her to be so willing, so cooperative. Though she hadn't yet decided if she would be.

"Anything you wish, Aoife. Well, anything you wish that is in my power to provide." With this, he bowed his chin and waited.

Declan waited for her to speak, attempting to ignore the twitching inside his gut that seemed to count down the time he was possibly wasting here. She at least seemed amenable to the idea of helping him, but he didn't know what she might demand in return—or if he could even deliver on any of those demands. And he was sure there wouldn't be just one thing on her list. He watched her as she took her time and turned back to study the deep blue of the sea. Her lips pinched as she thought, and he was nearly convinced she was taking her sweet time just to toy with him.

"Well," she started. He had to settle his foot, which wanted to tap out the impatience coursing through him. *Get on with it, girl!* his thoughts screamed at her, but he forced his features to remain calm.

"Yes?" Too sharp. Too eager. He needed to rein in this urgency before it scared her away.

"Two things." She was still facing the sea, and he wondered what her eyes saw beyond that horizon. Hope? Escape? Fear? Her voice cut through the rambling thoughts. "I'd like a change of clothes."

He dropped his head to the side and looked her over. Though she certainly wouldn't pass for a man in her current attire, the clothes fit her well and didn't make her look terrible. "And what is it I could provide for you? We are fresh out of more feminine garb."

"Is there not a crew member who might be of similar stature who might loan me something else?"

"Look around, miss." He bit back his frustration, trying to stay as polite as possible. He needed her cooperation, after all. He waved a hand over his shoulder but didn't turn around. "Does it look like we have changes of clothes? Or that we launder our garments often? Plus, you're only with us until tomorrow."

"Oh." Part of him felt sorry for her. A very small part. It must not have been easy to leave behind a life of luxury and comfort, of closets and chests full of clean clothes. But life wasn't easy. And the sooner she learned that, the better. He waited for her inevitable snark at this, some comment about the way they looked or smelled. But he was a little taken aback when she said, "Well, in that case, I shall learn to appreciate that these clothes fit so well. Plus, they are quite a bit easier to maneuver in than all the skirts. I just wish they weren't so dreadfully hot."

He almost wished she'd said something snippy, because these useless statements did nothing but waste his time, and it took every ounce of his willpower not to grab the woman and shake her, telling her how precious little time he had to come up with a feasible plan!

"What's your second demand?" Declan's words came out clipped, and he was sure she would hear the urgency in them. *And probably drag out her answer for spite.*

This time she turned toward him and, in doing so, ended up a few inches closer. He could smell the last remnants of perfumed soap on her skin, though this did nothing but irk him more. She didn't belong here, and he kicked himself for allowing her to remain—information or no. When she straightened, growing an extra inch, her eyes boring into his, he had to admire the fearless side of her that would dare stand up to a pirate captain, especially one now armed and capable of tossing her overboard with little effort.

"Let me help." Brave and unwavering, her answer caught him off guard. But he recovered quickly.

"You are helping."

"You know what I mean." Indeed he did, but that didn't mean he wanted to give in so easily. "Let me stay aboard after you hire the new crew. Let me go with you to free them." The bravery she'd shown a second ago seemed to be starting to slip, as though she were pushing herself to face a demon she desperately wanted to run from. These emotions and her close connection to the council could cost them though. Even if she sought to sever her bond to her family, she was a liability, and he couldn't take the risk.

"No." Even as he said it, he regretted it, but he'd find another way. He had to. He could do this without the information she had. "I can get what I need from somewhere else."

"Okay then. In that case, I believe our conversation is done, yes? I'd like to enjoy the fresh air in silence for a bit." And with that, she shut him down.

How had he lost control of this situation?

Regardless, he'd prepared for this possibility, in case she'd been unaware of the existence of the fae or unwilling to help. He'd already had the backup plan ready, although it wasn't a particularly good one. He would need to take a little longer in Foxhaven. Have his men ask around, collect information, perhaps pay for some, but even then he wasn't entirely sure anyone outside the council would know what he needed.

And now that he had to resort to this alternative plan, he'd need to prepare for the work ahead when they arrived in port tomorrow.

Turning, he quickly made his way to his cabin, signaling Tommy—who was standing on the quarterdeck pretending not to have been watching his failure with Aoife—to follow. Back in his cabin, he slumped into his chair, leaning back and looking at the ceiling. His quartermaster came in without a knock, silent with trepidation, uncertainty playing on his face.

Declan wanted to remain calm. To be that put-together, calm-under-pressure captain he portrayed to everyone else, but he couldn't. A growl escaped, though he kept it quiet. It was one thing to let his closest friend see him lose it. Quite another to have the crew hear him as he did. His hands clenched into fists so tight he half expected to draw blood from his palms as his arms shook from the tension. He lifted them to his forehead before dropping them. Tommy waited, lips pursed and brows raised, like a parent waiting for a toddler to finish a tantrum.

One second more, and Tommy spoke. "So it went well then."

A single laugh erupted from Declan. "Well, it wasn't a complete waste." He brushed a knuckle against his nose, beginning to relax now that he'd gotten the initial frustration out. "We now know the fae are there."

"She's seen them?" Tommy took half a step forward.

"She didn't say as much, but she might as well have. When I mentioned them, she seemed to get lost in a memory. And when I requested her help, she didn't deny her ability to do so."

"Or she was playing you just to get what she wanted."

"She wanted clothes."

It was Tommy's turn to laugh now. "Well, I mean, we could have maybe offered her something from the last chests we lifted, but there's not much, and little that would fit her."

"Yeah. I told her no. Plus, she won't be here long."

"That's all she requested? Clothes? Seems like we could have offered to at least buy her some new clothes in Foxhaven if that's all it took."

"If only." Declan let out a breath. He eyed his quartermaster, who couldn't hide his curiosity at all.

"Oh?"

"Aye. She wants to help."

Tommy's brow furrowed. "Wait."

"Yeah, I know. That's what I told her." Declan gave thanks that they were close enough to share thoughts without unnecessary words.

"So she wants—"

Declan finished his sentence, "—to come with us."

Tommy had no words at first. He seemed to be mulling over his response, choosing his words wisely. "And you said no?"

"Of course I said no."

"Of course. How foolish of me." Tommy paused a second and then added, "But why exactly did you say no?"

"Too complicated."

"Well, that's a given—"

"No, I mean, her involvement makes it even more complicated. You didn't see…didn't hear…" Declan had never struggled with words this much before. Usually they rolled off his tongue with ease and precision, but now he felt all tied up in knots, unsure how to explain or describe any of this.

"She's really done a number on you, hasn't she?" Tommy might have looked amused, if it weren't for the concern on his face.

"What?"

"I've never known you to stumble over your words, and I can only assume—"

"It's not that," Declan said, interrupting again. "It's nothing to do with her. It's this whole insane situation we're in. And she—"

"So it is about her."

Declan picked up the closest thing on his desk—a book—and threw it at his friend, who didn't budge, didn't even blink, as it hit him square in the chest and fell to his feet.

"Regardless, we need to hammer out this alternate plan that doesn't include her," Declan said, holding his quartermaster's gaze.

"Aye, Captain. Sure thing. We'll want to bring Mikkel into the conversation though, yes?"

Declan thought for a moment, roughing a hand over his jaw. "I don't know."

"You need the crew to know what we're after. And right now, they're sailing blindly."

"They will know. Eventually. When the time is right." Declan hoped it would be enough. For now, he didn't need the crew more nervous than they already were with a woman onboard. And he had no doubt they'd be even worse off if they knew where they were ultimately headed. Even he couldn't deny the twinge of fear he was experiencing at having to face the evil lurking beneath the surface of the Black Sound.

"Fair enough. So the plan." Tommy had just made a move to sit in the chair in front of the desk when the door creaked open.

"Excuse—" Declan started to reprimand the intruder but stopped when Aoife walked in.

"Oh, sorry, Captain. Tommy," she said, her gaze flitting about the cabin awkwardly as a blush spread across her freckles, readily visible even in the dim light inside.

"How did you know my name?" Tommy turned toward her with what Declan could easily assume was his oft-used inquisitive expression.

"Lucky guess?" A second passed, and she added, "I overheard it yesterday. At the door. And just now I recognized your voice. Connected the dots, as it were." She trailed off. Perhaps she realized she'd been rambling.

"Eavesdropping isn't polite," Tommy muttered as he turned back to Declan, shooting him an amused look.

Aoife spoke up again. "Apologies. I didn't mean to. Difficult to ignore noises when you hear them."

"Uh-huh." Declan wasn't convinced, but he ran back over his recent conversation with Tommy to determine if she might have heard anything she shouldn't have.

Aoife fidgeted again, still standing in the open doorway. "Shall I come back later?" She didn't seem too eager to go back out to the deck. Even though it would help the seasickness, he had no doubt the sensation of prying eyes was far from comfortable. He should have forced her into the discomfort. She'd need to get used to the feeling if she were going to insist on being out on her own away from the council. And yet, there was something that kept him from doing just that. Something about the look in her eyes. It reminded him of an innocence he'd lost in himself long ago, and part of him—some part of him he'd tried hard to forget—wanted to help her preserve that piece of her. If he could.

Declan stood and motioned for Tommy to follow suit. "No, you're welcome to stay here for the time being. We can take our conversation to the officers' quarters."

Tommy's face contorted into a look of amused confusion, but he complied. Declan moved swiftly around his desk and nudged Tommy toward the door as Aoife stepped to the side so they could pass.

"There's some food in the dining room if your stomach can handle it," he said to her. "Tea too, but be careful this time. I don't want to have to ask someone to clean up any unnecessary mess."

Before she could glare at him, he was out the door and had it shut behind him with a resounding click of the latch.

"I think you're right. We need Mikkel in this discussion so we hire the right talent in Foxhaven tomorrow." He was already speaking before he turned to find Tommy standing there, arms crossed and gaze prying him with a silent demand to know what had just happened.

But Tommy said nothing and didn't make any show of moving to find Mikkel for their meeting. Declan could offer some explanation, but he didn't owe that to his quartermaster, friend or not. He was the captain. And right now they had more pressing matters than discussing how he chose to treat an obnoxious stowaway.

The sun had long ago set behind Declan, but he remained at the prow, watching the sea darken before them, the horizon disappearing as the sea and sky faded into each other. They still had a day of travel left, maybe half a day if they had some good luck.

Luck. What a ridiculous notion.

Declan had spent the better part of the afternoon strategizing with Tommy and Mikkel in the quartermaster's cabin. And he was now confident they had at least half a chance of getting the information they needed from the men who frequented Foxhaven. While it didn't provide the same security and rest as Port Morshan, Foxhaven served its purpose for the pirates. Declan preferred it to Morshan, and the need to watch his back and keep up his guard didn't bother him in the slightest. He could take care of himself and didn't have to worry about any rulers demanding his services as payment.

In fact, Foxhaven barely had any sort of ruler. The man in charge, Porter Rogerson, had stumbled onto the shores, quite literally, about thirty years back. He'd been captain of a merchant vessel from Caprothe, and their ship had been tossed about so violently in a storm that he and the quartermaster had all but given up any hope of surviving when they'd landed on the tiny island south of Turvala. They'd found little more than a handful of weather-torn buildings that had long since been abandoned, but they somehow managed—over many years—to turn that beaten-up beach into a thriving port, which Rogerson still ran much like he had run his ship. Half drunk and stupid.

But it was to the benefit of the pirates, who were able to do business with no outside interference and had some semblance of protection from the cannons Rogerson had stationed along the entrance into the port, which fired at anyone who threatened his stronghold here.

Morshan might provide rest without fear, but the council had also forbidden pirates from hiring crew within their port, leaving Foxhaven as the best place to recruit new hands. It was unusual to find pirate crew switching ships, but in Foxhaven pirate captains could find disgruntled former merchant sailors looking to get out from under the heavy hands of their oppressive captains and earn a higher wage.

Declan clenched the wood of the railing as he looked toward that next port far off in the distance, not yet visible. He needed more than mere bodies to fill the holes in his crew. He needed those who weren't perturbed by the name of his ship. Men not ruled by superstition and fear. Or men not afraid to die. It wasn't always one in the same.

With a sigh, he scrubbed a hand over his face. The recruiting would actually be the easy part. Gathering the information would prove far trickier.

The only people who might have some knowledge of the council hall would be those who had actually been there, or those who worked for those who had been there. The pirate lords didn't stop in Foxhaven, at least not often, so he couldn't bet on their crews being around to pry the information out of. But the ships in their fleets, the ships that provided them with the additional bounty they used to buy their way into the council's inner circle, those were Declan's in. Those men would be more likely to talk, more likely to have heard stories from the lords' ships, or to have possibly stepped foot in those halls themselves.

He'd tasked Tommy, Mikkel, and Gavin with splitting up and each going to a different establishment in port to find the men. Declan knew his best bet would be to find men who worked under Saarin, Madigen, or Tiernen, as those lords were matched to the ladies of the current ruling council and would have visited more recently.

If he were lucky, perhaps the other three unmatched lords might have their ships in port. Perhaps a bit of final fun before their matching. Except two of those matchings wouldn't be happening now, and the remaining heir was too young to be matched yet. And so Declan couldn't count on that bit of fortune. Plus, he hadn't lied when he'd told Aoife how stupid those lords were. He wasn't even sure how they'd managed to build fleets large and successful enough to pay the high tax to become lords.

The sky had darkened around him, all remnants of the sunlight gone below the horizon, and a speckle of stars twinkled overhead. The crew was quiet. The ship was quiet. If there was one benefit to having them all on edge with Aoife aboard, it was this, that he could actually have silence.

He could think.

But he'd left Aoife alone for too long, and as little as he wanted to deal with her incessant rambling, pointed comments, and way of looking like she wanted to stick her tongue out at him, he didn't like the thought of her having too many hours alone in his cabin with his stuff.

With one more look out over the black sea, he sucked in a final breath before heading back to the cabin.

He half expected to find her asleep as he had the previous night, lying like a rag doll with one booted foot hanging off the edge of the bed. But although she was in bed, she wasn't sleeping. She was reading.

He stood in the small doorway of the bedroom for what felt like several minutes, staring at her without her looking up. He studied her for a while longer. Even with her hair chopped so haphazardly, she was cute. Pretty, in an adorable sort of way. Freckles danced across her cheeks and over her nose, peppering her cream-colored skin that clearly hadn't been in the sun much. She seemed so much younger than she was, and it was hard to believe they were actually so close in age. Had he met her under other circumstances—had he not long ago given up on such a future for himself—he might have hoped to catch her eye.

He shooed the thought away.

They hadn't met before, and with her being an heir, they never would have. Even if he had stayed home in Morshan with Cait, they never would have met under any pleasant circumstances. And it did him no good to wonder about what could never have happened. And would never happen.

"Is it good?" he asked, not bothering to warn her of his presence with a throat clearing. But she didn't startle, nor did she look up from the words she was reading.

"Quite." As much as her rambling and overuse of words annoyed him, this single one cut sharper into him, sending tension through his jaw.

"What is it?" He remained in the doorway, though all he wanted was to crawl into the bed and rest. Perhaps have a dreamless sleep for once.

She held up the book so he could read the spine. *Legends and Myths of the Aisling.* His eyes went large, and he turned back to the main room. He'd forgotten the book had fallen at Tommy's feet when he'd thrown it at him like a child. Neither he nor Tommy had picked it up, and now she had it. What had she read? Did she know what he was seeking? Why he wanted—needed—the fae?

"Ah, good bedtime stories," Declan said, hoping he sounded casual, with no hint of the worry stirring within. "Beware of some of them though. They lead to nothing but nightmares filled with evil and terror."

At that, she finally looked up and over the book, her eyes twitching the way they always seemed to when something sparked her curiosity. "Oh? Is that what bothered you so much in your sleep last night?"

He'd walked himself right into that question.

"No." He approached the bed and sat on the edge, leaning down to take his boots off. This felt strange. Too domestic. Too normal. Too much like the times he'd watched his father and mother go through a similar routine back home, when he'd hidden behind the curtain in their doorway, thinking they didn't know he was there. But they'd always known, and they'd always called him in for bear-sized hugs and good-night kisses. The memory was too strong, and it pushed Declan to stand, his boot unlaced but still on his foot.

His hands began to shake, and he hoped she didn't see. She'd think him mad. Not that he cared what she thought really, but he'd spent so much time keeping those stupid memories at bay. He wasn't ready to have them resurfacing. Not now. Not ever was preferable, but certainly not now of all times.

"Are you okay?" Aoife asked. He mulled over her words, searching each syllable for any hint she was goading him or mocking him for his ridiculousness. But he found only care and concern, which was decidedly worse.

"I'm fine." He sounded anything but fine.

"Are you hungry? I think I left you some of the salted meat and fruit from dinner. The man who brought it was nice enough, though he seemed really eager not to spend more time with me than he had to, and when I asked his name, he ran out in a terror. I half expected him to start screaming, as if I were a ghost!"

Declan normally would have rolled his eyes at her uncanny ability to string so many words together into what seemed like a single breath, but now he welcomed the noise to drive away the memories.

He looked over his shoulder at her. Her focus remained on the book, though she seemed to be merely avoiding him rather than actually reading. "That would be Philip. He doesn't talk much as it is, but I'm not surprised by his reaction. The crew is nervous with you here."

"Ah, that explains a lot actually." With this, she shut the book, keeping her finger trapped in the pages to hold her place. "All day I felt the crew staring at me, but they kept their distance. Even Collins, who seemed fine with me yesterday. Was it really only yesterday?"

"I know. Time with you seems to drag on and on. I feel like we should have a full moon overhead already." He walked around to the other side of the bed—his side of the bed—unlaced the other boot, and nudged both off as quickly as he could before the memories could return. Settling onto the feather mattress, he propped himself against the aged wood of the headboard. He had started to close his eyes when her voice snapped them back open.

"Is life always so boring on a pirate ship?"

He closed his eyes again as he answered; he didn't need to look at her to carry on a conversation. "Were you hoping for more action?"

"A bit, yes."

"Silly girl." He wanted to laugh but decided against it.

"Perhaps." Her tone was almost mournful. "It's just not what I expected. *You're* not what I expected."

Declan opened his eyes now and found her studying him. The green of her irises pulled him in, threatening to pull him under. This was getting trickier with each shared word. He didn't want connection. He didn't want her looking at him this way, as if she could see the parts of him he never showed.

"I'm sorry to disappoint." He clipped the words short, his eyes piercing hers. "I could offer to throw you overboard if you wish. That would certainly gain me some extra clout with the crew."

Pursing his lips, he looked at the wooden beams above the bed, as if he were pondering doing just that.

"That's not necessary," she said, and he happily sensed some real fear—however faint it might be.

"Or I could take advantage of you being in my bed right now."

He moved before she could, grabbing her by the arms. Lifting her easily, he swung her over him until he had her pinned down on the feather bed, his full weight holding her down. The book—still in her hands—pressed against his sternum, and his face hovered only inches from hers. He considered all the ways she could retaliate and prepared himself for any of them, but she merely lay there, with a look of shock and fear in her eyes. He pressed his hips harder against hers and licked his lips. It was a show, and yet there was a small part of him that wanted to do exactly what he was threatening. He shoved the feeling away, just as he needed to do to her.

"If I didn't know any better, I'd think you wanted this. Wanted me." His words came out low, a hoarse whisper against her ear as he leaned down further. Though she shuddered a bit under him, she said nothing. She didn't do anything. He let his breath warm her ear, let her hear his tongue brushing over his lips once more before he spoke, his words coming out as more of a purr than a growl. "Don't beg for action if it's not what you want."

And with those words, he retreated, releasing her and returning to his side of the bed. It was too hot to sleep under any blankets, so he rolled over onto his side and did his best to calm his breathing, longing for a dreamless sleep. She still hadn't moved, still lay there where he'd forced her down. He couldn't stop seeing the fear in her eyes, but he reminded himself it was for the best.

The seat Declan sat on was rickety and needed to be mended once again. His father had been meaning to get to it, but there were other tasks requiring his attention around the pub.

His mother's voice wafted through the room as she counted up the money from the night's business. It was nearly morning, and most children would have been in bed at this hour, but most children didn't have parents who owned and ran one of the only pubs in the port.

While most kids went to the local school, Declan and those whose parents kept irregular hours were schooled at home. As the government and all businesses on Cregah were run by women, it fell upon the husbands and fathers to handle everything else, including the education of their children.

And so it was that Declan was sitting at his spot at the bar, dangling his young feet and trying not to hit the wood, lest he get a reprimand from his mother, while spinning one of the coins a customer had tossed to him. He watched it spin and spin and spin until it lost momentum and fell.

He didn't hear the door behind him open, but his mother was around the bar in an instant, informing whoever had entered that they were closed.

But these weren't customers. And before Declan could turn around, his mother was out the door with them. He didn't know if she'd gone willingly or if they had dragged her. All he knew was that his mother now stood between two men who were muscular and nearly twice her size, but she didn't look afraid. Her chin was held high, her posture pin-straight. Even through the old waves of the glass window he could see her pride and her fortitude.

Declan moved to call for his father, but by the time he found his voice, it was too late. His mother was gone, being dragged out of sight.

His father came running, dropping the crates he'd been moving in the back storeroom, and tore out the door. He looked one way and then the other, his vision no doubt hindered by the pre-dawn fog and darkness.

Declan stayed behind, frozen on the stool, wrapped in absolute silence.

Cait wasn't there. Out with the boy she was courting for the better part of six months. She wasn't there. To help their parents. To help him.

Declan was shaking as he woke from the dream. The memories.

Another night. Another nightmare. Always the same. It seemed the harder Declan fought them, the more persistent and intense they became. Even after all these years, that day still plagued him. The helplessness. The weakness. The utter despair.

He'd never seen his mother again.

Later that evening, the two men had dared return to the pub. Declan had seen the dagger gleaming in the moonlight as his father stalked after them, but he hadn't been able to stop it. To stop his dad from taking revenge. To stop the people in the street from dragging his dad off to the council hall for justice. To stop himself from taking the blade from the body when no one was looking.

Cait had refused to go to Morshan's local authorities to file a grievance, insisting instead that the council would not be able to help. He'd hated her for that. For her absence. For her apparent indifference. He'd only stayed at the pub in hopes his parents would one day return, but after a year, he gave up, going down to the port while his sister slept in search of a crew in need of a cabin boy. And it was then, at the age of ten, that he'd been hired to work on a ship alongside another young boy named Tommy.

Years later he'd learned of his parents' likely fate.

And only then did he choose to forgive Cait, even as he vowed never to return home.

Keeping his eyes closed, he tried to steady his breath and calm his nerves. With how little sleep and rest he managed, it was a marvel he'd survived all these years and come to captain his own ship. Either he had become accustomed to this exhausted state or it gave him the gruff edge he needed for the job.

Aoife stirred beside him, and the beginning rays of the morning sun warmed his closed lids. The bed shifted as she rose. Her timid steps were a bit more even today. Perhaps her sea legs were finding her sooner than he'd expected. He turned over and propped himself up on his elbow to watch her, his vision slowly coming into focus. Through the doorway he could see her make her way past the desk to the table where Philip had come in earlier to drop off some food and tea. The peppermint had seemed to quell her nausea, at least. Last thing he wanted was to have his cabin smelling vile if her sickness overtook her.

The silence hung in the room as thick as the fog from his dream. He cleared his throat, the gruffness cutting through the air, but she didn't turn and didn't acknowledge him.

Indifference. Good.

This was decidedly better than the closeness he'd risked last night, which he'd had to cut off.

His stomach grumbled, pushing him to get up and put his boots on. He strode over to the table and grabbed a piece of meat and a slice of cheese. She didn't look at him. Didn't seem to notice him. She merely sat staring at, but not seeing, the cup of tea before her. He opened his mouth to make a comment, an extra insult to emphasize his point from the night before, but before he could, an alarm rang out from the deck.

"Sails!"

Declan bit back a curse as he turned, not bothering to wait to see how Aoife reacted to the news. She wanted action, didn't she? Perhaps the crew was right and she indeed was a curse.

He had barely reached the door when it burst open and Tommy rushed in.

"Captain." He was nearly out of breath, but seeing Declan was already on his way, he stopped short and turned on his heel. Declan followed close behind, stopping only to secure the door behind him.

On the quarterdeck, they made it to the stern as Tommy handed him his spyglass and pointed. Declan might have given his friend grief for pointing out the obvious sails on the horizon, as if Declan were blind and couldn't clearly see them, but this wasn't the time.

Were these friends? Or another pirate lord come to cut them off at the knees?

"Who do you think it is?" Tommy asked, leaning close so the crew—who had all but stopped their sailing duties to wait for an order—wouldn't hear. Time stood still, the ship eerily silent aside from the random flapping of a sail and the lapping of water at the hull.

Declan mumbled an "I don't know yet" as he looked through the glass, trying to find any clue as to who followed them, but they were still too far off and had not raised a flag to signal them. Not a good sign. A friend would have likely raised the flag of peace to let him know they weren't a threat. A flag of warning came much later, when the approaching ship was close enough that escape wasn't an option.

If that warning wasn't made with guns instead.

"Could it be Grayson?" Tommy asked, squinting at the horizon. As if that would help.

"Perhaps. We haven't run into him in ages."

Last Declan knew, Captain Callum Grayson had his crew plundering ships heading to and from Larcsporough, south of Cregah. A far riskier set of ships to take on than those to the north, as they were often larger, with larger crews and more guns to better protect the precious cargo brought from the south.

"Think he knows what we're after?" Tommy asked.

"Probably best to assume? But we don't even know if that's him following us or not."

"What's the call, Captain?" Gavin piped up behind them, but Declan kept his eyes locked on those sails.

Declan's answer was for Tommy instead, his voice remaining low. "Any estimate for when we'll be in Foxhaven?"

"Should be ahead of schedule with the way the winds have been. After lunch? Perhaps?" That was at least good news. And Declan could use something good these days.

He called over his shoulder, "Stay on this heading. We treat them as though they have no business with us."

"Aye, Captain," Gavin said, his hesitation evident.

"We simply don't have the crew strength to risk another fight," Declan said to Tommy, the two of them still watching the other ship.

"You don't owe me any explanation, Captain. I trust you."

"What is going on?" The question rang out behind them, and they turned to find Aoife about to step foot onto the quarterdeck.

"Hey! You're not allowed up here!" Tommy barked at her.

Aoife gave a quick glance at Declan. "Apologies. I didn't know." And with that, she retreated down the stairs.

Declan's jaw clenched. She couldn't just stay put. Not that he'd told her to. He turned to Tommy.

"Go get her back to the cabin. If things go badly up here, we need her out of the way. I can't have more of the crew getting killed by her being underfoot."

"Aye," said Tommy with a dip of his chin as he turned to follow the command.

Declan once again looked at the approaching ship, closer now. Were they using the same wind? There was no way the *Siren's Song* would outrun that ship, as it was bigger, faster.

Through the glass once again he tried to make out the ship, attempting to recognize the figurehead or any defining features, but they were still too far away. His heart sped up with the adrenaline that accompanied the thought of the inevitable encounter.

"Mikkel!" he called, knowing his bo'sun would be nearby waiting for the order. And indeed, Mikkel appeared in a fraction of a second, coming up on his left.

"Cap'n?"

"Have the men at the ready, but keep weapons hidden. We don't want to show our hand too soon."

"Aye, sir."

Roughing a hand over his stubbled chin, Declan ran through the different scenarios that could happen, and while he loved a good fight as much as the next pirate, if he were letting himself be honest, he couldn't risk the delay or the manpower this time.

Let this work out. Let something work out.

He needed something to go right.

The hand on Aoife's elbow squeezed tighter, though she wasn't struggling in the slightest. She rolled her eyes at the way the crew seemed to scurry away from her while still keeping their eyes firmly fixed on her, as if she'd actually put a hex on them if they lost track of her. How did they manage to keep the ship running if they feared her presence so much?

They must really respect their captain if they hadn't given in to their fear and thrown her overboard.

Or they fear him.

She swallowed hard at the memory. The look he'd given her as he'd held her down. Hard. Cold. Hungry.

Tommy's grip on her elbow felt too much like Declan's hands on her arms, and bile threatened to surface from the pit of her stomach.

She hadn't expected that from him, had thought him more respectable.

The whole thing had caused shame to burn in her chest, as if it had been her fault he'd acted that way. She hoped no one would ever know the position she'd been in, with his hips digging into hers, his breath in her ear. Though she knew, somehow, she hadn't done anything to deserve it.

But the shame was minuscule compared to the anger that seethed within her. She'd tried to keep it at bay, needing to remain in Declan's good graces lest he follow through with the threat to throw her into the sea. She needed to make it to land. From there she could find passage to Daorna, look up Adler's family. Perhaps find work and start over.

Tommy led her back to the captain's quarters, shoving the door open and guiding her inside. She expected him to fling her in and shut the door on her without a word, but instead he stepped in after her, closing the door behind him. Her nerves were on edge in an instant, spine straightening and chin rising as she tried to ignore the quivering in her gut and prepare herself for whatever he was about to do.

As Declan was preoccupied with whatever was happening on deck, she couldn't rely on his so-called protection now. And though Tommy had seemed innocent enough when she'd encountered him before, Declan's actions had shown her how little she could trust her instincts. Or anyone else for that matter.

But Tommy didn't step toward her, didn't make a move to attack her or further subdue her. His amber-colored eyes studied her as he pulled the gray wool cap from his head, letting his brown hair fall across his forehead. He began to shake his head slightly at her as he wrung the cap in his hands.

"What is it?" Aoife asked, her brow rising a touch with the question.

He let out a sigh through his nose as he chewed on the inside of his lip.

"I can't tell, miss, if you're going to be the thing that brings this crew down…" He dropped his gaze to the floor and paused.

"Or?"

"Or the thing that saves our captain."

Those were certainly not the words she'd expected. She racked her brain for any sign that Declan needed someone, especially a runaway girl, to rescue him. What could a pirate captain—especially one with his reputation—need saving from?

"I don't understand." Part of her wanted Tommy to stay so he could explain further, while the rest of her wanted to be left alone until they made it to port.

What business of hers was it anyway? Declan had made it quite clear he didn't want her to stay, and Tommy, of all people, should know of her impending departure. And yet he'd still said those words.

"Most wouldn't understand." Tommy leaned back against the wall beside the door. "I don't think the captain would even understand."

"Careful. He might make you walk the plank for suggesting such a thing." Aoife wasn't actually sure if that were true.

"Nah." He shook his head again, his lips in a tight line.

"So you've voiced this thought to him then?" She braced herself against the back of the chair Tommy had sat in the day before, crossing her ankles.

"Of course not. I don't have a death wish, you know."

"But you just said—"

"Making people walk the plank isn't really his style," Tommy said with a wink that seemed forced, though his words held a hint of humor in them, like he might laugh at any moment.

"But he listens to you. Trusts you."

"To a point. But I know the limits of our friendship, and I know how to stay on his good side."

"In his shadow. So that's where you like to be?" Aoife knew she tiptoed in unsteady territory with that, but if she was in danger anyway, why not? Tommy didn't seem all that menacing anyway. Then again, neither had Declan until last night.

"It won't work, miss." The corner of his mouth lifted up into a smirk so similar to Declan's it made her stomach flutter against her will.

"What won't work?" She widened her eyes, hoping she looked innocent enough.

"Oh, don't pretend you aren't playing me. I'm a pirate." He waved a hand in the air by his head. "I know all the tactics and the sleights of hand and the turns of phrase."

"I was merely curious, Mr. Murphy." She stumbled over her words, cursing herself for not being more cunning.

Tommy let out a single laugh. "Flattery will get you nowhere either."

"I only said your name. How is that flattery?"

"I'm no mister. Just Tommy. Even to you. To everyone really." He stopped and looked at her more closely. "Wait. How'd you know my last name? And don't claim eavesdropping. No one uses—"

She tossed her head toward the desk. "It was written on a piece of paper over there."

He looked again like he might laugh at her. "Don't let the captain know you're poking around."

She kicked herself for the slipup, cursing her tongue for getting her caught. Again. She needed to change the subject. "So, why do you think I might save him? And from what?"

Tommy rubbed his temple, his eyes falling to the floor as his hand moved back to rub the obvious tension from his neck. "I shouldn't have said anything. It's really not my place."

"What is it with pirates doing that?" Aoife couldn't hide her irritation. "Or is that more in line with men in general, pirate or not?"

"Doing what exactly?" The space between his brows creased in what appeared to be genuine confusion, with no sign of the feigned ignorance Declan always played up to goad her.

"You say something curious, and then when asked for clarification or elaboration you claim inability to speak on the matter. You can't do that! It's maddening to the person you're speaking to. Leaving them hanging! Leaving them with nothing but their curiosity to plague them!"

The confusion vanished from his face, replaced with an amused grin, and she realized she'd been rambling again. Something her mother had always chided her for, something Lani had always teased her for. Lani. She pushed the image of her dead sister aside.

"Well, pirates do like to cause people consternation; that's for sure. But I promise it wasn't intentional. This time."

"So why mention it at all?"

"Mere slip of the tongue, I'm afraid. I'm not as calculated and controlled as Dec—" He stopped himself and cleared his throat. "Excuse me. As Captain McCallagh. My thoughts tend to slip out if I'm not too careful. And apparently I wasn't careful enough just now."

Before she could push for more information, he was nodding his head and turning for the door, giving her a final command to stay put before he was stepping out the door.

Her mind was in a whir, and she couldn't find the words to get him to stay and explain.

What could this captain need saving from? She worked her way through all the puzzling pieces of information she'd collected. The short schedule he was on and the urgency that obviously plagued him. The disdain in his eyes when he looked at her, as well as the obvious stress he was under. The worried dreams she'd witnessed on his sleeping face two nights in a row now. The book of legends that she was sure had something to do with all of aforementioned, given how he'd tried to hide his reaction upon finding her reading it.

And how could she save him exactly?

She wasn't anything more than a useless former heir, probably being chased down by the council she'd fled from. She hadn't saved Lani. She was doing a piss-poor job of saving herself. She was under no delusions that she could save anyone, let alone a pirate captain.

Once again alone in the captain's quarters, she turned and looked around. She'd already explored every inch of the space—as much as she had allowed herself to without disturbing anything. Like Tommy, she would prefer not to incur the captain's wrath unnecessarily.

She'd been instructed to stay put, but the air in the cabin was stifling. Despite that her legs had steadied, her stomach had not, and she needed fresh air to calm it. Moving to one of the back windows, she propped it open. She breathed the sea air in deeply and stared at her feet, letting each breath calm her nausea. Though it could only do so much.

The ship was still moving, and faster now.

She forced her eyes up. If she could find the horizon, it would help. But her view of the horizon was disrupted by the sight of another ship. A larger ship, its massive sails full and impressive. It was approaching fast.

Now she knew why she'd been instructed to stay in here. And she felt like an idiot for not realizing that was what the warning call had been about. She really didn't know anything about sailing, did she?

Her gut tensed—and not from the rolling of the sea—urging her to run and hide under the blankets or beneath the dining table. But she froze, her eyes locked on the ship as it came up on them.

And then they were slowing.

The other ship had caught up, and Declan had simply given up? What if they'd been sent by the council to hunt her down and bring her back? As bizarre as that was to think about, it made sense. Her mother might not be able to explain the disappearance of two heirs within as many days. Would she?

The ship stopped its steady rolling and now bobbed atop the sea. Footsteps sounded overhead, and voices shouted. From here, even with the window open, she couldn't make out whether they were friendly or angry.

Aoife closed the window and tiptoed back to the door of the cabin. She stopped midway across, just past the desk, and turned. There had to be something in the room she could arm herself with, in case this was not a friendly meeting between pirates. A dagger. A knife. Something. In the dining room she spotted a fork but no knife. It would have to do. She slipped it into her sleeve to conceal it, hoping she'd be able to get it out in time if needed.

The ship seemed incredibly still as she opened the door to the cabin. There'd be nowhere for her to hide, with the midmorning sun shining brightly across the deck. The crew was scattered about, leaning against railings and standing in huddled groups here and there, but no one turned to look at her. That was a first. Instead they all stared to the left, no doubt at the large ship that had come alongside them, its sails lowered, as the *Siren's Song*'s were, to keep them steady.

Tiptoeing past the stairs, Aoife spotted Declan and Tommy standing at the railing, watching and waiting, their eyes lowered to the water, not looking at the deck or the many crewmen present. Her heart pounded, her eyes flitting about. What was going on? Was this something that happened often at sea? She really hadn't studied up on pirate politics at all before she'd fled, though she wondered if that would have done much good at all.

She leaned against the banister of the stairs to the quarterdeck, trying to hide herself as best she could, but still, no one seemed to notice her presence. A few minutes passed, and no one seemed to breathe or even mutter a word. Some of the crew looked a little antsy, but she didn't see any weapons in their hands. And for a brief moment she wondered if pirates ever fought at all. They seemed so pleasant and unassuming.

Aoife marveled at the silence of the crew. They all seemed to hold a collective breath as Declan and Tommy stepped back to allow two men to climb aboard, and she wondered where they'd come from and how they'd gotten here from their ship. Maybe a small rowboat or something. So odd. She'd always imagined them swinging over on ropes.

She took in a deep breath and waited. Waited for them to call her forward and hand her over. But it didn't happen. From this vantage point she couldn't see Declan's face and tried to read his body language instead, but he looked as he always did. Confident. Brave. In command.

It was Tommy who stole a glance her way, his eyes widening ever so slightly when he spotted her at the railing, but he gave no indication to the men around him that she was out of the cabin. She moved an inch or two, shifting her weight to get more comfortable, as her hip was starting to ache from the uncomfortable position. But as soon as she fidgeted, Tommy's hand tensed by his leg, fingers splaying wide as he gestured for her to stay put.

This time she would listen.

Declan's hand rested on the pommel of his sword as he worked to keep his stance casual and unassuming. Captain Callum Grayson stepped forward, his quartermaster close behind him.

"I wasn't sure you'd stop for us, McCallagh," Captain Grayson said, working out the kinks in his neck as he stepped toward Declan and Tommy.

"Almost didn't." In a more civilized society there would have been a shaking of hands, but not among pirates.

Declan could have raised the yellow flag, claimed illness or plague aboard his ship, but he'd decided it better to use this encounter to his advantage. Any interaction with a friend at this point—especially since Aoife refused to help—could give him information he needed to free the Bron sisters.

He kept his head up and his back straight, forcing himself not to let the weariness and fatigue and stress show. The crew of the *Curse Bringer* stood much like his own crew: steady, waiting, ready to act if this meeting turned sour.

Callum, barely five years Declan's senior, stood a few inches taller and had an air about him that demanded obedience. He'd built quite the name for himself over the years, managing to buy a larger ship than all of the other lesser captains who remained unbound to the pirate lords.

"You can tell your men to stand down, by the way. We aren't here in ill spirits." Callum didn't bother to look around at the crew as Declan thought he might, instead keeping his gaze firmly locked on Declan.

Declan drummed his fingers on his blade's hilt out of habit, but he didn't move to give Tommy the command. They both stood, eying their guests. "So what spirits do bring you here then?"

"Can't an old friend merely pop in to say hello now and then?" A faint smile spread across Callum's rough face, though his dark eyes remained serious, dangerous, seeming even more so given the severe cut of his black hair and the white scar that ran from his jaw to his left ear. "How long's it been anyway?"

"Two years, I believe. Since the fleet we took on up north."

"Right, right. Good time indeed. I always wondered why we didn't partner up more often." Callum's eyes gave a slight twitch as he spoke, and Declan got the distinct impression he was being baited.

"We did work well together. One of the best bounties we've secured. Gave us enough for the crew to have quite a worthy rest afterward." Declan shifted his weight, trying to read Callum's expression but coming up empty. He'd simply have to ask outright. "Did you have another partnership opportunity in mind?"

"Perhaps, perhaps." Callum leaned toward Declan and lowered his voice so only he and their quartermasters could hear. "I've heard rumors you might be working on something. Something big."

"Well, you know what they say about idle hands."

Callum straightened, lifting his chin. "Actually, no, I don't. Regardless, I want in."

"Without even knowing what it is?"

Callum's grin spread wider as his brows rose. "I didn't say I didn't know."

"You shouldn't believe everything you hear." Declan worked to keep his expression blank, though he could feel Tommy tense up beside him.

Again Callum leaned in. "I hear you're going after the Csintala Dagger."

Declan let out a laugh. "I didn't take you for one to believe in children's stories and myths, Grayson."

"Play the fool all you want, but I know it's true."

How does he know? Who would have told him? He pushed those questions aside.

"Why would you want in?"

"Why wouldn't I? It's a legend. The prestige alone that would come with finding it? Retrieving it? And to use it—"

Declan interrupted. "If you can even trust the stories to be true. They very well might be fabricated. Exaggerated to delight children."

"Aye, true enough. But still. I want in." Callum rocked back on his heels, one hand on the hilt of his sword and the other hovering at his stomach. Such arrogance and confidence emanated from the man, the kind that came with years of laying waste to smaller ships and knowing he could do so here with a mere flick of that hand.

Declan pondered this request for a moment, doing his best to look bored as he looked up toward the sky. He could use the help, for sure. But he couldn't share this bounty with any other captain. He needed to hand it over to his sister—if he decided to do so. And he couldn't trust anyone—not even an old *friend* like Callum—not to divulge secrets to the council or take the dagger for their own use.

"I'm still trying to wrap my head around why you'd believe such tales about me."

"Dominic here asked the same thing," Callum said, nodding to his quartermaster. "But it's a McCallagh thing to do. Chasing after more than just the usual and the mundane. You always were a kid with an eye for adventure, for more than the status quo."

"I've grown up since then. I'm a bit more practical now." Friend or no, Callum couldn't be trusted, and Declan certainly couldn't ask him for any insight into the council hall or the fae. Not without bringing more suspicion upon himself. But this encounter hadn't been for naught. If Callum had heard the rumors, then they were spreading far, and if the council didn't know he was searching for the dagger, they would soon.

Whether anyone believed he had gone mad or was truly looking for the dagger was beside the point. People were talking. And that didn't help him in his need for secrecy.

Callum cut through his thoughts. "You have gotten a bit taller at least. But I still see that same wild kid in your eyes, McCallagh."

The time was creeping by, and Declan was antsy to get Callum off his ship and get underway. "Well, I hate to break it to you, but you've been misinformed. We're merely on our way to Foxhaven."

At that, a thump sounded behind him, and he and Tommy both turned. Declan's jaw tightened. What was she doing out of the cabin? Two days. She'd only been on board two days, and she was indeed proving to be a liability. The ship wasn't even moving, and Aoife had somehow lost her balance and stumbled on the deck. She looked at him and Tommy, her eyes wild with fear and worry as she quickly glanced away.

"And who is that?" Callum asked, trying to see around Declan.

"Just someone we're giving passage to Foxhaven."

"So you're a ferryboat now? Since when do pirates give people rides?" Callum's face had such amusement written all over it that Declan wanted to punch it off him.

"Since this pirate decided to." His words came out with more of an edge than he'd intended.

Callum took a step forward, but Declan stepped in his way, pressing his hand against the other captain's chest.

"I merely want to meet the man you allowed aboard your ship, McCallagh. No ill will here, as I said before. Unless you have something to hide." Callum's eyes narrowed at him with the challenge.

"I'm a pirate. We all have something to hide. Friend or not, this is my ship, and you will not take another step on it without my permission."

Declan could feel the tension mounting around him. Tommy kept his eyes on Dominic, who was an older gentleman, old enough to be Callum's father, weathered by the years at sea but also toughened by them.

Callum lowered his voice once again. "Indeed, friend. But I won't hesitate to overrun your ship and sink it to the bottom of the sea. Even for something as silly and trivial as you not allowing me to talk to someone."

Declan knew it was possible. The *Curse Bringer* had far more crew members. His mind whirred with his options. He could kill Grayson right here, with a swift jab of the dagger he carried at his hip. And Tommy would have the older quartermaster taken out within a fraction of a second later. But how would their crew respond? No doubt Callum's bo'sun would take charge and have them attacking swiftly.

It's what his own bo'sun was trained to do.

Time ticked by, and he needed to make a decision soon. If Callum knew of his search for the dagger, had he also heard of the runaway heir? Quite likely, and Declan wasn't sure what Callum would do if he learned she was here.

Before he could respond, Callum was waving Aoife over to join them. Declan turned toward her and saw she'd already taken several steps in their direction. "Stop!" He hoped she'd listen. For once. And not do anything stupid.

But it was too late. "A woman?" Callum burst into laughter. "Declan, you fool. You're a complete and utter fool. You let her on board?"

Declan turned back to Callum, his jaw clenching tighter. His desire to punch him grew stronger with every word the man spoke. Declan could feel his crew's disapproval growing. He was risking possible mutiny by going against their wishes and allowing her passage. But he was the captain, and he was in charge. For now.

"You know who she is, right?"

"Do you?" Declan challenged.

"Aye. It's all anyone's talking about right now. The Cregahn heir who fled."

It didn't make any sense to Declan. Why would the council let word of that spread? But he could use this to his advantage.

"And you believed those stories too?" Callum remained quiet, his eyes on Aoife, who had frozen mid-step. "Honestly, Callum, has the salt air gotten to your senses to make you accept every tale you hear?"

"If she's not the heir, then who is she?" Callum's eyes flicked back to Declan's and held them with such an intensity his mind nearly went blank from it. But he wasn't that young kid anymore, and he wasn't easily intimidated.

Declan opened his mouth to answer, but before he could, Aoife began speaking behind him. His stomach clenched as he turned to see her inching toward them, her chin high and regal despite the ridiculous outfit she still wore. "I am the heir, but I did not flee."

Tommy shot her a questioning look before catching Declan's gaze as a smile started to pull at the corner of the quartermaster's lips.

"Oh?" Callum asked.

"I was sent."

"And why would they do that?" Callum's eyes narrowed.

Aoife stepped between Declan and Tommy now, only a foot away from the captain of the *Curse Bringer*. She didn't flinch. Didn't back down. Didn't show any of the fear Declan—or Callum—might have anticipated. "Because there's word of rebellion and dissent, that some are working to overthrow the council."

Declan blinked at her, wondering if she was making this up on the fly or if she—and the council—knew about his sister's organization and their plotting.

"But they'd never send an heir to uncover that information. That's why they have the pirate lords, after all." Callum spat the words out with disdain.

"The lords are losing favor with the council and can no longer be trusted. Not fully anyway, and certainly not with anything of this magnitude."

"But you're just a girl."

"Don't let my looks deceive you."

Callum studied her for a bit as if he were chewing apart her claims in his head and testing them. Declan and Tommy shared a glance around Aoife, who, regardless of how clumsy she was, did put on a good show of being fearless and determined. Perhaps he should consider keeping her on board.

"I'll hand it to you, Miss—I'm sorry, I didn't catch your name."

Aoife didn't say anything, but merely urged him with her sharp stare to continue.

"You are a decent liar, and you might even make a good pirate someday. But I'm better. And my sources are more…reliable." Callum rubbed a hand over his beard and turned to his man. "What shall we do, Dominic?"

Dominic's voice came out as gruff and weathered as his face. "I say we take her home. No doubt her people miss her and need her back on their shores."

"Aye. My thought exactly," Callum said and turned back to Declan. "So we'll be doing just that." He leaned in close once again to speak only to Declan. "Should help you earn back favor with your crew too, McCallagh. They look about ready to toss you to the depths."

Callum gave a nod to Dominic, who made a move toward Aoife,

but Tommy was immediately there, his blade now drawn and held against Dominic's neck. Callum looked from Declan to Tommy and back again, as if expecting Declan to call his man off and out of the way. But Declan met Callum's stare, his mind ablaze with the possibilities of how this could pan out.

"You will not touch her, Callum. She goes where she pleases. She is her own person." He could feel the questioning daggers from her eyes beside him, but he continued. "We promised her safe passage, and you know my word—"

"Is not the word of a true pirate. You're a fool, Declan. Wave of my hand and my men will be firing all our rounds into your ship, taking the girl, and leaving you as fish food."

Declan knew his crew was growing more anxious by the minute. If it were up to a vote, she'd be handed over without question. But he couldn't send her back. As much as she irked him, he wouldn't subject her to the cruelty of the council should they get their hands on her, even if it might lead to a possible mutiny among his men.

In an instant, Declan had his own dagger out and up, but instead of killing Callum then and there, he merely pushed the point into the other captain's neck. Blood trickled out around the blade and slid down the man's skin, but he didn't flinch. Neither man moved.

Declan spoke first. "You will not. I see your bluff for what it is, Callum. You want that dagger, and you know I'm the only way to find it."

Callum was equally as fast with his own blade, using it to swipe Declan's away before pushing himself into Declan's face, their blades crossed between their chests. "Does that mean you've reconsidered?"

"Aye." Declan shoved Callum off, pointing his dagger at the man's chest. "We share the spoils. But I run the operation. I call the shots. And I decide when and where and how you engage."

"You're asking a lot," Callum said, sheathing his own dagger while eying Declan's. "But I accept. How can I be of service?" He gave a grand bow as he spoke.

Declan lowered his own blade, securing it as he said, "We could use some information, if you know anyone who can help. Particularly about the dagger's location and who or what might be guarding it."

"You don't already have that?"

Declan shook his head. "I have hints and clues. Guesses really, but we'll want to be certain before we make a move to take it."

Callum lifted his chin. "And I assume you won't be divulging any of these hints or clues?"

"You'll know when you need to know." Declan called for Tommy to lower his weapon and release Dominic.

"So you're on to Foxhaven," Callum said. "And what of the girl?" Declan gave another shake of his head. "Ah, a need-to-know basis, is it? Fair enough. Do with her what you will. We'll head back to Morshan and see what we can dig up."

"Be quick about it. We are on a short timeframe," Declan said, and as expected, Callum's eyes widened.

"How short?"

"Thirty days."

"That's plenty of time to get information out of someone."

"Thirty days to retrieve the dagger."

Callum's expression tightened as he no doubt tried to work through all the pieces. "And do what with it?"

Declan chewed on the inside of his lip while he studied the captain. Callum would need to know just enough to keep him on track but not enough to piece it all together. Though Declan hadn't managed to figure out Cait's plans yet himself.

"To bring it back to Morshan." He knew Callum had a million more questions, but they'd need to wait. He held up a hand to stop him from asking any of them. "That's all you need to know for now. So if you'd like in on this, you'll take it and get to work. We will meet you back in Morshan in five or six days."

"Very well, Captain." Callum gave a short nod and waved at

Dominic to depart, but before he backed away himself, he stepped close to Declan. "I find out you've crossed me, and I won't be quite so cordial next we meet."

The threat hit its mark, cutting off the air in Declan's throat, but he refused to let the trepidation show on his features as Callum walked off.

As soon as the two pirates were off the *Siren's Song* and rowing back to their own ship, Declan's crew released a collective breath, as if they'd been holding it for the entire exchange. But they were far from relaxed, and a nervous energy buzzed among them.

Declan ignored their stares as he spoke to Tommy. "Talk to the men. Answer any questions they have. I'm sure they have plenty."

"Aye, sir."

And with that, Declan grabbed Aoife's arm and dragged her back to the cabin while the crew stared after him.

Back in the captain's quarters, Aoife shifted in her seat. Her arm throbbed where Declan had grabbed her, but she hadn't bothered to fight him as he escorted her back to the cabin and pushed her inside. That encounter hadn't exactly gone as planned—not that she had really had a plan at all. Still, it could have gone better.

Much better.

She still had the fork lodged in her shirt sleeve, and it poked her wrist whenever she moved. Declan's eyes were fixed on her. They bored into her as if probing and prodding to find out what secrets lay within. He drew in a breath and released it slowly, his hand lifting to swipe the hair away from his forehead. She waited for the yelling, for the reprimand, for the lecture about how stupid she was.

But it didn't come. Instead, he laughed.

Not in a mocking way, but in a way of pure amusement. Had he lost it? Completely gone mad? There was nothing funny about this situation. She'd outed herself as the heir, and the other captain hadn't believed any of her lies. Soon the council would know where she was and who she was with, and they'd hunt her down and "take care" of her.

And here he was laughing.

She cleared her throat, trying to cut through his laughter, snap him out of whatever madness had taken hold of him.

"I'm sorry," Declan said between his chuckles. Another deep breath cleared the last of the laughter away, and he seemed to put every bit of effort into calming himself down.

"I don't see what is so funny about this." Aoife forced the words out through clenched teeth, her anger rising with every word. "This is serious, and you're here chuckling like an imbecile."

Something in her gut begged her to back off before she stepped too far over the line, but she ignored it. She was already so far beyond every line ever drawn for her by people in power. She wasn't going to let this idiot of a captain keep her from stepping up and speaking her mind. She had nothing left to lose. She was already being hunted—probably by every pirate in the Aisling. What did it matter if she was thrown into the depths by this captain or killed by those hired by her mother?

Declan didn't seem put off by her comment though. "Oh, but there's much to laugh about here."

"I disagree, Captain." She spat out the last word, hoping it would sting him, but it seemed to have little effect.

"Of course you do. You have no sense of humor."

"I do when the situation calls for it, but I see nothing funny about those pirates knowing who I am—"

"And whose fault is that, miss?" All humor vanished from his expression, his stare hardening with the cold intensity that haunted her whenever she closed her eyes. "I believe we told you to stay put, stay hidden. But you couldn't. You couldn't follow a simple command intended for your safety. So excuse me while I distract myself with a bit of laughter and try to see the humor in a situation that altogether sucks. Because of you."

His words stung more than she wanted them to. Why did she want his approval or his admiration? He was nothing but an awful, heartless pirate who would never care about anyone or anything but his own ridiculous plans to retrieve some dagger.

She stopped, her mind flitting back to a section of the book she'd read the night before. A dagger. *The* dagger. Was Declan truly seeking the Csintala Dagger? She'd assumed it was simply a legend, obviously, as it was in a book of children's stories and make-believe. But was it true?

Aoife lowered her eyes to her hands in her lap. The fork still poked her wrist, but she dared not remove it in his company and incur further ridicule. Not that a fork would have done her any good had Declan agreed to give her over to Callum and his crew. She had no doubt Callum wouldn't have shown her the same courtesy or given her the same accommodations Declan had.

And yet Declan looked at her as though he wanted to toss her overboard himself, to be rid of her and her mistakes and missteps. Why was he helping her and protecting her?

"So the dagger's real?" It came out barely above a whisper, and she waited, breath held, for him to snap at her again. As much as she hated him, she hated him being cross with her more, though she couldn't understand why it hurt as much as it did.

"Aye. It is."

"And can it really do what they say? Is it really enchanted?"

His silence seemed answer enough, but that was ridiculous. Impossible. But an image of the fae sisters flashed briefly in her mind. The fae had magic, so maybe the stories of this dagger were true too.

"And the shield? Does that exist too?" she asked.

"If it does, I haven't been told. Nothing beyond what that book said." He looked as bored as he sounded.

She leaned forward. "But you know where the dagger is, don't you?"

He answered with a silent dip of his chin, his eyes burning into her, challenging her to look away. She didn't.

"And you sent Callum off to get information you already had."

"To keep him busy."

"Why didn't you let him take me?" It was the question she worried most about asking, partly because she had been so close to being handed back over to the council, but also because she feared his answer wouldn't be what she hoped.

He roughed a hand behind his neck, as if to buy himself time, perhaps thinking of an excuse or a lie.

"Because..." He cleared his throat before continuing. "If anyone's going to be rewarded for returning you to the council, it's going to be me. Not him."

She'd expected as much, but the disappointment still fell heavy in her gut. She forced herself to not let it show in her voice though. "Of course. Just as I thought."

"Then why ask?"

"Because I wanted to hear you say it aloud, I guess."

Declan narrowed his eyes again at her. "Did you think I did it because I care?"

She held his stare, refusing to look down again as she searched her brain for the answer. Had she thought he cared? She had hoped. When he'd stood up to Callum for her, a burning ember had caught and ignited in her chest, though she couldn't understand why.

Why did she care what Captain McCallagh thought of her?

And yet, she couldn't deny how it stung to know he didn't care, how her heart seemed to cave in on itself a bit.

He'd made it clear the other night, hadn't he? But she'd begun to wonder if maybe the desire she'd heard as he purred in her ear had been real and not merely an act. And she hated herself for liking it, for wanting him to make good on his threats. Hated herself for the way her stomach flitted uncontrollably when he looked at her.

A knock came at the door, and Tommy poked his head in. "Captain, we'll be arriving in Foxhaven soon." He raised an eyebrow as if to say something more without words.

Declan waved him inside and turned back to Aoife as Tommy stepped inside and shut the door with a soft click.

"Aoife, I don't think I need to warn you of what ill-fate awaits you if you tell anyone what we're after." He paused, almost as if daring her to argue, but she remained quiet. "The pirates you'll encounter in this port are a different breed entirely. Not like us, or even like Callum. And certainly nothing like what you've witnessed when the lords dine in your hall."

Aoife swallowed her fear and worry, but her stomach grew more uneasy with each word he said.

"You'll need to have your wits about you," he continued. "And we won't be there to help if you get into a sticky situation."

"And what am I supposed to do there?"

He thumbed his nose before crossing his arms over his chest, his expression dripping with indifference. "You might have thought about that before you trespassed on my ship."

"There wasn't time." A simple fact Aoife had repeated in her head over and over again when she chided herself for getting into such a mess.

"Even with little time, one can stop and think and plan without relying so much on their emotions driving them to stupidity."

Mess or not, she was damn tired of being called stupid by this pirate.

She unclenched her teeth and glared at him. "I'm sorry, Declan, that we aren't all cunning masterminds like you. We don't all have the ability of shutting down all feelings and pushing away all human ties so easily. Do you think it was easy to leave behind the only home I've ever known and the only family I've ever had? Even though I know the truth now, they're still the only people I've ever loved. Those ties are not so easily severed for most of us."

She heard Tommy shift, his breath seeming to scrape against his throat. Either he had words he wanted to add, or he merely wanted to escape this uncomfortable situation. She didn't know which, but she didn't feel sorry for him in the slightest. He followed this captain. Did his bidding. Gave him his loyalty.

Declan eyed her for a moment, but something in his glance made him seem bored, as if he weren't on some daring quest for an enchanted dagger but was simply sailing about on a sunny afternoon. "Fair points, I suppose." And then his expression hardened a bit. "But you'll need to check those emotions here. Be on your guard. Watch your back."

"Why bother giving me advice?" Aoife had zero ability to be gracious to him.

"You know? I don't know." He raised his hands in an exaggerated shrug. "I'm done. Tommy, get her out of here. We'll be arriving soon, and she can wait out of my sight and out of my hair."

"Aye, Captain." Tommy moved to lift her by her elbow out of the chair, but she shook him off, shooting Declan one final glare before turning toward the door. He didn't notice. He was already done, as he'd said, preoccupied with whatever book or journal was on his desk.

"I can walk myself, Tommy." And without another look at the young captain, she walked out of his cabin and his life.

25

Aoife

Aoife stared at the port before her, her fingers clutching the glass vial of black sand at her chest. For the last two days, she had tried to prepare herself, to imagine what Foxhaven would look like, but she never could have painted it with such clarity and vibrancy. While Morshan was a town of order and peace—at least on the surface—Foxhaven was decidedly the opposite. She could tell that simply from her view aboard the ship.

Standing on the deck of the *Siren's Song*, which was now anchored in the bay, Aoife waited for the men to prepare the boats that would take them ashore. She tried to take it all in, but there was too much to look at. And so much to listen to.

Everywhere along the beach men arranged cargo into wagons while women came to offer them drinks, greeting them with kisses and low-cut dresses that could barely keep their supple bodies contained. Beyond the beach, ramshackle buildings of every size and shape were erected in what appeared to be no particular order whatsoever, as if the builders had simply started putting up boards wherever their eyes happened to fall.

The buildings weren't painted with the drab and mundane beiges and tans from back home, but rather wore every color under the sun and sea. A bright purple one-story structure stood beside a pink and teal two-level building with a large wrap-around porch and multiple balconies framing its second-floor. Weaving among all the buildings were people of equally diverse appearances, from tall men with skin as dark as Aoife's hair to petite women with olive skin and sleek black hair in braids down their backs.

And the smells.

Even from the ship she could smell the aromas of foods and spices wafting out to her and mixing with the brine of the sea. Her stomach gave an appreciative growl. As much as she'd hoped Declan would keep her aboard, the fresh fruit they'd enjoyed from Morshan had dwindled quickly and likely wouldn't be available forever. The thought of having a warm meal that wasn't sea-hardened and tough was incredibly appealing.

She'd never even imagined a place like Foxhaven, and it made her heart race a bit.

Someone came up beside her, nudging her elbow with his own. Tommy.

"He hates me." She cringed at the words that spilled out of her, not knowing why she'd said them. Of all the things she could have said... But she couldn't deny—even with the marvel that was Foxhaven before her—that Declan's final words to her weighed heavy.

Tommy only gave a hum in response.

"Why didn't he want my help?" She turned her head a fraction of an inch to find him staring toward the shore. Why did this man follow such a captain? Tommy was kind and funny, always seemed in good spirits, unlike Declan. And why waste those good looks on a ship full of men?

He could have a wife and a whole brood of children to play with and raise up. And yet here he was, wasting his handsome face and warm heart on this ship.

Thankfully, her traitor of a tongue didn't say any of that to him.

Tommy kept his gaze ahead on the teal waters of the bay. "He did, Aoife. And does. But like everything else, he wants it—needs it—to be on his terms."

Aoife breathed the briny air deep into her lungs, her stomach responding once again to the delicious smells it carried. The mere sight of Foxhaven overwhelmed her. So many people. So little order. She didn't even know where to begin once she was ashore, and the crew had already insisted she be one of the first off the ship.

"Where do I go now, Tommy? I have no skills, unless they need me to recite some Cregahn poetry or explain the details of the Muirnaughton Treaty." She looked down at her smooth hands, untouched by any manual labor, a stark contrast to the weathered wood of the railing they rested on. "I don't fit in here."

"Aye. You don't. But were you born to fit in, Aoife?"

It seemed such an odd thing for him to say, but it felt genuine and caring all the same. Perhaps, had things been different, had Declan been a pirate lord, Aoife and Tommy might have met in the council hall and planned their own escape like Lani and Adler had. She swallowed hard and ignored those thoughts.

"Don't flatter me, Tommy."

"I'm not. Simply stating a fact." He glanced at her from the corner of his eye. "Council ladies aren't meant to blend in. You were born to rule and to lead, not hide among pirates."

"But I didn't fit in there. And I doubt I will here either."

"Why all the preoccupation with fitting in anywhere?"

His question hit a sore spot. She'd only ever belonged with her sister, with Lani. And then she'd betrayed her. Without her, where did she belong? Where was her place? And why wouldn't the thoughts of her sister stay hidden, locked away in her mind? She hoped that would happen with time, hoped she'd be able to move on and not live with this ghost and guilt forever.

"We all want to know we belong, Tommy. Whether it's in the shadow of our captain"—she paused to smirk at him—"or in a new land of strangers. Or in a council of rulers. We weren't meant to be alone. We weren't meant for solitude. But what's the point of being among people if you can never be comfortable? Be yourself?"

"Ah, I see what you mean." Tommy glanced past her toward the men starting to gather for debarkation. They'd just had rest in Morshan, but apparently all were eager to partake in whatever pleasures lay ashore, the notable difference today being the sheer number of weapons they had on their persons. She'd never seen so many blades of various sizes tucked into belts and boots and slung across backs and chests. "Well, if you're going to fit in, or at least try to, you'll need this."

Aoife glanced down at Tommy's hands, which held a small dagger. No, too small to be a dagger, though she didn't know what to call it. Weapons identification wasn't exactly a course they offered to council heirs. Or to anyone from Cregah.

"Take it." Tommy held it up a little higher.

Aoife wrapped her fingers around the hilt. A simple but handsome design with a serpent was carved into its handle. It fit her hand perfectly, as if it had been made for her, but that notion was preposterous. She lifted it tentatively, resting the end of the blade in her left palm as she examined the design closely. "Whose was it?"

"I don't know. We took it off a ship we looted a couple months back, and for some reason I kept it. Of all the goods that ship carried, this one seemed to call to me, as if it wanted to be in my possession. Perhaps it was trying to find its way to you."

"Are all pirates so superstitious and weird?" she asked, not taking her eyes off the gift.

He laughed. "Maybe. A bit."

"Where do I keep it?"

"On you?"

"Well, yes, I got that, but where? You know, I'm more accustomed to wearing dresses and tunics, not whatever you call these items. And I'm not used to concealing weapons on my body."

"Who said you needed to conceal it? It might be better to display it so people know you're armed."

He took the blade from her and held it in his teeth, using his hands to undo the buckle at her belt. Her heart nearly stopped as she wondered what he was doing, but with a few quick movements, he had slid a sheath onto her belt and refastened it, pulling it tight around her waist. He wiggled his brow at her as he slid the blade into the leather.

"I don't even know how to use it." She dropped her gaze to the deck, unable to look him in the eye, to let him see she wasn't as strong as she pretended to be.

"The pointy end goes in the other person."

She managed a half smile before her nerves took hold again and kept a laugh from emerging. "And where do I go? There's so much here. So much to see and smell."

"Smell?" Another laugh. "It can be overwhelming the first time. Or the tenth time, if I'm honest. But may I recommend you head to Lucy's."

Something tightened in Aoife upon hearing the name. Not that it was an intimidating name in itself, but what sort of establishment did this Lucy run? Her consternation must have shown on her face, because Tommy laughed again. "No, no. It's not what you're thinking. She runs one of the best eateries in port, and I'm sure she would have a spot for someone to help in the dining room."

"How do you know she'll have a spot open for me?"

"Well, let's just say most of the women prefer the other, more lucrative positions on the island." He winked when Aoife wrinkled up her nose. "Hey, don't look down on them or their customers. They've found a place they belong and fit in. And isn't that what we all need?"

Of course he'd found a way to throw her words back at her. "Lucy's. Okay. And where do I find her exactly?"

"She's in the yellow building in the middle of that mess over there." Tommy pointed off to the right a bit, and Aoife hoped she'd be able to make it there without needing to use the blade now hanging at her waist.

"Thank you, Tommy. For being so kind. I'm sure Declan wouldn't approve of your helping me."

Tommy turned and stepped away from the railing but noted over his shoulder, "He's the one who asked me to."

An hour later Aoife stood on the shore of Foxhaven, not caring that her feet were still getting wet from the tide as it came in and washed out.

She couldn't move.

If she had found this port overwhelming while on the deck of the *Siren's Song*, it was much more so when standing on the outskirts of it. Crew from Declan's ship moved around her, careful not to come into contact with her, as if she had some plague or disease.

Or bad luck. They couldn't have that rubbing off on them.

"Hey! Lass! Are you going to stand there all day?" A voice sounded up the shore, as rough and gravelly as the face it was paired with. The man had stopped moving bottles and trunks from his boat into a small wagon already overflowing with goods. He smiled at her, his teeth broken and chipped, a nasty shade of yellow. "If you're looking for work, I might have some for you." His blue eyes twinkled at her as his tongue wet his lips. She was sure the work he offered was of the less reputable variety.

Declan had been right when he'd said these pirates weren't like those she'd met thus far. What had she gotten herself into?

"No, thank you." She cringed at how formal she sounded. She'd never fit in here. "I have work lined up already."

She forced her feet forward, up the beach, refusing to look at the man as she passed him, though she saw him give a shrug as he laughed.

No one else spoke to her as she weaved around the various crews and island workers. Some eyed her briefly with curious looks. She hoped she'd find Lucy soon and that perhaps the woman might have some clothes she could change into. She hadn't even done anything other than lounge about and sleep in these, and they were already grungier and smellier than she was comfortable with. Though she supposed that did help her blend in a bit.

She had expected walking on the sand would be difficult after being on the ship, and she was right. While the soft white sand of the beach didn't help matters, she found the boardwalk and cobblestones no easier to traverse. She wondered how many people she passed assumed she was drunk, despite it being just after midday. Among this lot, though, that would earn her less ridicule than the truth—that she simply hadn't found her land legs yet.

Aoife didn't know where to look as she walked, and she imagined she appeared ridiculous as she looked from one colorful building to the next, her eyes wide and curious. She tried to guess what business or family might reside in each building—if families even existed on this island.

There were no signs anywhere, and it was impossible to determine whether something was a pub or a brothel or a clothing shop. But she soon realized that shops—whether selling clothes, weapons, or food—displayed their wares, albeit haphazardly, in the front windows. It was nothing like Morshan, where merchants displayed their goods in bright, orderly arrangements, showcasing the items' appeal to entice the residents to come in and buy. Here in Foxhaven it seemed the goods were merely stacked in front of the windows, as if the shop owners had stored the items without realizing customers could see the piles.

She tried her best to ignore the shops from which delicious smells drifted and seemed to seep from the pores of the buildings themselves. Her stomach growled at her, demanding to be filled, but she could wait until she found Lucy and her eatery.

Tommy had slipped her just enough copper coins to get her a first meal and maybe a short swig of rum, but it was up to her to earn all the meals and drinks that followed. She wondered if she'd ever see him again. Or Declan. Ass that he was, she couldn't ignore the small bit of gratitude she held for him. After all, he hadn't taken advantage of any of the numerous opportunities to be rid of her on their way here.

Or taken advantage in any other way, for that matter.

Aoife glanced back toward the beach, trying to peer over the bustle of people milling about. She thought she caught a glimpse of the captain and his quartermaster climbing out of a rowboat, not stumbling at all as they trudged up the beach toward the town ahead. Foxhaven seemed much bigger now that she was among the buildings. Big enough for them to avoid her if they desired.

She turned back to the mess of buildings, stifling a laugh at the sheer nonsense of how they were laid out, with the stone roads meandering between them not in a precise grid but in a mess of angles, all of different lengths, with some ending abruptly at a building, as if the road builders had gotten tired of laying cobblestones and decided to erect a building instead.

Ahead she spotted a building with three levels that had to be Lucy's, as it was the only sunny yellow one amidst the rainbow of colors around her. She picked up her pace, her heart speeding up to match her steps. She'd sneaked aboard a pirate ship and stood up to Captain Callum. She could do this. She could approach this Lucy and request a job.

And maybe lodging. She'd need that too.

Within a few moments she was standing in the doorway staring at a sea of people crowding around tables and standing along the walls with mugs of beer and mead in their hands. A few glanced up at her but then wrote her off as nothing special as they returned back to their meals and their conversations. She inched her way through, muttering apologies as she bumped into people—and wondering if pirates normally apologized for such things. How would she ever find Lucy in this mess? She looked around for someone who seemed to be working rather than eating, a server or a barmaid or someone carrying dishes or taking orders.

There, in the far corner. It had to be Lucy. Or at least someone who worked for her and could direct her to the lady. The woman was young, not much older than Aoife herself. Her dark face, with skin the color of the sands back home, was framed by tight curls haphazardly but attractively tied up at the crown of her head. She displayed a joyful demeanor that Aoife would not have expected for how busy she appeared to be, chatting with customers, clearing plates, wiping down tables, and letting others know their food was coming.

She wasn't dressed like the other women in port but wore clothing similar to Aoife's—a men's style but cut for a woman to make room for all the curves—only more colorful. Lucy's had hints of color throughout, including a turquoise sash around her waist she used to wipe down her hands now and then. Instead of an off-white linen undershirt, hers was bright pink, the color of the tropical flowers that grew in the gardens at the council hall.

Aoife realized she was standing in the middle of the crowded room, staring, just as the other lady's eyes met hers. The woman approached with the same smile beaming across her face, and Aoife lost all her words.

"Welcome! I'm Lucy, owner of this little establishment. You're new here, aren't you?" The woman had a hint of an accent Aoife had never heard before.

Aoife cleared her throat, her mouth suddenly dry, as if she'd taken in a mouth full of sand on her walk from the beach. "I am."

"I knew it. I knew I hadn't seen you around. I mean, I get a lot of people in here, so you'd assume I wouldn't be able to remember everyone, but…" She reached a free hand up to tap her temple. "My mama always said I had a memory like an elephant. Whatever an elephant is. We had them back home, I suppose, but I never saw one."

Aoife couldn't help but smile. Lucy would be easy to like, and Foxhaven might be a place she could fit in after all.

"Come. Standing in the middle of the room won't do either of us any good. Let's find you a table and get you some food. You look like you haven't eaten in days." Lucy waved a hand as she turned toward the back of the room. Aoife wasn't sure where she'd be able to find an empty table, but she supposed Lucy would know where one was.

She followed Lucy to the back corner of the room where a set of wide stairs led up and around to the second floor. Aoife had assumed these would be Lucy's quarters, but instead it was another large dining room. Unlike the first floor—with its simple tables and chairs—this upstairs dining area was a mishmash of different furniture. Mismatched armchairs with high backs and cushioned seats were scattered around low tables, while the high tables had stools surrounding them. This room sat empty, however, which Aoife attributed to the jump in temperature as they ascended. On the far wall overlooking the street below, the windows were all open to let in the sea breeze, but it wasn't enough to make the room comfortable in the slightest.

As if reading her mind, Lucy commented, "I know it's hot, but it's quiet. Come, sit. Let's chat and get you some eats." She led Aoife to a set of armchairs perched right in front of the open windows, and Aoife was pleased to discover that it was at least somewhat cooler over here. She sat down tentatively as Lucy plopped into the chair opposite her.

"Don't you have to work?" Aoife cringed a little at the silliness of her question, but Lucy didn't seem to notice as she tossed a glance toward the stairs.

"They'll be fine for a bit. Don't you worry about them. It's mostly regulars anyway, and they're a fairly patient lot, considering their profession."

"Pirates," Aoife muttered.

"Aye. And you're not one of them." Lucy tapped against her pursed lips.

"How'd you know?"

"It's a tad obvious."

Aoife's face burned. It wasn't obvious to her. She wondered what the giveaway was. Was it the clothes? Her hair? Again, it was like Lucy could read her mind. "I mean, you look the part, sure. The clothes are on point, wherever you got them. But they're too clean, for one. And two, you look too sweet. Too innocent."

"Maybe I'm just a new pirate." Aoife fought the urge to shrink in her seat and instead sat up straighter.

"Are you?"

"Well, no."

"But you did arrive on a pirate ship."

"How did you—"

"Girl, the only ships that stop here are pirate ships, so either you rowed here yourself—unlikely—or you got passage on one." She lifted her hand, her fingers finding a loose curl to fiddle with as she clicked her tongue. "Let me guess. McCallagh's ship."

"How do you do that?"

"Do what?"

"Know everything without me telling you."

Lucy's hearty laugh bounced around the empty room. "It's nothing magical, sweetie. Mere logic and powers of deduction is all."

Aoife must have looked skeptical, because the woman leaned forward then and continued to explain.

"I've lived here—owned this place—for the better part of seven years."

Aoife looked her over, earning her another chuckle.

"I know, I look younger than I am. Still. I've gotten to know most of the captains sailing the Aisling. And Declan? Well, he's one of the only ones I could imagine allowing someone such as you to stow away. And in one piece."

"I'm still surprised he didn't throw me overboard, or worse," Aoife said, glancing down at her hands as she wrung them. She didn't want to talk about Declan. She wanted to start a new life, free of him, since that was what he apparently wanted as well.

"Oh, no, that's not his style. I know, I know. His *reputation*. But it's not hard to see it's all show. Doesn't reach his heart."

"You think the stories are lies?" The thought had crossed her own mind a few times.

"Oh, no, they're quite real. He's certainly done all they've said. But the boy's not like the rest. Even if he hides it well enough from everyone else, I can see the truth. Plus, he's not one to bloody his hands unnecessarily. He's far more likely to do what he did. Drop you off here with naught but a dagger and my name."

"He didn't give—"

"Ah, but he did. Through Tommy, I imagine."

Aoife's jaw dropped a fraction of an inch, and she stared dumbly at the woman, who responded with another round of boisterous laughter as she once again settled against the high back of the threadbare armchair and crossed her legs. "Again, girl, it's just observation and what I know of Declan and his crew. Nothing special about me."

Aoife smiled at the woman and said, "My name's Aoife."

Her smile vanished as soon as she realized her mistake. She should have given an alias. But Tommy hadn't instructed her to do so, so perhaps she was safe. Perhaps Aoife wasn't that rare of a name and no one would connect her to the Cregahn Council.

"I knew an Aoife once." *See? Not rare.* "Or was it Evelyn?" Lucy stared at the ceiling, as if it might hold the answer. "Not that it matters either way. It's nice to meet you, Aoife. If Tommy sent you to me, I can only assume it's because you're needing more respectable work than what is offered elsewhere."

"Yes. And lodging too. If you can point me to a boardinghouse or—"

"Oh, nonsense. You'll stay here. The upstairs has two separate apartments, so you'll have some privacy. And I'd really appreciate the help. I have two cooks who stayed on with me after they got too weary of the sea life—Marco and John. They're nice enough and work hard. But they won't bother you none. I'll be sure of that. The patrons on the other hand… Let's just say, keep that blade handy. You won't have any trouble while here, because they know I'd wallop them if they caused trouble in my eatery. But out there?" She pointed to the street below. "That's another story altogether."

"How have you survived all this time if it's so dangerous?"

"Ah, yeah. One rule of Foxhaven—you're responsible for your own safety. Ain't nobody gonna save you here. So I hope they taught you to use that thing." She dipped her chin toward the blade still tucked into Aoife's belt. Aoife's worry must have been written clearly on her face, because Lucy rolled her eyes and groaned. "They didn't. Tommy, Tommy, Tommy. What was that boy thinking, sending you off on your own with a blade you don't know how to use?"

"Well, I mean, he told me to put the pointy end into anyone who bothered me."

Another hearty laugh. "That's a good start at least, I suppose. Perhaps I'll have Marco or John teach you a bit. In the meantime, let's get you some food. I'm guessing you had nothing but cold, sea-hardened morsels for the past few days."

"Yes, please."

Without another word, Lucy was up and out of her seat, rushing down the stairs. Aoife turned to look out the window at her new home.

If it was really as dangerous as Lucy had said—and Aoife couldn't imagine why the lady would have any reason to lie about it—she had no desire to ever leave these walls. But she hadn't escaped one prison just to hole herself up in another.

Someday she'd need to venture out and explore a bit. If this was to be her new home, she'd need to own the fear and subdue it. She swallowed hard, unsure and afraid, wishing—despite herself—that Tommy and Declan were here to teach her instead of these two cooks she hadn't yet met.

They were wasting their time here in this port, and that bothered Declan. They'd been here two days, and while Mikkel had found another twenty men to fill in their ranks, he still didn't have the information he needed. Mikkel was back on the ship, getting the new crew situated, and here Declan was, counting down the last hours of their final day in port with nothing to show for it.

He kicked the cobblestones with his boot as he leaned, arms crossed in front of him, against the porch railing of Michaelson's Pub. It wasn't the best establishment in the port—that was Lucy's—but having sent Aoife there when they'd arrived, he had no desire to see her, no matter how superior the fare was.

Still, no matter how he tried to ignore it, some part of him wondered how she was doing and if she had settled in all right. It was better this way. Even if ill manners got him more grief from Tommy than he would have liked, at least Tommy had successfully gotten the hint and backed off about the lass.

He didn't have the luxury of relationships. That was for other men on distant shores. Not for pirates. Their relationship was with the sea, and maybe with the goods they took off others' hands.

This was what he wanted. Solitude. No responsibility. No ties or connections.

Then why are you doing all this for Cait then?

A groan rumbled in the back of his throat. He'd been asking himself that question since they'd left Cregah.

Technically he had never actually agreed to do this for Cait. She'd assumed. And should he somehow manage to retrieve the dagger from the Black Sound, there was no contract—written or otherwise—between them requiring he hand it over.

But could he betray his sister like that? That was the question. She'd given him so few answers, so little information. And though he knew it was for his own safety and the safety of her people, it stung how she didn't trust him.

There was no need, however, to make up his mind yet on the matter.

First get the fae.

Then get the dagger.

Then decide what to do with it.

But that first step was proving to be a great deal harder than he'd anticipated.

Movement came from his right, before the clearing of a throat announced who approached.

"Any luck?" he asked as Tommy came up beside him and mimicked his relaxed stance against the wooden rail.

Even after days of disappointment, the man seemed to be in good spirits, serious but not downtrodden.

Unlike Declan.

"Luck's got nothing to do with it, Captain."

"Any developments then?" As annoyed as Declan was, he had to admit he was thankful to have someone as steadfast as Tommy beside him, someone even-keeled. It was one of the main reasons he'd asked him to be his quartermaster in the first place. That and because Tommy was the only other pirate he trusted.

"Just a few tidbits here and there. Nothing concrete. And all the stories and rumors we're gathering contradict each other. Some say there are two sisters; some say three. Others claim they've seen them, but only once and in passing, and they could have been shadows. My guess? The fine booze they serve up there at the council hall isn't helping their memories. And those men have only been there once, on the rare occasion their lord allowed them to."

"I knew it was a long shot."

"It's tough trying to go on hearsay. We only get one chance at this. We can't risk it on shoddy information and drunken tales."

Declan gritted his teeth and looked down the narrow street, away from his friend, but didn't answer.

Tommy waited for a breath, then another, before finally saying, "We need to—"

"I know." Declan scratched at the back of his head, his gaze lowered toward the stones at his feet. "But I don't like it."

"Maybe her terms will have changed. I mean, perhaps life here has turned out better than expected and she'll offer up her knowledge with no strings attached."

"One could hope, I suppose. But it will be my last resort. I want to try once more before I give up using another route."

"We've exhausted all routes." Tommy's cool demeanor was fading quickly, his expression darkening by the second. "Why are you so against asking for her help? Are you so proud?"

"Watch it, Tommy. I mean it. I have my reasons, and pride's got nothing to do with it. Leave it."

Tommy raised his arms in surrender. "Fine."

"And we haven't exhausted them all. Another ship came in this morning."

"Yeah. I saw that. The *Duchess*, wasn't it? Don't they sail in—"

"Lord Madigen's fleet. That's right. They're his second most trusted crew after his own."

Tommy's eyes narrowed. "You know the *Duchess*'s crew doesn't partake in places like Michaelson's though." Tommy gestured to the building behind them.

Declan breathed out a sigh. "I know. Lucy's. Which we will be going to anyway if this doesn't pan out, so it saves us some extra walking."

"Lucy will be glad to see you, I bet." Tommy gave him a nudge, but Declan just rolled his eyes before he pushed off the post and started walking, not bothering to see if his friend followed.

Lucy's was only a five-minute walk away, but with the meandering nature of the streets it could have taken considerably longer had they not been so well acquainted with the town. Declan kept a decent pace, his eyes always watching, observing people as they passed, sizing up potential threats, looking for those who didn't recognize him and might see him as an easy mark.

Though Tommy was beside him, they walked in silence—another reason he had hired Tommy. He could be silent. Too many people had to fill in the silence with small talk and awkwardness. The thought brought images of Aoife and her incessant chatter to mind.

It had been too quiet the past couple of nights without her talking or humming to herself or asking asinine questions. He'd told himself it wasn't her he missed but more the distraction she'd provided.

The yellow building came into view as they rounded a corner, and he took a deep breath without slowing. It was midafternoon, but Lucy's main dining hall remained nearly packed day and night as various crews mingled with the locals who lived and worked here.

He and Tommy stepped inside and paused. Eyes turned to them, and Declan waited. A tense hush fell over the room, as if announcing their arrival. Some of the customers glanced away hurriedly; others seemed confused by the sudden change.

"Oh, ho, ho! Look who has finally graced my doorstep!" Lucy's cheerful greeting boomed through the dining room, and the patrons—any concerns now quelled by their hostess's reaction—returned to their conversations and their meals. "Come in! Come in!"

She waved them in but then stopped short, her smile dropping as she placed a hand on Declan's chest. "Now, wait a minute there, Captain. You're not here to take back my girl, are you?"

"And which girl would that be?" Declan kept his expression blank.

"Don't play dumb with me, Declan. I know well enough you and Tommy sent Aoife my way. Here to talk to her?"

"No. We aren't."

Tommy chimed in. "Not yet anyway."

"Good, because she's busy workin'. You can talk to her after dusk. Most of the folks these days head to the other pubs for a better booze selection once it gets dark. I don't mind. Gives my feet a rest."

"Fair enough, Lucy. We are, however, looking for someone else. Perhaps you've seen them?"

"And who might that be?" Her smile brightened as she straightened.

"Looking for some royal blood." He hoped she'd understand his meaning, and given her many years of working for and with pirates, he had little doubt she would.

"You know I can't divulge that kind of information, Declan." She kept her voice level, almost raising it so those around could hear her clearly, as she glanced around the room at the full tables. "Though, I do have a table upstairs with your name on it, if you're interested."

Declan looked over the diners, wondering if any of the *Duchess*'s crew was here in this room. But that ship carried double the men his did, making it impossible to know every face. And with everyone seated, it was too difficult to catch the colors they wore at the waist.

Again, he hoped Lucy understood they weren't seeking just any member of the crew, but the officers.

Tommy answered for them. "That would be great, Lucy. And don't mind us. We know our way. We'll let you get back to your customers."

She patted Tommy's cheek. "Thanks, love. I'll bring some food up to you in a bit." Lucy turned away from them but called over her shoulder, "It's good to see you both though!"

Declan nodded toward the back of the eatery before leading the way to the stairwell. The air became sticky and heavy as they climbed the stairs and left the loud chatter behind.

The upstairs hadn't changed at all, not that it had been that long since they'd stopped in. Certainly not the seven years he'd waited to return home. The room had the same mix of furniture that always made him laugh. Even with how worn each item was, Lucy kept everything impeccably clean and inviting. He often wondered where she found the energy and time to keep things looking so nice, though he'd never ask her.

Declan walked over to a low table tucked into the corner near the windows, but there was little breeze and not much to be done about the heat and humidity. Tommy shifted uncomfortably in his seat, undoubtedly from said heat. "Why can't they be sitting downstairs?" Tommy mumbled so low Declan wasn't even sure he'd heard him correctly.

"Some people prefer quiet. At all costs, I suppose." He kept his chin down as his eyes took in the dining room and the smattering of guests.

A man dined alone by the windows a couple of tables down from them, huddled over his plate and not seeming to notice that anyone else occupied the room. Two women, locals perhaps, sat at a high table near the far wall, talking quietly as little laughs peppered their conversation. It would have normally been a welcome sound, jovial and carefree, but now it only grated on Declan's nerves.

His gaze came to rest on three men sitting in the armchairs a few tables away. Two of them leaned forward, their heads close together as they spoke in hushed tones. No laughs from that group. The third sat with an ankle crossed over his knee, leaning back as he steepled his fingers under his chin, his face hidden under a large brimmed hat that had not been taken off. All three wore a purple sash at their waists—indicating their loyalty to Lord Madigen—along with the gold fabric that marked them as crew of the *Duchess*.

Tommy must have noticed them too, because he nudged Declan's boot with his own and carefully angled his head toward them before working the kinks out of his neck. Declan gave an almost imperceptible dip of his chin in acknowledgement.

These were the officers they'd been hoping to find. He'd need a good plan to address them and get them talking about their last trip to the council hall. He checked his pocket watch and almost groaned. It was getting late. In a few hours he'd have to give in and turn to Aoife for help. He didn't want that.

Tommy leaned forward, elbows resting on the table, eyes darting to the side to look at the three officers one more time before he spoke. "What's the plan?" He thumbed his nose.

"I'm working on it."

"Well, we need to work faster. Maybe Lucy could help."

As if on cue, steps sounded in the stairwell, and Lucy's warm humming filled the room. No one turned toward her, no doubt used to the way she always entered a room with a tune and a smile. She balanced two plates on one arm and three mugs in the other hand. Declan could have smiled at the sight of his old friend and how nothing seemed to dampen her spirits, but he was too restless and grumpy.

Lucy approached and set the two plates before him and Tommy. "Maybe some food will fix that sour demeanor, McCallagh. Eat up. I'm sure you could use this after whatever drivel you've been eating the last months you've been away."

He looked over the meal as he accepted the forks she offered, then looked up at her. "Where's the pie?"

She gave a laugh and a shake of her head. "You think I forgot? I got slices already set aside for you downstairs, Declan. Don't you worry."

"This looks great as always, Lucy," Tommy said and began shoveling forkfuls of meat and gravy and potatoes and green vegetables into his mouth.

Another booming laugh escaped their hostess. "Don't eat too fast there, Tommy. Your captain here may need you to be light on your feet yet, and eating like that won't help." Tommy only nodded, but he did at least allow himself to swallow fully before taking another bite. "I'll have some drinks for you in a bit."

And then she was gliding away, the three mugs in hand as she approached the three officers of the *Duchess*. She wasn't unfriendly with them, but Declan noted how her behavior changed as she became just a hair more formal and subdued, but she spoke loudly enough that Declan could hear her side of the exchange.

"How was everything? Satisfactory, I hope." The pair paused their conversation, and each gave her a nod. The third didn't move or speak. "I brought you some of our latest batch of mead. I've had rave reviews about it, even from those who prefer the rum and whisky at other establishments. On the house, of course."

She set the large mugs down on the low table and took up their plates that held mere remnants of the meal they'd enjoyed. "If you need anything else, just holler."

If they responded to her at all, Declan couldn't hear, and then Lucy was heading toward the stairs, smiling once more at Declan before disappearing below.

Declan ate slowly, or at least more slowly than Tommy, monitoring the officers in his periphery the whole time. As they drank the mead Lucy had presented, he noticed they became visibly more relaxed—even the silent one. Lucy returned once without a word, bringing two mugs similar to the ones she'd provided the officers, but filled with water instead.

He and Tommy finished their meals and sipped on their waters, requesting refills a few times as they watched the three *Duchess* crew members.

After a little over an hour, all three officers were leaning in, chattering loudly under the hats they still wore, not bothering to keep their voices down. Even the more somber one was joining in. They'd let their guard down as Declan needed, but he couldn't assume anything. It could all be for show.

But they sounded off, different, not what he'd expected. They lacked the gruffness of Callum and most other officers, not displaying the same crudeness as the average crew member. But as officers, their notable air of formality was expected, even after a few drinks.

But no, that wasn't what set these voices apart. They were higher. Like boys who hadn't yet matured into manhood, yet their bodies were the size and shape of grown men.

Except they weren't.

Declan turned to Tommy and whispered, "They're women."

Women. How had Declan missed that?

He kicked himself for being so ill-informed and naive. He'd heard of some crews employing women, but to have all your officers be women? It was unprecedented. Not that it changed his mind at all. In fact, it perked him up a bit. Female pirates might be allowed more freedom about the council hall, able to see more than the average pirates were able to.

"Of course they're women. You didn't know?" Tommy's expression was almost comical as he whispered back, and Declan couldn't keep from tightening his jaw in frustration. "I thought you knew. Hell, I thought everyone knew. You do know their captain, Casey Halloran, is a lass, too, right?"

"Well, I do now. How did you know and I didn't?"

"I thought it was common knowledge. I mean, I guess Casey isn't clearly a feminine name, but—" Tommy shrugged and pulled the corners of his mouth down. "I honestly thought you knew. But I suppose it makes sense you didn't. People don't really talk about it anymore, since Captain Halloran has an affinity for cutting out tongues for shit talk. Everyone's been pretty hush about it for years. And it's not like we've had any encounters with them ever. They always seem to be sailing in the opposite direction as us."

"You're rambling. Stop it."

"You know I chatter when I feel bad."

"Hence why it happens so rarely," Declan said. Another shrug. "Well then, how the hell did you hear about it?"

"I heard back when we were cabin boys."

Declan's eyes went wide. "That long ago?"

"Yeah. I overheard the officers chatting about some female captain and how her officers were women. Not all of them, mind you, but two of them. Her quartermaster and her sailing master though. They couldn't understand how men could stomach serving under them, but I suppose when you have such a ruthless reputation and a few big hauls under your belt, the men stop caring who's running the ship as long as their pockets continue to be lined and their bellies fed."

"You said two of her officers are female."

"Aye."

"So who's the third sitting—" Declan cut his words short as his stomach tightened. Why hadn't he anticipated this? The third, more aloof one, had to be the captain. Captain Halloran. She wouldn't be as easy to sway or trick into giving up information, and he certainly couldn't risk her going to Lord Madigen or demanding to be cut in on the prize like Callum had.

"So," Tommy started, "now what?"

Declan ran his fingers under his stubbled chin. His mind raced from option to option, but nothing he came up with would work. Except maybe one thing. A long shot, but desperation burned behind his sternum.

The two officers stood, their captain remaining in her seat. This was his only chance, his last hope of not having to crawl back to Aoife and beg for her aid. With a nod to their captain, the two officers made for the stairs. Declan sent Tommy off after them with an angle of his head and a raised brow. Tommy asked no questions but acted swiftly to follow, likely already devising the smooth lines he'd use to get them chatting with him.

Declan, too, rose and made his way over to where Captain Halloran sat.

This was far from an ideal location to have such a talk, but only the single man by the window remained, preoccupied with watching people on the streets below. Declan stopped a few feet away from the captain. She didn't move or acknowledge his presence.

He cleared his throat before speaking. "Captain Halloran? I've never had the pleasure of meeting you in person."

She looked up at him, and even in the shadow of her large hat, she was beautiful in a dangerous way. Her eyes, a mix of browns and golds, reflected the light of the chandeliers overhead as they burned into his own. Her dark skin showed the wear of the sea, but not in an unattractive way, not the way older men wore their years of sailing. Where others appeared weathered and worn down, her lines gave her a look of refinement. Experience.

If Tommy had heard of her all those years ago, she had to be at least ten or fifteen years Declan's senior. But she was still a pirate, and he knew how to deal with other pirates.

"And you are?" It was the first he'd heard her voice clearly all evening, and it sounded like honey dripping from her lips, but with hint of an edge, like poison slipped into a sweet treat.

"Captain McCallagh. Of the *Siren's Song*." He gave a bow of his head.

"Ah. I've heard of you." She rested her hand at her cheek as she looked him over.

"Good things, I hope," Declan said with a slight smirk on his lips.

There was no laughter in her words or eyes as she asked, "Do pirates ever say good things about one another?"

She had a point, and given the lengths he'd gone to ensure his name carried weight, he was glad to hear she'd at least heard it uttered. "May I sit?" He gestured to one of the now empty chairs across from her.

Captain Halloran tipped a shoulder up in a shrug but didn't say a word. Lowering himself into the chair, he leaned back, his mind racing through the possible paths this conversation could end up on.

He opened his mouth to speak, but she beat him to it. "So, Captain McCallagh of the *Siren's Song*, I assume you haven't gotten the information you need yet."

Declan sucked in a breath and stilled but forced his features to remain calm. He could play dumb, but he imagined that might get him into trouble with this pirate. No doubt she'd heard his crew had been asking around. "Nearly."

She let out a single laugh and leaned toward him, pushing the brim of her hat up a bit. Her eyes seemed to dance with danger and intrigue. "If that were true, you wouldn't be risking this little conversation with me, pup."

"Risking what, exactly? Merely introducing myself to a captain of such great esteem."

"Don't mock me, boy," she said, her words losing all their sweetness. "I don't deal well with being toyed with."

"So I've heard." He cleared his throat. He needed a new tactic with this one. If the charm hadn't worked, perhaps honesty might. "To be perfectly honest, Captain, I didn't know you were a woman until this evening."

"And you thought you'd come scoff at me to my face."

"I thought I'd come chat up the woman who has grown men cowering at her name and has earned a place in Madigen's fleet."

She didn't say anything. Her eyes scanned his face with such intensity it took every ounce of will not to squirm and look away.

With another breath, he pulled his lips into a tight line. "But I can see I've wasted your time, and mine. Apologies." He moved to rise, hoping she'd stop him. But she didn't. "Good evening, Captain."

He lowered his chin once more and strode off toward the stairs. He hoped Tommy had fared better with the officers, but that hope was slim. He'd need to find Aoife after all, and he wasn't looking forward to that.

He'd made it down three stairs when Captain Halloran called out to him, "McCallagh." He continued down a few more steps. He didn't want to seem too eager.

She called again, "Declan."

Hearing his first name used by someone he didn't know at all made his muscles tense. He came back up the stairs and stopped at the top, resting against the half-wall. "Yes, Captain?"

"Get over here." Her tone had lost some of its edge, and she gestured to the seat he'd just vacated.

Declan did as requested but didn't speak as he returned to his seat. Leaning back in the chair as he waited, he forced himself to relax and appear far more patient than he felt.

"I knew your parents." She showed no emotion, stating this matter-of-factly, as if she were noting the color of his jacket.

Memories threatened to rush forward, but he slammed the door closed on them. "A lot of people—a lot of pirates—knew them."

"They were good people. It's a shame what happened to them."

"Yes, well, that's the way of the world, isn't it?"

"And your sister. Cait, was it? She still runs the family business, doesn't she?" Something about the way she said *business* had Declan's skin prickling.

Halloran didn't seem to be talking merely about the pub, but certainly his parents hadn't been involved with the Rogues back then. Though, would Declan even have known? He could look back through his memories, but no. He wouldn't risk letting those out, wasn't sure he could handle it. Especially not here and not now.

"Aye. The pub is still up and running. Doing pretty well from what I could tell last I was in."

The captain breathed deep. "I'm glad to hear that."

"Why are we talking about my family, exactly?"

"What would you rather discuss? The weather? The sea? The council? Or maybe the fae?"

Declan narrowed his eyes at her. It would have been one thing for him to bring those last two up, but for her to already know what he sought? How did she know? He'd been clear with the men to be discreet, ordering them not to mention the fae or the dagger in their questions but to only ask about the council in general, as if they were merely curious about what it was like to visit the hall.

She let out a laugh. "Oh, don't worry yourself, Declan. Your men didn't screw up. It's not hard to figure out what you're after and what information you need." Her words didn't quell any of the anxiety rising within him. If she knew, who else knew? And there remained the question of how.

"Are you offering to help me then?"

A scream pierced the air from somewhere in the streets below, the sound carrying through the open window, but he fought to keep his attention on the deadly captain before him. He had no desire to lose an appendage for disrespecting her.

She didn't blink at the scream either. "Not in the way you desire, I suppose. You know, Declan, it wasn't easy to get where I am. No one helped me. No one offered me aid. I clawed my way to this position and my ship."

"And killed many in the process. You have quite the reputation."

"Yet you didn't know I was a woman." The gold in her eyes flashed. Was that an inkling of humor within them, or was he imagining it?

He sighed. "No, I didn't. I suppose everyone is too afraid of you to note that bit of information anymore."

She sat and stared at him for a moment in the silence. He waited, his pocket watch becoming a burning weight at his side. He was wasting too much time here. He needed to find Aoife and get moving if he was going to stay on task.

Twenty-five days left. To get the fae. To get the dagger. To get back to Morshan.

"You know, I always admired your parents. I wouldn't mind seeing their work succeed."

His glance flicked to the man still sitting by the window before returning to her. "The pub is a blessing for those who stop at the island."

Halloran leaned forward now, her voice dropping into a whisper. "I can't give you what you need, Declan. Can't risk Madigen discovering I helped you. But I can tell you, you must not fail. And you must not trust anyone. They know what you're seeking, and they're looking for her."

Declan's breath caught. Aoife. He fought the instinct to look around the room, as if the mere mention of her would call her up here.

Captain Halloran continued. "Find her. Take her with you. It's the only way to keep her safe."

Declan thought of mentioning how he didn't care what happened to the girl, play it cool, but before he could say anything, the captain was standing.

"Good luck, Declan. Truly." Then she was across the room and down the stairs, leaving Declan alone with all she'd said.

Don't trust anyone. Keep her safe.

Why did the girl's safety matter so much?

He glanced back to the man still sitting by the window and wondered how much he'd heard. Was he a spy? Or was he merely a local enjoying a quiet meal alone?

Surely he could trust Tommy, whom he'd known all these years. Callum perhaps. But that was already a shaky alliance.

Who could Captain Halloran have been warning him not to trust?

Her words threatened to drive him to paranoia. Had that been her intent all along? Distract him enough so he'd fail?

Humming came from the stairs. Lucy.

Declan's mind raced, tripping over itself as he thought back through all the encounters he'd had with the owner of this eatery. She'd always been friendly. Too friendly? The captain's words had him second-guessing everything. But perhaps that wasn't a bad thing. He couldn't be too careful.

"Declan! Where did Tommy get off to? I didn't see him leave."

"Ah, he went off to get the crew ready to sail," he lied.

He might be a pirate, but he hated lying to a friend. Though perhaps she wasn't as good a friend as he'd imagined. He looked toward the window before turning back to Lucy, who was now clearing the mugs from the table in front of him. "Where's the girl? I need to speak with her after all."

Lucy stood upright, a flash of surprise written on her face. "Oh! Dear me, she's gone, I'm afraid."

"Gone to where exactly?"

"Cregah, I believe. A couple big guys came in not five minutes ago and said they were to escort her home."

"And you let them? She let them?" The echo of the earlier scream pierced him. Had that been Aoife? Tommy had given Aoife the dagger, right? Had she lost it somehow? Failed to use it? He cursed himself for not having Tommy train her a bit on the use of a blade.

Lucy's eyes were wide, her jaw hanging open until she snapped it closed, and he didn't have the time to pry answers out of her.

Aoife was gone.

His only hope of getting that dagger, gone. He jumped up and ran down the stairs, not quite sure which way he was heading, only knowing he needed to find her. And fast.

Out on the street, Declan skidded to a stop on the cobbled stones and glanced down one side and then the other, his heart beating wildly and his breathing ragged.

No doubt they were heading toward the water if they were planning to cart her back to Cregah and the council. Without a second thought, he took off at a run, taking the shortest path there. With any luck, perhaps he could cut them off at the shore.

If only he knew which ship they were from.

Or what they looked like.

Or anything.

He rounded a corner and slammed into someone. He bit back a curse and nearly screamed at them to watch where they were going before he realized it was Tommy.

A look of concern washed over Tommy's face. "What's wrong? Where's the fire?"

"She's gone. They're taking her back to Cregah." Fear dripped from every syllable, and he was glad when Tommy didn't mock him for it.

Without another word, Declan was off, running again, with Tommy right behind him.

They wove through the streets looking for two pirates escorting a poorly disguised woman. At least Aoife was on the short side. It shouldn't be too hard to find two big guys walking with a short one between them.

The sunlight was quickly fading as they ran, and it seemed time was stacked against them. As always.

As soon as they rounded the last corner the buildings gave way to the shore, nothing but sand greeted them. All the crews had apparently packed up and retreated into town for the evening.

No one. No crews. No kidnappers. No struggling girl.

It was almost eerie to see the beach so deserted, but then again, perhaps this was normal for Foxhaven. He wouldn't know, having always been in town with the rest of the crew come dusk.

Their boots had barely touched the sand when words pierced the night air, causing them to freeze.

"I said, let me go!"

Aoife. At least she hadn't given up yet.

Declan scanned the beach but still didn't see them. He and Tommy both looked down the edge of the town, waiting to see from which street they would emerge.

"There!" Tommy said, barely over a whisper. He pointed to his left at the two men stepping out from between a pair of buildings a few hundred yards away, with Aoife in hand. Tommy moved to run, but Declan reached out an arm, holding him back.

"What are you doing? We have to get her!"

Tommy's urgency and desperation echoed in every bone and muscle of Declan's body, but he fought it back, his jaw clenched. He'd wanted to be rid of her, and he'd known something—perhaps not exactly like this but something similarly unpleasant—might happen. But knowing the possibility and seeing it unfold were two vastly different things. Seeing her now, struggling against her captors, stumbling on the sand, he could sense her fear. He balled his fists, wanting to ram them into the men's faces, to grab her from them and make them pay for hurting her.

The need to protect her stormed inside him, a battle raging despite his effort to suppress it and shut it up. He couldn't let himself care about her. About anyone. But the need to get her didn't mean he cared. No. It wasn't a matter of caring or protecting. It was a matter of winning. A matter of success.

If he were to get the fae, he needed her. That was all he saw being dragged toward the shore—his one chance to succeed.

"Aye, we do. But they haven't reached the water yet, and we have the upper hand here. I don't want to risk going in without a plan."

"We don't have all night, Declan. Hurry the hell up." For a brief second Declan questioned why Tommy cared so much. He wasn't jealous, of course. That would be preposterous. No, this was Tommy. And assuming he actually knew Tommy—and could trust him—it was likely a mix of wanting to get the dagger and not wanting to see Aoife hurt. He'd always had a rather un-pirate-like way of caring about other people's well-being, unless they had a ship full of goods.

He allowed himself a few more seconds to think, ignoring Tommy's irritated stares as his mind raced to formulate a plan. His mouth contorted into a devious smile. "I'm thinking Lady Gem's Tavern. Two years ago?"

Tommy gave him a hard look, as if hunting down the memory in his mind, and then looked around. Behind them. And then at the men leading Aoife toward the shore. Taking a single deep breath, he squared his shoulders before jogging off and disappearing between the buildings, shaking his head and muttering curses as he went.

Listening to Aoife continue to struggle with her captors, he would have laughed at her growls had she not been in such a predicament. He gave the trio another once-over. The men were of similar height, but the one on the left was long and lanky. He gripped Aoife's arm with spindly fingers. The other, lumbering close behind them, appeared to have stolen some extra rations on his ship.

He watched them for one more moment. No signs of drunkenness. No stumbling in the sand like Aoife had. They had their cutlasses drawn, but all their attention was focused on the girl and keeping her from fleeing.

They hadn't yet noticed him. Nor did they notice when he drew his own cutlass.

He moved forward, making his steps uneven. He leaned to one side, his head lolling a bit as he stumbled along his way. He'd seen enough drunks—and been one often enough himself when he was younger—to mimic their ambling gait with astounding perfection whenever needed.

"Keep moving, girl," the larger man barked from behind her.

Though Declan couldn't see fully what was happening, the man must have reached up to strike her because his friend piped up. "Don't hit her! You know the orders. We can't return her already bro—" His words cut off in a howl. "She bit me!"

"I'm not—going—back!" Aoife huffed. Declan looked up to see her wriggling and pulling against the man's grip, but it didn't loosen.

Declan had made it within thirty feet of them when he opened his mouth. Not to speak, but to sing. Loudly. And not well.

"Take me away to Lagley-place…" He tossed his head about and looked toward the sky as he sang, his cutlass hanging limply by his side. "…where my fair lass awaits me." Another stumble and a half. "Been fightin' and killin'…" With those words, he gave his cutlass a haphazard swing from left to right, sending him teetering ever closer to Aoife and the men, who had now stopped to stare at him.

Amateurs.

"Get back, you!" It was likely the lanky one who had spoken, but Declan couldn't tell for sure. He lifted his head to look at them and lazily smacked his lips. Aoife had stopped struggling now, her expression one of confusion and amusement, which made sense given the spectacle he was making.

He forced his gaze to look through the man so his eyes appeared glazed over as he burst out into more of the song. "Been fightin' and killin' and drinkin' for so many years…" From his left came movement. Not a threat, but Tommy.

"Oy!" Tommy burst out from between two buildings, running toward Declan with a perturbed look plastered on his face. "What the hell are you doin' out here? We've been lookin' all over for you!"

Declan swung his head to face Tommy before rolling his eyes with such drama he knew Tommy would never stop mocking him for it back on the ship. He ignored his friend and went back to singing as he moved, or fell, a few steps closer to Aoife and the men, who were still standing and watching him.

The lanky man interrupted his song, which had become more of a string of gibberish and half words set to his own made-up tune. "Why don't you head back to whatever drunken hole you crawled out of?"

Declan was now within six feet of them. So close he could smell their unwashed bodies mingling with whatever scented soap Aoife had used that morning. Was that Aoife's heart pounding in her chest, or was it his own? It didn't matter.

"C'mon, Captain." Tommy inched closer to him, like a man approaching a wild animal. Declan swung his cutlass across his body until it pointed, wobbly and unsteadily, at his best friend's face. Tommy stopped and raised his hands in surrender.

Declan glared as he spoke. "Don't you *c'mon, Captain me*, boy. I do what I want. Where I want."

And with that final, slurred and barely intelligible word, he moved with a controlled swiftness so at odds with his drunken act that the lanky man had no time to react before Declan's cutlass met his throat. The curved blade—meticulously maintained and perfectly sharp—sliced through his neck as if it were made of soft cheese instead of bone and tendon.

At once, the man's grip loosened on Aoife's arms as his knees gave way, his body falling to the sand at the same moment his head, now severed, fell with a dull thud at Aoife's feet.

Declan waited for her scream, but it never came. Instead she stood frozen, blood sprayed all over her shocked face, her hands shaking at her sides, her eyes staring at Declan but not quite seeing him.

Tommy came up beside him, his dagger now drawn, pointed at the man who stood behind Aoife and his now dead partner. The pirate's hands flew up, mirroring in an almost comical manner how Tommy had looked seconds earlier. He backed away, his feet stumbling in the soft sand as he retreated slowly.

Declan kept his cutlass trained on the man, trying to ignore Aoife's intense glare from his right. "We'll be taking her with us."

The man gave a string of nods. "Take her. She's all yours."

"I suggest you get to your ship and leave." The man's gaze shifted between Declan, the bloodied cutlass, and his fallen friend before he took off, tripping and falling as he struggled to navigate the sand and return to whatever ship he called home.

Tommy leaned close to Declan. "You think it's wise to let him go?"

Declan wiped the blood from his blade onto his pants before sheathing it. "Who said I was letting him go?" A slight gesture of his head in the man's direction had Tommy moving, dagger in hand, as he ran to take care of the loose end.

He didn't bother waiting to see how Tommy managed, knowing it would be quick and silent. Tommy's specialty.

Aoife hadn't moved, and her captor's blood now dripped from her chin, but she made no sign that she noticed or cared. Declan had occasionally seen this behavior in newer crew members, the first time they saw action, especially during the moments after their first kill.

Though, in those instances, this vacant stare and frozen stance came later when the adrenaline had worn off. He'd offer them rum or bourbon. Something to calm the nerves as he spoke to them, assured them it would get easier, and reminded them they were free to leave at the next port if they couldn't stomach the work.

In all his years as captain, he'd only had two men take him up on that offer. And he had not begrudged them for knowing themselves well enough to make that choice.

But he couldn't give her that same offer.

He needed her, as much as he hated to admit it, as much as he had hoped for another option. He couldn't succeed without her help, and if she was truly going to insist on helping—not just with devising the plan but with its execution—he needed her to be able to handle whatever bloody messes they encountered.

He approached her with caution, hands up so she could see he meant no harm, but she still seemed to be looking through him. He didn't dare look down at the body to his left or to the head that lay between them. Instead he walked to the side first, hoping she would turn so she wouldn't have to step over her dead captor.

"Let's get you back to the ship and cleaned up."

She blinked and turned to face him, her feet shifting as he'd hoped. "What—what just happened?"

A part of Declan he'd worked so hard to contain pushed to get out, urging him to comfort her and protect her, but he shoved it back. He needed her to trust him, but he wouldn't let himself care. He couldn't. "We saved you. You're safe. But right now, we need to go. Tommy's waiting for us."

Reaching into his pocket, he pulled out a bit of cloth and handed it to her. "You can clean up further at the water." She took it and wiped it across her chin and forehead, smearing the man's blood, but at least it wasn't dripping anymore.

He offered her his arm, making a point not to grab her and cause her to panic. She waited. Hesitated. And he tried not to let his growing impatience show. If he moved too quickly, pushed her too soon, it would spell disaster for his plans. Better to be calculated, patient.

"Don't worry," he said as she slowly weaved her hand under his arm and let it rest on him, "blood can be washed away."

Aoife dipped her chin in gratitude and walked with him in silence back toward the ship.

Cait paced the small room that had become her home, or as close to one as she'd allow. The paintings she'd hung all those years ago—a poor attempt at dressing up the place and making it more comfortable—were now slightly askew and in desperate need of dusting.

This office had been her mother's, and she'd found it by chance only a few weeks after her parents' deaths. Her mother had left few clues as to what they'd been doing beyond running the pub, and as a teenage girl nearing adulthood, Cait had been preoccupied with courting prospective partners and had had no time to worry about her parents' dealings.

All she'd found was a cold room with old furniture, little comfort, and a nearly empty desk. Yet there she'd felt a connection to her mother, and there, below the Morshan streets, she'd found she could think and grieve in peace.

But it never did feel like home.

Not that it needed to. She only came down here when she needed a break from all the noise or needed to conduct business meetings, but even those had been few and far between of late, as most business was being conducted in coded messages passed along to her team via trusted messengers.

Declan had been the first guest here in months.

And now she was waiting for her second visitor in less than a week.

She glanced at the clock on the desk.

He was late. *Typical.*

Lucan was always late. But she hadn't promoted him to her second-in-command because of his punctuality.

He had a knack for strategy, an ability to think beyond the obvious and see all possibilities of a situation, weighing them faster than anyone else could. And he wasn't bad company.

A series of knocks sounded at the door.

Two. One. Three.

His knock. The one he'd insisted on using so she would know it was him. She'd mocked him for it at the time—had it really been four years ago?—but now she was thankful for it. Those men hadn't come back to the pub since they'd stepped in a few days ago, but ever since, she'd been jumpier than usual, sure to go straight upstairs after working, in case anyone was watching the apartment.

Cait opened the door an inch and whispered into the dark gap, "What's the password?"

"Pie." He uttered it with such deathly seriousness that she only barely managed to contain her laughter.

"You're an idiot."

She opened the door further, holding it at arm's length as she leaned against the frame and blocked his entry.

Lucan didn't move but rather waited in the dark hallway, his finger tracing the thin scar that ran along his hairline. He could have passed for a pirate, choosing to wear the standard garb of sailors rather than the simple garments favored by the locals.

She'd once asked why he hadn't scurried off to join a crew. While he'd claimed it was due entirely to his devotion to protecting the people of Cregah—like all members of the Rogues—she'd learned later that he had a distinct fear of water.

Good for someone who lived on an island.

Lucan flashed her a wink and dropped his hand. "You know you love me."

She merely shook her head. It might have been a casual remark, but it still pulled on a frayed thread in her heart. Had she met Lucan back then, before that night, she would have most certainly fallen for him. Unlike the boy she'd been courting—out of duty and not actual interest—Lucan might have stirred in her the dream for a home and children. For a simple life on these black sands.

If she was honest, she'd been almost grateful to have a reason to end things with the other boy, if only it hadn't come at such high a price.

But Lucan. Lucan wasn't like everyone else. He was one of the good ones. Solid. Loyal. And handsome. With eyes of melted chocolate that displayed the strong kindness and fearless humor he carried within.

The kind of man she would have chosen as a true partner.

But they hadn't met back then, and perhaps it was for the better.

He'd grown up on the other side of the Binbrack mountains and had only ventured to Morshan after his own family disappeared—his younger brother, his sister, and both of his parents.

He'd traveled here to file a complaint for suspected violence against them and to open an investigation into their disappearance.

The council had seen him in the public hall, had listened to his case and his evidence. They'd vowed to look into it, to have their lead security officer investigate, but he'd later learned they never did. They didn't even have a security officer. Or any kind of team to lead investigations. Every time he returned to inquire as to the status of the case, he was told it was ongoing and no leads had been found yet.

He'd come into Cait's pub then and tried to drown himself in rum.

With her parents dead a year and Declan newly gone, she had seen her own misery and grief mirrored in his glossy eyes across the bar. She'd let him sleep off his hangover in the back storeroom, giving him a blanket and a pile of rags for a pillow. She'd sat with him that whole night, allowing herself to doze off as she sat upright against the storeroom wall. When he'd awoken the next morning, his head pounding and an anger burning in his gut, she'd managed to convince him not to go after the council hastily.

For weeks after her parents' deaths, she'd been plotting and planning.

But she'd been doing it alone.

Until Lucan.

In that storeroom, seven years earlier, they'd joined forces, resurrecting the Rogues after the council had effectively wiped them out with her parents' disappearance. They'd never become more than friends and allies, but he was right. She did love him. Like a brother. She would never let herself love him as anything more.

"Aye, Lucan. You know I do. What took you so long?" She waved him inside and let him pull her into one of his classic bear hugs before they entered the room together, arm in arm as if they were taking a stroll through the village instead of plotting to overthrow their rulers.

"Thought I had a couple louses following me, so I had to take a few detours. If they were tailing me, I lost them around Carver Street."

"You lost them at the Ruby Inn? I should have known." The Ruby Inn—one of the more upscale brothels in the port, known for the respectable women and men they employed—wasn't like the whorehouses she'd heard peppered other ports in other lands. It was clean, well-kept, and meticulously managed by Ruby Rosewater, an older woman Cait had admired as a young girl, if only for her beautiful dresses and the jewels at her neck. Neither of which meant much to Cait now.

Lucan gave her a shrug. "They should be having more fun now than they would be here."

"I won't take that personally," she said as she walked over to the sofa.

This might be a business meeting, but nothing said it had to be formal. Plopping herself on the worn sofa, she let her head fall against the back of the cushion, one arm flung across the armrest. Lucan sat beside her and tapped her knee with his hand.

She didn't move her head but eyed him from her relaxed position.

"Now's no time to take a nap," he joked, but his smile didn't reach his eyes.

"I know, but I'm so tired."

"That worried about him?"

"No. I mean, yes. Sort of. But it's not only that. It's everything. Everything is riding on him, and…" She broke off with a sigh and pinched the bridge of her nose, as if the action could force her emotions to get in line and under control.

"It's only been a week, and you've done everything you can to help him, Cait. You know that." All the humor from moments before was gone, his words now acting like the big hug he'd offered at the door, wrapping around her for comfort and reassurance.

"I know, but…" Why couldn't she finish a sentence right now? She'd never allowed her vulnerability to show around any other member of the Rogues, and certainly not around the pub or even in front of Declan.

But Lucan had been there when Declan had not. But could she blame Declan for leaving? Initially, she'd remained out of obligation, telling herself she was being a good daughter, doing the responsible thing. She'd cursed her brother's name for so long, but in the quiet moments when the pub was empty, with only the sound of her rag on the bar for what seemed the millionth time, she let herself admit—if only internally—that she was mad she hadn't been the one to leave first.

As stories had come in of the new Captain McCallagh, who'd

named his ship the *Siren's Song*, she longed to be the one sailing in his place. She'd tried to ignore the tales the pirates brought into her pub of the young captain and his crew who undermined the pirate lords, hit merchant vessels before the larger fleets had a chance, and left gruesome messages carved into their victims for the lords to find.

Whether or not the stories were true mattered little to Cait. No, she couldn't blame her brother if he truly did dastardly things, not after what he'd witnessed as a boy. But she wished it were her captaining that ship, having adventures, feeling the sea breeze on her face, seeing distant lands.

Adventure. Excitement. Something beyond the mundane day-to-day activities of the pub, with the same faces and the same voices and the same everything day in and day out.

"I know that look," Lucan said, snapping her back to the present. He flashed her one of his most dashing smiles, his eyes gleaming with humor once again. "You're dreaming about ditching me again, aren't you?"

"That obvious?" The corner of her mouth pulled back into a half smile, but his own faded.

"Don't sell yourself short, Cait." His words once again seemed to wrap around and hold her like her mother used to. "Your actions here matter. We each have a role to play. Don't let yourself ever believe that yours is less important because it's done in the shadows."

He was right. Of course he was right, but there was a difference between knowing something logically and actually believing it. She wondered if there would always be a tiny piece of herself, tucked somewhere behind her ribs, that ached and yearned to be free of this place, to be free of the pub, to be free of the routine.

She took a deep breath, wishing the air rushing into her lungs would alleviate the ache within. It never did.

"Speaking of our roles," she said, sitting up. Placing her elbows on her knees, she looked him in the eye. "Have we any word from Maggie?"

Lucan watched her for a moment longer, his gaze burning into hers, as if he were checking to ensure she was truly okay. She'd never be okay though. But she wouldn't look away. Her raised brows urged him to let it go and get back to work.

He cleared his throat before answering, and had it been anyone else, she might have thought it was out of embarrassment of getting caught staring. But Lucan was rarely embarrassed.

"Aye. She got word to me yesterday. The hall is abuzz preparing for Captain Madigen and Captain Halloran. Word is the council has been scrambling to come up with an excuse for there being only one heir now."

"What of the rumors we heard? Is there any truth to them?"

"She believes so, but she says she needs more time."

"She'd better hurry. Twenty-five days. We need to know if it's true."

Lucan leaned forward and once again looked her square in the eye. His hand moved to rest on her knee, but at the last moment he retreated. She pretended not to notice, instead focusing on his words. "Maggie knows. The whole crew knows. We're working tirelessly. Trust that. Trust the team we've built."

Cait needed to move. To think. She pushed to her feet and began pacing along the same path she'd worn in the rug over the years.

"What have we heard from the twins?" She didn't look at Lucan as she asked, instead staring blankly before her as she continued to pace.

"They're currently keeping an eye on Captain Grayson and his crew. They arrived in port yesterday. Eva said she heard your brother's name mentioned a few times, and Aron is seeing what else he can learn about their role, if they're involved at all. Think Declan might have brought Grayson in on the job?"

Cait roughed a hand over her face. Sands, she was tired. So tired of the years spent working to bring the council down, to reinstate actual peace in her land. And now she'd entrusted the most important part of the plan to her younger brother. Would he be stupid enough to tell another pirate about it?

Her mind raced from thought to thought as she tried to determine what logical explanation there could be. She had assured Lucan and the Rogues that Declan could be trusted, but she had been racked with doubt, unsure if she even knew her brother anymore. But there'd been no other option. And there still wasn't. If he had indeed brought Grayson into his confidence, she'd need to trust there was a reason for that.

"Make sure the twins stay on their guard. Captain Grayson knows the rules of Cregah, for sure, but he's not above using whatever tricks he has to get folks aboard his ship to do as he pleases. If he suspects they're following him, I doubt he'll hesitate to deal with them in his own disgusting way."

Cait surely hoped Declan hadn't been so stupid.

She felt Lucan's eyes on her before she heard him speak.

"And are we certain about the timeline?"

Her feet stopped moving, and her shoulders slumped as she fell back onto the sofa. So much was riding on this and on her. The fate of her whole land was at stake.

"Honestly? I'm not certain of much these days, but what are our options?" She raised her arms out to her sides. "We have none."

She gritted her teeth, grinding down years of bitterness and frustration until her jaw ached.

Another deep breath had her turning toward him. It wouldn't do them any good if she let the weariness and worry overtake her. No. She was the leader of the Rogues. She had rebuilt this team, picked up where her mother had left off, recruiting fourteen people to help save their country.

She wouldn't fail. Couldn't fail.

"I've heard the same thing from multiple sources, so it's unlikely they've all collaborated. Last I heard, King Kilmeran is still gathering a fleet in Caprothe's main port. He's up to eight, perhaps ten, ships now. Maybe more. We need Maggie to dig a little deeper. As best she can without being found out. We need to know when he is meeting with the council. If they are, in fact, planning to overturn the Muirnaughton Treaty and partner with the king instead, all the lands of the Aisling Sea are in trouble."

"Why would they?"

Lucan's question came so quietly, Cait wasn't sure if he was asking her or himself, but she answered anyway. "If the king truly has the resources to take control over the Aisling lands, the council will want to do everything in its power to maintain its sovereignty. They might offer the aid of the pirates. But what would they gain from doing that? We've been playing the long game, taking our time instead of gaining any foothold against them. We haven't loosened their death grip on us in the slightest. Not yet. So why? Why would they?"

She stopped. A memory from the other night in the pub echoed in the back of her mind. "There were mumblings in the pub, but…"

Lucan's gaze lingered, a silent nudge for her to spit out the words.

She rushed to her feet with a curse. "What if they're right?"

Lucan's mouth had dropped open, and he was looking around the room as if there were someone else who could provide the answers she wasn't sharing. "Cait! What if who's right? About what?"

Another curse, and then she was shaking her head. "It can't be. No." She began pacing again.

"Damn it, Cait." He was standing now, grabbing her arms and forcing her to look him in the eye. "What is it?"

"I only caught a portion of it and chalked it up to the typical boasts of latest hauls. Basic pirate banter. They had just sailed from the west. Not sure whose ship they were from—I didn't recognize them—"

She was rambling but was too busy sorting through her jumbled thoughts to care what her words sounded like. "They mentioned a shield."

"A shield? That's a bit odd."

"Right? Really odd."

"No one uses them. Haven't since the war. They're nearly impossible to come by." Lucan's face contorted with confusion as he obviously tried to fit the pieces together.

"Lucan. What if the king has the counter to the dagger? The shield? What if he's using that as his bargaining chip? What if he's using that to get the council to partner with him? It's the only way they'd ever call off their pirate goons. Thanks to Maggie, we know they know we're searching for the dagger. And this whole time we've been trying to ensure we got to it first. We completely failed to see that they might find the shield."

Lucan dropped back onto the sofa, saying nothing, staring blankly ahead. Cait resumed her pacing. She couldn't fall apart. The Rogues, her people, the entire nation needed her to hold it together. They could still win—it was up to Declan now—but there were so many other variables it made her head spin.

"We need Maggie to confirm the date. Best to assume the worst here. Assume he has the shield. So Declan needs to get us that dagger before then. He should be returning to Morshan soon for the first step. Assuming all went well with him in Foxhaven."

"The fae." Not a question. "We could have gotten him the layout from Maggie, right? Saved him time?"

"No. Maggie's access is limited, unfortunately. And while she's able to overhear conversations, she hasn't had the chance—and likely never will—to explore and find where the fae are being held."

"Does Declan know we have her on the inside?"

"Not yet. But I'll let him know when he makes port."

Lucan glanced at the clock on the wall, as if it could tell him when Declan might arrive. "I hope he hurries."

"Me too."

Aoife's next day and a half was a blur. The familiar images of Lani being hauled away were now joined by the memories of being sprayed with blood, and dull thuds of the crew outside jolted her awake whenever she was able to doze off.

To his credit, Declan had given her time to process the events in Foxhaven. He had allowed her to remain in bed—his bed—for a full thirty hours following the ordeal on the beach. He'd brought her food, small morsels, to nibble on as she could manage. He offered a steady hand whenever she needed to get out of bed to tend to her needs.

How did one recover after seeing such a sight?

She could still feel the warmth that had smacked her face when the blade had struck. She could still feel the way her heart had seemed to stop, as dead and lifeless as the man before her, before resuming with a roaring pounding against her sternum, her stomach launching into her throat. All her will was spent keeping the bile contained.

But most of the time she slept, drifting in and out of dark dreams, and tried her best to give her mind and body the rest it needed.

She couldn't stop the scene from replaying in her mind. The sound of their voices. The smell of their filth. Her thoughts berated her for not even getting her blade out when they attacked. Tommy's first words to her after the attack didn't help drown out her internal admonishments.

You did good.

But she hadn't done good.

They'd sneaked up on her as she'd been taking the trash out the back door. She'd only had enough time to drop the bags onto the ground before one of the men lifted her up and whisked her down the alley, her screams trailing behind her. Not that anyone on that damned island would care about a woman's screams.

Damn pirates.

She'd certainly fought as best she could—even without the blade—to get free from those men, but they were much stronger than she was, and the soft sand had been far from helpful in her efforts to pull free.

And then there was the matter of what had happened before that.

She'd been delighted for the opportunity to bathe and wash her clothes while ashore. And Lucy had been kind. But looking back, Aoife could see where the woman had been a bit too eager to know about her history and her past.

Had Aoife said too much? She wasn't sure. She'd admitted to being from Cregah but saw no harm in sharing that fact. It didn't necessarily indicate an affiliation with the council, after all.

But she hadn't anticipated the woman walking in on her while she washed, and she hadn't been able to hide the marks of the council. Lucy, to her credit, had played it off well enough, not giving away any hint that she knew what the swirls of black, like smoke rising from Aoife's wrists, indicated. Lucy had only remarked how interesting they were, how she'd never seen anything like them, and then asked if Aoife had gotten them in Cregah or while visiting another land.

They'd seemed like harmless questions that could be tiptoed around easily enough, but still, she hadn't been able to shake the feeling that Lucy wasn't the sweet person she claimed to be.

You did good.

Those were also the last words Tommy had said to her before he'd been whisked away to his officer duties, leaving Declan alone to care for her.

At first, his quiet patience had been appreciated. But by the second morning she wished for things to return to some semblance of normalcy.

A quip. A retort. A bit of banter. Even an insult would be better than the deafening silence.

He had been even more aloof than usual the next morning. Not cold or harsh. But distant.

She had sensed him about to speak several times, but words never came. She would turn in time to see his mouth snapping shut and his gaze shifting. She wanted to ask him what was going on, but she couldn't find her voice, held back by the small part of her that still feared him.

She'd been stupid and naive to think he wasn't a real pirate. Even after he'd threatened to take advantage of her, she hadn't truly let herself see what he was capable of.

But witnessing him kill someone. So quickly. So efficiently. So mercilessly. Anyone would have been frightened, but her fear was minuscule compared to her sense of gratitude. Perhaps she was an idiot. She told herself he'd only done it for his own gain. He needed her help to free the fae, and she couldn't let herself believe he actually cared.

And yet, part of her hoped.

At times it almost seemed as though there was a change in how he looked at her. But it was likely just her imagination and her own yearning for companionship making her see what she longed for. She wasn't hoping for love or a family like Lani had risked everything for, but friendship. A friend would have been nice.

With her sister gone and her remaining family untrustworthy, she had no one, and she was tired of being alone.

Tired of lying in bed watching the morning sun light up the dancing dust motes with nothing but the feelings welling in her chest for company. She couldn't sort through them on her own, couldn't process them within her own mind.

She needed to talk them out, to have someone listen, to discuss them so she could best understand.

Short of an actual friend, maybe she could seek out the one person on the ship who seemed okay with her. Tommy. They'd only spoken a few times, but that was more words than she'd shared with the rest of the crew. And he'd never insulted her, so that seemed promising.

She hoped he'd be able to help her. She needed to work through all of these thoughts before she could be useful. And she desperately wanted to be useful.

Swinging her feet to the floor, she peered out the window and willed herself to stand steady as the ship lolled along the sea. Two days on land had sent her back to square one when it came to finding her sea legs. And as they would be arriving in Morshan tomorrow evening, she needed her legs to cooperate.

The cabin was empty.

Based on the state of Declan's side of the bed, he hadn't slept at all, though she had vague recollections of his body next to hers during the night, trying to keep a respectable distance.

She moved toward the door, hoping Tommy would be easy to find among the crew. But she stopped at the sound of low voices.

A tingle crept up her spine as she recalled the last time she'd been in this exact position, hearing these two men talking on the other side of the door. She should walk away and respect their privacy. And she nearly did. Until she heard her name.

"Aoife needs you, Declan. I know you don't want to hear it or believe it." It was Tommy. Of course. The only person Declan would ever let speak to him like that.

Declan's voice came out low, harsh. "You're right. I don't want to hear it."

"I know you care. I can see it. But you're too damn scared to admit it."

Declan seemed to growl his next words. "Watch it, Tommy."

"Or what? You'll push me away? Like you do everyone else?"

She wished she could see how Declan reacted to being challenged in such a way, and she half expected him to give up there, but then he spoke.

"I can't protect her." It was so low and muffled she wasn't sure if she'd heard him right. Surely that's not what he'd said. He had protected her. Multiple times even.

"You already have," Tommy said, echoing her thoughts. Before Declan could respond, he added, "I know you have your reasons, but it might be time to leave them behind."

More words followed, but far too quiet for her to hear.

"Maybe, Declan, you need her too. For more than just this damn dagger."

The door creaked under the weight of a hand, sending Aoife scurrying back to the bedroom—thankfully with little stumbling. As she sat on the edge of the bed, blankly staring out the window, she pondered the words she couldn't have heard correctly.

Surely they would not have had such a private and personal conversation in such an open space where anyone could have overheard. But the crew had always seemed to have a certain respect for their captain, along with a healthy dose of fear, not wishing to suffer his reprimands if they dared to defy him.

You need her too.

The words bounced around her mind as footsteps thudded across the main room of the cabin. Then silence. She waited to see if he would say anything, and when he didn't, she turned.

He wasn't in the doorway as she'd expected. He wasn't even looking at her. Rather, he was standing behind his desk with a hand on the back of his chair. He stood there, unmoving, for what seemed like an eternity, looking like the weight of the entire Aisling Sea was crushing him, drowning him.

She desperately wanted to ask him what he was thinking, but she didn't know how to break the silence that had been lingering between them since she'd returned.

Glancing back at the window, she waited. She still wanted to go find Tommy so she could talk to somebody, but now that Declan was in the room, she couldn't convince herself to leave him. So she waited. The silence stretched on, even as he pulled out his chair and it groaned under his weight. She had a strange urge to get up and go to him, not merely out of curiosity, but out of kindness.

You need her too.

He'd helped her. Even though he'd said he wouldn't, he had. He'd told her she'd be on her own, but then he'd been there when it mattered most. He'd saved her, and whether he'd done it for his own personal gain or for her well-being, she didn't care. And now she couldn't get past the silly and absurd notion that he was the one in need of saving now. But what could she do?

Aoife turned her attention back to Declan, who was now leaning back in his chair with his elbows on the armrests and his fingers steepled under his chin. She opened her mouth to speak, but it was his voice that filled the room instead.

"Come here, Aoife." It wasn't harsh, but it wasn't warm either. However ridiculous it seemed, she could have sworn he sounded nervous.

Moving as quickly as she could, thankfully not toppling into him when she passed the desk, she took a seat in the chair opposite him. She bristled at the memory of the last time they'd sat here together, the way he'd looked at her with such loathing, the way she'd spat her words at him.

Declan cleared his throat, pulling her out of her thoughts. He pushed a piece of paper toward her, along with a pen and ink. "I need to know where the fae are inside the council hall. Can you draw it?"

"That's it?" She didn't move. She only stared at him, hoping he couldn't hear how her heart thumped in her chest. He was still as handsome as he had been that day in the cove, even if his gray eyes seemed dulled by exhaustion and stress.

He leaned his head to one side, and a piece of hair slid into his tired eyes. Something inside her stirred. She didn't know where it came from. Maybe it was Tommy's words earlier, but looking at him now, she wanted to lean toward him, to move his hair back into place, to hold his face in her hands and whisper that it would all be okay. As if this pirate captain needed her reassurance. It was as foolish as thinking he was nervous around her.

Yet a hint of those nerves lingered in his question. "That's what?"

"After all this silence, no 'How are you'? No 'Glad to have you back'? No talk of the weather and other pleasantries? Just back to business?" She tried to make the words lighthearted and carefree, to get them back to their old bantering ways. She hoped he'd allow it.

A smirk slowly spread across his lips as he leaned on his elbow, his head propped casually on his hand. She had to remind herself how to breathe, which was utterly ridiculous. It wasn't like she'd never seen him smile before, but after days of seeing nothing but worry and fatigue in his features, this classic smirk of his brought some life back into his eyes and made him look more like the dashing hero than the cruel pirate.

The smirk still played on his lips. "How are you, Aoife? We're indeed glad to have you back. The weather has been altogether too hot." He gestured to the paper once again. "Now, draw."

"I'm—" *Fine* seemed like an odd word to use when she was still struggling to suppress the images from the other night. So she didn't bother saying it. “I’m glad to be back.” A light laugh bubbled up from her. He’d played along with her, which was quite unexpected, but not unappreciated. When had she gone from wanting to annoy him to wanting to make him smile?

Back at Lucy’s, she’d tried to stay mad at him but failed. He’d been rude and callous to her before she’d left, but still he’d had Tommy take care of her. Declan had ensured she would have some form of protection. And try as she might, she hadn’t been able to keep from missing him and the ridiculous smirk he wore.

Every time she had walked into the main dining room of Lucy’s, she’d hoped he would be there with Tommy or Gavin. Hoped he’d stop by to see how she was getting on, to make sure she was safe. But he hadn’t, and her heart had sunk a little with every disappointment.

She’d missed him. Beyond her better judgment, and despite the harsh words she’d shot at him right before they parted ways, she had. But now she was here. She could be useful. She could help.

She scooted her chair closer, taking the pen from him. “You have a nice smile, Declan. You should smile more.” She kept her face lowered so he would hopefully not see how she flushed at the words.

“I can’t. It would ruin my reputation.” Was that a hint of humor she detected? She hoped so.

“Well, you can just smile for me when we’re alone then.” Her flush deepened, and she leaned closer to the paper before her.

She began to draw the outlines of the council hall. Each line she created, marking out her old home, tugged at her insides with an intensity she hadn’t expected. She thought she’d gotten past missing home, but then she remembered it hadn’t even been a week since she ran. Such a short time.

She missed these halls, missed Lani, even missed her mother to a point.

Silence settled between her and Declan, but she didn’t know how to fill it, so she kept her mind fixed on the lines she drew, each one adding to her anxiety as the questions swarmed her mind. Would Declan take her ashore when they went back to Cregah? Would she actually walk through the hallways she was marking on the paper? She had asked to be included, after all, but now she wasn't sure she'd be able to go through with it if he invited her along.

"Why did you run?" Declan asked, his voice low and careful. It was certainly not a question she wanted to answer, especially when she was only barely holding on. She didn't want to lose it in front of him.

She stopped drawing and looked at him, steeling herself and hoping her voice wouldn't crack under the emotions. "If you want me to finish this map, you'll need to find something else to talk about."

He didn't respond, and his eyes didn't leave hers. She couldn't tell if he was challenging her or if he was merely hoping to find the answers somewhere within her.

She lowered her head again. "I'm sure you can come to your own conclusions."

"I have considered a few possibilities." As he talked, she resumed her work, hoping to get this over with so they could move on to other topics like daggers and books. "Perhaps you couldn't stomach being matched to any of the eligible lords. Which would make sense. Or life at the council hall had become so stiflingly boring that you sought adventure on the seas. Or maybe you'd done something dastardly and were attempting to run away from your own guilt."

Her hand tightened around the pen, sending the nib ripping through the paper as she pushed down too hard. Dropping the pen, she sat up, pushing away from the desk.

"So that's it then? Guilt?" Declan's eyes narrowed at her as he leaned back in his chair, arms crossed behind his head.

She didn't say anything, merely stared back at him, trying to find the words to throw in his face, but her mind was drawing a blank. Yet again she was unable to do anything but chide herself for being so obvious and giving away too much.

Declan's features softened a bit, but his next words came out with an edge. "You don't have to tell me, of course, but if it has anything to do with the council and my need to get in there to get the fae, it might be best for me to know. Surprises get people killed."

Aoife looked down at the lines she'd drawn on the paper and swallowed hard. Her mouth went dry, and she fumbled over what to tell him and how to push the words out. After spilling Lani's secret to her mother and then revealing too much to Lucy about her past, she didn't trust herself to speak. Why couldn't there have been classes on tactful speaking, on how to formulate sentences to avoid saying the wrong thing? Those would have been far more helpful than the lessons on the local flora of the island.

Declan's voice once again cut through her thoughts. "Did you steal jewels from the council ladies? Get caught with one of the pirates during a dinner? Kill someone?"

Her chin shot up then. The smirk he had donned faded in an instant.

"Ah."

She couldn't read his expression, couldn't determine what he thought of her. Would he admire her for having killed someone? He was a pirate, after all. Or would he mock her for having betrayed her country's dedication to nonviolence? She lowered her eyes, worried—however foolishly—that he could see the betrayal written in the depths of her eyes. "Not exactly."

"How do you not exactly kill someone?" She could hear that smirk of his in his words.

"I betrayed my sister." Her voice came out a whisper, scraping against the dryness of her mouth as she spoke. It was the first time she'd given the truth a voice, and the sound of it being uttered for others to hear, no matter how quiet and no matter how small the audience, sent a fresh dagger of guilt straight into her gut.

"I see. What was her name?"

"Lani." Barely over a whisper.

Declan shifted in his chair, and in her periphery she saw him lean forward, resting his forearms on the desktop. She waited for the mockery or for more questions about what had happened to Lani, but as a pirate, he had to know what the council did to people who broke the laws.

"Well now," Declan began, "if you betrayed Lani, who I assume you were quite close to, how can I be sure you won't do the same to me?"

"I didn't—" She cut herself off. It didn't matter anymore what her intentions had been. All that mattered was what had happened. No, she'd never meant to tell, but she'd put herself in the position to easily fail her sister, and her sister had been the one to pay.

"You didn't what? Intend to betray her?" Aoife gave a nod, keeping her eyes lowered but no longer seeing the page before her. "Intention or not, it happened. How can I be sure that tongue of yours doesn't get us into trouble? How do I know you didn't divulge something during the two days you were in Foxhaven? After all, someone learned who you were, where you were, and what reward could be fetched for your retrieval."

The earlier fear returned, along with a tingling of panic. She fidgeted in her seat, and her words tumbled out. "I won't. I haven't. I would never."

"You claim such things, Aoife, but your history provides little reason for me to trust you. And this time there are far more lives at stake. More than just an heir and her lover."

Aoife startled at that and stared at him again. She hadn't mentioned what Lani had done, or that anyone else had been involved. "How did you—I never mentioned—"

His jaw tightened, the movement so slight and subtle she wondered if she'd imagined it. He gave a casual shake of his head. "Gossips, remember? Pirates trade in more than just gold and trinkets. We trade in news as well."

"But the council never would have allowed that information to get out." She had an unnerving feeling he was hiding something, but she couldn't work out what it was, and it drove her mad, the curiosity and the not knowing.

Declan shrugged a shoulder. "They may think they control everything and everyone, but things are learned, and those things are whispered around."

Aoife froze. Declan knew more about Lani than she'd expected. If he'd heard whispers about her, then he might know who… She snapped her head up, her eyes boring into his. "Who whispered it to you?"

"Why, so you can get revenge? I don't rat out my sources, Aoife. Unlike some of us in this room, I have honor."

She couldn't suppress the scoff that burst from her. "Honor?! You're a damn pirate." Her mind flitted back to the night he'd pinned her to the bed and threatened her, sending a shiver across her shoulders. How could Tommy have ever claimed Declan cared for her? How could she have started to believe he might? Why did she even want him to?

He didn't move. Didn't blink. Didn't register any reaction. "More honor than a spoiled and naive heir who got her own sister killed."

His words hit their mark, sharp and painful, stinging her in the chest.

She had wondered if he'd thought so little of her. Now his words confirmed it.

Worst of all, it was true.

She was spoiled. She was naive. She was responsible for Lani's death.

Her lip threatened to tremble, and she clenched her jaw tight in order to stay it.

She wouldn't lose face here. Not in front of him.

With a huffed sigh, she shot to her feet and slid the chair back, its legs scraping as they moved from the worn rug to the wood beneath.

She couldn't look at him, couldn't let him see how he'd hurt her.

How could she have ever thought he would change?

She stumbled around the chair, trying to hold herself together as the ship's movement made her exit less than graceful.

If he mocked her, she didn't hear it, not through the pounding echo in her mind calling her all the names he'd thrown at her.

Spoiled.

Naive.

She was almost to the door when she heard his chair move against the floor.

"Aoife." All the edge had left his voice.

And she stopped. Sands help her, she didn't know why she stopped. But something in the way he said her name kept her feet planted, unable to continue in their retreat.

"I'm sorry."

Her chin dropped to her chest, her shoulders drooping under the weight of the words she'd never expected to hear him say. When she didn't turn, he repeated them.

She shook her head, eyes still lowered as her body betrayed her will and turned to face him. She raised her head only enough to look at him through her lashes.

Remorse shone in his eyes, more than she'd ever thought him capable of.

Perhaps Tommy had been right after all.

"I shouldn't have said all those things," he said, barely louder than a breath.

She looked at him squarely now, confused by the change in him. Was he playing her now, or was all that she'd overheard accurate? Did he care about her? Did she care about him?

She thought about telling him it was okay, that all he'd said was true, but she couldn't bear to admit any of it. It was difficult enough to acknowledge it herself. Even if he was playing her for the fool, using her to get the dagger for himself, she wanted to help him.

Regardless of all the times he'd put her down, she wanted to make him smile more, to see his nightmares cease, to see him content and free of the stress and fatigue he constantly wore.

He gestured to her chair, a silent invitation to come back and sit.

She obliged, pulling herself closer to the desk before she looked at him again. "Careful, Declan. You don't want to ruin your reputation. Who would fear a pirate who cares?"

She mimicked his classic smirk, hoping it hid how her insides still stung, rubbed raw by the reminder of all she'd done wrong.

"Good thing it's just the two of us here then." His smile slowly crept over his lips, as if he wasn't sure he was doing anything right in this moment.

She lowered her eyes, unable to look at him as she whispered, "Thank you."

"For what?"

Wringing her hands, she forced her next words out, hoping her face wouldn't flush when she looked at him. "For the apology. And for saving me back in Foxhaven. I know it was only because of the fae and the dagger, but thank you all the same." Some small part of her hoped he'd tell her she was wrong, that he'd done it for her and not for the treasure.

But those words never came. He only nodded. A silent *you're welcome.*

With a deep breath, Aoife had the ink flowing on the paper once again, but the silence that settled between her and Declan squeezed her heart. After so many hours of his silence, she needed them to talk.

"I've only met the fae sisters once," she started. Images of them flooded her mind—their long limbs, graceful bodies, otherworldly beauty, and the eerie and magical lilt to their speech, that made it seem as though they could put you in a trance simply by speaking. "They didn't move about freely, as far as I know. But their room wasn't locked either. We don't have locks in the council hall."

"If they could leave, why wouldn't they?" Declan's question seemed more for himself than for Aoife, but she answered anyway.

"Maybe they have nowhere else to go?"

She watched Declan ponder this, chewing on it as if it were a piece of dried meat.

"Perhaps." Again, his voice was low, and his eyes stared at his desk beneath his creased brow. "Did you enter the room they were in?"

Aoife thought back to that day, and her body tensed as it relived the hesitation she'd experienced as a child. "A step or two. Not far though."

"Did you smell anything odd?" Such a bizarre question, but he had to have a reason for asking.

"It's been so long. But I don't think so."

He traced a line across his forehead as he looked at nothing, and Aoife could have sworn she could see the gears turning in his mind. He mumbled a few words, and she wasn't sure she'd heard him correctly. "No chains. No locks. No iron."

"At least none that I could see."

"Interesting. There could be iron in the walls." It seemed he was talking to himself, as if Aoife were a spirit or a voice in his ear rather than a person sitting with him.

She almost hated to interrupt, but the question still nagged at her. "Still, that would only affect their magic, right? It wouldn't keep them from leaving. And their room looked rather comfortable, as if they had every accommodation they could want. Books. So many books. Puzzles and games and paints. I didn't see anything there that kept them in that room physically though. Almost like they didn't want to leave."

"For five hundred years? It seems unlikely."

Aoife couldn't imagine spending a lifetime, especially one that spanned centuries, confined within a single building, let alone a single room in *that* building. Surely they would have wanted to leave. There had to be something keeping them there. But what?

Declan straightened in his chair, and his eyes locked with hers. "What do you know of the fae in general? What did they teach you about their kind?"

"The basics, I suppose. Long life. Heightened senses. And they're strong," she said.

"That's an understatement. They are damn near unstoppable physically. And the ones with magic…"

"But the iron suppresses that, right?"

"Yes, but only the magic. It doesn't affect their senses or their strength. So even if the council hall's walls have an iron core, they still wouldn't need their magic in order to escape. So something else is keeping them there."

"And you know what that is?"

He leaned forward, his eyes now alight, almost excited. "Their word." Aoife must have had a confused look on her face, because Declan gave a small laugh. "I see you're following." That smirk played on his face again.

"Not at all." Her face heated again with further embarrassment. How she'd thought she would be of any aid to him on this job, she wasn't sure. But like hell she was going to give up.

He didn't seem annoyed but rather elated that he might have made the breakthrough he needed for this plan to work. "There have long been rumors that the fae can't lie, but there's a theory—an old one, passed on through whispers—that it's not true. Those whispers claim, rather, that when a fae says they will do something, they are firmly bound to that word. Nearly impossible for them to betray it. If the council procured an agreement from the fae sisters, it might have allowed the council to hold them all these hundreds of years while still having access to their powers."

"Like a powerful sense of honor?"

Declan only nodded.

"If that's the case," Aoife said, her pen still hovering over the paper, "which it might not be, how do you plan to get them to break an unbreakable vow?"

"Nearly unbreakable," he reminded her.

He reached into his chest pocket and pulled out a piece of paper.

Aoife reached for it, thinking he'd hand it over to let her inspect it, but he didn't move.

"Don't you trust me?" Aoife asked, though his expression plainly indicated that he, in fact, did not. She dropped her hand. She couldn't blame him. If her whole plan had been resting on a piece of paper, she wouldn't hand it over to someone with ties to the enemy either. "What is it exactly?"

He flipped it around so she could see the wax seal that kept it closed. It was a deep green—almost black—imprinted with a symbol she didn't recognize. "This," he said, "is—I believe—a message from the fae who fled to Larcsporough."

Aoife's eyes went wide. "But all the fae perished—aside from the three sisters at the council hall. None survived the Aisling War."

"That's what you've been taught, what everyone on Cregah is taught."

The words threatened to pull the air from her lungs, but she recovered quickly. What was it to learn another lie when so many had been told already? The last threads tying her to her old life continued to fray. They'd break soon enough.

She leaned forward to get a better look at the fae insignia. "What does it say?"

"I don't know. I won't open it. If the sisters saw I'd tampered with it, they wouldn't believe whatever it contains. And there'd be no point in trying, as it's likely written in their ancient tongue."

"So how do you know it doesn't say something like, 'Don't trust this man'?"

"Because I trust the woman who gave it to me."

Aoife's chest tightened against her will. What he said made sense, and while she understood why he couldn't trust her, it still pained her to know he trusted someone else at the same time. And another woman at that. Was she jealous? She had no claim to Declan, nothing that said she was the only woman who could help him, and yet jealousy seemed the only logical explanation for the way her insides twisted. It was the same way she'd felt when Lani or Darienn received praise from the council or when she'd thought of Lani getting a life in Daorna that she couldn't have herself.

She hated this feeling because she knew better, knew logically it was stupid and wrong and immature, and yet she still couldn't stop it from creeping up.

"I trust her because she's my sister." Aoife looked up to find Declan's features as soft as his tone, which acted like a salve to ease the burning pangs within her. She kicked herself for being so transparent, but she couldn't deny how appreciative she was that he apparently cared how his words affected her.

"I didn't know you had a sister."

"I wouldn't expect a council heir to worry herself over family trees of the common folk. And I don't know that she acknowledges it readily, except with her close friends." Aoife noted how he stumbled over the word "friends" but wrote it off.

"And how did she acquire this exactly?"

"I don't know. And I didn't ask. She only said it would be the key to getting them to help." He tucked the letter back into his jacket pocket. "Now, how do we get to them to deliver this message?"

Aoife released a breath and straightened up in her seat. Turning the paper around on his desk, she pushed it closer to him. "I've drawn the hall to the best of my memory, but it has been a long time since I ventured into that wing. While it wasn't outright forbidden, one encounter with them was enough to keep me away."

"Not *outright* forbidden?"

"*Frowned upon* would be a better phrasing. But I got the impression that Mother didn't want to draw attention to it, and a strict rule to not go there would have done just that. Plus, they kept us busy. Classes and meetings and outings. There wasn't much time to explore and get into trouble."

"So what's our in? How do we get in and out without alerting the council?"

"The next meeting with a lord was scheduled for this week. It would be the only time you and your men could enter the hall without raising suspicion. These meetings are the only time men are allowed beyond the public chamber and inside the main residence."

"But crews know each other too well. If one of the men noticed us, they'd know immediately we didn't belong."

Aoife flashed him her best version of his smirk and waited.

"You know something I don't," he said.

"Surprising, I know. I'm trying to relish this moment."

"Well, don't relish too long; we're running short on time."

She clicked her tongue at him. "Always in such a hurry. But if I remember correctly, Captain, we still have a day and a half of sailing to get back to Morshan, so we do have some time."

A roll of his eyes had her basking in her triumph.

"This was a special meeting scheduled," she continued. "I don't know why—they don't tell us much—but I know there will be more than one crew in attendance. If we—I mean, you—can somehow pretend to be a member of the opposite crew if you ever get confronted, that could work? No?"

Declan rubbed his stubbled chin as he thought over her words. He stopped and met her gaze. "I'd need to know which crews. Each crew wears a particular color."

"I only know one of the crews—Lord Madigen's. But for the other, I only know their colors. My mother always insisted we wear something that honored our guests. The garment she had made for this dinner was the prettiest I'd ever seen." Aoife paused. Declan stared at her, annoyance and amusement dancing around in his gray eyes. "Violet."

Declan froze, his face going blank. He sat so still she half expected him to keel over in his chair from lack of breathing.

"What? Who is it?"

A second passed. Another. And then he blinked but remained still, seeing through her as he spoke. "The *Duchess*."

"Who's the duchess?"

"Not who. What. It's the ship. Captained by Casey Halloran."

"Is that a problem?"

"No. In fact, it could work to our advantage."

Before Aoife could ask for clarification, Declan was pushing back from his desk and standing. Without another word, he was across the room and out the door, leaving her alone to wonder how this Captain Halloran could help and whether he would let her in on the plan after all.

Declan had been thankful for the distraction of further honing the plan with Tommy, Gavin, and Mikkel. His mind kept threatening to pull his thoughts back to Aoife and the sorrow and guilt that had swirled in her eyes when he'd broached the topic of her sister.

She wasn't as acquainted with death, had been sheltered from it her whole life, while Declan seemed destined to be its eternal companion, his hands and heart forever stained by it.

He still remembered the first lives lost because of him, though they had not been killed directly by his hand.

He'd been so young, too young and innocent, when they'd died. Had he been faster, stronger, maybe he could have stopped it, could have kept his parents safe.

His hands clenched the worn wood of the quarterdeck's railing. The sun was inching its way toward the horizon in front of them. They'd be in Morshan in another day, and they still had a day in port before the dinner was scheduled. He'd need to get word to Cait for her aid in securing some items for this plan.

Without thinking, he reached a hand up to his left breast pocket, as if to ensure that the fae letter was still there. Not that there was any chance for it to have been lifted by anyone, and no one on his ship would dare such a thing anyway. It was true he didn't know what the letter said. Cait didn't know either. But she'd found it among their mother's belongings, in an envelope addressed to Cait. He hadn't pried into what their mother had written. Her simple directive to use the letter to free the fae from their vow was enough for him.

How, he had no idea. His knowledge of fae lore was shaky at best, but he had to go on the little bit he had.

He only hoped he really could trust his sister. And his mother.

His memory of her had blurred over the years, and though he could sometimes hear her voice on the wind, he often wondered if that was truly how she'd sounded or if his mind had twisted and mangled it into something false. He'd spent so long pushing the memories away. He needed to do it again now.

With a stretch of his neck he headed down to his cabin, where he found Aoife lounging in bed with a book. A sense of déjà vu washed over him. Too much like that moment a few days ago. He shook his head to clear the feeling, but it refused to budge, lingering at the edges of his thoughts, like a tingling along his skin. It had him clenching his jaw as he approached her. He didn't dare sit this time. That hadn't worked well for keeping memories locked away, so he settled himself against the doorframe.

If she'd noticed him, she didn't let on, and for a moment he simply watched her. She appeared fairly well put-together given the ordeal she'd been through in Foxhaven. Although the sun was setting in front of the ship far from the windows of his cabin, it still cast a warm glow through the room. He tried to think of what Aoife had looked like back in that cove with her hair long and her features smug and haughty.

Now she looked… He wasn't sure how to describe it, actually. More carefree, perhaps. While she was at Lucy's he had missed the rough ends of her hair that matched her fiery spirit.

"It's not nice to stare, you know," she said, not looking up from her book.

"Funny, I recall telling you the same thing."

She laid the book down in her lap and pursed her lips before she said, "So you should know better."

"Guilty as charged." He shifted his weight, hoping she would assume it was out of habit and not an indication of how nervous he was while trying to figure out how to speak to her. This shouldn't be so hard, but he couldn't even remember how long it had been since he'd played the role of *nice guy*. Charming guy, yes. Snarky guy, obviously. But genuinely nice guy? A light laugh escaped him.

"What's so funny?" She bit her thumbnail. A nervous habit he'd never noticed before.

"Nothing."

Before she could push him for an actual answer, sounds from the deck interrupted. A noise he hadn't heard in months. Not since before their latest defeats. Hands beating against barrels, a steady pulsing and shifting before the voices started. Gavin's tenor was the easiest to identify. Mikkel's accent became thicker as his baritone joined in.

Aoife stood and inched around the bed toward him, her brows high and her eyes glistening. "What is that? Music? Why are they singing?"

"Can't pirates have fun?" He shot her a challenging look, as if he were accusing her of being the one incapable of such fun.

"Of course, I suppose. But with everything going on, it seems like an odd time for it. Doesn't it?"

A deep breath was his only answer. He counted backwards. Waiting.

Five. Four. Three.

Steps sounded outside.

Two.

One.

The door to his quarters shook under a banging fist.

"Yes, Tommy? What do you need?" The question was more for Aoife's sake than his own. He already knew the answer. Knew it with the first sounds of his crew's music.

Aoife sidled up to Declan's side just as his friend and quartermaster burst in, a huge smile on his face.

"You can't stay in here, Captain. Nor you, Aoife."

"Last I checked," Declan said, his face steeled, "I didn't take orders from you."

"Ah, but if you refuse, you may end up with a mutiny on your hands." Tommy waggled his brow at his friend before shooting Aoife a wink.

Declan tried not to bristle when a wave against the ship sent Aoife stumbling into him with the cutest exclamation he thought he'd ever heard. Her warmth sent his head swimming. Somehow she still managed to smell sweeter than anyone had a right to on a pirate ship. It was almost as if her body naturally produced that sugary scent. He couldn't think straight as she grabbed onto his arm to steady herself, but at least he was able to ignore Tommy's silent accusations at seeing her hanging onto him so close. Too close.

Declan pushed her away, trying not to be too forceful as he helped her find her footing again, and he glared at his friend, a silent denial that anything was going on.

Aoife looked from Declan to Tommy. "What's going on out there? Why all the music?"

"He didn't tell you." Not a question.

"I might have, had you not so rudely interrupted," Declan said. He tried his best to look bored, but it was hard to keep up the ruse when the joy in his men's voices was streaming in through the open cabin door.

"Right. I don't believe you." Tommy turned to Aoife, a mischievous look in his eyes. "It's our dear captain's birthday."

Aoife turned to him, her face bright with that glorious smile of hers lighting up the entire room. He shook the thought away. No. She was only a means to an end. A tool in his arsenal. A member of his team for this job. But that damn smile. Those lips. He forced his gaze up to her eyes, which didn't help much at preventing his thoughts from wandering further.

He cleared his throat. "What? It's not my real birthday."

Tommy cut in. "Just the one that really matters. The day he became a pirate."

"Pirates celebrate such a thing? I had no idea." Again with that coy smile directed at him.

Declan nearly made a joke about how little she knew about pirates at all, but Tommy spoke first. "Most don't, but I like any excuse to piss him off." He lifted his chin in Declan's direction.

"Well, not too pissed off though. I mean, you still have your head, right?" Aoife asked. Declan and Tommy both turned toward her, and while Declan managed to conceal his own shock by keeping his mouth shut, Tommy's mouth flopped open like a fish. "What? Too soon?" she asked.

"No," Declan said.

Tommy finished his thought. "Just unexpected is all."

"What he said," Declan offered.

"It seems the best way to move on is to learn to laugh about it," she said, sounding resolute despite the twinkle flashing in her green eyes. Sands, she was adorable, and more of Declan's inner guard began to crumble. Before he could chide himself for thinking such nonsense, she was grabbing his elbow and dragging him out after Tommy toward the activities outside. He didn't bother fighting her.

Birthdays had never been a big event at the council hall. The council ladies didn't give gifts or have cakes made, though Aoife had heard such traditions were still held by the families in the villages around the island. Instead of celebrating with parties, she and Lani had marked their birthdays in their own way, jotting them down in the back covers of their favorite books—the ones they were allowed to keep, that is. They would exchange small gifts. A sparkling rock they'd found in the garden or a weed's bloom from the lawn.

Even amid the revelry on the ship, she missed Lani. Her laugh. Her teasing. She didn't blame her sister for keeping secrets, for wanting to keep Adler hidden, for needing to keep their plan under wraps. She shouldn't have forced her to tell, should have honored Lani's privacy instead of taking it personally. Maybe then she would still be alive.

But then you'd still be at the council hall preparing to be matched, preparing to serve in a corrupt council.

She would have gladly done it if it had meant Lani could be somewhere safe, building a life. It would have been a worthwhile sacrifice. Perhaps she could have changed things from within.

But now her only hope was to escape, run away, leave it to someone else, someone better, to address the problems.

After she helped Declan.

She watched him from her perch on the lowest of the steps leading up to the quarterdeck. She had followed him and Tommy out to join the festivities but had only made it to these stairs before deciding to hang back and let them have this time without her butting in.

Sure, she'd been invited, but it was blatantly clear she was an outsider here. And if she was being honest, she was content to simply observe.

If anyone had asked her what her thoughts on pirates were just a week ago, she wouldn't have had anything nice to say. It wasn't that they'd been rude to her at the council dinners, but they certainly hadn't been what she'd describe as friendly or cordial. And if she hadn't witnessed Declan use his blade—seen the blood on Tommy's dagger—the other night, she might have had a hard time classifying them in the same category as all the pirates she'd previously met.

The music continued. It pulsed through the wooden planks of the ship and up her boots. She couldn't keep from moving to the beat. And even with a hint of seasickness still lingering in her belly, she was comfortable and at ease. It helped that the crew seemed adequately distracted by the party and forgot to be wary of her unlucky presence.

Declan's gaze flashed to hers, and she looked away, hoping he hadn't noticed her staring.

A few of the crew members, who were likely new based on how awkward they appeared, crowded together next to the railing, watching their shipmates dance and laugh and sing a song Aoife didn't recognize.

It had her thinking back to Declan singing on the beach in his faked drunken stutter. She smiled and shook her head at the thought. He'd looked completely mad.

"Having fun?" She hadn't heard Declan's footsteps over the music's thrumming, but thankfully she hadn't been startled either. She didn't particularly want to blush again in front of him.

Peering up at him, that unruly lock of hair being blown into his eyes by the evening wind, she wondered what had shifted in him. Was it merely his birthday that had him smiling down at her? Not a smirk, but an actual smile. And they weren't even alone.

"I am. But you, Captain, should be careful." She pretended to look around with suspicion. "The others might see you smile."

"Good thing most of them are too drunk to notice or remember." He settled himself on the step next to her, a polite distance away so no part of them touched. Disappointment flickered somewhere inside of her before she could shoo it away. That kind of thinking would get her nowhere. Nowhere good anyway.

Never before had she given any thought to romance or love. Matching, sure. But that was purely political, a requirement of her status. It wasn't the same as building a family, fostering a relationship. More like an alliance or a business partnership. One that would produce another heir to the council.

It hadn't been until Lani spoke about a future with Adler that Aoife had even considered the possibility and let herself wonder what it might be like, if only to better understand why her sister was willing to risk everything to attain it.

And that little bit of inquisitiveness had opened some small gate within her that she'd never known existed. And she couldn't quite shut it completely. Having Declan sitting close and smiling, being kind even, didn't help. She couldn't ignore that future Lani had painted. A family and a life of peace and quiet in the Daornan hills.

While she didn't want that life specifically, she couldn't quiet the damn niggling voice in the far reaches of her heart that asked, "What if?"

But that *what if* wouldn't include Declan. Or any pirate for that matter.

What kind of family could one care for on the seas, waging battles, pillaging merchant ships, and chasing after enchanted daggers?

Adler had supposedly been ready to give all that up—set aside his life of adventure—for her sister, but she couldn't imagine Declan, or anyone in his crew, walking away from it all. She glanced around the deck at the smiling faces, noticing the true camaraderie among them, the way they laughed and joked and pushed each other and hugged while they sang. How the new members were welcomed and pulled into the festivities by the veteran crew.

This was their family.

And it seemed far more functional, healthier than the one she'd left behind.

Here she sat on the outskirts, a spectator looking in on something she could never have. And why should she yearn for it anyway? Everyone she had thought cared for her had deceived her. Could she trust anyone again after that betrayal, after being fed lies her entire life?

But Declan had always been honest with her. Even as he kept information close and guarded, he hadn't lied. *That you know of.* She grumbled internally, frustrated by her inability to find any footing in her current situation. Where did she stand? Who could she trust? She'd trusted Lucy, and look where that had gotten her.

Yet there was something about Declan, Tommy, and this crew. She couldn't explain it, but somehow, some part of her kept pushing her to trust them.

Noticing as Declan moved to face her, she wondered if he'd asked a question she hadn't heard while she was lost in thought. She turned toward him. "What?"

With a shake of his head he turned back to watch his men, a too quiet "nothing" escaping his lips.

She wanted to nudge him and ask him what thoughts he was mulling over, but the music and laughter was growing louder as the merriment continued and the rum flowed.

Tommy rushed over with two mugs, careful not to let any of it slosh on Aoife. He placed one in her hands as if it were being served in delicate china rather than sea-weathered tin. He was less careful with his captain's, but Declan didn't seem to mind when some spilled over his hand.

"It's not the best rum in the Aisling," Declan said. He took a long sip. "But it's not the worst either." He raised his mug toward her as if his words had been a toast. Tommy had already escaped back to the crew, and Aoife didn't bother to see where exactly he'd run off to. Declan was staring at her again, as if daring her to taste it already.

"I wouldn't know either way."

"The council doesn't serve rum?" She didn't sense any teasing in his tone.

"Not to us, no. It's reserved for our guests only."

"And what did you fancy council folk drink at these dinners?" There was the teasing she'd expected—and hoped for, if she were honest—and it took every ounce of will to not let herself smile or even think about how much she'd missed hearing him speak the past couple of days. While his change in demeanor confused her, she wouldn't complain. It was nice to have him not scowling at her all the time, even if she still refused to believe he truly cared about anything more than her ability to help him.

"Wine mostly."

"Wine? Really." He seemed to ponder that information as if it were the key to something, though she had no idea what clues it could possibly give him. "They don't produce wine on Cregah."

She gave a slight shrug as she stared into the amber liquid in her cup. "Well, to be fair, they don't produce much of anything on Cregah."

"True enough." Declan tipped his mug back and downed the last drop before motioning toward her untouched drink. "Try it. One sip. If you don't like it, you don't have to finish it."

"Well, I'd hate to be rude," she said as she lifted the cup to her lips.

"That's a first."

She flashed him a glare over the rim as the liquid reached her mouth, and then in one swift motion she tipped her head back, sending the syrupy blend of sweet and spice down her throat. It coated her tongue and burned as it traveled, settling like a warm fire in her stomach. When she lowered the mug, now empty, she caught him staring, his features contorted in a way she'd never seen.

"Oh, settle down, Cap'n. I've had rum before." She struggled to keep her smug smile from spreading but soon gave up trying and let herself beam at him.

"But you said…"

"I said I wouldn't know whether it was the best or not, and that's true. And no, I never had rum at the council hall. But I had a few glasses during my brief time with Lucy. She said it would help calm the nerves."

Declan laughed quietly as he shook his head at her. She did enjoy surprising him. Maybe he'd stop underestimating her. Maybe she'd stop underestimating herself too. That would be a nice change.

"Would you like more? I believe Gavin and the crew stocked up in Foxhaven. We should have plenty, though by the looks of the crew, it might not last long." It was her turn to chuckle at him. He was rambling a bit, which was rather unlike him. Perhaps this was what the real Declan was like when he wasn't wound so tightly. The rum seemed to help more than just one's nerves. Or perhaps it had simply changed the way she saw him.

Regardless of the cause, she was happy to see his moodiness dissipating, even if she knew it would only be temporary.

"Are you trying to get me drunk?" She flashed him her best attempt at a coy smile, but she had no idea if she was pulling it off or not.

"Of course not, Aoife. Then I'd have to carry you back to bed."

The image his words conjured up had her head swimming, and her face warmed with a flush of embarrassment. She hoped it was too dark for him to notice, but then she could always blame the rum for the heat in her cheeks.

She handed her empty mug to him with a nod and said, "You're the captain. You could have one of your men do it for you."

"Certain tasks should never be delegated. Carrying women to one's bed especially." He snagged her mug and held it up without taking his eyes from her. Tommy was there in a heartbeat to refill it for his captain.

No word of thanks from Declan. No words at all actually, and Tommy was gone again.

Aoife was trapped in Declan's gray eyes as she took her mug back from him, unable to turn away despite the discomfort of being stared at. What was he seeing in her? She couldn't look away, as if there were some tether holding her in place.

It was Declan who broke first, blinking a few times before turning back to watch his men dance around the deck and sing loudly to the beat of the music. They didn't have proper instruments and were instead beating their hands on barrels and stomping their feet on the deck. The deep richness of their voices mixed in perfectly. Aoife had never heard anything so lovely and enchanting.

She couldn't keep her shoulders from bobbing to the beat, and she let her eyes slide closed as she took another sip. Her mind wanted to take her back to those moments during which she and Lani had danced around her room to no music at all, and she found it difficult to keep the memories at bay. Lani would have loved this. She would have been grabbing each young crew member, insisting they dance with her under the stars while the sea moved the ship as if it, too, were in on the dancing.

Tears pooled in her closed eyes, and she hoped they wouldn't spill over, but just like her memories, they wouldn't be deterred. A single drop escaped. Then another. She hated this. Hated crying in general, but especially in front of others. In front of him.

A hand brushed her cheek. Her eyes flashed open and caught his gaze again. His hand hovered between them.

"I'm sorry." His voice came out in a low and gravelly whisper. He cleared his throat before adding, "For everything you've been through this past week. I'm sorry."

She hunted for any sign that he was teasing or mocking her, but there was only genuine sympathy and care written on his face. It was such an extreme change, so drastic a shift from her earlier encounters with him that she felt bewildered.

"Are we becoming friends?"

Clearing his throat again, he gave her the slightest of nods. "Perhaps we are."

"I'd like that," she said.

"And you can call me Declan."

She looked around and leaned in to whisper behind her mug. "But what would the crew think if they heard that?"

A small huff of laughter escaped as he lifted his shoulder. "Well, only when we're alone then."

"So when we're alone, you'll smile. And I'll call you Declan." Another nod. "How scandalous, Captain."

"You're a goofy drunk, you know that?"

"Who said I was drunk?"

"So you're just goofy then."

"Only with my friends." She bumped her shoulder against his and shot him a smile. She expected him to smile back, but he didn't. A flash of something else washed over him. Something she couldn't quite place. Was he that uncomfortable being her friend? Before she could mull it over too much, the look was gone, and he was downing his own rum and standing.

He looked down at her, and part of her wished he'd reach out a hand, invite her to dance. That was foolishness though.

"I'd better go mingle with the crew a bit. Are you okay here?"

A few quick nods told him she was fine.

"Don't have too much."

"Of course. I'd hate for you to have to carry me to your bed." *Our bed.* She shoved that thought aside as he walked away without another word.

Were they becoming friends? She wondered if it was okay to believe that were true. She'd wanted a friend. Someone to truly talk to. But she still worried it was all a ploy, a ruse. A way to keep an eye on her until she could help him rescue the fae. Would he ditch her then? Would she be left to fend for herself in some other port or in some other land?

Those thoughts were too much for what should have been a fun evening, so she forced them into a far corner of her mind and tried to watch the crew as they beamed at their captain and clapped him on the back. Tomorrow they'd be arriving in Morshan again. Tomorrow she'd be helping him with the final preparations for the rescue.

But tonight? She'd drink.

She beckoned Tommy over for another fill, and he obliged.

"Last one. Captain's orders," he said with a wink. He nearly walked away, but something in her expression must have caught him off guard, because he stopped and knelt in front of her, a hand on her knee and worry tugging at his brow. "Are you okay?"

"Of course." Her gaze flashed to where Declan stood by the deck's railing talking to a couple of the new crew members, and Tommy's eyes followed.

A sigh filled the space between them. "Be patient with him, Aoife." She started to ask him what he was talking about, but he cut her off. "He's lost a lot. Been battling himself and his mistakes for as long as I can remember. But I'm glad he has you."

"Friends are a blessing, to be sure."

"Aye. Friends. It's what he needs right now, I think." And with a pat of his hand on her leg, he was standing and walking away.

Aoife couldn't remember much the next morning. Tommy had effectively cut her off per Declan's orders, and yet the three mugs she'd enjoyed eventually caught up to her.

Her head ached, and this was made worse by the gentle swaying of the ship. Still, it wasn't as bad as the time she and Lani had sneaked a bottle of wine after dinner one night and downed the entire thing together in Lani's room. They had managed to avoid their mothers' wrath by hiding all evidence in the kitchen waste bin, but they'd both had to claim food poisoning the next morning to get out of their lessons.

No, this wasn't as bad. And yet it was worse.

No matter how hard she tried, her memories of the evening remained dim, as if she were trying to view them through the rum she'd consumed. It was as though she was still swimming in the drink, unable to get her mind to the surface to think clearly.

"Good morning."

Declan.

She cringed as each syllable pressed against her aching mind. Some part of her urged her to make a smart remark, but she could only manage a shush through her teeth.

He laughed, sending new waves of pain through her head.

"I told Tommy not to let you have too much."

She didn't dare move as she opened her eyes. At least her vision seemed to be clearer than her mind, and she tried to focus on the knots and swirls of the wooden ceiling above her. Drawing in a deep breath didn't do much to clear the fog.

He chuckled beside her again, and from her periphery she could see he was lying on his side atop the blanket, propped up on an elbow as he stared.

At least he was clothed. Mostly. She had to work to keep her eyes from drifting noticeably down to his bare chest.

She realized she still hadn't said anything to him, but she couldn't quite figure out how to get her tongue and teeth and breath to cooperate.

"Did you have fun at least?"

She managed to turn her head, wincing again at the stab of pain the movement caused. "I think so?" She tried not to cringe at how horribly pathetic she sounded.

"You seemed to, from what I can remember seeing."

"What? What did I do?" Her eyes went wide as her brain continued to refuse to recall any memory of what she'd done.

"You don't remember dancing with Tommy? You both nearly fell overboard at one point."

The memories started to come back little by little. Dim images of twirling and spinning. The faint sound of her giggles and Tommy's laughter mixing with the unceasing beat and songs of the crew.

Her cheeks warmed. Had Tommy wanted to dance with her, or had she forced him to? Had she looked as much the bumbling fool as she felt while replaying the night in her head?

Another wince and cringe had Declan breathing out a silent laugh.

"Don't worry, Aoife. The crew will probably stop talking about it by the time we leave Morshan again."

She maneuvered to her side, ignoring the way the movement sent her head swimming again, and looked at him. "It was that bad?" She raced through all the possible embarrassing scenarios she could think of. Oh, she hoped she hadn't done anything too ridiculous. It had only been three mugs. How full had they been? She didn't think it had been that much. But now, as she pushed her mind to work, harder than it desired in this moment, the embarrassment settled inside her as heavy as the rum had.

She was going to be sick.

She forced the bile down, not wanting to lose her stomach contents in front of him.

"Honestly?" He lifted his brow, and she waited for his sharp teasing, but she didn't see any hint of ridicule in his eyes. "You were fine, Aoife. A perfectly respectable lady."

"But I almost fell overboard." Her expression twisted with the embarrassment.

"So did half the crew. They were much further gone in the rum than you. It's going to delay us a bit getting into Morshan today, but—"

"Won't that ruin all your plans?"

"Not all of them. And to be honest, I'm thankful Tommy and Gavin arranged the festivities. The crew needed it. I needed it."

"Wait. What happened?"

He shot her a questioning look. "What do you mean?"

"Where did the Captain Mc—I mean, Declan—I know wander off to? He wouldn't have been so nonchalant about a delay or anything upsetting his precious timeline."

He sat up fully then and roughed his hands over his face, the stubble on his jaw looking extra scruffy and appealing. Were such thoughts acceptable among friends? She wasn't sure.

He turned to her again, his arm now resting on his bent knee. She forced herself to keep her eyes on his face and not his bare chest and the scars that peppered his tan skin. Ignored the way her mind pondered what that chest might feel like.

"I suppose seeing you being dragged across the sand in Foxhaven forced me to get things in perspective."

"But you're a pirate. And one with quite the reputation, so I hear."

"A reputation I worked hard to achieve. But that doesn't mean I don't have a heart."

"I don't understand. Doesn't time still tick by? Don't you still have a deadline to meet?"

"Aye. But perhaps I came to realize if we don't enjoy ourselves a bit, if we don't keep our mind focused on the good things we have—or could have—then what is the point? Is success worth losing sight of everything worth living for?"

She mulled over his words and bit her lip as if chewing on what he'd just said. "Are you saying I'm a good thing you have?" *Or could have,* she added to herself. Her face warmed again at that thought, and thankfully he looked away without seeming to notice.

For a moment she thought she saw the more vulnerable side of him peeking out from behind the tough shell he had created. But his eyes hardened and his lips stiffened as he slid his mask back into place and faced her. "Perhaps. Though that depends on what happens at the council hall in a couple days."

"So our friendship is completely riding on my successfully helping you; is that it?"

She had meant it to be teasing, but her rum-addled brain couldn't keep the bitterness from soaking into her words.

He didn't seem to have an answer, and before she could push him further, he was moving, swinging his legs off the bed and walking away.

36

Declan

Declan made his way across his quarters toward breakfast, painfully aware that he'd left Aoife's question hanging in the air unanswered.

He'd spent all evening watching her dance and laugh on the deck with Tommy, pondering how a friendship with her might work. He was still at a loss.

And here she was asking if their relationship would end if she failed at the council hall. How could it end if he wasn't even sure it had begun? Yet he had the sinking suspicion it had begun against his will.

Something in him had snapped when he took that pirate's head and freed her, creating a connection, a link between the two of them. Whether it was friendship or not, he didn't know, but a life without her around? Unacceptable.

Despite this, though, he had no idea how to be her friend.

She wasn't like Tommy or Gavin or anyone in his crew. And she certainly wasn't like any of the other women he'd occasionally entertained himself with over the years.

But he couldn't admit to her that he didn't know how this would work. Nor could he silence the nagging in his gut that urged him to see the other options.

He'd been unable to completely hold back the memories of his parents. Ever since he'd rescued her, they'd plagued him, unwilling to stay locked away no matter how many times he shoved them aside. The way they'd always talked and shared everything. The tender kisses he'd witnessed and the silent glances that had passed between them. The gentle strokes of fingers as they worked together or the little touches whenever they crossed paths.

They'd had friendship and romance, perfectly balanced and intertwined.

Until the end. And his father had run out the door that night without hesitation.

These images didn't merely haunt Declan, they were changing him. He'd spent so many years ignoring them, pushing people away and keeping everyone outside the wall he'd constructed.

And now that wall was crumbling down as the memories pushed against it.

Friendship. Romance. He welcomed the first, but the latter seemed impossible. Not something destined for someone like him.

Pirates didn't fall in love, didn't raise families, didn't tie themselves to anything but the sea and the hunt.

"Did you get lost?" Aoife called from the bedroom. At least she didn't sound quite so pained now.

He didn't bother looking toward where she still sat on the bed, instead calling over his shoulder, "Would you like some breakfast?"

"I'm not sure I can stomach anything yet."

He picked up a tin plate and piled an assortment of items they'd stocked up on in Foxhaven onto it. A banana. A roll. Some hard cheese. No pie though. He'd missed out on the slices Lucy had set aside for him, as he had run out to save Aoife.

She'd better be worth it.

He carried the plate back into the bedroom, setting it down before her.

Aoife had managed to sit up. With her slender legs crisscrossed before her, she eyed the food he'd presented before picking up the roll and tearing small bits off, testing each morsel before selecting another.

Even with her hair a choppy mess—the ends pointing out in all directions, some strands sticking up in the back where they'd gotten stuck in place as she slept—sands, she was adorable.

Thoughts warred inside him. Tommy had insisted they needed each other, and Declan had resisted. At least outwardly. But he'd been considering the same thing before Tommy ever uttered the words. And it was more than just practicality. Yes, he needed her help to rescue the fae, and she very plainly needed him to keep her from being whisked back to the council.

But he'd seen something spark in her last night. Even before any drop of rum had passed her lips. He'd seen it in her glances and in the slight turning down of her lips when he'd kept some distance between them while sitting.

It had been brief. So brief he'd been sure he imagined it.

Had she felt the tether that had formed between them after Foxhaven? Or was it only on his end, born out of his innate need to protect those around him—a need he'd spent years refusing to accept? Yet he couldn't quite figure out what that connection meant for them. Would he turn her down if she pursued a romance?

In this moment, as the sun shone on her sleep-mussed hair and her freckles stood out more pronounced across the bridge of her nose, he wasn't so sure. But she'd never seemed interested in him in that way, and she was the one who had suggested friendship.

So friendship was what he'd settle for. That was the easier option anyway.

"What are you thinking?" Her question startled him out of his thoughts. He hadn't noticed her look up at him, and he had to blink a few times to clear his mind from all he'd been pondering.

He needed a lie, but one eluded him at the moment, and his brain sent out the first words he could muster. "How to be friends with you, actually."

Aoife's laugh split the air, short and sweet, and he found he thoroughly enjoyed it. "Is it that hard to do?" She went back to studying the bread she held, then muttered, "Friendship shouldn't be hard."

If she only knew.

But she had a point, didn't she? Friendship should be easy. Like with Tommy. Why did he want to control it, as if it were a ship to be captained?

Maybe it would be better if he let it ride the waves on its own, let it develop naturally, without force or planning.

Stop overthinking things, Declan.

Trust yourself.

Trust her.

"I suppose you have a point," he said. He leaned his back against the wall and crossed his arms over his chest, hoping he looked more relaxed than he felt.

She lifted her gaze to his again, a mocking smirk tugging at her lips.

"Did you have many friends at the council hall?" He didn't realize until after the words were out that he'd accidentally stepped onto shaky ground. *What a friend you're proving to be, jackass.*

"Only Lani really."

He'd expected to see her face drop with the mention of her sister's name, but her calm expression didn't waver.

He'd sat with her for two nights after rescuing her in Foxhaven, had watched her tremble in her sleep, battling the nightmares that pulled at her features and tensed her jaw. At first he'd assumed it was merely because of the kidnapping and the beheading, but she'd whimpered her sister's name multiple times.

It had twisted his gut, and he'd wondered how he could possibly rescue her from that.

And wondered why he felt such a need to. But here she sat, her grief and guilt still dancing at the edges of her green eyes that seemed far more confident now. But this change hadn't arisen from the rest he'd allowed her.

This change had come overnight. Perhaps the music and the dancing and the revelry was what she'd needed too, though it made little sense to him how frivolity could heal such deep wounds.

"What about you? Is Tommy your only friend?"

"Aye, I suppose. He's my oldest and closest, to be sure."

"How'd you meet?"

He'd never told the story to anyone. No one had ever asked. Whether that was because of his reputation or simply because pirates didn't care, he wasn't sure. It wasn't hard to recall though.

"We were both cabin boys on a ship."

She looked at him, brows raised in expectation for the rest of the story, and he stifled a laugh. He'd known that answer wouldn't suffice. That was precisely why he'd given it.

"And?" she asked.

"And what?" Toying with her was delightful indeed.

"That's it? You were both cabin boys, and that's the whole story behind your friendship."

"Pretty much."

"But how did you end up on that ship? How did he? Where did he live before? And how did you acquire the *Siren's Song*?" The questions rushed out of her, and he had to use every ounce of his will to appear bored.

"Oh, well, you didn't ask any of that."

Aoife rubbed at her forehead and temple. Such frustration building. This was too easy.

"Fair enough," she said. "Would you answer them now?"

"Very well." He paused to think. How much should he divulge? How much of it really mattered? And did he have any right to tell part of Tommy's story for him?

"I left home—don't ask why, because I won't explain—and joined the first crew in need of a cabin boy. The *Reckoning* was a larger ship, and the bo'sun had already employed Tommy that morning, so we were both new to the crew. And new to sailing and piracy as well. He was born on Cregah, across the Binbrack Mountains, but why he left and how he ended up in Morshan, you'd need to ask him."

He expected her to push him on that, to challenge his silence on Tommy's past, but she didn't. "And this ship? Your becoming captain? How'd that come to pass exactly?"

"After being cabin boys for a couple years, we worked our way up through the crew. We had several hard voyages on that ship. Some of the merchant vessels that captain chose to intercept did not willingly submit to the pirate flag. It's rare for them to engage in a fight. Most don't employ fighters and don't protect their vessels with cannons and the like, but a couple we ran across did. One in particular cost our crew dearly. Even though we had disabled their ship with our own cannons, when we boarded them, we found they weren't harmless sailors but fighters. Each and every one of them. And good ones too."

He looked toward the window and out to the sea at the lines his ship made as they sailed on. He could almost feel the adrenaline that had coursed through him that day.

"The officers all fell, and the captain was badly wounded, but Tommy and I were able to get him back aboard the *Reckoning*. We had just enough men to sail, and our ship hadn't taken much damage, but our captain refused to go to any of the better-known pirate ports. Instead he directed us to a land we'd never heard of. A tiny port nestled in a cove. It may have been home for him once. He refused our help in tending his wounds, and Tommy and I were left sitting there in an unfamiliar port with a bunch of confused crewmen watching our captain limp away. Never saw him again, and while he'd given us no indication he planned to return, he also hadn't uttered any farewells, so we waited there. For three days. It was Tommy's suggestion to take the ship as our own. He had no desire to be captain but insisted I could be one of the best. We met with the remaining crew, took a vote, and they named me their new captain. To make a name for ourselves we changed the ship's name. You know pirates and sailors in general are a superstitious lot. This ship's name is meant to drum up fear and stop people short. And it does just that."

It was the most words he'd managed to get out without her interrupting him, and had he not found her staring at him wide-eyed, hanging onto every syllable, he might have thought she'd begun to daydream and had stopped listening.

Drawing in a long, slow breath, she sat back a bit, dropping the roll onto the plate. "Well, that's a lot to digest. How old were you when you took command?"

"Fifteen." Though he'd been fully aware of how young he was, recalling the story aloud now—and seeing Aoife's eyes widen—made the reality of it sink in deeper.

Silence settled between them as they studied each other, and he wondered where the conversation might lead. He had so many questions for her as well but didn't want to risk undoing whatever healing had occurred for her. Before he could settle on something to ask, she was speaking.

"My story is far less intriguing."

"I find that doubtful. Heir to the council? Running away? Trespassing on one of the most feared ships? And then challenging their captain time and time again? Sounds intriguing to me."

"See? You already know the whole story." She blinked up at him, a smile threatening to spread across her lips.

"Do I?" How much could he ask? How far could he push? Surely there couldn't be any harm in simply asking. If she didn't want to talk about it, she could brush it off as he had with her questions about Tommy's past.

As if she could sense his thoughts, she asked, "What do you want to know?"

So much. Too much, perhaps, and he'd have to choose carefully. "Were you close with your mothers?" He wasn't sure he'd worded it correctly, not sure how they referred to the councilwomen.

"Not really. It isn't what I'd call a family, exactly."

"How would you know?" He didn't ask it to be harsh, and he hoped his tone came across as softly as he intended. She didn't even bristle at the question though.

"Lani and I ventured often enough into Morshan, and we would see the families there. We were taught in our lessons, too, that marrying and having children was allowed for the people of Cregah, that preserving the old ways of the familial units was beneficial for their well-being, but the council was different. We had a different purpose and role, and a family would only distract from that duty."

He couldn't help but think back to his childhood. Having a family had, indeed, been good for him. Even during times when food was scarce and income from the pub had slowed to a trickle, he had never felt lacking. He had never doubted his parents' love for each other or for him and Cait. And it had been a happy life, until it ended.

How sad that she hadn't experienced any of that herself.

He shifted his weight against the wall.

"You've been standing a long while, Declan," she said, gesturing for him to sit with her.

He eyed the open space beside her on the bed, and his feet throbbed as if they'd heard her invitation and begged him to accept. It felt too close for friends though. Surely he could handle standing for the duration of a conversation, so he muttered an *I'm fine* and didn't move closer.

"Suit yourself," she said with a twinge of laughter.

She could mock all she wanted, but he'd finally gotten history locked away again in his mind, and he didn't want to risk it flooding out again.

"Did you ever wish to be away from it? You know, before you ran?"

"No." He hadn't expected such a quick answer, but then again, she had only learned about the council's secrets a week ago. Why would she have ever felt the need to leave when she'd been taught it was her duty to rule?

He wanted to ask if it was only the guilt that had pushed her to leave, but he didn't know how to broach that yet. So he switched to something else. "Did you have any hobbies? Or were those prohibited as well?"

"So many questions, Declan. If I didn't know better, I'd think you were interrogating me, digging up information to one day use against me."

Declan flashed her as menacing a look as he could manage, setting his jaw and lowering his brows along with his tone. "If I were interrogating you, you'd know. And you certainly wouldn't be sitting on a feather mattress munching on my food." With a loud exhale, he let his face melt into a more relaxed state. "This is what friends do, yes? Get to know each other? Or have you changed your mind on the friendship?"

"You won't get rid of me that easily."

"I've pretty much given up any hope of being rid of you, Aoife." He thought he saw a flash of hope in her eyes, but it could have easily been amusement or a mocking thought.

"We were allowed certain activities. Music, art, and reading, but only within limits."

"Limits?"

She swallowed, and a slight change came over her, like a cloud had passed by the sun, though it still shined on her through the window. "Certain books were forbidden. One of my favorites, a novel of love and adventure, was found by my mother. She took it and promptly threw it into my fire. I tried to salvage what I could after she left, but it turned to ash so quickly. I told myself it was for the best, that Mother had good intentions and was only looking out for me. But I never quite forgave her for that. I've looked for more copies of the book. Whenever we'd go into the little bookshop in Morshan, I'd hunt for it. But you know they get so few books into port these days. I never found it again."

"What was the title?" He'd never let the crew know, aside from Tommy, that books were one of his favorite prizes from their plundering. In fact, Tommy had instructed the crew to bring any they found to him first, and he would discreetly deliver them to Declan after they had sailed on.

It was a long shot, but perhaps he had it somewhere in his cabin.

"*The Mercenary's Bride.*" Her cheeks flushed, and he knew it wasn't the title that caused that reaction. Though it wasn't anywhere on his shelves here, he knew the book and had read it once, long before he was old enough to do so. It was indeed a tale of adventure and romance. Heavy on the latter.

"And why is that one among your favorites?"

"It was a life I'd never have for myself. Sailing the seas. Going on daring missions—"

"—being touched by a man?" The words spilled out before he could think better of them. And regret immediately washed over him. This didn't seem polite conversation, but again, he wasn't sure what was appropriate between friends.

You're a pirate. Forget propriety!

The warmth in her face deepened, but she looked him squarely in the eye—to his surprise. "Well, yes. I suppose that wasn't part of the life I was meant for. At least not in that way."

What was that life like for the heirs? To have a business partnership with their match and not romance? No family or mutual love like he'd witnessed between his parents? To have physical intimacy be not for pleasure and closeness but for the continuation of the council only?

Not that he had an issue with children. When he was younger—much younger—he'd even dreamed of one day finding a wife and having more than the two kids they'd had in his family. But then he'd learned that was the limit the council had placed on family size, and he couldn't understand it. He couldn't understand why his parents would choose to live in a land where families were told what they could and couldn't do in their own homes.

But his parents had rightly quieted him, instructed him to never express discontent or utter ill words against the council. It hadn't made any sense to him. In a land of peace and nonviolence, why did his parents fear them so?

He'd eventually learned.

"What was your favorite part of the book?" He needed to get his mind off his parents, but this question didn't exactly help.

Before he could stop it, his traitorous mind had him seeing his mom finding him with the book and pulling it out of his hands, telling him it wasn't for young eyes. He hadn't understood her, but then she'd explained certain aspects of married life, and he'd found it repulsive, though he still hadn't understood why she wouldn't let him read it. It wasn't as if it had pictures depicting any intimacy, but she had insisted, telling him he could perhaps read it in a few years if he was still interested. He hadn't dared cross his mother, and so he'd waited patiently.

Aoife answered his question with her own. "How can I pick just one? Have you read it? I'd hate to spoil it for you."

"Aye. A long time ago."

"Well, then, perhaps the part where Marko rescues Lorelai from the bandits. Or where he teaches her to fight. Lani and I used to pretend we were in her place, learning to protect ourselves from dangers beyond our shores, going on wild adventures with our one true love. Perhaps…" Aoife's eyes lowered to her hands then, and her words became rough with emotion. "Perhaps that's what Lani risked everything for. What she saw in Adler. A chance for the adventure we'd read about. For the love we'd witnessed on the pages of books."

"And you never did? Never dreamed of that, I mean?"

"No." Another quick answer. "It was a fantasy. Something to be read on the page, as real for me as the dragons and elves in fantasy stories. Something I'd never see or feel in real life."

"So I suppose I shouldn't tell you that dragons and elves are far from fantasy?"

Her eyes widened and then darted around the room, as if one of the fantastic creatures might be hiding somewhere in his cabin. "What?"

"Well, I don't have any here." He couldn't contain his laughter. "But yes, they are very much real."

"Have you seen them? With your own eyes?"

"No." Her face dropped in noticeable disappointment. "They've long left the Aisling Sea, but we once stumbled across signs of them. There are old dragon lairs on the islands around Foxhaven actually. The gold has long since been plundered, but you can still see the scorch marks from their fires and deep gouges from their claws. Can still see the bones of their victims. Apparently no looters wanted to take those."

"And the elves?"

"Evidence of them is harder to find. It was actually Mikkel who told us what we were seeing while we were taking a rest in a tiny coastal village in Turvala. The markings looked like natural designs in the trees, but he explained it was their old language. How he knew about them, he never said, and we never pushed him."

"Why did you believe him then?"

"You know how you can tell when someone is being genuine and when they're not?"

She nodded.

"Had you seen the look in his eyes when he explained it, you never would have questioned him either."

A breath fell from her. "Dragons and elves. Real. I can't… In all my days I never would have imagined. Do you think they'll ever return?"

"I'm happy for the dragons to stay gone." Indeed, it was already hard enough to be waging an endless war with the pirate lords, and now his sister's fight against the council. What would all that look like if dragons returned? "But the elves. I heard they were a formidable force in the Aisling War."

"Why did they leave?" The question seemed more for herself than for him, which was fine, because he had no answer. But if he'd had to guess, he would have assumed their desire to escape was for reasons similar to his own. The Aisling Sea brought nothing but trouble. He couldn't blame the elves—or the fae—for abandoning it.

Yet he hadn't been able to sail off yet.

"And why haven't you left, Declan?"

Startled, his eyes snapped to hers. "What do you mean?"

"Well, you don't seem to be as attached to the Aisling or any land bordering its waters." He racked his brain for what might have given her a clue, or what might have indicated that the rest of his crew *did* have an attachment. An attachment he lacked.

"I don't think I follow."

"It's hard to explain. Tommy and the rest of the crew seem at home here, on the ship, on the Aisling. Even when I witnessed them in Foxhaven, they seemed content, as if there was nothing missing for them. But you"—she swallowed hard—"you always seem to be elsewhere. And I don't think it's merely being lost in a daydream or in thought. It's as though your mind is on distant lands you've never seen, on adventures you've yet to take, and on a life you have only been able to imagine."

Silence spread out between them once again.

She'd seen all that in him during the few days they'd spent together. How should he respond? Words eluded him. His mind seemed to stop, frozen by her observation.

Only Tommy knew of what he yearned for, and yet this girl had picked up on it so quickly.

She lowered her eyes again, the blush returning. "But I suppose I could be wrong. Lani used to give me such grief for all the fanciful tales I'd devise for each of the servants in the household, or for the people we'd meet while in town."

"You do have a wonderful imagination. Surprising for someone raised to lead the council. Surely you must have had some inkling that something wasn't right about them."

Would she realize he was changing the subject? Did he care if she did?

"So we're talking about me again?" Her eyes flitted to the ceiling, as if the answer to his non-question was written among the knots and grooves. "You're right. There was an inkling, but I didn't know what it was at the time. An odd feeling in my gut, but I always shoved it aside."

"I'm surprised by that. I'd think your curiosity would have pushed you to do otherwise. Gotten you into trouble, as it tends to do."

"I didn't say it was shoved aside easily. But I trusted my mother. How was I to know I shouldn't? She was all I knew as my family—and yes, I know that word isn't adequate, but again, it's the only word I have for it. I mean, she never raised a hand to me, obviously, but the look in her eyes and the tone of her tongue could hurt as much as any strike. At least I imagined it to be so."

"What of your sisters? Did they ever question?"

"Lani was not as passionate for our service on the council. I'm not sure why. We all received the same education and upbringing, but council life never seemed to appeal to her. Even before she told me of her plans, I could sense it in her, even if I couldn't pinpoint exactly what plagued her. She always had a sad look, even when we were joking and laughing. It was as if she couldn't fully be happy, forever cloaked in a shadow. It wasn't until she spoke Adler's name to me that I saw that shadow lifted. For the briefest of moments."

"So why did you turn her in?" The question was out before he could leash it, his thoughts given life before he could stop them. Aoife recoiled as if slapped. "I'm sorry. I shouldn't have—"

"No, it's not your fault."

Why was she consoling him? He was the one being an uncaring ass.

You're a pirate, aren't you? Why bother with apologies?

"It was a callous thing to ask," he said.

What is happening to you?

She relaxed once again, her grief and pain seemingly soothed somehow. "But it's the obvious question, isn't it? Even if you hadn't asked, I'd know you were wondering." She paused and wrung her hands in her lap.

Would she provide an answer, or would she change the subject? Whatever she chose, it would be her decision. He wouldn't force that information from her, because it didn't matter. Not in the end. And not for the job they had to do, despite his insistence to the contrary days earlier.

"I didn't mean to," she whispered, but unlike the last time she'd said these words, all defensiveness was gone, leaving only remorse dripping from each syllable. Almost as if she were speaking to the one she'd wronged and not to a pirate captain.

Declan waited. The minutes dragged on, but they might have been seconds. He wasn't sure, and he dared not look at his pocket watch for fear of offending her.

The silence became unbearable though. He needed to say something, but he had no idea what that might be.

She finally rescued him by speaking first. "It's not as though they forced it out of me."

He wished she'd look at him so he could see what she might be feeling in this moment. Even with her gaze lowered, he could see her eyes darting along the bed in front of her.

The next words flowed out of her like water released from a vessel, the stopper pulled and the words eager to be heard.

"My mother asked to speak to me, to ask why Lani and I had been quiet at dinner. I wanted to find a way for her to be with Adler without having to run away in secret. I wanted her to find that life with him without having to sneak around and lie. I'm no good at deception though. I think you know by now how my tongue betrays me. I always manage to say the wrong thing, and at the wrong time. Lani…" A pause. A hard swallow. But she didn't continue that thought, leaving Lani's name hanging in the air between them even as she finished the story. "I merely asked if any other council lady had ever fallen in love. I should have known what questions that would lead to, known that my mother would not believe me when I claimed it was hypothetical."

"And has anyone? Fallen in love, that is?" Declan's words sounded dry and hoarse. Why he asked the question, he wasn't quite sure. It was not as if it had any bearing on his situation. But perhaps Aoife's curiosity was rubbing off on him a bit.

"She didn't give me a name, but yes, a sister of her mother's."

"What happened to her?"

"She was removed from all council records, her name stricken from the histories. Exiled."

Declan winced at the word. *Exile.* On Cregah that meant death. But had it always? Aoife's grandmother's generation was far before his time, and he couldn't recall if the executions masked as exiles had started that long ago or were more recent, but he wanted to believe it was the latter.

Aoife interrupted his thoughts, echoing them. "I don't know if it was true exile back then. Or if it had already become what it is today. Regardless, I didn't know any better. To me, exile was preferable to sneaking away."

"So you told her what Lani was planning?" It felt so odd to say the girl's name, as if he'd known her as well as Aoife had.

"Not intentionally. Even with the thought of exile, I didn't feel it was my place. I was planning to try to change Lani's mind and get her to reconsider the possibility of requesting to be let out of her obligations to the council. Surely a land of peace would honor such a request. But it was my mother who pushed. Asked me if *I* had fallen in love."

A faint pink colored her cheeks again, but she fought it with a shake of her head, as if that could remove the coloring. "Then it was a slip of my damn tongue that said, 'Not me.' And she immediately knew it was far from hypothetical and I was speaking of one of my sisters. Even had I not said Lani's name, I think she would have guessed it."

"Why?"

"Lani and I were never close with our other sister, Darienn." She said this as if it were obvious, as if no one in their right mind would ever be close to this other girl.

"Why not? She that hideous?" He hoped he'd get even half a smile out of her, but she didn't seem to catch his poor attempt to lighten the mood.

"The opposite actually. She's gorgeous. But different."

Aoife worried the inside of her lower lip with her teeth but kept her eyes locked on his. She ran a hand through her tangle of hair and down her neck as if this sister's name had stirred up uncomfortable memories.

"It's hard to explain. She's intense. Cold and distant, though I assumed that was due to how Lani and I ignored her and pushed her away. Now, I'm not sure. It might simply be her nature. Darienn always seemed to be calculating, plotting something, though I thought she was just odd. Our mothers all knew we didn't get along. And it wasn't that we fought at all. We just…didn't talk."

"Ever?"

"Never. Not in many years anyway. And not until after Lani… Darienn came to my room. It was bizarre, honestly. I mean, after years of tolerating each other in silence, she looked me square in the eye and spoke. I had just learned the truth about Lani, after overhearing the staff talking in the kitchen. I wasn't sure what to do. I felt so lost and confused."

"And that's when you decided to run?"

"Not initially. I thought maybe it wasn't true. Maybe it was mere servant gossip. Fantastical stories and daydreams of bored staff longing for excitement. But the more I considered it, the more I realized how ridiculous that notion was. And Darienn all but confirmed it. How she knew, or how she'd come to suspect, was beyond me. I still don't know. But I knew what they would expect of me. And if it were true, if they were killing instead of exiling, if they were lying to our people and insisting on peace when they practiced the opposite? Could I live like that? Could I take up that mantle?"

"But maybe you could have changed it from within?" Surely she had to have considered that option.

"I thought that, for the briefest of moments, but in the end I let fear take over. Fear and self-preservation. What good would I have been to my people? I couldn't trust myself not to screw up and get myself exiled in the process. I'm no eloquent leader. I'm no eloquent anything, actually. Were my people on Cregah really in danger? I only ever went into Morshan. And everyone always seemed happy, content, taken care of. I wanted to believe my people weren't all that bad off. I already had so much guilt from Lani. So I guess I deceived myself. All those years of being lied to, and I was doing it to myself, convincing myself my people would be okay, even if I couldn't stay."

Declan's jaw clenched at the word *stay*. He'd run off, abandoned his sister, claiming he'd wanted to leave all of it behind, and yet he'd stayed close, choosing to remain on the Aisling.

She continued, seemingly unaware of the tension roiling within him. "I left, thinking, perhaps hoping, that the majority of people, as long as they didn't break the council's rules, would not be in any danger. But I wouldn't have any part in even one more exile."

Her eyes now brimmed with tears, which caught the sunlight from the window, and Declan had the urge to go to her, but he fought it.

He was a friend, but to touch her, to wipe away the tears that now escaped down her freckled cheeks, would be crossing a line he dared not. He'd done it last night, yes, but the gesture would feel different, more intimate, here in the privacy of his cabin. He didn't want to give her the wrong impression.

"But the *exiles* will happen whether you are present for them or not. Simply ignoring them doesn't make them go away, and unfortunately—" The words lodged in his throat.

He'd heard the stories. He'd seen the mass graves himself.

They haunted him almost as much as his parents' deaths, had him refusing to return home.

She needed to know the truth. He needed her to know. He needed to tell her.

But her steady tears, the lip on the verge of trembling… He couldn't.

"Unfortunately what?" she asked, timid and wary.

Tension filled his jaw as he looked at her, trying to keep the faces and the bodies from surfacing in his mind. Anger burned in his chest as he muttered the only word he could manage.

"Nothing."

She'd been right earlier. He wasn't tied to this sea or to Cregah, yet something kept him here, hindered him from leaving, continued to give him excuses to stay.

But could he do any good? Did he want to?

The rum-induced fog finally cleared from Aoife's mind, only for Declan's unfinished sentences to create a new cloud of questions she had to wade through. She wanted to give him the benefit of the doubt, trust that he had his reasons for not telling her everything.

She ripped off another piece of the roll he'd handed her and placed it on her tongue. Sands, she missed butter.

Even without looking up she could see that Declan's shifting was becoming more frequent. His feet had to be hurting. They'd been talking for hours. Without bickering. Without interruption. She nearly smiled at the thought of their budding friendship, but his refusal to rest his feet and sit beside her kept it hidden.

She tried not to take his decision personally.

Tried and failed.

They'd been silent for the last few minutes. She had no idea if he was watching her, but she didn't need to look at him to digest all he'd told her.

She had learned more about him over the last couple of hours than she had in the past several days. At that thought, a small half smile pulled at one corner of her lips before a breath of a laugh escaped.

"What's so funny?" he asked.

Embarrassment warmed her cheeks, and she tried to shake it away as she raised her chin.

"Nothing."

Another laugh tumbled out as she realized she'd given him the same one-word answer he'd offered moments before. She lost herself in his stormy eyes, trapped by their intensity, as she waited for his teasing comment.

But it never came.

He simply looked at her—no, looked *into* her, as if she were a puzzle he needed to figure out. An intense gaze, but not altogether uncomfortable. In fact, something in his expression seemed to be inviting her to stay, and she very nearly inched closer to the edge of the bed toward him. But she stopped herself when he cleared his throat and pulled his attention down to the floor.

With a blink, she shook away any hope the moment had sparked within her. *You're letting your imagination get away from you.* She needed to keep her head if she was going to be of any help to him.

She also needed to know more about his plans to find the fae.

"If I might ask…" she said, propping an elbow on her knee so she could lean her chin on her palm.

He offered a hum of approval for her to continue before looking up, his head falling to the side as he did.

"Why the short timeline anyway? If the dagger does what the legends claim, why the hurry?"

Rubbing a hand on the back of his neck, Declan raised a shoulder before answering.

"I don't know much actually. Kind of par for the course in our line of work. You get used to only being told the bare minimum."

"Even from your sister?"

"Especially from her. We aren't particularly close, and that's my fault." He didn't look away as she expected. His gaze held fast, but his eyes were now devoid of any of the emotion she'd seen in them earlier, their previous fire replaced with a cold nothingness, as if he were guarding himself.

"And that doesn't bother you?" She couldn't imagine being okay with not being close to a sibling, and then Darienn's face flashed in her mind, rebuking her for judging him. "I mean, she's your only sibling, yes?"

"Aye. Just the two of us, but we have our own ways of dealing with…"

His voice trailed off, and he turned his face toward the windows and the sea beyond.

She watched him intently, wondering if the wall he'd built would ever come down, even if only when they were alone. She'd seen it start to give, bits of it falling away, always to be patched up swiftly. And he showed no sign of letting it falter again now.

Turning back to her, he offered, "Let's just say, going back to Cregah brings back memories I'd rather keep locked away." He stiffened, as if bracing himself against her possible push for more information.

"So why did you go back?"

This question got him to relax slightly, and he raised a brow. "Your turn to interrogate me then?"

She tossed him a shrug and one of her mocking smirks, which at least earned her a small laugh from him before he drew in a deep breath and answered.

"It was the closest port after we were hit hard by one of the lords up around Helles Island. My men needed care, and they wouldn't have made it to one of the farther islands. Morshan was it. I planned to stay aboard the ship, but my sister got word to me. She knew I was seeking the dagger. And her…"

Again he trailed off. He kept doing this. Leaving sentences incomplete, as if his tongue steered him toward paths in the conversation his mind didn't want to go down but was late in catching up.

He still didn't trust her with certain things, and she was trying to be okay with that, but she couldn't deny that she'd thought things were changing last night. And this morning.

Yet he still paused, edited his words, and it irked her, lighting a fire in her gut that wouldn't be quenched no matter how she tried to talk it down and reason it away. Why should he trust her? He had little reason to. At least not fully.

He continued his sentence, though it was obviously altered from what he'd originally planned to say. "Her running the pub keeps her from going after the dagger herself. She requested I bring it to her."

"And you agreed?"

"She had information I'd failed to gather myself. Namely, the dagger's location and a plan for how to retrieve it. So yes, I agreed. But I hadn't decided if I'd follow through."

"Such a pirate thing to do. Say one thing and do another."

Aoife hoped he'd hear the humor she intended, but if he did, he didn't let on.

Instead his gaze hardened, like her words had struck a nerve. *But he is a pirate. Why should that bother him?*

"You said you hadn't decided. Past tense. Does that mean you've decided now?"

"Perhaps. I might be leaning stronger to one side now."

Her brow tightened as curiosity took over. "What changed? What pushed you to a decision?"

He didn't answer but nodded in her direction.

Her. She'd been the catalyst. But which way had she swayed him? She had her assumptions, but her instincts were so off-kilter, she didn't quite trust them.

"And?"

"And what?"

She groaned out a sigh, knowing he was toying with her. He knew full well what she was asking. Still, she clarified. "Which way are you leaning?"

"Well, it is still tempting to take the dagger for myself so I can leave the Aisling. I wouldn't need to spend more years preparing. I'd simply be able to leave and have successes and triumphs in all the seas beyond. But no. I'm not sure now if I could enjoy any of that, knowing what was going on behind me. Some pirate I am."

"You know, a pirate once told me that pirates do, in fact, have honor and a heart. I'm apt to believe him, because he seemed pretty sure of that fact."

"I see what you did there."

"But do you believe it or not? Or were those words about honor another well-crafted lie fed to an irritating stowaway?"

He didn't answer. Not that she had expected him to. She was once again swimming in the grays of his eyes as they locked onto hers, and she wished she could know what his mind was mulling over.

What was he seeing in her? Did he see her as a friend, as she had begun to see him? Or did he still see her as a nuisance aboard his ship? She didn't think it was the latter, but she couldn't tell if the friendship budding between them was completely genuine.

Did it even matter?

All she needed was for him to trust her enough to let her help.

To get the fae.

So he could get the dagger.

So they could stop the council from killing her people.

This was too big, too important, too impossible.

How could they ever dream of succeeding?

That single question brought the weight of everything slamming into her like a wave against the ship's hull.

It sucked all the oxygen from the room. With both hands, she clenched the blankets, but she kept spiraling as the panic rushed in.

Even with her eyes squeezed shut, the heaviness in her chest wouldn't subside. The tension increased, and the sensation of a million legs crawling over her skin overtook her.

For the briefest of moments she worried what he might think, seeing her losing it. But the panic had its hold on her. Pulling her under.

It didn't matter if he saw.

Nothing mattered except getting it to stop.

Ending it.

Surviving it.

Through her pounding heart and shallow breaths she heard the two steps he took toward her. Felt the bed shift.

She opened her eyes to see him moving her plate out of the way as he knelt on the ground before her.

His hand reached for her knee, his touch light but still reassuring.

"Breathe, Aoife. Slow. Steady." His voice melted over her, and she did as he suggested, his words not a command but an encouragement. His tone was far from that of a ruthless pirate, but more like a caring friend, and that thought helped calm her.

"There you go," he said.

Her heartbeat slowed. Breathing became easier, and she could have almost cried at how quickly the panic began to ease up.

"What happened just then?" he asked. "One minute you were asking about lies and irritating stowaways—" He flashed her favorite smirk. "And the next, you're acting as though someone punched you in the gut."

She needed a moment before she could explain it with any coherency, and he waited with more patience than she'd anticipated.

"It's all simply—" No, that wasn't the best way to explain this. Why were words so damn hard sometimes? "It's too much."

"What is?"

Aoife stared at her hands, fidgeting with her fingers, trying to ignore how his hand remained on her knee.

"All of it." She lifted her chin, but her gaze darted around the room, as if the words she needed would be found in the air. "The fae. The dagger. The council. It's all so much. How can you—we—hope to succeed?"

As he drew in a breath, she wondered if he'd react with the same panic she had experienced. But he didn't. Of course he didn't. He was a pirate. And a young one at that, constantly fighting against the odds to make a name for himself and find his footing amongst the other ships and fleets.

He was used to being challenged, and that was all this was. Another challenge.

"We might not," he finally said.

Well, that wasn't reassuring. Surely he wasn't finished. She scowled at him, and he shook his head at her before flashing her another of his smirks.

At least one of us is in a good mood.

"But—yes, there's a but," he continued. "We will certainly fail if we don't try at all. So we will push forward, one step at a time, doing the next task set before us until all are complete."

If he'd said these words to her a few days ago, they would have aggravated her, but now she understood the comfort he offered. Though this didn't quite quell her concerns. "Don't you have to plan for the later steps too though? Doesn't that get overwhelming?"

A shrug seemed to be his only answer until she jutted her chin out at him, pressing him to explain.

"It only gets overwhelming if you let it. Yes, you see the big picture in your periphery. You calculate the possible paths that might present themselves along the way, but if you let the overall mission shadow the task at hand, you'll stumble and fall. Just like you almost did when you forgot how to breathe."

"So focus on the next task."

"Aye."

"Which is?"

"Shopping."

Declan could barely contain his amusement as Aoife sat staring at him, her mouth hanging open.

She repeated the word. "Shopping."

He nodded in return.

"But how?"

"Well, we use these things called coins, and merchants give us goods in exchange for them."

A groan rumbled in the back of her throat. "Apparently the next task at hand is actually to drive me mad."

She seemed to be trying to hold onto her irritation as much as he was trying to contain his laughter, and soon both of them lost their respective battles, if only for a moment, smiles creeping across their lips.

She looked away first, as if suddenly aware of how close they sat and how his hand still lingered on her knee.

He pulled it away with some reluctance. She only wanted a friend, and he could be that for her. He shooed away the teasing, taunting thoughts of having more.

With her hands raised, she gestured to her attire and reworded her earlier question. "How do we go shopping without being recognized? If they found me in Foxhaven, they'll surely be looking for me in Morshan. Yes?"

"Indeed. But we won't be shopping in the normal sense." She began to protest but then snapped her mouth shut. She must have realized he wasn't quite done explaining. "Remember, I grew up in Morshan. I know how to maneuver around without being seen. And we won't be going to any shops. They'll be coming to us. In a way."

He waited for her to object, to demand more information, to insist he tell her every minute detail of the plan, but whether she was beginning to trust him more or simply too tired to argue, he wasn't sure. She merely nodded, lips pursed in acceptance.

She once again glanced down at her lap, keeping him from seeing the green of her eyes under her lashes as he studied her. What he wouldn't give to get a glimpse into her thoughts.

Every passing second with her made the nagging desire within him grow more and more impatient, urging him to acknowledge the possibilities, and he could no longer suppress the images of his parents doing life together, side by side as a team.

When all of Cregah had believed women should rule and men could not be trusted to do anything but destroy and tear apart, he had seen his mother and father live as partners. Equals. He'd fought against this notion of partnership and marriage for too long. It only ended in heartache. Death.

Happiness couldn't last. Love and peace—supposedly valued—weren't allowed on Cregah except within the council's limits.

Could he risk opening his heart to someone as his father had, as his mother had? Could he risk opening himself up to someone—taking that leap—while the council still existed, still preyed on its people and crushed everything good?

He breathed deep, but it wouldn't clear away the warring thoughts in his mind.

Focus on the task at hand. Focus.

He needed to distract himself, to shut up the voices.

"Do those attacks happen often?" he asked. He hoped she'd understand what he meant. His words had not come out quite as eloquently as he'd planned.

Aoife angled her head to one side as her lips twitched a little. Would the mere mention of the panic attack trigger another? He held his breath until she gave him a string of small nods, her eyes looking into his again.

Was that shame in her expression? Her eyes began to gloss over with the start of tears. His fingers itched to reach for her again, but he managed to refrain.

"I used to," he said. "Get those panic attacks, I mean."

She showed no surprise even as she asked, "When?"

"When I was younger, before I left home."

"So long ago. And never since then?"

"Rarely since. It was as if the sea and this life gave me a distraction, perhaps. Not a remedy for what hurt, I suppose, but more like a curtain being drawn so I could no longer focus on what had plagued me prior."

He was tiptoeing along an uncomfortable line, but he couldn't stop, like some part of him was desperate to let her in. The wall within him started to give again, but no, it wasn't failing. Rather, it was as if he was standing atop the wall and reaching a hand toward her, inviting her to join him on the other side.

Would she want to learn more? Would she want to see the real him? Her curiosity would likely insist she accept whether she truly cared for him or not.

But she didn't pry.

Instead, she offered her own story.

"I've gotten them my whole life. Only Lani knew about it. Or if our mothers and Darienn knew, they never let on. Lani was the only one who ever tried to help, much in the way you did. She'd remind me to breathe, sitting beside me until it passed."

"What caused them?"

"They seemed to happen whenever I got overwhelmed. When the pressure became too great, I'd lose myself. Forget how to function. It felt like the weight of the council was sitting on my chest, pressing in from all sides, like my heart might be squeezed until it burst."

Declan waited for her to continue, mostly because he wasn't sure what questions to ask now. He wanted to understand but had little idea how to proceed. Before today, he hadn't witnessed one of her episodes, not that he'd been with her during every moment she'd spent on the ship.

"How often?" he asked again.

Did she hear the concern in his voice? Would she understand he asked as a friend, or would she assume he was looking for any possible hiccups in the upcoming mission? She was becoming difficult to read. All these new thoughts and feelings seemed to be clouding his ability to assess her.

"Every so often." She must have seen the twitch at the corner of his eye, because she immediately elaborated. "Once or twice a week actually."

That regularly. It took every ounce of will to keep his mouth from falling open. Even after his parents' deaths, his panic attacks hadn't been that common. Once a month, if that. And they'd been unbearable when they came upon him. He couldn't imagine living with them at such frequency.

"And since you've been here?"

Her head once again dipped down, her eyes falling to her fingers that were worrying the blanket at her feet. Declan hoped—as silly as it was—that perhaps the sea and his ship had done for her what it had done for him all those years ago, distracted and suppressed the inner demons that took hold without notice. But he knew that was unlikely.

"This was the third."

She'd hidden them well. He'd never noticed. He hadn't been here to help. Though, looking back at their early days together, he knew he wouldn't have likely offered help had he witnessed them.

"I'm sorry." It was all he could think to say.

No hint of sadness or distress remained in Aoife's eyes. The greens and golds seemed warmer somehow, reminding him of the hills outside Morshan where his family used to picnic in the summer evenings, when the sun would hit the rolling waves of grass.

Such happy yet somber memories.

That's what her eyes brought him, what caused the twinge in his heart as she looked at him now. Looking into her eyes felt like returning to the home he desperately missed. And the shock of that realization threatened to suffocate him, ripping the breath from his lungs.

How long had he spent trying to leave the Aisling, and his past, behind? And now here, this girl, who had dared to stow away on his ship, seemed to be calling him to stay, without her knowing or realizing it. He was getting lost in those eyes that so perfectly mirrored the beauty of their shared home of Cregah. The rich greens. The gold of the sun. Even the black of her pupils reminded him of the black sands of its shores. Home.

"It's okay, Declan. Truly." Her words snapped him back to the present.

"I'm sorry all the same. You shouldn't have had to bear those on your own."

"And you would have aided me somehow had you known?" She flashed that smirk at him, the one he knew she put on to mock him.

"Perhaps. But perhaps not. We will never know now."

"Aren't you worried these attacks might impact the task at hand?"

"Shopping? No. We can handle panic as we shop."

"You know what I mean, Declan. How are we going to retrieve the fae from the council hall if I might freeze up at any moment?"

Declan looked at the ceiling, biding his time. He already knew his answer, but he didn't want her to know he'd already formed a contingency plan.

Aoife spoke again before he could reply. "You've already thought of that, haven't you? Already planned for that possibility during the short moments we've sat here together."

"Aye. It is part of being captain. When potential—" He didn't want to call it a 'problem.' That would indicate something was wrong with her. "When potential obstacles present themselves, one must devise remedies or solutions. And I prefer to identify those early rather than wait for them to spring on me in the heat of the moment. If possible."

"And what is the remedy for my…condition?"

"You speak of it as if it were a deformity of sorts."

"Isn't it?" Shame swept across her face as she tugged her bottom lip between her teeth.

"A deformity would imply that it's something innately wrong with you, and that is far from the case. These attacks are not you. They do not define you. And while they can seem insurmountable, they are not."

"But I've never been able to predict them. Or prevent them. They crop up with no warning. Where is my distraction? My curtain to hide what haunts me? The sea obviously is not helping me in the same way it helped you."

Declan couldn't help but smile at her rambling torrent of words, and he almost hoped she'd continue.

Almost. There wasn't quite time for that though, as he could see the edges of the Cregahn coastline in the harbor creeping past the windows. They would be docked soon.

"Aye. For me it was a distraction, but I've learned from others that while we may not be able to prevent them, we can learn to suppress them when they happen."

Her eyes widened, a sparkle he hoped would never die shining in them upon hearing his words. "Can you teach me?"

"Perhaps. But first, we must prepare to go ashore."

As if on cue, the crew began to scurry about out on the deck, announcing their arrival in Port Morshan.

Aoife tried to be patient, but Declan's offer to help her with the panic attacks was too enticing to be forgotten so easily.

Focus on the task at hand, Aoife.

She tried to do as her thoughts instructed, but it was difficult not to ponder the secrets to conquering her malady.

They do not define you. His words echoed in her mind. All these years she'd felt ashamed, like something was wrong with her, like something within her had gone awry as she was formed or as she grew. Some mistake or error in her very nature. But Declan, in one brief conversation, had given her another option. It was a sickness. Something from outside herself that attacked and took hold.

It was not her. It was a foe. And all foes could be defeated.

Declan had already stood and crossed the room to prepare to head ashore. He slid a dagger into an ankle sheath hidden within his boot and then another at his hip. His cutlass he left atop his desk.

"Are you ready?" he called, peering at her from the main chamber.

She was still getting used to this new rapport, his gruffness and rude tones now calmed and softened. It would have been more off-putting if she hadn't found it so welcome and endearing. She had been the one to suggest friendship, after all, and she found herself almost giddy to see he had so willingly obliged. How things had changed in a matter of days.

Her imagination rushed ahead of her though, with images of a possible future popping up against her will. A life on this ship, serving on his crew. Or a home on a distant, unknown shore, with a quaint cottage and a small garden and a love all her own.

She pushed the images back into the far recesses of her consciousness. She needed to focus, not get lost in fantasies and daydreams. Especially those that were far from likely to ever happen.

Stretching out her neck, she stood and found her footing more quickly than in the past. A glance down at her sleep-rumpled clothes had her hoping their shopping plans—whatever they might be—included acquiring a change of garments. Approaching Declan, she tried her best to smooth out the fabric at her waist.

"And how does this *shopping* know to come to us and where to find us?"

Had he some secret pirate method for sending word to the shores ahead of them? It seemed unlikely, but pirate life seemed intent on surprising her at every turn.

"Telepathy." Declan's expression was dead serious. She searched his eyes but found no sign of jest in them.

"Really?" If elves and dragons were indeed real, perhaps this form of magic existed as well.

"No."

Her shoulders slumped. With a roll of her eyes, she smacked him with the back of her hand. He'd fooled her. And she'd fallen for it so easily.

She did her best to recover some semblance of self-respect, but his deep laughter—so carefree—was impossible to ignore. All she could do was shake her head, purse her lips, and wait for him to settle. This was taking too long.

"Are you done laughing at me?"

Declan composed himself, sucking in a gulp of air before he spoke. "I think so. Your face though." His smile grew.

"What about my face?" She wondered what he might poke fun at this time. As much as she wanted to be annoyed with him, she was finding it increasingly more difficult. This lightheartedness was such a change. And not an unwelcome one.

"You're just so cute when you fall for things."

Cute.

She tried to dissect the word, peeling back the meanings as she knew them. She'd never been called "cute" before and had only heard the word used by the women in town regarding babies or children's paintings. Was it an endearing term? Or was he calling her childish?

"Don't worry, Aoife," he explained. "It's a good thing."

"What is?"

"Being cute."

She started to challenge him, ask him why he'd bother clarifying such a thing, but he spoke again. "You looked concerned about my words is all. A little hurt even."

While some of the mirth was still present in those damn sea-gray eyes, there was a flash of tenderness again. Something moved in her gut, but she couldn't determine what it was. A warmth settling in, grounding her. Comfort.

Again, future possibilities whirled in her mind, but she now began to see him beside her in the various scenes. She tried to blink them away, but each was replaced with a new one. And in each she found him to be more of a companion than a friend. Holding her hand. Brushing her hair from her forehead. Placing a kiss on her cheek.

She clenched her eyes shut. No. This would do her no good right now. Would only cloud her ability to do what needed to be done. He was a friend, and he could only ever be such.

"Are you okay? You look hurt again." The previous amusement still hovered at the edge of his words.

"I'm fine. Just trying to focus." Another stretch of her neck, though it didn't need it. "Are you going to answer my question now? With the real answer?"

"What's the fun in that?"

She answered him with a frown, earning her another laugh.

"Okay, okay. Gavin's getting word to them as we speak."

"How did he know to do that?" He raised a brow, and she quickly interrupted whatever he was about to say. "And don't say telepathy again."

He clicked his tongue at her. "Always so curious to know my ways. If you insist on knowing though, I gave him the command this morning. While you were still sleeping off last night's fun."

A knock sounded at the door, and without looking away from her, he gave the command to enter.

Aoife turned with some hesitation, taking another moment to drag her eyes away from Declan's. Tommy stood there, a look of curious expectation on his face. If he suspected anything was happening between her and his captain, he didn't voice it. But it seemed more and more obvious that he sensed something in the air.

And it didn't seem to bother him.

"Captain. Aoife. When you're ready..." He gestured with an arm toward the door, inviting them to lead the way out of the cabin into the sticky air of Morshan.

Declan reached for her, his hand hovering at her waist, warming the air between them. When she turned toward the door, his hand made contact with the small of her back. Not at all unwanted. Warmth bubbled up into her chest.

As she stepped forward, his hand fell away, and the resulting emptiness and longing tingled along her spine. She hoped Tommy couldn't see it all written across her face.

The feelings resisted being pushed away. She was as desperate to ignore them as they were to pester her, but it would do her no good to become preoccupied with hidden meanings behind every move and touch.

He was merely being kind. A friend. Just as she had claimed she wanted.

Cait looked around at the nearly empty pub and the handful of afternoon regulars. Word had come an hour earlier by way of one of the young kids from the docks. The note sealed with Declan's siren insignia in black wax had provided nothing more than a list of items, a location, and a time. And the instruction to come alone.

He hadn't given her much time, but it hadn't been an issue. Each Rogues member took a shift at the pub in case of just such an occasion, when Cait might need them to run an errand.

She hadn't paused to question his list of items but had jotted them down on a scrap of paper, which she'd tucked into the folds of a napkin before sliding it—and a small glass of rum—to the girl, Kira, seated at the bar. A slight dip of Kira's chin had confirmed she understood.

The girl had been part of the Rogues since she'd moved into Morshan from one of the southern villages over a year ago. Her whole family had vanished while she was at the secret market to sell medicines banned by the council. Finding her home eerily empty, all their belongings gone, Kira had fled with nothing but the items she carried.

For days Kira had stayed off the roads, sticking close to the trees to avoid whomever the council had sent for them. When she'd made it to Morshan, Cait had found her standing in awe of the town, her jaw hanging open at what must have been a marvel to see.

It was how they all looked when they arrived. Eyes wide. Jaw agape. Like a child standing before a buffet of decadent desserts after years of eating nothing but bland porridge.

Cait had heard stories about the other villages on Cregah.

Morshan was the anomaly.

Despite the inevitable underlying layer of filth, which plagued all port cities, Morshan was well-kept, and its people lived well. The paint on the buildings was as fresh as the abundant food provided to the residents by the council. Brightly colored gardens adorned the grounds of each home, the blooms covering the smells of the many travelers who visited and left their muck behind.

But life in Morshan was as much a facade as Cait's maintained residence above the pub.

As false as it was, she knew the people in this town were blessed in a way. While they too lived in fear of exile, they didn't suffer the same hardships as those elsewhere. The starvation. The sickness. The poverty.

No business remained open on Cregah without the council's blessing, and the council in turn used these establishments to provide everything to the people. Most of the money earned by the merchants and business owners was paid back to the council via monthly dues, but few complained, because it meant the residents always had access to food, medicine, clothes, and wares brought in by the pirates.

The very drink Cait offered was supplied by the same pirates who would later come in and drink it. If they realized it, they didn't care.

The same was not so in other areas of Cregah, where the little food the council distributed was usually rotten by the time it arrived on the carts hired to deliver it. Medicine was nonexistent, and most other items were scarce.

The once prosperous nation had slowly deteriorated as the council changed its focus during the centuries following the signing of the treaty. Eventually outlawing more than just violence, they'd closed the markets where locals had sold their goods, insisting everything could be provided by the pirates who had signed the treaty—goods they would then distribute to all the people.

But they'd either been unable to do this for the other towns on Cregah, or they'd lied and had simply been neglecting the people out of heartlessness.

Cait wasn't sure which it was.

Not that it mattered in the end.

She was determined to see that the people of her beloved nation didn't have to live in fear and poverty any longer. So every time a Rogues member encountered someone who hadn't arrived by ship, they sent them on to the pub so Cait could chat with them, ensure they weren't a spy from the council, get them clothed, fill their bellies, and give them hope.

She'd done so with nearly fifteen individuals, but for each person she helped, she knew there were many more who never made it to her, who still suffered back in their home villages.

Kira, in fact, had been the last to come her way. A year had passed, and no one new had arrived.

Cait didn't want to know what was keeping more from getting here. But she suspected many didn't want to leave their homes, no matter how bad life got. It was their homeland. Hard. But beloved all the same.

Kira had trusted Cait and readily stepped into the Rogues, eager to do whatever she could to take down those who had stolen her family from her.

And now Cait was trusting her to round up a few of the others around town, to discreetly secure the items from Declan's list, and to get it all back to her office on time.

She glanced at the clock above the bar. Kira had been gone over two hours, and Declan would be expecting her soon. She could only hope they'd been able to locate everything he needed.

The door opened behind her, and Kira entered. A quick nod told Cait all she needed to know.

She tossed the towel she'd been holding to Kira, who took her spot behind the bar. No one in the room took note of the exchange and would likely have thought nothing of it even if they had, as it was not unusual for Cait to leave the pub for a bit now and then to run errands or to take a break, and these slow afternoons were the ideal time to do just that. But just to be sure, she made a point to voice her plan to head upstairs for some rest before the evening rush of revelers.

While she'd taken the door from the street with Declan last week, she couldn't use that entrance in the middle of the day when shadows were scarce and eyes were watching.

At the back of the pub, in the storeroom beside the stairs that led to her childhood residence above the business, a hidden door barely wider than her shoulders led to an underground passage.

She knew most of those currently in the pub, but she still didn't trust them not to rat her out. One never knew when the council might call in a debt from any of the pirates who frequented Morshan's streets, no matter how many times they came to the pub or how friendly they were.

Loyalty on Cregah was bought, not earned. And the council had more to offer the pirates than the locals of the town did.

But she had to keep up the ruse.

She trudged up the stairs with heavy and tired steps until she reached her room and placed a bag of sand on the bed, causing the floorboards to creak, alerting the patrons downstairs that someone had settled in for some rest.

Leaning against the wall, she removed her boots with care and then returned the way she'd come, carrying her boots under her arm as she kept to the edge of the hallway and the stairs, the boards remaining silent under her weight.

The back wall of the bar hid the stairs and storeroom well enough that no one would notice her tiptoe around the corner and slip into the hidden passageway, replacing the wooden door above her head.

It had been that secret doorway, discovered years ago, that had sparked a sense of adventure in her, temporarily easing the grief over her parents' deaths.

She'd entered it without hesitation, not even bothering to wonder where Declan had run off to. He hadn't handled the loss well, which was to be expected for a kid so young and so enamored with his parents—as most kids were apt to be—and she'd had no notion of where he went or how he spent his time.

She should have kept better track of him, but they had never been close, and if she knew nothing else about her brother, she knew of his need for space.

And she'd been more than willing to grant him that as she explored that passage, her fingers tracing the wooden walls that transitioned to stone as she descended the stairs.

She'd tried to mentally picture where the passage led, but as it had turned one way and then the other, every twenty or thirty feet, she'd lost track of all sense of location or heading. After thirty minutes of tiptoeing along, she'd come to a split in the corridor. Nothing differentiated one way from the other. No difference in light or scent or air.

During that first venture into the passageway, she'd gone left and found herself in a tunnel that narrowed until ending abruptly at a sharp drop-off into the Aisling Sea just northeast of the docks, hidden by the trees that sprang out along the rocky cliff face.

She later discovered the other corridor led to her mother's office, and it was that one she needed to take now. And quickly.

A small lantern sat on the bottom stair, and she lit it as quickly and quietly as she could.

While she could have made the trip in the dark, the way having been etched into her mind after so many years of using this path, time was not on her side, and she'd need the light to navigate the uneven ground beneath her feet more quickly.

With her boots back on her feet and laced up, she ran ahead, hoping to get there before Declan arrived.

It was risky having him use the street entrance, but it would raise fewer alarms than having them enter a near-empty pub and then disappear into the back. When that entrance wasn't hidden in shadows, it sat nondescript among a row of shops and eateries.

Declan was a skilled enough pirate. He should have no problem getting around without raising suspicion.

Cait reached the top of the stairs and heard voices on the other side of the door.

Apparently, he hadn't come alone.

Her feet slipped on some loose pebbles as she hurried to unlock it for him. She pulled the door open a crack to verify it was Declan who waited for her. She had just begun to open it wider for him when a girl—the one from the pub that night—stepped around him and moved to enter.

Cait didn't budge as she looked at Declan. How could he have been so stupid to bring her here?

"I see the *come alone* part only applied to me?" She put an edge into her words.

Declan leaned in, his face hovering over the girl's shoulder as he whispered, "I couldn't very well leave her on the ship."

She needed to get them off the street, but something twinged deep in her bones. If this girl undid all their years of work, if she were actually a spy sent from the council…

Cait stepped aside and ushered them in, but once the door was locked behind them, she didn't make a move to lead them to her office.

In the dim light of her lantern, she searched the girl's face, as if something there might provide a hint as to her identity and motives.

The girl twitched under her stare, her eyes flicking to Declan, her body shifting closer to his ever so slightly.

Well, this is an interesting development.

Declan was the first to break the standoff. "I can vouch for her, Cait."

Cait turned to him but didn't soften her tone a bit as she said, "You'd better, because otherwise it'll be our heads."

Without another word, she turned on her heel and led them down the hallway.

She pushed her office door open and gestured for them to enter, following her idiot brother and the girl inside before locking the door behind them. Turning, she found them standing in the center of the room. The girl—a full head shorter than Declan—was looking about.

Cait strode past them, trying to ignore the tension in her limbs that reminded her how those men had come looking for this girl last week.

She motioned to the chairs before them. "Please, sit."

Cait settled herself behind her desk as it struck her how similar this was to the last time she'd hosted him here.

She watched intently as Declan ushered the girl to one of the proffered seats. He showed her such care, such genuine grace. Had her dear brother, the ruthless pirate, gone soft? Surely it wasn't a ploy. He had no reason to act any part in front of Cait, and there was no one else to play to.

Unless he was playing the girl.

"I don't believe we've met," Cait said, raising her brow in invitation to the girl.

"Aoife," the girl replied, with no hint of the meekness Cait expected. "Cascade."

That name. No wonder that pair of pirates had been looking for her.

"An heir then," Cait said, catching how Aoife shifted at the word and how Declan reached for her. He stayed himself, pulling back with apparent reluctance.

"Aye," Declan said. "A most valuable addition to our side, I think." His expression betrayed none of the feelings Cait was certain lay behind his behavior. "Did you manage to acquire the items we needed?"

"I believe so, but to be honest, I only just arrived when you did. I haven't yet had a chance to review what my crew collected."

"Funny you call them your *crew*, almost as if you wished to be a pirate yourself, sister."

She ignored him, needing to keep that longing from distracting her. With a bob of her chin, she gestured to a haphazard pile of fabric on the table against the wall. "A curious assortment you requested, Declan. Not easily acquired. It's not as though we can go to the market or a local shop to find these, you know."

"Aye, but if anyone could do it, you could, Cait," he said and then stood to go inspect the goods. "Plus, at least we only needed garments and cloth. Nothing too large and hard to conceal."

Cait watched Aoife, once again inspecting her for any sign the girl wasn't a runaway but a spy. She scolded herself for letting Aoife into this room, into this life of hers, behind the veil of secrecy.

But Declan had a knack for sensing traps. He would never have brought her—warming feelings or no—had he thought she might betray them.

At least that's what Cait needed to believe.

"So, Aoife. How has life on a pirate ship treated you?" She tried to give her as warm a smile as she could muster, but she didn't know how well she pulled it off given all the doubts and worry that wouldn't quite dissolve.

Aoife seemed to startle, her eyes blinking below her scrunched brow, as if she couldn't fathom why Cait would bother talking to her.

"The food could be better, but the company—" Her words cut off, and she looked to Declan, seemingly out of habit.

The warming feelings are mutual then.

Cait's eyes narrowed with this suspicion, but she recovered quickly, hoping Aoife wouldn't realize how much she was learning with this encounter.

"I hope they're treating you well. There are far worse crews and ships you could have stumbled upon."

Something flashed across Aoife's features. Pain. Fear even.

What happened to her this past week?

"Indeed," Declan said, returning to his seat. "Far worse crews. Everything looks to be in order." He gave a nod toward the table.

"Given the list, I can assume you plan to enter the council hall and pass for a member of one of the crews in attendance tomorrow evening?"

A nod from him. Another glance at him from the girl.

"It would benefit you to know, then, that I have someone inside the council hall who can help." Cait ignored how Aoife's eyes widened at this ever so slightly. "She can't—won't—help outright for risk of being outed, but she can help you get in at least."

Cait explained how the servant's entrance would be left unlocked and how they were to station their lookouts in the hallways. Aoife tensed as she spoke, and Cait couldn't help but wonder how the girl would manage with being back home. She had so many questions for her.

Why had she fled? Did she know the truth about the council? Was she truly ready to betray them?

Surely Declan had asked her all of this, and Cait had no choice but to trust him. Time was ticking by, and this was the only play they had.

With all of Declan's questions answered and the plan laid out, he moved to gather up the clothing they'd need for their ruse.

Cait followed them to the door, watching as Declan ushered Aoife out in front of him. Had she not known otherwise, she would have suspected him to be a doting lover, not a pirate of wild reputation.

Once Aoife stepped out into the darkened hallway, Cait grabbed Declan's elbow. He turned his chin over his shoulder, as if unwilling to let Aoife completely out of even his peripheral vision.

"Declan. Be careful."

He flashed her that stupid smirk of his. "Where's the fun in that?"

Cait lowered her voice to a whisper. "With her, I mean."

His eyes twitched, and Cait couldn't tell if he was questioning her meaning or challenging her words.

"I mean it." Before she could comment further, warn him of how dangerous it was to get too close to Aoife, he gave a final nod and was gone.

Cait stood in the doorway long after they'd exited and shut the door to the street at the end of the hallway behind them. She'd need to go lock it again, of course, but she couldn't yet, frozen by new fear and worry, not just for the mission at hand, but for her brother's heart as well.

All the preparations had been made and the crew briefings wrapped up, but Declan still hadn't been able to shake the odd warning from his sister. Throughout the entire evening, he'd been distracted by her words.

If Aoife had noticed his quiet demeanor, she hadn't let on, hadn't pushed him to explain it. Perhaps she assumed he was merely nervous over the task ahead, fearful their plan would fail.

He should have been thinking of the plan, but he told himself it was solid and set, with little need to worry over it further. His men knew what to do, and Aoife would be by his side the whole time so he could ensure she didn't stumble or falter.

Or get in the way.

He swept that thought aside, a remnant of his former opinion that she was nothing more than a nuisance. She remained clumsy and awkward, but despite the trouble that could cause, he didn't hold it against her as he once had.

Pacing, he trod the familiar path in his chamber that had worn the old carpet down to its threads. With Aoife relaxing in the bedroom, working to calm her mind before they left for the council hall, he was left to his own thoughts.

And they plagued him, like a swarm of flies that wouldn't leave no matter how often he shooed them away.

None of this worrying would help them in their task. It would only bring cloudy thinking and poor judgment. He needed to be prepared, focused. But every time he managed to get Cait's warning firmly tucked away, it slammed into him again.

Be careful with her.

What had she meant? There were two obvious messages there, and it behooved him to consider both. He needed to protect Aoife and ensure nothing happened to her but also be watchful and guarded. He'd never gotten the sense from Aoife that she secretly worked for the council; he'd pondered the possibility only once, early on during her stay aboard the ship.

Still, what would going back there do to her? Would her loyalty be swayed?

He needed to prepare for all possibilities, but that latter one—her turning against him in the end—the mere thought of it felt like a dagger tip at his breast. A warning of the pain it would wrought if that happened.

He roughed a hand over his chin and then behind his neck. A desperate attempt to clear his mind and push away the anxiety all these thoughts brought on.

A rustle of fabric behind him made him turn. Aoife leaned against the archway between the main room and the sleeping quarters. With her arms crossed over her chest and her legs crossed at the ankles, she displayed a surprising amount of swagger. She was getting quite good at mimicking him, which would help in this next adventure. He needed her to look every bit a pirate tonight.

"You look—" she said before stopping to chew on the inside of her lip, as if the word she'd planned to use had evaded her. Or she'd thought better of saying it.

Declan didn't feel like bantering, but he couldn't risk having her worried about him or knowing he was preparing himself for her possible betrayal. "Dashing? Handsome beyond measure? Irresistible?"

The last word was out before he could stop it. The tension between them had been palpable since the night of his birthday, and he had little doubt she felt it too. He didn't need to tug at that invisible connection, but he couldn't seem to resist doing so either. And every time he toyed with it, tiptoed along it, letting a hand linger on her shoulder, allowing his gaze to settle on her body, or whispering a delicate word in her ear, it only grew stronger and more adamant.

Be careful with her.

Yes, his sister must have intended it as a double-edged warning. But with the look in Aoife's eye now, after he had planted a seed of desire with those blasted words, he wondered if he should have been more careful with himself.

This would end nowhere good.

Or it might be the one good thing in your life in years.

And there. A spark of hope somewhere deep in his chest. It was small but bright. And while he couldn't afford to give it the oxygen to burst into flame, he couldn't bear to blow it out completely either. What harm was there in a dream? A dream of hope and love and family.

It took him a second to realize Aoife had never answered him. How long had they been standing here studying each other?

Aoife dropped an ear to her shoulder, looking the epitome of calm and collected as her fingers tapped against her arm. "Well, I was going to say, 'tired' or 'worried,' but…"

He held a breath and realized the books had gotten it all wrong when they spoke of hearts stopping in anticipation. Because his now thundered in his ears as he waited to hear which of his previous words she would choose to elaborate on. If any.

A light sigh escaped her lips before she added, "Your suggestions would apply as well." Her chin dropped, and she pulled her eyes down, as if the part she was playing had become too difficult to maintain and the embarrassed and awkward girl within had stumbled out. He thought he heard her add a whispered "always," but he couldn't tell now, with her lips hidden from view.

He must have heard correctly though, as a flush of pink washed across her cheeks, nearly hiding the freckles below her eyes. He wondered if her skin warmed noticeably when that happened.

"No point in being embarrassed by merely agreeing to the obvious, Aoife." He hoped making light of it would be better than ignoring it altogether, wash away some of the tension mounting between them.

Lifting her head, she said, "I'm not embarrassed." But her features said otherwise as the pink only deepened. Something sparked in her eyes, but he couldn't quite tell what it was. He knew what he hoped it might be.

A teasing smile tugged at her lips. "I'm merely worried all this talk of your irresistibly dashing good looks will make your head swell to the point we won't be able to enter the council hall doorway."

"Then I suppose we'll need to find another way in?"

"Or I could cut you down a peg or two." Declan waited. She seemed to be studying his face, looking for some piece of him that she could insult. He nearly laughed when a full minute passed. And then another.

He was the first one to speak. "Surely you can think of something negative to say about me?"

"It is just so hard to choose one. There are so many." She tossed her head, as if she'd forgotten the hair she would normally fling behind her had been chopped off.

"Liar," he said.

Aoife moved away from the doorframe and took a step toward him. Then another. She'd at least gotten better at walking aboard the ship—at least while they were in port. She kept her eyes lowered as she reached a timid hand toward his chest. He froze, his breath trapped in his lungs as Cait's words echoed in his mind for the millionth time.

Be careful with her.

She knew where he kept the fae's letter. Would she be so brazen as to take it from him now, when he had his guard down? Had she been playing him this whole time?

He couldn't risk haste, so he waited and watched her hand slide into his jacket. It wasn't the letter she pulled out but his pocket watch.

The chain it was attached to pulled taut as she held it in her hands and flipped it open. "It's nearly time."

With a click of the watch's clasp, she added, "We should get ready."

Aoife's fingers tingled as she fumbled with the purple fabric they'd acquired from Declan's sister. He had gotten it tied around his waist, but she'd insisted on fixing it to keep it from looking ridiculous. With no mirror aboard the ship, it was a wonder the captain managed to look halfway decent most days. *More than halfway.*

She shushed the thought. Though, what harm was there in admitting his good looks? None. Like admiring the beauty of a sunset on the sea or the rocky cliffs of Cregah overlooking the black sand of the cove.

But those couldn't reach out and touch her.

For the past day and a half she'd been racked with confusion over this new desire to have him near, and those damn visions of a future together invaded her thoughts when she least expected.

She huffed a sigh in frustration before realizing he would hear it and have no idea what she was thinking.

"It's just a sash, Aoife. No need to get angry with it."

She refused to admit what was truly bothering her. "But it won't sit right. Blasted thing!"

"We are pirates, you know. We don't have to look perfect."

"Yes, but you're walking into the council hall. You're expected to look somewhat put together and not like you just strolled in from mercilessly pillaging merchants for the past two months."

"Aw, if only that was how I'd spent the last months." There was a longing in his voice, and she realized she had little idea what he'd been through recently.

When she looked up at him, she found him facing the window, his attention on the setting sun.

Out there was where he belonged. On the sea. Not on this island or in a council hall. The realization fell in her gut like a weight dropped into the ocean. And all those visions she'd struggled to be rid of seemed to vanish in an instant, as if they'd been squashed by that weight.

She straightened her shoulders. "You'll be able to get back to that soon." She'd expected to feel free, the weight of her longing lifted by the confirmation that it was the sea he wanted, not her. But it had been replaced with something decidedly worse.

She should have tried harder to keep those thoughts at bay. Then she wouldn't feel such deep disappointment now.

"Not soon enough."

His words pricked her heart. How he must long to be away from her. She had thought she'd seen the same hope echoed in his gaze, but she had clearly misunderstood.

She would not let this distract her. There had never been any future for them. They were cut from a different cloth. Destined to tread different paths. And those paths had only converged temporarily for this one shared mission and goal.

And that goal was what she needed to focus on now.

"Aye. I suppose that's true," she said, now reaching up to adjust his shirt and jacket and brush lint off his shoulders, anything to help her avoid his gaze. "But we will get the fae, get the dagger, crush the council, and get you on your way to distant seas and new adventures."

She ignored the sight of his shoulders rising as he took a breath. Ignored the way that breath sent tingles down her spine when it swept across her forehead.

"Is that all," he said. Not a question.

"Simple as that." She lowered her hands then and took a step back to look him over. "That'll have to do."

He reached behind him and grabbed the gold sash from atop his desk. "Your turn."

It had been one thing to be touching him, but to have his hands on her and around her waist, straightening and adjusting her garments? Sands, help her. The ghosts of her hope threatened to rise from where they'd been trampled.

No, she would let them rest in peace.

There was nothing in his touch that indicated they were anything more than two friends preparing for battle, and the last thing she needed was to have her head muddied by a dream that could never be.

Her breath hitched as he moved his hands behind her and pulled her closer with the gold fabric at her waist, causing her to stumble. She nearly fell into him but managed to catch herself before her hands made contact with his chest again.

"Already getting into character, I see."

She could hear the smirk in his words, but she dared not look up, unsure what his face might do to that damn hope she'd laid to rest.

"Do you pretend to be drunk often in your escapades?" She tried to sound casual, but her voice trembled slightly as she spoke. "It seems to be a common ruse for you."

"It is rather effective, I must say."

They stood mere inches away from each other now, and the heat of his body mixing with the stickiness in the air would have normally made her uncomfortable, given the many layers of garments she wore. But now she was thankful for all the barriers between them. If only Tommy or Gavin or anyone else would knock and save her.

They were too close. Altogether too close. Each breath caused his scent of sea and spice to nudge at the ghosts of her dreams. She needed to get out of here before she lost herself to something she could never have.

His hands moved to adjust her jacket, just as she had done with his, but where her hands had brushed along his shoulders, his went up along her neck to straighten out the collar.

She closed her eyes at the touch and hoped he didn't read too much into it. She simply couldn't bear to look at him while his skin touched hers.

His touch lightened but didn't leave, even after it seemed all the necessary adjustments must have been made. She felt ridiculous standing there, eyes closed, arms dangling lifeless at her sides. But she didn't trust herself not to look even more foolish if she moved. Hopefully he'd read it as her final effort to prepare mentally for the night.

The warmth of his hands and feather lightness of his fingers trailed across her shoulders and down her arms. And when his hands met hers—a breath of a touch she couldn't quite be sure was real and not imagined—he whispered her name.

A hum of a response was all she could manage as she forced her eyes to open and take him in. What she had expected to see, she couldn't say, but it certainly wasn't this. The longing she'd seen in his face earlier, when he'd been looking at the sea, had returned.

Now directed at her.

Everything disappeared—the cabin, the ship, the council, the fae—as if nothing else mattered but the man before her. Her mind went blank yet whirred with a million thoughts. Such an odd sensation to feel empty and full all at once. Full of hope and desire and fear. As if the touch of his hand and her name on his breath had fully resurrected every dream and hope that had been dashed away.

And she didn't know what to do with any of it.

This had never been a part of the plans for her life, and now all she had to do was dare to reach out and grab it, to take it for herself. *Like a pirate.*

Her hand twitched, and a tingle went up her arm as it brushed against his fingers. All of time stood still and yet rushed by too quickly. The stormy grays of his eyes held her. She found herself drowning in them, even as she realized she'd never truly breathed until now.

Was this what love felt like? A confusing yet thrilling, tangled web of emotions and sensations? To be both wholly vulnerable and yet firmly secure, to feel weightless and yet grounded, to want time to both cease and yet hurry up, to savor the moment and yet to yearn for everything the future held?

Declan's fingers laced with hers. He was no longer the rough pirate she'd met in that alley or the one who had attempted to scare her away.

This was Declan. Not Captain McCallagh. And while he might insist those men were one in the same, she knew the truth. He had opened a door in that wall within him and beckoned her to enter.

And she gladly did so.

When his hand grasped hers, the warmth of him engulfing her, she handed herself over to it. Whatever this meant, whatever this would bring, whatever was to come, it would be okay. As long as he was here.

She didn't flinch when he moved again, as he brought himself closer to her. His face—dashing and irresistible indeed—inched toward her, and she dared not move, for fear it would release him from whatever spell he might be under.

He held her captive with one hand and reached the other to her chin. Every bit of her seemed to freeze as the edge of his finger lifted her face to meet his. He paused, his breath tickling her skin, and then all of time vanished as his lips found hers.

It wasn't like their first kiss, behind the pub. Where that had been forceful and frightening, this felt like coming home, like finding the one place she belonged after living her whole life off kilter.

Light and gentle, his lips moved on hers, and she melted ever deeper into them. Tingling pinpricks danced over her skin, uncomfortable and delightful at once. Like his kiss had finally woken her from a deep slumber. Like all the tales she'd read about in books. Now she understood why kisses held so much power—the power to break spells and conquer curses. Reaching her free hand up to his neck, she held him against her, as if he might disappear like an apparition or a dream if she dared let go.

Declan moved his hand from her chin to her waist and then around to the small of her back, pressing her still closer to him.

And then he stopped. Before she could protest, his lips pulled away, his breath rushing out of him. In his eyes she found an odd mix of satisfaction and sadness.

Had she done something wrong? Did he regret it? She didn't know what to say or what to do. All she knew was there was no friendship here. All remnants of hope for that less complicated arrangement had been dashed away.

"Well," she said, breathless and awkward as ever. Licking her lips and then biting them, she searched for any words to say, trying to read his thoughts. And failing.

His hand left her back and reached up to his lips, and she wasn't sure if he was trying to wipe away the feeling of her kiss or capture it as if he could tuck it away in his pocket. If there was any regret, she couldn't see it, especially not with his fingers still grasping her hand, clinging to it like a lifeline.

"That was…" He paused, and self-doubt rushed through her again.

But before he could possibly hurt her with the truth, she finished his sentence. "Unexpected?"

"Not altogether unexpected. I've been wanting to do that for a few days now."

Leave it to a pirate to be so brazen and forthright.

"Truly?" Her brow creased from surprise. She could not seem to grasp onto anything witty or charming to say, lost in this new reality.

"Aye. I tried to ignore it. Told myself it would never work out. But…"

"You failed."

"You don't make it easy, you know."

Aoife's mind whirled, and the whole room seemed to shift and rock around her as she was thrown off-balance by this development. When had things changed, and how had this happened? It wasn't that she was against it. Not in the slightest. But it threw another complication into the already messy situation. A delightfully wonderful complication, but a complication nonetheless.

"But what? How? When?" Her thoughts manifested against her will and tumbled out before she could stop them.

She didn't even care when he let out a string of light laughs. She would have laughed too, if she'd had any control over her voice.

But he didn't answer her. She found no hint of an answer in his eyes either, which never left hers.

Aoife gave his hand a squeeze, like she was reassuring herself that he was, in fact, holding her. It wasn't her imagination. Wasn't one of those dreamy visions that had vanished earlier.

"I was convinced you didn't care," she said.

"I didn't want to," he said. Her pain at hearing these words must have been visible, because he added, "Want to care, that is. This—" He lifted their clasped hands a bit for emphasis. "This was never something I wanted."

Her chest hurt as if his words had stabbed her. And again her features betrayed the sting as she winced.

"Nothing is coming out right, Aoife. See what you've done to me?" He seemed to be trying hard to right himself as he stumbled about with his speech.

But she thought she understood, even without his ability to articulate it clearly.

Just as she had never let herself dream of anything beyond her duty to the council, never once giving thought to love and family, he hadn't either. Not only that, he had spent years actively pushing those dreams away. He hadn't been raised with everything set out before him, hadn't been destined for a life of service to the country. He had the freedom to choose for himself, even if his choices were limited under the council's rule, yet he'd denied himself the possibility of love and intimacy, choosing instead a life on the sea.

"Why? Why would you not want this?"

"It's complicated."

"I'm sure I would understand. If you let me."

"And I will. At some point. But right now—" His eyes darted to the window, where the sky had been painted with the deep pinks and oranges from the setting sun. "We need to head ashore and crash a dinner."

Of course this would have to wait. Once they finished at the council hall, they'd have time to navigate this new course.

"You ready?" Declan asked, dipping his head down an inch to better look at her.

A gulp, a nod. It was all she could muster as the nerves hit her. She could do this, and she would.

With Declan beside her, she could face anything.

The walk to the council hall wasn't as long as it was uncomfortable. It was only a mile from the edge of Port Morshan, but Aoife had suggested a different path than the one commonly used.

This path had been hers and Lani's. A lost and forgotten trail. She'd never known what it was for, but as it led from the port to the servant's entrance, she and her sister had imagined many a fanciful tale about its purpose and use.

Walking the path with Declan now—Tommy and Gavin following close behind, each donning the same purple sash she'd placed around Declan's waist—she couldn't remember any of those stories they'd made up.

She tried to focus on her steps, careful not to make too much noise on the twigs and rocks. How were her steps so much louder than the men's? They were certainly heavier than she was, but she found herself occasionally turning to check and make sure they were still with her. Maybe when this was all over she'd ask for lessons on stealth.

Why she might need stealth as a skill in the future, she didn't know, and at the thought, a short burst of laughter escaped her before she could stop it. She clamped a hand over her mouth and flashed Declan an apologetic look.

He merely shook his head, an amused grin on his face.

They hadn't touched each other since leaving his cabin, and this did nothing but stir up the familiar self-doubt, which told her how he probably regretted what had happened. After all, he'd said he never wanted it.

A small voice pushed against that doubt, insisting he was simply focused on the task at hand and didn't want to raise questions from the two men accompanying them.

Yes, that was the voice she wanted to believe. If only the doubt wasn't so much louder.

She tried to push it away as they walked. They needed to hurry if they were going to make it to the hall before the sun had completely set and they could no longer see where they were going. The pirates might be stealthy, but she doubted they had the ability to see in the pitch-dark of Cregah at night. Especially in these trees.

Another laugh threatened, but she held it back. Her mind was not making this trek easy, and she needed to keep it in check if she were going to succeed at not getting them into trouble once they were inside.

After another five minutes, they arrived at the edge of the forest that bordered the council hall grounds. Aoife nearly stepped out into the open in her desperation to get this over with, but Declan reached an arm across to stop her. Her body reacted to his touch, a single, quick chill through her nerves.

The sensation was hard to ignore, though she managed, focusing instead on the building before her. Everything she'd hoped to avoid—all the memories, the dreams, the regrets—slammed into her as if she'd run face-first into it.

The panic was building, and she felt as though her heart were racing, but she knew it was an illusion. How many times had she been sure her heart would thump right out of her, only to find her pulse normal and steady?

It's all in your head. You can control it. Focus. Breathe.

With eyes closed, she began to count her breaths. Tommy and Gavin must have stepped closer to them, though they remained silent, and she wondered if Declan could tell what was happening. The last episode hadn't been as bad because he'd been there, with a hand on her knee and a reassuring word of understanding.

But he didn't touch her now. He only leaned close to her ear and whispered, "Breathe. Focus. It's okay."

Such simple words, but with each one, so low she was sure only she could hear it, the panic eased. It didn't leave completely, but it let up enough that she could open her eyes and peek up at him.

In the dimming light, the gray of his eyes were more pronounced, like the sea under a sky of thick clouds.

"You okay?" Again Declan kept his voice low, but the other men inched forward as if to check on her.

"Yes, better. Thanks." She wanted to say more, to remark how she'd known this would be hard but hadn't expected it to hit her so soon. But now was not the time for long, drawn-out conversations.

She turned back toward the council hall. Creeping ivy obscured the gray stone walls, covering the windows and stretching out like spindly fingers eager to squeeze the life out of anyone who entered.

It had been her home, but now as she looked upon it, she saw it for what it was. Not a home, but a prison. Not a place of warmth and love and family, but one of service, duty, and control.

And for the first time since she'd run, since she'd turned her back on the council, she grasped the truth.

She hadn't killed Lani.

They had.

Melina was no more her mother than Tommy was her father.

Tommy. Gavin. Declan. This could be her new family.

Pirates.

Who would have thought? Lani would have found it to be such an adventure, completely out of character for Aoife, who only ever read about romance and danger but never dared seek it out herself.

Pirates had killed her sister. And whether they had done so willingly or not, she now wasn't sure.

Declan hadn't given her the name of her sister's executioners, but even if he had, she didn't know what she'd say if she ever met them. She wanted to believe she'd forgive them, tell them the comforting words she told herself. It wasn't their fault, just as it wasn't her fault.

Would she tell them it was okay? Tell them she understood? Or would she hold onto resentment and anger?

Later, she told herself. *Focus on what's at hand.*

Now was not the time to let her mind wander, yet she'd done just that. Still, the men waited with surprising patience.

"There," she said with a nod toward a small door in the side of the building, tucked between a pair of bushes. "That's where we enter."

"You ready?" Declan asked, and she knew it was meant more for her than for his men.

Another nod was all she could muster.

"Remember the plan. It's all an act, but don't overdo it. Just pretend you're back on the ship." He shot her a wink, and had they not been about to infiltrate the home of the ruthless rulers of their nation, she might have smacked him or pinched him for it. Instead she settled for an exaggerated roll of her eyes. An expression she'd only ever dared share with Lani.

For you, Lani.

A deep, calming breath washed those words down into her belly, and she hoped she'd remember them no matter what happened within those walls tonight.

The four of them crept out of the trees and over the small metal fence, not wanting to risk making the gate squeak by opening it, and then moved across the lawn and between the bushes toward the servant's entrance.

Aoife held her breath as Declan pressed the lever on the door's handle. If Cait's spy hadn't come through, their whole plan was ruined.

But the door opened with ease, and she stepped inside with Declan close behind her, the warmth from his hand hovering over the small of her back.

Thankfully the men had spent every spare moment memorizing the map she'd drawn. They had no room for error.

The hallway before them was wide and bare, devoid of any decoration, as it was designed for carrying in large deliveries of goods. On the left sat the door leading to the pantries and the storehouses for the dry goods. On the right lay the kitchen, its open doorway allowing the scents of the roast pork and fresh bread they'd served for dinner to waft toward them. Aoife's stomach rumbled in response, and she pressed a hand to it as if that could quiet it.

There was none of the usual gossip and chatter of the kitchen staff, but the kitchen wasn't empty either. A solitary voice sang in a low tone.

Stopping at the edge of the doorway, they didn't plaster their bodies against the wall but leaned back casually in case someone should turn the corner up ahead and find them loitering.

Declan had his forehead against the wall, as if he were sick from too much drink, while Tommy and Gavin pretended to be having a whispered conversation. Aoife turned away from them to peek into the room.

Marta, the old cook who had hated her—hated everyone, actually—stood at the worktable in the center of the room slicing up a variety of fruit pies for the dessert course in the great hall. Her wide back was to Aoife, making it difficult to hear the words of her tune, but at least she wouldn't see them as they stepped past.

Keeping her eyes on the ill-tempered cook, Aoife reached back to tap Declan on the hip. He, in turn, alerted his men, and they moved down the hallway as stealthily as they had on the path outside. When it was Aoife's turn to move, she tried to mimic their quiet steps. But either her shoes weren't made for sneaking around, or she was incapable of being quiet. Her steps thundered in her ears as she rushed as fast as she could past the doorway with her eyes shut tight, unable to risk checking to see if the cook had heard and turned.

She passed the door and ran smack into Tommy's back. Her eyes flashed open. The men were all staring at her with odd looks of amusement on their faces.

Aoife nearly breathed a sigh of relief until she realized the cook's singing had ceased. Then the woman said, in a tone much nicer than Aoife had ever heard when she'd lived here, "Hattie? Is that you?"

Aoife held her breath and listened for footsteps or any sound that indicated the cook was coming to check out the noise. But they had spent the last day and a half preparing for this very situation. Maybe not the cook finding them, but someone. It was inevitable given how many people were currently crammed inside these walls—two pirate crews in addition to the regular staff.

But the cook never came to investigate, and Aoife finally released her breath when the quiet singing started again.

Fifteen feet ahead, the hallway came to an end and split. The hallway veering right led to the front of the council hall and ultimately to the large dining room where the banquets with the lords were held. To the left lay the residential section of the hall, with the chambers of the councilwomen and their heirs on the second floor, the staff quarters below those.

The room where the fae were housed was, as best as Aoife could recall, in the center of the first floor, tucked amidst the rooms of the staff, as if they were more than mere cooks and maids and attendants but also guards.

Without a word, Declan drew their attention and gestured for them to head down the left hallway.

The only sound as they moved through the hallways was their own breathing. And Aoife's footsteps. Though at least they weren't quite as noisy as they had been earlier.

While they had anticipated the staff being occupied with the dining guests, this heavy silence unnerved Aoife. Had her home always been so eerie, or did it merely seem so now that she knew what the council did to their own people?

What they'd surely do to them if they were caught.

When the hallway branched off again, Aoife hoped she'd remembered this labyrinth correctly. Tommy and Gavin stopped, taking up their predetermined stations against the wall, once again slouching back casually. Aoife gave them one last glance and a shake of her head. While Tommy had his back to the wall, chin tipped down to his chest and eyes half closed with faked drunkenness, Gavin rested his shoulder against the wall and pretended to be chattering incessantly to his friend.

What he was yammering on about, she wasn't sure; as it was too soft for her to make out any of the words. But the way they fell into their parts so quickly and effortlessly made her think they could have been actors in a theater troupe instead of pirates.

She turned back to find that Declan had already started down the hallway to their right. This one was also empty and quiet, though shorter, with only one door on the left. She repeated the turns in her head, visualizing the map as she did so. *Left. Right. Left. Left. Left. Right.*

Declan made his way quickly and with such ease that she wondered if he were mentally reciting the turns as she was.

Each hallway they took looked the same. No artwork on the walls. No windows. Only door after identical door with lanterns perched between them.

As a child, Aoife had thought it must have been the worst chore to have to light each of them every evening, only to put them out again every morning. Day in. Day out. Monotonous. Boring. Though she had never met the women tasked with this job, she'd often imagined them as being the youngest and most hated among the staff.

They made the final turn into a long corridor just as one of the doors opened and a young woman stepped out. She wore one of the nicer uniforms reserved for these dinner gatherings, her red curls pinned neatly upon her head. She couldn't be much older than Aoife, if that, but as soon as she saw the two of them, her sweet face scrunched into a frown.

"What are you doing here? You're not to leave the public areas!"

Showtime.

Aoife blinked and dropped her shoulders in an exaggerated slump as she smacked Declan on the arm. "I told you," she hissed. "We were supposed to take a right, not a left!"

Declan ignored the servant and turned fully toward Aoife. His words came out slurred to perfection, "And why would I take directions from a lass?"

With a hand on her hip, Aoife shook her head and clicked her tongue. "Not just any lass, mind you."

His gray eyes rolled as his head fell to one side, heavy with exasperation. "Yeah, yeah, yeah. A lass from the *Duchess.*" Contempt dripped from the last two words.

The woman moved toward them, her hands shooing them to turn back the way they'd come. But they continued to argue.

"Why did I ever trust an imbecile from the *Dark Star*?"

He wagged his brow. "Because this imbecile is rather dashing."

Aoife didn't have to fake the flush that spread across her cheeks as she remembered the last time he'd called himself that. And what had followed.

All the pretend frustration vanished as if blown away by a breath, and she mimicked his earlier eye roll.

From the corner of her eye she saw the girl standing with arms still raised, glancing between the pair of them, surely wondering whether they would pay her any attention.

Before the girl could admonish them again, Declan had his arms around Aoife's waist and was pulling her to him. Her hips slammed against his so hard they both crashed into the wall behind him. And an instant later, his lips were on hers.

This was no act, hadn't been part of their plan, but she couldn't argue with his improvisation as his lips beckoned for hers to part so his tongue could caress hers.

Sands, she never wanted this to stop. Was this what she might have missed out on had she stayed? Never to be kissed with such passion and need?

She couldn't imagine a life devoid of this. Nor did she want to.

Wrapping her arms around his neck, she let herself melt into him, relaxing into his embrace, her entire body sighing with satisfaction. With her eyes closed and her mind threatening to get swept away by this moment with him, she could only imagine how perturbed the servant looked, how she must have thrown up her hands one final time as she muttered "whatever" and stormed off.

Even after the girl's retreating footsteps had quieted, Aoife remained entangled with Declan. She wanted to savor this, but they had too much to do.

She chuckled against his lips when she heard the girl's exasperated groan. She must have found Tommy and Gavin lingering in the other hallway and not even bothered to try to make them leave.

Declan released her, and with great reluctance, she leaned away from him.

He spoke first. "Do you think Tommy and Gav used the same tactic to distract her?"

"That would certainly give her something to gossip about with the other staff."

He took a step back, and she immediately regretted the loss of warmth as his arms fell away from her body. She lifted a hand to her lips.

Now was no time to get lost. In the hallway or in those damn eyes of his.

Declan brushed her hand with his, and with a tilt of his head he motioned for them to continue on, but Aoife couldn't move as she took in what they now faced.

A hallway lined with doors. All indistinguishable. Door after door.

Her memory seemed cloudier now, fogged over by the damn kiss.

Declan watched her, more patient than she'd expected—more patient than she deserved. She had one job. One task. But standing in this hallway, facing a sea of doors, her stomach tightened.

She was going to let them all down. Not just Declan and the crew, or Cait and her rebels, but all of Cregah. All the people who lived in fear because of the council. She felt the weight of all these lives upon her shoulders.

Declan gripped her hand. His fingers wove between hers and gave a reassuring squeeze, his thumb tracing tender circles along the back of hers.

"Breathe, Aoife." A whispered reminder. She breathed it in deep. "We'll check each one if needed. You said they don't leave their quarters, so we might hear them stirring within if we listen closely enough."

"But there are scores of doors to check, and that's in this hallway alone. What if I got the wrong one?"

"Then we'll check the next one, and the next one, if needed. This is only the end if you give up now."

Time was against them, and Aoife could almost hear the ticking of Declan's pocket watch mocking her as she fumbled forward.

"It will be near the middle of the hallway," she said, adding a muttered, "I think."

They started down the corridor, which was narrow enough they could keep their hands clasped as they listened at each door on either side. Most of the staff would be tending to the dinner. At least that's what she hoped. She wondered how much she had gotten wrong about the home she'd grown up in. Did she really know anything about it?

One door after another, they slowed down, listened, and moved on. They moved as quickly as they dared, but Aoife worried they'd miss it. The fae might hear them coming and choose to be still to keep them from stopping.

"This is pointless, Declan. We are never going to find them." Aoife turned toward him, but he didn't stop. Dropping her hand, he left her standing in the middle of the hallway as he proceeded to continue listening at each door. "We don't have time to check them all."

Declan stopped, turned, and narrowed his eyes at her. Not from anger, but desperation. "No, Aoife, we don't have time to *not* check them. We don't have time to stop."

The possibility of failure pressed in on her, and she chided herself for wanting to give in to the hopelessness of the situation. She wanted to be brave and daring and optimistic, but the odds were stacked against them.

And then those odds worsened.

A low whistle drifted down the corridor.

Tommy. A warning.

Someone was coming.

Declan and Aoife looked at each other, but she didn't find her panic mirrored in his face. Rather, his expression reflected the confidence she longed to possess herself.

Grabbing her hand without a word, Declan pulled her down the hallway and around the corner to the right at the same moment she saw someone enter the hallway they'd been searching. She didn't see who it was, but no doubt the person had seen her and Declan.

This corridor was darker than the others, with only a single lantern lit at the far end. Aoife could have sworn a chill swept over her.

Their pursuer was ambling toward them. Slow. Steady. Like the metronome Aoife had used when learning to play the piano as a child.

She peered into the darkness. She'd been here before. This was the hallway. Not the previous one.

Declan leaned an ear against the first door and tried the handle. Locked.

He whispered, "We need to find an open room to hide in. We can't risk a fight here."

Aoife didn't answer but moved past him to the door in the center of the hallway. Shrouded in such darkness, it would have been easy to overlook and walk past.

Declan, seeing where she was headed, picked up his pace to match hers.

Please let it be unlocked.

All those years ago, she'd felt this same pull, a silent voice within her bones calling her forward.

Not bothering to listen for movement, she reached for the handle, but it turned before her fingers could touch it.

The door swung open, and as the footsteps grew ever closer behind them, she reached down deep for any drop of courage she could find and pulled Declan into the room, closing the door behind them with a nearly silent click.

Even the dim light of the hallway hadn't prepared Declan's eyes for the darkness that enveloped them in the room Aoife dragged him into. He blinked once and then opened his eyes as wide as he could, as if that would get them to acclimate faster.

He felt ridiculous, but at least Aoife probably couldn't see him doing it.

A voice greeted them, a whisper of a song wafting toward them. "Sorry for the lack of light, Captain. Maura, could you remedy this for our guests?"

No answer came, except for the silent lighting of a lantern at the far end of the room.

The sight before him rendered him speechless.

The room was far larger than he'd expected, with enough space for the three sisters to live comfortably. To the right sat a living area, with a sofa and three armchairs surrounding a large hearth that stood cold and unused. Behind that lay a dining area and a small kitchen, where the dishes from their last meal filled the sink, waiting to be cleaned. He assumed the door at the far end led to a washroom, while the three doors to the left were likely bedrooms.

The council must have built this room specifically for the fae sisters who served them. Which meant they really had been living here for more than five hundred years. While he'd heard this was the case, seeing the evidence of it sucked the breath out of him. To live in a single room for so many years. How had they managed? Surely they would jump at the chance to come with them and be free.

The melodic voice pulled Declan's attention back to the room's residents. "Welcome back, Aoife. We wondered when you might visit us again."

The most beautiful woman Declan had ever seen stood before them, and though she had addressed Aoife, she was looking squarely at him. Red curls the color of autumn leaves, fiery and bright, framed a face that could have been angelic if not for the mischievous turn of her pink lips. Her eyes, a more vibrant blue than seemed possible, like the bluebirds that had sung outside his childhood window or the lilies his father used to surprise his mother with on her birthdays, bore into him with such an intensity it was like being suffocated.

"I hadn't planned to come back," Aoife said with an edge to her voice. Declan wanted to look at her, to determine what emotion had sharpened her words, but he couldn't pull his gaze away from the beautiful fae before them.

The fae clicked her tongue. "I'm sorry to hear that. Your last visit was cut so short. We never even had the chance to properly introduce ourselves." She raised a slender hand to her chest. "I'm Renna. The oldest. And these are my sisters, Bria and Maura." She motioned to them with the grace of a dancer. Even her movements were beautiful.

And potentially deadly.

The thought snapped him back to the task at hand. He couldn't let himself be so enchanted. Needed to play his hand with care here.

But before he could do anything, Aoife was speaking again, giving a nod in his direction. "This is…"

"Captain Declan McCallagh," Renna said, finishing the sentence for her.

It hadn't registered when she'd called him Captain earlier, but now, upon hearing his whole name on the fae's breath, his skin pricked with unease. All the time he'd spent studying fae lore hadn't adequately prepared him for their abilities. Did this mean he'd been wrong about the possibility of iron-core walls? He hadn't heard that the fae sisters—or any fae for that matter—possessed mind-reading capabilities, but somehow they knew who he was. And likely they knew why he was here.

"How did you know?" Aoife asked.

Maura and Bria moved closer to their sister, as though their sharp fae senses didn't make it possible to hear the conversation from anywhere in their quarters. But they stayed behind her, waiting.

"We may not leave this room," Renna said, "but we still hear things. Know things."

Declan spoke for the first time since they'd entered, his words coming out gravelly and rough. "You were expecting us."

He cleared his throat so he could continue, but Renna spoke again. "I would have thought that obvious since we opened the door for you without your knocking. But we will save you the trouble of begging. We won't be coming with you."

Though he'd expected as much, at least initially, his heart still plummeted into his gut, falling like an anchor into the sea. Cait's spy must have given them the heads-up, but had they told them what he carried? What he offered? And if not, would it help?

From his periphery he saw Aoife turn toward him, though only slightly, and thankfully she kept quiet, waiting for him to be the one to offer up their bargaining chip.

He straightened his shoulders, forcing himself to ignore the dreadful feeling of defeat that coursed through him. It wouldn't serve him well now, and all the years of working past his own fear, pushing through his insecurities to build his name as a pirate, had prepared him. At least somewhat.

Not taking his eyes off Renna, he reached his hand under his lapel as he spoke again. "I have something that might change your mind."

Curiosity flashed in her blue eyes for a moment before it was replaced yet again with that playful look a cat gives a mouse as it waits to pounce. "And what is that?"

The sealed letter weighed little and yet felt as heavy as the dread resting in his stomach. He held it up, keeping the wax seal hidden from her.

Renna took a step forward, her expression a strange mix of interest and boredom, and reached for the letter. When he lowered it into her hands, the seal of the fae now showing, she froze.

Bria and Maura inched forward to glance over their sister's shoulder.

"What is it?" Maura asked, but a gasp escaped her when she saw what her sister held. Bria's fingers reached up to her lips as if to stifle whatever might escape.

Renna still didn't move but stared at the paper in her hand, at the symbol of her long-lost brethren pressed into the wax. Declan thought her hands had begun to tremble, but she stilled them before snapping her chin up to him. All boredom had vanished from her flawless face, leaving behind only suspicion and what he worried might be malice.

"Is this some sort of trick?" She spat the question at him.

If nothing else, at least he had gotten the upper hand and was in control of the conversation now.

He pushed aside the snarky bravado he normally used and reached instead for the empathy he'd need to convince them. That side of him had been locked away for so many years, but Aoife had provided the key he'd needed, as well as the desire to retrieve it.

"I'd never dream of tricking you, Renna. As if a mortal—pirate or no—could hope to do it successfully."

Her features didn't soften, and her glare threatened to rip him apart. "Flattery? That's your play, Captain? Our kin are all dead. We are the last of our kind."

Behind her, Maura was shaking her head, and Bria had gone still, her eyes glazed over, seeing nothing. Renna's still burned into him, but he wouldn't let himself be intimidated, at least not noticeably so.

"It would appear they are not," he offered, with a nod to the letter in her hand.

"What does it say?" she asked, no hint of kindness in her words. Only guarded suspicion. And a hint of what sounded to Declan like hope.

Declan lifted his shoulders half an inch. "I do not know. You can see for yourself the seal is not broken. I dared not intrude or break the confidence of those who entrusted this to me."

Silence fell among them, his heartbeat the only sound in his ears, pounding out the precious seconds as they passed. The dinner wouldn't last forever, and if they delayed too long they risked running into more staff in the hallways on their way out. But could he rush the fae without risking their refusal to even consider his request? Would their centuries-old hearts understand—or even care—about the urgency of the situation?

Before he could search for the words he needed to spur Renna into action, her sister, Bria, spoke up. "Open it, sister."

Maura chimed in with her sweet, innocent voice, a stark contrast to Renna's intimidating tone. "Time is not on our side here, Renna."

Renna didn't look at either of her sisters, her gaze firmly set on the letter in her hands. If she heard their words, she gave no indication.

Declan felt Aoife stir beside him. He wanted to grab her hand, reassure her that the seconds passing were well spent to allow Renna time, but he couldn't risk them knowing about the growing bond between them. Not yet. If the stories he'd heard were true, information needed to be carefully guarded to deny the fae any ammunition for their trickery.

Aoife cleared her throat quietly, and Declan closed his eyes, waiting for whatever words she was planning to utter. He fought back the urge to stop her, pushed back against the old thought that she was nothing more than an awkward girl with a lack of tact. He'd promised himself he would trust her.

Several seconds passed in silence, pushing Declan to steal a glance toward her, but she didn't look to him for approval as she had done so often in the past. Whether that was because she was worried he might stop her, he wasn't sure, but he hoped she was starting to trust herself just as he was learning to.

"Renna," she started. The fae didn't look at her, didn't even flinch at the sound of her name. "I know what it's like to be lied to. To have those you've trusted—those you've served—keep the truth from you. But avoiding the truth won't change that betrayal."

Renna lifted her head. Her eyes burned into Aoife, but Aoife didn't falter. More seconds ticked by, and Declan quieted his breaths as he waited, as if any sound might ignite the tension in the room.

"I'm not avoiding the truth." Renna's tone had a bite to it, but it was not quite as sharp as before.

Aoife must have noticed her words had lost some of their edge, because she said, "Then I would humbly ask you to please open it. Read the words from your kin. I know minutes to you must mean very little compared to the centuries you've lived here, but as your sister mentioned, time is not on our side this evening. Please."

At that, Bria and Maura inched even closer to their sister, offering light touches of encouragement on her arms before Renna slid her slender finger under the paper's edge and broke the seal.

Declan managed to keep himself from craning his neck to see over the edge of the paper and look at the writing the fae sisters now read. He startled when Aoife's fingers brushed his own, and he risked another glance at her, then gave a nudge of his head to dissuade her from moving closer, adding a warning to his eyes and hoping she wouldn't see it as a rejection but merely a precaution.

She gave him a small smirk in understanding before moving to clasp her hands in front of her.

They waited. Another breath. Then another. The sisters stood as still as stone, only their eyes moving as they read.

And then, Renna looked from Maura to Bria. Though Declan couldn't be sure, he could have sworn the sisters exchanged quick nods, but perhaps that was only what he hoped to see. Before he could ponder it further, the fae were moving.

Renna handed the letter to Maura, who moved to the back of the room and held it up to the lantern's fire, turning it to ash on the stone floor, while Bria rushed over to a trunk sitting against the wall nearest their bedroom doors. Renna stepped toward him and Aoife, the earlier tension and intimidation in her eyes now replaced with undeniable hope and promise.

She kept her voice quiet, as if worried someone in the council might be listening. "We will come with you. We will help. We have been alone for too long, deceived for too many years, and they will not hold us one second longer."

With that, the fae donned the cloaks Bria had retrieved, and Renna motioned with a hand for Declan to lead the way.

Aoife couldn't hear the three fae sisters as they followed her and Declan out of their room, though she sensed their presence all the same. She tried to focus on Declan ahead of her. They were almost done. Almost out. At least with this first step of the plan.

A smile threatened to spread across her lips. She'd helped. She'd managed to encourage them to read the letter, and while it had ultimately been the letter that had convinced them to help, her pride fluttered in her chest all the same.

Declan motioned for them to stop at the corner, and with her breath held, Aoife placed a hand on his back, more for herself than for him. His warmth reassured her, calmed her heart, and also kept her from running into him and pushing him out into the open before he could ensure the way was clear.

He stepped away, and before she could frown over the space between them, his hand was in hers, pulling her around the corner. A shiver went through her at his touch, those pinpricks once again dancing over her skin. She hoped she never ceased to respond to him in this way.

In the fae's quarters, it had been necessary to avoid touching, but what had changed now, she didn't know. And she found it hard to care. Curiosity be damned. She melted into his grasp as he claimed her as his own, paying no mind to their audience.

They'd barely made it halfway down the long corridor when she heard footsteps. Instinct had her feet turning to stone, unable or unwilling to move from where they stood, even as Declan kept walking. Or tried to. Refusing to drop her hand, he couldn't get far with her now frozen in place.

He turned, perhaps to offer some encouraging word or maybe explain his superhuman pirate hearing, as he appeared unconcerned by the feet rushing toward them. Before he could do either, she saw Gavin and Tommy turn the corner with a woman on their heels.

Yet the sight of them didn't bring any comfort, as their eyes were wide with urgency.

In an instant Declan had turned to face them. "What is it?"

Tommy didn't answer until they reached them, his body fidgeting to keep moving despite the obvious tension in his jaw. "Maggie here came to warn us. That girl who found us loitering went straight to the banquet hall to ask the crews to come retrieve their drunk mates."

"You can imagine how well that went," Gavin added.

Declan glanced over his shoulder at Aoife and asked, "Is there another way out? We can't go back the way we came."

Aoife blinked, giving her head a few quick shakes. "I'm not as familiar with the servants' areas."

He looked past her to the fae, but they must not have been any more help, because he met her gaze again quickly, raising his brows in question, urging her to think harder.

She hated letting him down, but the girl, Maggie, must have been the one Cait had working on the inside. She nudged a chin toward her. "Perhaps she knows of one."

"I do, in fact," Maggie said, her voice carrying the slightest hint of an accent from some other region of Cregah.

Declan looked back at Maggie and hesitated. Though Aoife couldn't see his face, she could imagine his broody eyes boring into the young girl, pondering whether to trust her or not.

A small bob of his chin was his only answer, and then they were all moving again, back the way she and the men had come, turning left instead of toward the entrance they'd used earlier.

Declan still gripped her hand, pulling her along. But this wasn't right. Maggie was leading them toward the council's meeting rooms, where she and her sisters had done their lessons. She was taking them closer to the councilwomen and their guests, not leading them away.

Her heart thumped in her chest, as loud as her feet against the stone floors. Panic settled in her throat, and she wondered how she would breathe past it. But fainting in the hallway certainly wouldn't help, so she forced her feet to keep moving.

Maggie opened a door and ushered them all inside a dark room.

Aoife didn't need to look around to know she'd brought them to the library. The last place she would have chosen. This room was in the middle of the council hall. No access to the outside. Silence hung like a heavy shroud, so quiet that the pounding in her chest seemed to fill it with its quickened booms. Her hand grew sweaty and clammy within Declan's.

They halted and waited for their eyes to adjust to the change in light, but it was not long before Maggie set off again.

She led them to a corner of the library that Aoife had never explored. There she pulled a book off a middle shelf and reached a hand into the now vacant spot. Whether it was a button or a latch, Aoife couldn't determine, but whatever Maggie did released the shelf from where it was locked into place. She pulled it toward them.

Aoife's jaw fell open. She'd lived here her whole life and had never known this doorway existed. How many other secrets existed in her former home?

Maggie spoke in a hushed tone as she motioned for them to enter the dark passage. "This leads to the outside. You'll come out behind the bushes next to the front stairs. You'll need to be quick and stay hidden. The bushes only provide so much cover, so be careful. I'll try to buy you some time."

Before they could ask anything more, she scurried away between the bookcases that stood in the middle of the room. No doubt heading toward the banquet hall.

Declan considered their little band. "Gavin. Sisters. You first."

Aoife's feet itched to get moving, her legs restless and tingling with the need to escape and survive.

Declan had barely turned to the sisters before they were brushing past Gavin to head into the passage, with Gavin needing no further encouragement to follow.

Tommy stepped aside, gesturing for Declan and Aoife to go next, but Aoife hadn't even moved when a dagger appeared at Declan's throat.

Another man came up behind Tommy, grabbing his arm.

A third, who was surprisingly fast given his stocky frame, rushed past Aoife, sliding between her and freedom.

A rough voice, deep and sultry, filled the library.

"Leaving so soon?"

46

Declan

The edge of the dagger bit into Declan's skin as he moved to face the source of the voice. He gave Aoife's hand a final stroke with his thumb before he released her. As much as he wanted to hold onto her, he couldn't risk their connection making this worse.

He caught only a glimpse of the pirate guarding him and ignored the handful of other crewmen he could see, focusing instead on the man standing twenty feet away, whose purple sash looked black in the dim light.

"Madigen," Declan said, keeping his tone flat, uninterested.

"Lord Madigen," the captain corrected, lifting his chin, causing the deep shadows to shift across the rough planes of his face.

Declan raised a brow and pulled the corner of his mouth into a smirk before he offered a nod, ignoring the dagger's pinch as he did so. "Excuse me. *Lord* Madigen. What can we do for you, sir?"

The pirate lord's jaw tensed, his weight shifting as he glared at Declan before looking at Tommy and then Aoife.

Something sparked in the lord's eyes. "You're looking…different… Ms. Cascade."

Declan bit back the urge to tell the man not to even utter her name, as if he had an exclusive claim to its use. Yet the sound of it on this pirate's despicable tongue, with possessiveness coating each syllable, had him feeling prickly and more on edge than he already was.

Aoife's voice came out clear. "Let them go. Now."

Lord Madigen sneered at her, a devilish smile with no hint of kindness. "Afraid I can't do that. You see, I'm tasked with protecting the council. Especially you, and unfortunately for this lad and his crew, they made the poor decision to not only kidnap an heir to the council but—"

"They didn't kidnap me," she interrupted. "I ran. Stowed away on his ship."

"I would have thought my daughter to have better taste."

Declan's hands tensed, eager to pummel the smug look off the man's face, but he kept silent and still.

Madigen continued. "Regardless, the young captain here allowed you to stay aboard, took you to Foxhaven, I believe. When he should have brought you back home."

That word—*home*—twisted Declan's gut. No doubt it did the same to her. He wished he could reach back and reassure her it was all going to be okay, but he couldn't even risk a look in her direction.

It was a dangerous dance they performed here. Any misstep and Madigen could end them all.

"Well…" Aoife's voice faltered, causing a surge of panic to hit him as he anticipated her next words. "I'm back now. So let him go."

Declan blinked, slowly and deliberately. He knew she was only trying to buy time—or at least he hoped that was her plan—but the thought of her staying here while he ran knotted his stomach even further. He couldn't leave her. Not with them. Not here.

"Had you let me finish though," Madigen said, his voice growing more oily with each word, "you'd know this wasn't merely about you, miss. He has also kidnapped the Bron sisters, who have resided under the protection and care of the council for five centuries."

"You mean enslaved by the council?" Aoife asked, every word a challenge.

Madigen clicked his tongue. "What lies they've been spreading. You really ought to be careful who you trust."

Declan turned to look not at Aoife but at Tommy, who had remained quiet, not even shuffling a foot or clearing his throat. The man behind Tommy—one of Madigen's crew, no doubt—gripped one of Tommy's arms, and likely held a blade at his lower back. The man's eyes didn't meet Declan's, and he was too busy keeping his attention on his own captain that he didn't notice when Declan gave Tommy the silent order.

Whatever Aoife had been about to say got cut short, turning it into a sharp gasp as Tommy pivoted away from his captor at the same time Declan raised an elbow enough that he could slip out from under his captor's arm, pull the knife from his boot, and drive it into the man's stomach.

The man doubled over, and Declan looked past him, his gaze meeting Aoife's. With another nod toward the pathway behind them, he told her to run, then pushed the man to the floor.

She didn't turn, didn't leave, didn't listen.

Of course she didn't listen.

Before he could scold her though, she reached into the folds of her sash and pulled out the dagger Tommy had given her, ready to help however she could. He might have been proud of her for finding such courage and confidence had his stomach not twisted with panic over her remaining in harm's way.

But he could still protect her.

With his bloodied knife in hand, he turned with Tommy, and they prepared for the rest of Madigen's crew to approach.

But they didn't. He'd expected them to be slow with the rum from dinner, had anticipated they wouldn't be ready for a fight—especially not on this island, let alone here at the council hall—but he hadn't prepared for what now greeted them.

Madigen hadn't moved. Neither had any of his men.

The captain didn't even seem put out by the sight of two members of his crew writhing on the bloody library floor. In fact, he looked downright bored as he motioned for a few of his men to retrieve the injured.

Declan waited for the man to start clapping slowly at the display he and Tommy had put on. It was what he probably would have done in this situation. But instead Madigen merely stood there, arms crossed in front of him, waiting.

A door opened somewhere in the library, and the sound of footsteps filled the room. From between the bookshelves to his right, three women stepped forward.

A mature and regal woman led the way with her nose in the air. She held her hands at her waist, clasped together in a grip as tight as the dark curls pinned atop her head. Behind her a girl who wore her youth with an air of arrogance held the arm of his sister's spy, whose face showed no fear despite the danger she found herself in.

The older woman spoke, keeping her focus solely on Declan, her lips pulling into a wicked smile. "You're back. And I see you've gotten blood on my floor."

This whole plan had gone badly rather quickly.

Aoife still gripped the dagger in her hand, but the arrival of her mother and Darienn shook the confidence she'd managed to unearth.

And they'd caught Cait's spy.

If they saw Aoife—or the secret passageway still open behind her—they didn't show it, both of them staring intently at Declan and Tommy, who stood in front of her.

No one moved. No one even seemed to be breathing.

Such was the attention the councilwomen commanded.

Melina's voice pierced the still air. "Are you trying to get away without paying?" She didn't let him answer. "In fact, it appears you chose to collect a fee from me instead. By taking our fae."

Before Declan could respond—and before Aoife could think better of it—words came pouring from her mouth. "They aren't your fae, Melina."

Her mother swung her glare to Aoife, her lips pursed. "Such disrespect. I might have assumed this stemmed from the company you've been keeping, Aoife, had you not chosen to abandon your station all on your own."

"Not on my own," Aoife said. She nodded toward her sister. "Darienn suggested..."

Darienn straightened but didn't look at all surprised to have been ratted out. Melina remained unfazed, her expression shifting into one of pity rather than surprise.

"Oh, you are so easily swayed, Aoife. Darienn offered an out, and you readily took it. Though I suppose it is to our benefit you exiled yourself. The council requires a dedication you apparently lack."

They'd tested her. And she'd fallen for it.

But how she'd gotten here was of little consequence compared to what she had yet to do.

She stepped up beside Declan, her hand inches away from his, though she dared not reach for him.

"My dedication is to our people," she said. "Not to you or the council. Where are my aunts anyway? Babysitting the other crew?"

Melina laughed, ignoring her questions. "Is that why you ran? You could have stayed. Might have used your power to change things. Yet you fled. Like a coward."

"But I came back." Why she bothered to defend herself to this woman, she didn't know, but she couldn't stop herself.

"And look where you ended up. Caught in the act of betrayal. A failure. Again. As I always expected." Melina's words cut into her, each syllable increasing the pressure in her chest.

Even in the dimness of the library, the coldness in Melina's eyes was clear, a stare so icy it seemed to freeze every muscle in Aoife's body, tightening her joints, closing up her throat.

She couldn't move, except for the pulsing in her jaw as she fought to keep her shame from slipping out as tears.

She's just goading you, trying to get under your skin.

It was working.

She had no response, no retort. She merely stood there and took it, let her mother's words of disappointment coat her like the grime on her skin. This woman's favor was far from what she craved, and yet the insults still stung.

Melina focused again on Declan. "Back to the matter of fees, Captain. I assume you still do not have the means to pay, so it will be a service once again?"

When Declan didn't answer, Aoife looked to find him watching her instead of her mother, as if Melina hadn't asked him a question. His expression clearly asked if she was all right.

She swallowed and attempted a smile to assure him she was fine.

But the snap of Melina's fingers cut through their moment, drawing their attention, as Darienn shoved Maggie forward into Melina's grasp. "It seems one of my staff isn't quite as loyal as we require. She helped you. Did she not?"

Declan drew in a deep breath, not rushing to answer. "We worked alone."

"It's not polite to lie, Captain McCallagh."

Aoife nearly scoffed at such a statement coming from this woman, but she managed to hold it in.

Her mother continued, "Regardless of what you say, we know Maggie here works for the Rogues. We know she's been spying. And for that, the punishment is *exile.*"

Aoife looked at Maggie, but to her credit, the girl didn't whimper or beg. If anything, she remained resolute, firm in their cause, confident in the task she'd been given. Even if it meant her certain death.

"No," Declan said, and Aoife swung her head to look at him, her eyes wide, but he didn't register her existence. His features were as stern as his tone, with no sign that Melina intimidated him, even as the remaining men of Madigen's crew stood guard around them.

"No?" Genuine amusement laced her mother's words, though it didn't play on her face.

"You heard me. I won't do it."

Now the smile Aoife had heard in her mother's question spread across her lips, devilish and dangerous. "You pick an odd time to grow a conscience, McCallagh."

They stood there, staring each other down, until Melina's smile faded, melting away into a snarl that made her look every bit the animal Aoife now imagined her to be.

"Well, if you won't—"

"I'll do it," Tommy said, interrupting her, not taking a step forward but standing tall as he offered his service in place of his captain's.

Declan started to protest, but Melina stopped him with a raised hand.

"How noble a gesture, Mr. Murphy. But that won't be necessary."

Another snap of her fingers, and the spy—Maggie—went rigid, her eyes widening, her mouth dropping in a silent and final gasp before she fell forward, revealing the handle of a blade protruding from the back of her neck and the pirate who had been hidden behind her in the darkness.

Aoife tried to scream, but the sound lodged in her throat, and she froze. Her mother had ordered the kill personally, and in the council hall no less.

She wanted to squeeze her eyes shut, but they, too, remained unresponsive to her commands, leaving her to stare at the lifeless body of the girl lying on the library floor.

Melina drew in a breath and addressed Declan again. "Well, since you refused that job—not that it did Maggie any good—it seems I'll need to find another task for you."

Still staring at the fallen girl, Aoife barely heard the conversation going on before her. She should pay attention. She needed to be ready, in case she needed to act, but she felt just as she had on the beach in Foxhaven.

As if she were standing in the midst of a dream, begging her mind to wake her up and erase all the blood and death from her vision.

But with every blink, the scene remained.

It was no dream.

Her mother's clicking tongue knocked at the edges of Aoife's mind, pulling her back to the present, even though her eyes remained lowered.

"What am I to do with you, McCallagh? How shall I collect for this visit to our shores?"

"Let me deal with this one?" Declan said, and those words managed to pull her out of her shock enough to find him pointing his blade in her direction.

"I'm listening," Melina said.

"You've exiled one heir already. You can't risk exiling another without raising more suspicion with the people. Make hers look like an unfortunate mishap, an accidental drowning or a fall down some stairs. She is rather clumsy, after all."

"An interesting proposition," Melina said, her gaze shifting between her and Declan. "Unfortunately, I can't trust you to follow through. I doubt this heir will be as easy for you to kill. Unlike the last one."

Aoife's attention snapped to her mother and then back to Declan.

What had she said? The last one. Not as easy to kill.

Was this another trick? Another test?

Declan met her gaze, but she couldn't read whatever emotions those grays held.

His throat bobbed as he swallowed. His jaw tightened.

No.

Not Declan.

Lani?

Declan?

Her mind sped out of control, her head shaking as her eyes searched his for the answer she needed.

But he didn't speak, didn't even open his mouth to try.

Her sister. Her…whatever Declan was to her now.

Had he been the one? The one tasked with killing Lani?

She opened her mouth to ask him, but it was her mother's words that filled the silence. "Oh dear. He didn't tell you, did he?"

Someone breathed a laugh. Maybe Darienn. Maybe Lord Madigen. Or one of his men. Aoife couldn't tell.

She could only stand there gaping at Declan, begging him to refute it, but he only stared back at her.

There. A flash of what Aoife swore was shame burned in his eyes, but it was gone as quickly as it had appeared, his expression tightening and all emotion washing away.

He turned to Melina, his voice reverting back not to the Declan she'd fallen for but the captain who had wanted to be rid of her. "Of course I didn't tell her. I needed her to trust me. She's just a means to an end."

"We'll see about that," Melina said, but the words sounded distant, as if Aoife were hearing them from underwater.

This had been their plan—for Declan to deny any emotional ties to her, to insist he'd used her—if they got caught.

But that was before.

Aoife couldn't focus on any of the thoughts that now swarmed her.

He'd lied. He'd killed Lani and hadn't told her. Ever. Not in all the hours they had talked.

What else had he lied about? Had his kisses been an act? Had it all been a ploy?

Her chest caved in on itself, the air becoming thin around her.

She couldn't breathe. Couldn't stand.

Her knees wobbled, but she forced them to steady, willed them to keep her upright.

Tommy, standing on her other side, inched toward her. Feeling his shoulder brush hers, she turned to him. His expression displayed a mix of so many emotions—sorrow and confusion and remorse and helplessness.

Had Declan fooled him too?

Her vision blurred. She couldn't think straight. Couldn't sort all of this out. She could turn to Declan, demand answers, but she knew he wouldn't offer them. Not here.

Her hand itched to both grab his hand in hers and slap him across the face, but neither were particularly good options given the circumstances.

Something moved in her periphery. So lost in the buzzing within her mind, Aoife hadn't heard the door open or the footsteps approach.

A pirate wearing a gold sash had entered, someone from the *Duchess*. And by the display of confidence, this was likely Captain Halloran herself. Her face remained hidden behind the brim of her large hat as she leaned toward Madigen's ear.

Melina looked over at them. "What's happened?"

Halloran straightened as Lord Madigen cleared his throat and answered. "The fae got past their crew."

This should have brought relief, but nothing could ease the ache that now plagued Aoife.

"How did that—" Melina started, but she raised a hand as if batting away an annoying insect. "It doesn't matter. You can redeem your crew and their utter failure to protect my property by handling her."

Aoife's stomach turned to lead under her mother's glare.

No!

She wouldn't meet Lani's fate. Or Maggie's. She wouldn't be *dispatched* or *exiled* or whatever her mother wanted to call it.

She looked at Declan, but he still wore the cold mask he'd donned. It had to be an act. Another ruse.

She'd thought he and his crew were more like actors than pirates, right? Surely this had to be another one of his well-executed plays.

Captain Halloran stepped toward her, the sash around her waist swaying with each slow, confident step.

Aoife's heart thundered painfully against her chest as she waited to see if Declan would protest or Tommy would step in, as they had with Captain Grayson. As they had on the beach in Foxhaven.

But neither moved.

No one moved, except for the approaching captain.

Aoife adjusted her grip on her dagger and raised it, not knowing exactly how she'd defend herself against this captain—and in a room full of Lord Madigen's crew—but she wouldn't go easily.

If Declan and Tommy wouldn't help her, she'd help herself.

Captain Halloran had gotten within ten feet when Declan finally faced Aoife, his eyes still as hard as steel, with none of the warmth they'd held less than an hour ago.

Declan glanced down at the dagger in Aoife's hand, then met her gaze once more before giving the slightest shake of his head.

No.

He wanted her to stand down. To not fight.

Her thoughts warred inside her. After all the times he'd told her to do something and she hadn't listened, only to have things fall apart, should she listen this time?

Beside her Tommy whispered her name, and she turned with reluctance, avoiding looking at the captain who now stood close enough to strike.

Why hadn't she been grabbed yet? Why was Halloran waiting?

Her skin crawled. Was this how a mouse felt while the cat toyed with it?

Tommy held her gaze and mouthed a silent *don't.*

Her brow creased. He couldn't be telling her to give up. Could he?

Before she could even think to lower the dagger, a hand gripped her wrist so hard she dropped the blade to the floor.

The captain pulled her close, turning until they were both facing her mother. A blade she hadn't seen in the captain's hand poked her in the ribs.

"I can do it now. Here. Make the boy suffer to see the girl die." The woman had a voice that was rough in Aoife's ear, like sandpaper against her skin, sending a shiver through her she hoped would go unnoticed.

She would be brave. Like Maggie had been.

Declan and Tommy remained quiet behind her, and even though Aoife knew it was the smart play, it still stung to have them not fighting for her.

She was once again that stowaway on a ship of pirates who wanted her gone. Utterly alone. A nuisance. A bother. No one worth their time or energy.

They had the fae. They wouldn't need her now. There was no reason for them to save her.

There'd be no rescue.

The hand on her wrist tightened. The knife at her back pushed harder. But Aoife forced herself to hide her fear, to choke it down, to steel her expression as best she could. She wouldn't give her mother the satisfaction.

"No. Not here, Captain Halloran," Melina said. "As much as I'd enjoy seeing McCallagh's pain, I won't do that to Lord Madigen. He has so few accomplishments. Seems cruel to remind him of yet another failure. Take her to the usual place. It's time for her to be reunited with her sister."

Aoife's screams of protest echoed through the hallways as Captain Halloran dragged her out into the night, her desperation and fear so much greater than it had been in Foxhaven.

Declan's gut twisted, squeezing ever tighter like a snake around its prey. It took every bit of his energy to keep the torment from showing.

Though he faced Melina still, her face blurred as his mind forced him to replay the image of Aoife, the way she'd doubted him, the way she'd doubted every moment they'd shared.

How could she have so easily believed his act tonight? How could she have so easily believed the mask he'd had to wear?

He had meant to tell her about Lani, about how he'd been forced to take her life, about how her sister's face and her pleas for mercy had been haunting him more than all the nightmares he'd carried since childhood.

He had planned to tell her, but the timing had never felt right. The words had never felt enough, they could never do his remorse justice.

And he'd stupidly kept the truth hidden.

Would she ever forgive him? Would she listen to his apologies?

Here, standing before her mother, he vowed to the sands he'd never stop begging for that forgiveness.

Melina shifted her weight and dropped her head to one shoulder. "Now for the matter of payment. It's getting late, and I'm growing weary of this interruption to our evening."

"What do you want?" Declan spat at her. His hand tensed, as if begging him to throw the blade into the matriarch's chest, but he talked down the urge. That would bring certain death at Madigen's hand, and he still had too much to do.

"You have my fae, and I know you didn't free them out of the goodness of your heart."

"You want them back? You know where my ship is. You have men at your beck and call. Why not take them back?"

She stiffened, her cold smile returning as she lowered her chin at him. "Because there's something we want more than merely getting those sisters back into the safety of our care."

Declan didn't even bother to stifle his scoff. "And what's that?"

"The Csintala Dagger. You will go. You will use our fae. And you will retrieve the Csintala Dagger from wherever it rests, and bring both—the blade and my fae—back to us."

He could play dumb, as he'd attempted with Callum, but that would only waste precious time. How far had Halloran gotten with Aoife already?

"And what if I don't? Are you going to have me *exiled*? What will stop me from taking the dagger and leaving the Aisling altogether?"

"Because we both know you aren't the ruthless pirate you have everyone believing you are. We both know you won't take the blade for your own benefit, not when you think so many people could be helped with its use."

Declan roughed a hand over his chin and scratched at his jawline as he thought through all his options. And their consequences. He needed to think faster. Never enough time. Time was always against him.

Melina spoke again. "And *exile* isn't in my plans for you. You don't deserve to be let off that easy, not for all you've already taken from us. Our fae. Our heirs."

She stepped toward him, brazenly close, as if daring him to strike and end her here and now.

"You see, Declan," she breathed, "Aoife isn't the only way to hurt you."

There was no snap of her fingers this time. Only the slightest movement of her chin as she gave the order.

It happened too fast. He didn't even see the blade as it flew through the air and hit its mark with the all too familiar sound of steel ripping into flesh. Tommy released a muffled groan, his hands clutching his stomach.

No!

Before Declan could move—before he could make a sound—one of Lord Madigen's crew stepped from the shadows behind them, ripping the blade from Tommy's gut and slicing it across his chest. He plunged it into his side, and Tommy gave another grunt of pain before the pirate pushed him away, pulling the blade out.

Tommy fell, his knees hitting the stone floor with a sickening thud that rang in Declan's ears as he sent his own knife flying into the attacker's face. The blade hit true, in the man's eye, sending him backwards, where he fell with a thud.

Declan rushed to Tommy, trying to put pressure on the wounds as best he could, but he didn't have enough hands.

He needed to think.

He cursed aloud as he fumbled with the knot in the purple sash at his waist, the blood—Tommy's blood—on his fingers making it harder to get a grip on the fine fabric.

Finally he got it free and yanked it away before wrapping it around his friend's abdomen as he moved the man's hands away. "You'll be okay, Tommy. It'll be okay."

Tommy winced as Declan pulled the fabric taut against him. "I've had worse."

"Liar." He tried to smile at his friend, to reassure him, but he couldn't.

Before he could grab more fabric to staunch the bleeding from Tommy's chest, that damn bitch's tongue clicked again, mocking him.

"Poor Declan. No matter how hard you try, you always fail, don't you?"

Declan didn't look up from Tommy, whose eyes blinked rapidly as if he were trying to keep himself conscious and present.

Melina stepped even closer. "The tourniquet will only do so much, but you can save him, you know. Get him to the fae. They can heal him. But you'd better be quick about it. He doesn't have much time."

Damn her!

He didn't want to admit it, but she was right. The gash in Tommy's chest was deeper than Declan had first thought. He needed help, and he needed it soon.

Never enough blasted time.

Declan growled as he pushed to his feet, pulling Tommy up and onto his shoulders. Holding onto his friend's arm and leg, he tried to ignore the warm blood seeping out of him even as it soaked his jacket.

Tommy's body went limp as he gave himself over to the pain and blood loss.

Declan could back up and take the secret passageway out, but that likely wasn't the quickest exit, so he moved past Melina, not daring to let his eyes meet hers, and then past Lord Madigen, who stepped aside.

"Oh, and Declan," Melina called after him. He stopped and turned, though every muscle screamed at him to keep moving, keep going. "If you fail? If you refuse, as you did earlier, your sister will be next"—she nodded toward Tommy's blood-soaked body—"and you may not be around to save her."

Cait.

Declan slammed his teeth together, pushing all of his anger into his jaw, and without another word he forced his legs into as fast a run as he could manage out of the hall and toward his ship.

He couldn't lose him. Not Tommy. Not the friend who'd been there through everything, who knew Declan better than anyone, who'd never given up on him.

Tommy would make it. He'd get him to the fae. Get him healed.

Tommy first. Then Aoife.

The two people he couldn't bear to lose.

Though he might have already lost her.

Captain Halloran didn't loosen her grip as she dragged Aoife across the lawn toward the wooded path, ignoring how Aoife's feet slipped and stumbled, pulling her still onward.

Until they were a hundred feet into the darkness of the woods.

The captain dropped Aoife's wrist and halted on the path.

Aoife's feet screamed at her to get moving, to take this chance to bolt, but her damned curiosity took hold. What was happening? What had she missed?

The captain backed off a half step. "I'm sorry if I hurt you. Take a moment to catch your breath."

Aoife rolled her sore wrist, but she refused to rub the pain away. Like hell she'd show weakness to anymore pirates.

"Who in the sands are you?" Anger seethed in her belly, and she hoped it—and not her anguish—coated her words as she spat them out.

"Captain Halloran—"

"Yeah, I got that much." Tension burned through her body, through her joints, down to the knuckles of her hands, and up into her jaw. A silent scream echoed somewhere inside, but she bit it back.

"You're a feisty one. I can see why Declan likes you."

His name echoed on Aoife's lips, a mere whisper she couldn't contain.

"Yes. Declan. You can thank him for this rescue." She gestured to the path ahead. "Speaking of which, we should get moving."

"Let me guess. We don't have much time."

"How'd you know?"

Aoife rolled her eyes but didn't answer as she started trudging down the path, hoping she could manage with the scant moonlight peering through the trees.

The captain caught up to her quickly and walked beside her in silence. A silence Aoife couldn't handle.

"So where are we heading, Captain? Not to—"

"No, not to the killing grounds."

"Is that what they call them?"

"It's what the pirates call them. I don't know if the council has an official name for it."

Aoife might have asked where it was, where her sister waited for her to join her, but she couldn't stomach it. Someday maybe.

"We're heading to a cove. It's hidden, secret—"

Aoife cut her off. "I know where it is." The image of him emerging from the teal water flashed in her mind. Of all the places…

They continued a few more paces before she spoke again. "You don't have to take me, you know. You can go on back, tell them I'm dead."

"Firstly, no, I can't. While time is short, I do need to allow for the time it would have taken me to complete the *exile*."

A shiver crawled up Aoife's spine, and she was glad the darkness hid her wince.

"Secondly? I promised Captain McCallagh I'd get you there personally, if needed."

He'd planned this.

Look at all options. Plan for all possibilities. He'd been prepared for things to go badly. He'd known Halloran would help.

And he didn't tell you that either.

How much didn't she know? How much had he kept from her?

"How?" She hadn't intended to utter the question aloud, but it spilled into the quiet night on her breath, and she sensed Halloran turn to face her as they walked.

"You'll have to ask him that."

"I don't know that I can. I—"

"No. You stop right there." The harshness of the woman's tone caught Aoife off guard, and her feet skidded to a stop. "Well, I didn't mean literally stop."

Sands, are all pirates snarky bastards?

"Look, Ms. Cascade, I don't know what in the sands is going on between you and McCallagh, and I don't want to know. That's between the two of you. This isn't a stroll with your girlfriend. You're not here to gush your heart out to me. I'm just following through with a promise to get you to the drop point where Declan will come to retrieve you. That's it."

"Fine! Sorry to inconvenience you," Aoife said, dipping her head forward in a nod before she stomped off down the path once again.

They continued on in silence with only the sound of their feet trampling twigs and pounding the dirt.

Aoife tried to focus on the rhythm of their steps and the difference between hers and the captain's. Each crack and squish of wood and earth underfoot. When that wasn't enough to keep the truth at bay, she resorted to counting her steps.

Fifty-eight. Fifty-nine. Sixty. Sixty-one.

He'd killed Lani. He'd lied.

A curse rushed out of her, and if the captain noticed—how could she not?—she didn't let on.

One. Two. Three. Four.

Aoife had to restart her counting five times before they reached the cove, and as expected, the sight of the sand, the tide, and the boulders they'd sat beside rushed at her, driving all the air from her lungs.

Breathe. Damn you. Don't let her see you fall apart!

She sucked in the briny air and forced her shoulders back, pushing against those damned images in her mind. But they wouldn't stay away, popping back up with each step she took toward the same boulder she'd chosen before.

Easing herself onto the sand, she looked back at the captain. "You waiting with me? Or what's the plan?"

"One hour. That's the most I can spare. He should be here by then. But if not, you'll be on your own."

As hard as it was to think of facing him again, the thought of being alone, of being abandoned, forgotten? It threatened to crush her.

She looked back to the sea, where the sliver of moon hovered above the water. All the peace she'd ever found here now seemed tainted, like mold creeping through a loaf of bread. He'd ruined it, this refuge. He'd taken it from her.

Just as he took Lani.

She'd thought she'd cried all the tears she could for her sister, but now, with the grief pooling again in her chest, she couldn't stop them as they pushed their way to the surface, gathering in her eyes until she could barely see the waves before her.

Captain Halloran leaned against the other boulder—Declan's boulder—and Aoife assumed she wasn't one for small talk. Not that Aoife would even be able to manage speaking now without her tears turning her words into a blubbering mess.

She'd have to face the truth at some point. Now was as good a time as any.

ꝏ

An hour later, Aoife had gotten nowhere with this new reality, her mind warring with itself, pulling her back and forth as it wrestled with whether she could trust Declan or not.

Captain Halloran shifted away from the boulder with a gruff sigh and stepped toward her. "It's time for me to go."

Aoife pushed herself up, ignoring where her body now hurt from sitting. "I thought you said he'd be here."

"He will."

"When?"

The captain's jaw tightened, and Aoife waited for the harsh words she could see the woman contemplating.

But they didn't come.

"Ms. Cascade," she said with a tone far softer than seemed possible for her, "trust him. He'll be here."

Aoife moved to protest, to remind this ridiculous pirate of her earlier words about being on her own, but the captain raised a hand.

"Look, I don't know him that well, but I knew his parents. They were good people, and if he got even an ounce of their honor, he will be here. They were not the sort to abandon the ones they loved. And I don't think he is either."

Love.

Aoife couldn't handle the word, not yet anyway, so she focused on the other question that had been nagging her since they'd stopped on the path.

"What happens to you when they find out you didn't actually…" She couldn't even finish the question.

"Kill you?"

Aoife nodded, hoping her discomfort didn't show.

"I'll figure something out." And with no other word, the captain left Aoife standing on the black sand to wait.

And she waited.

And waited.

Her thoughts tumbling around in her head with the ebb and flow of the waves before her.

He'll be here.

Aoife had no idea how much time passed as she waited. Minutes. Hours. Did it even matter?

What had happened back in the council hall after she'd been dragged away?

Her mind played out every scenario she could think of, her chest tightening as she envisioned Declan and Tommy cut down and bleeding on the library floor.

What would his crew do if that happened? Would Gavin take command? Would they go after the dagger? Would the sisters abandon them? Would the dagger ever be retrieved? Would her people ever be free from this tyranny?

The questions swarmed her, buried her, until she was sure they might suffocate her.

Footsteps in the sand behind her had her standing without thinking, not stopping to consider it might be one of Lord Madigen's crew coming to finish her off after finding out Halloran had helped her.

In the darkness she couldn't see who approached from the path, but the steps were slow and unsteady.

"Declan?" She called his name out of instinct, even as her heart ached at the sound of it.

No answer came, but whoever approached seemed to respond to her voice, picking up their pace slightly. As much as they could, perhaps.

She moved around the boulder just as he stepped out from the trees.

Or stumbled out of them.

And there he fell, his knees hitting the black sand with a soft thud. His chin dropped to his chest. In the moonlight Aoife could see it across his shoulders and back.

Blood. So much blood.

Declan's whole body ached, from his sore feet to his throbbing head. But nothing hurt him more than the sound of his name on Aoife's lips and the fear that she'd deny him the forgiveness he needed.

She rushed to him, as best she could in the soft sand, but stopped when he raised his face to look at her.

His hands itched to reach for her, to pull her close and hold her tight, but he couldn't move.

She lowered herself to her knees before him, just out of reach. "What happened? Are you—"

He couldn't look her in the eyes, couldn't keep his head from shaking as he answered. "Tommy."

"Is he okay? Is he—"

"I don't know yet. The fae are with him, working to heal him, but their powers are weak. So many centuries trapped in that iron prison. Their healing will take longer than usual, and the cuts… Deeper than we… He lost a lot of blood before I got him to…"

Declan stumbled over the words, unable to focus on anything other than the pool of sorrow and regret that had settled in his gut.

He looked up at her then, taking stock of every part of her he could see, desperate to ensure she was okay. "Are you hurt?"

"No," she said, but her eyes lowered to the sand between them.

He dared to inch closer to her but stopped.

"I'm sorry." The words felt empty as they fell out. Worthless. Pointless. Insufficient.

"That's it?" The bite in her response had been expected, but he recoiled from it all the same. "That's all you have to say? I'm *sorry*?"

When he didn't answer, no words sufficient to express his remorse, she stood with a huff and turned away from him.

No. Stop her. Get her back.

His thoughts urged him to his feet, the sight of her walking away from him pushing him to ignore the burning fatigue in his legs as he stood.

"Aoife, stop. Please."

She whirled around, and even in the darkness the pain and anger swimming in her eyes was clear. He needed to fix this. Needed her to understand, to forgive him.

She didn't say anything, only looked at him, her jaw tense and her mouth set in a straight line.

He took a step toward her, and when she didn't retreat as he expected, he took another.

He reached out a hand for her, but she pulled back.

"Don't—don't touch me." The words fell from her lips, dripping with the same poison echoed in her expression. He half expected her to back away from him, to curl back in on herself.

But this wasn't the same girl who had trespassed onto his ship and begged for transport.

She straightened, and though she stood a head shorter than him, she dwarfed him with that glare.

He took another half step toward her, until they were close enough to share the same breath.

"I should have told you," he whispered.

"Yes, you should have," she said, each word coated with malice, but she didn't back away.

"I can't undo it. I can't bring her back. I can't go back and fix it. But—"

"But what? You had no choice? You didn't know how to tell me?" She railed against him, shooting more daggers at him with those eyes that had enchanted him.

"Well, yes, honestly, to all of that. It's why I didn't want to come back to Cregah, why I vowed never to return. This is what the council demands of pirates who can't pay. If we don't have the money, we pay with services. Dealing out the death they can't with their own hands."

"How many?"

He didn't need to ask for clarification. He knew exactly what she was asking. But he couldn't find the strength to answer her.

"Declan, how many have you killed for them?"

That venom in her eyes ebbed enough for him to catch a glimpse of the pity he'd never wanted from anyone. But from her, he'd take her pity over her disgust.

He forced himself to hold her gaze. "Nine. Lani was the ninth."

"What were their names?"

Without hesitation he recited the list that haunted him relentlessly, the list that would never be quieted, never be shut out, always lurking in the far recesses of his heart. "Saoirse. Conor. Desmond. Kallie. Cillian. Eden. Sean. Regan."

"And Lani."

He nodded, still not letting himself look away from her. He deserved the hate she flung at him, and he wouldn't let himself avoid it.

Silence settled between them, and he could hardly bear it. He wanted her to yell at him, scream at him, push him away. Anything but this still and silent anger like a sleeping dragon waiting to devour him.

"You didn't mention Adler." A sad hope seeped into her gaze.

"What?"

"The pirate Lani was to meet. Adler. You didn't name him."

"Because I didn't kill him. He wasn't assigned to me. But, Aoife, I had no choice. You do what you're told or they come after your crew. I never wanted my men to be asked to do this, so I always took the orders upon myself, never allowing even Tommy to come with me."

Her jaw tightened, her eyes narrowing, and he braced himself for whatever torrent she was about to unleash.

"I'm not angry at you for that. For all you had to do for them. That's on them. But you should have told me!"

"I know—"

"No," she said, cutting him off, "I don't think you get it, Declan." She flung an arm toward the trees—toward the council hall. "Everything I've ever known, everyone I've ever trusted, has *lied* to me. Everything I believed was built on a false ideal. Everything I was taught was a charade. A hoax! I hoped you were different."

In his mind echoed the words he'd said so many times before. *I'm a pirate.* But he bit them back.

"And I know you're a pirate, but you are different, Declan. I see it. That's why this…" She trailed off as she shook her head at him.

"I'm so sorry, Aoife."

Still not enough. Still such shallow words.

"Were you ever going to tell me?"

He'd been dreading this question. More than her asking for the count and the names. This question. He couldn't lie to her again. She deserved the truth.

"I don't know. Maybe."

Swallowing hard, she clenched her teeth again, and tears began to well up in her beautiful eyes. He'd caused this. This was his doing. But he could fix it. If she let him.

He had to try.

"At first, I thought to, just to make you mad, to punish you for trespassing on my ship. But then I needed your help. And after Foxhaven, I couldn't bear to hurt you. I thought about telling you so many times, but I was a coward. And then you were happy, laughing, smiling. I didn't want to take that away from you."

"But you've just taken so much more than a smile or a laugh, Declan. I don't blame you for killing Lani. But I trusted you. And now—"

"Please, Aoife. I love you. I need—"

"What?" She backed away a step. "What did you say?"

"I said I love you, Aoife." He paused, but she only stared at him, her expression blank as her eyes searched his. "I didn't expect this. Didn't want it. But here I am, a wreck of a man, drowning in uncharted waters." He took a step toward her, and then another until they were inches apart. "You wrecked me, Aoife, and I'd have it no other way."

He dared to reach for her, marveling when she let him touch a finger to her chin, angling her face to him as he had back in his cabin.

"Please, Aoife, forgive me?" he asked, hope lacing each word. He swallowed, waiting for her to say something, to do something. "Say something. Please?"

He lowered his hand, leaving her staring up at him with no hint of her thoughts.

But when her head slowly started to shake, his heart plummeted.

"I can't." She took a step back from him, tears welling up in those green eyes he loved more than the sea. "Declan, I'm sorry. I just can't. Not yet."

And with those words, she left him standing there on the black sands, in their cove, while he stared after her as she made her way back to his ship.

Aoife didn't hear Declan's steps behind her on the path, but she didn't turn to confirm he'd given her the space she needed either.

Blinded by a mess of emotions, her mind a whir of thoughts refusing to settle, she didn't notice when the trees gave way to the quaint buildings of Morshan and her steps touched cobblestones instead of soft earth. She'd be lying if she said she'd never suspected Declan had been the one. He'd been in port that day. He'd looked distracted when he swam into the cove.

But she'd pushed all suspicion aside, sure he wouldn't hide something so important.

She'd been wrong.

Just as she'd been wrong about everything.

So naive. So gullible. Was there anyone in this world she could trust? At this point, she didn't even know if she could trust herself.

Her heart and mind had led her down the wrong paths time and time again.

Onto that ship.

Into the hands of those pirates in Foxhaven.

Into this mess with Declan.

The thought of his name caused fresh tears to spill over and trail down her cheeks. She wiped them away. Though no one was around to see, she had no desire to have the crew seeing her with such signs of emotion marking her face.

Aoife pushed herself forward, careful to stay in the darkened shadows with her head down, adding more swagger to her hurried steps—as if that might help conceal her identity—as she made her way down the narrow streets and around the few corners back to the docks.

Seeing the ship waiting at the end of the dock closest to her, the crew busy with final preparations to sail, she let herself breathe the salt air deep into her lungs before looking over her shoulder to ensure Declan was on his way.

He wasn't there.

Nothing but darkness lay behind her, the streets empty, all residents asleep, and the only noise coming from the various crews aboard their ships.

He'd be here. He'd show up.

She took the final hundred feet to compose herself, hoping the darkness would conceal any evidence of her tears. Thankfully, the crew barely acknowledged her arrival as she boarded. No sign of Gavin and the fae, but they must have arrived, as the crew was eerily silent. No doubt their newest guests made them more uneasy than Aoife had.

She began to make her way toward the officers' cabin, where the fae would be staying during their journey, where Tommy was likely resting while being healed, but she changed her mind. Declan had said the healing would take a while, and she didn't want to interrupt any progress they'd made.

As she laid a hand on the door to Declan's quarters—their quarters—her heart twinged with a spark of hope that maybe he'd used his pirate ways to get ahead of her, had arrived at the ship early, and now waited to surprise her here. It would be just like him to sit there behind the desk, with that smirk on his face, asking her what took so long.

But she opened the door to find the cabin dark, cold, and empty.

No one had been in here for hours.

A sharp bite of panic stung her chest, but she shook it away.

Declan can take care of himself. He's a grown man, she reminded herself.

Yes, a grown man who loves you.

Who lied to you.

Who you love in return.

Her mind bounced from one thought to the next over and over as she walked into the cabin and lit the lantern on the desk.

Each thought spoke truth. Even if everything else she knew was a lie, these truths remained, but she had no idea how to reconcile them all.

Love required trust.

How could trust exist without honesty?

But you love each other.

Her stomach tightened as the thought echoed within.

She didn't hate him. Even as her anger simmered, it remained in the shadows of her disappointment.

She'd let herself fall, let herself hope. Perhaps this was to be her life. A vicious cycle of trust, hope, and betrayal.

Would she ever be happy? Would she ever find peace? Or was this her punishment for what she'd done to Lani? Was this the debt she owed for her own betrayal?

These thoughts followed her into the sleeping quarters, where she slumped back onto the bed, her unblinking stare fixed on the ceiling.

She wished her mind would go blank, but it seemed bent on haunting her, stirring up the memories of how he'd held her, how his lips had caressed hers, how safe she'd felt with him. Her chest squeezed ever harder as each image gave way to the next.

He'd asked for forgiveness.

She'd declined.

At least for now.

She knew absolution was the right thing to grant him, the only way to move forward. Yet some part of her refused to take that next step.

He deserved to hurt as she did.

He deserved to feel that guilt of knowing he'd screwed up.

For how long, she wasn't sure. She only knew she couldn't give him what he requested yet.

So she closed her eyes and waited.

Maybe by the time he returned, she'd be ready to at least hear him out.

52
Declan

Declan stared into the trees long after Aoife had turned away from him.

What had he done?

Sands knew he'd made his share of mistakes in life, but this? He didn't know how to get himself out of this one. Normally he'd brush it off, focus on what mattered most—treasure, freedom, the sea.

But now Tommy was injured, Cait had been threatened, and Aoife…

The look she'd given him, that mix of betrayal and grief and anger, would torment him until his final breath.

He hadn't followed her, and wouldn't have even if his feet would obey. She needed space, and he could give her that much, at least for a little while.

He waited until the sound of her footsteps had faded, and then waited longer, not wanting his longer strides to bring him upon her before she'd made it back to the ship.

With one final glance at the cove—their cove—he made another vow to the sands and to the sea and to whoever might be listening above.

He would come back here to these shores.

And he would bring the dagger.

And he would end the council.

For the people. And for Aoife.

He wouldn't screw this up again. He would make it right. He would fix this.

Even if she never forgave him, he would make sure she was safe. That would be enough for him.

The walk back to Morshan took less time than he'd expected, each step matching the pounding of his heart as he tried to work out the words he'd say to her.

The dock came into view, but he realized too late that someone followed him. He'd been too distracted, wrapped up in his thoughts, to notice. Under the shadow of the next shop's awning, he turned sharply, his hand on the dagger at his waist, ready to use it if needed.

Nothing but darkness.

Had he completely lost his senses?

He searched the streets, glanced at the windows for any reflections, but still found nothing. He must have imagined it.

He turned back toward the docks, and that's when they stepped out. Not one of Lord Madigen's men as he had expected, but another captain, his face hidden behind the wide brim of his weathered hat. He now stood in Declan's path.

"Did you forget we were to meet, McCallagh?" the captain said, lifting his chin high enough that the dim moonlight glinted off the white of his scar.

Declan bit back a curse. He had forgotten.

"Aye, Callum—"

"Hold it right there. Callum is what my friends call me." He took a step forward. "You can call me Captain Grayson."

Declan made to protest, but Callum raised a finger.

"Now, Declan, I thought we were friends. But your actions prove otherwise."

Declan could see his ship over Callum's shoulder, his ship where Aoife waited for him, where Tommy was being healed. He needed to get off this street and onto that deck. He needed to lose Callum. Now.

"Apologies for forgetting the meeting, Captain—"

Callum stepped forward again, so close Declan could smell the rum on his breath and the grime that clung to his skin.

"This isn't about a meeting, Declan. You sent me on a pointless task to get me out of the way, to keep me busy, to keep that bitch of an heir out of my hands."

Declan forced his expression to remain blank, even as his hands fisted and his jaw tensed. He raised his arms in a shrug. "What can I say, Captain? I'm a pirate. It's what we do."

"Aye. Indeed. And so is this."

Callum gave a quick nod, and before Declan could turn to block the attack, the pommel of a blade slammed into the side of his head, and everything went black.

The door to the cabin slammed against the wall as it was thrown, and Aoife jolted upright. A pair of feet rushed in, and a glance toward the window told her it was nearing dawn. Had she really fallen asleep? She turned to the bed and found Declan's side still empty, untouched.

"Aoife?" Tommy's tone—urgent and coated with anxiety—filled her with dread.

It took her less than a second to rise and rush into the main room to meet him, sending out a "Tommy? Are you okay? I thought you were hurt."

Tommy stood alone, his face pale and lined with worry. "He's not here, is he?" he asked.

"What? No. Are you sure you're okay? Did they—"

"I'm fine."

He looked far from fine, but when she motioned for him to sit, he only shook his head, his eyes burning into hers.

"What happened, Tommy? What's going on?"

"Your mother. Had me nearly gutted in order to get Declan to agree to get the dagger for them. He carried me all the way here so the fae could heal me. As soon as I woke, I wouldn't let them touch me again. Not until I checked on him."

"Tommy, sit, please. You need to rest."

"No, I can't," he said as he began pacing the same path Declan always did on the rug. "The crew said they saw you arrive, but the captain didn't. We're running out of time, Aoife. What happened at the cove?"

Aoife answered his question with one of her own. "Did you know?"

A nod. A swallow.

Aoife's throat tightened. How many people knew what Declan had done and had hidden it? "Did anyone else—"

"No." He stopped her with the sharp word and a small shake of his head. "Only me. I'm the only one he allowed to shoulder those burdens."

"You didn't tell me," she said, with more sadness than anger.

"It wasn't my place, but I encouraged him to tell you. Told him you could handle it. He was supposed to, said he would. Perhaps after we got the fae. He never meant to hurt you, you know."

She knew, but it didn't make it any less painful.

Tommy cleared his throat and looked around the room once more. "You fought then? I'm assuming that's why you didn't return together?"

"I left him standing on the beach, but I didn't expect him to allow me to go off on my own. Not after Foxhaven."

"You didn't bother to check to see if he was following?" he asked, no trace of anger in the words, only concern for his friend.

Lowering her eyes, she shook her head.

Her thoughts raced as she wondered where Declan might have gone, what might have happened to him. There had to be someone they could contact for help. She snapped her gaze up. "Cait. Would she know?

Maybe he went to the pub?"

"He wouldn't have risked it. Not when we needed to be out. But if anyone has info, it would likely be her."

Tommy strode to the door and opened it but turned at the last moment. "You coming?"

Without a word she rushed past him out onto the deck.

But she stopped a few feet from the gangplank. A man she'd never seen before stood there, looking as though he was going to be sick despite their still being docked. Perhaps it was the news he brought that had him looking so ill, but she couldn't tell for sure.

Tommy stepped around her. "Lucan? What is it? If you're standing on a ship, it can't be good."

The man—Lucan—swallowed hard and gave a nearly imperceptible nod.

"Word from Cait?" Tommy asked. Aoife wondered if they shouldn't move this conversation somewhere private, as Declan would have. Tommy didn't usher him inside the cabin but stood, his fingers twitching at his sides, as if he were anxious to take action.

"Aye. He's gone."

Aoife's eyes went wide. "What do you mean he's gone?"

Lucan looked at her, but only for a second before his attention returned to Tommy. "Grayson. Grabbed him. Left word with Cait to get to you." He held out a scrap of paper, and the crew—frozen in place from his first word—now held a collective breath.

Tommy took the note, and Aoife glanced over, unable to read the scrawl of letters.

"What is it?" she whispered.

"Callum's going for the dagger."

Lucan spoke up. "If they try to go without the fae, they'll be killed. None of them will survive."

Aoife felt her heart thud to a stop. As if all of time had ceased to tick on.

"Tommy, we have to catch up to them, get him back," she said.

"Aye, but their ship is faster and has a head start."

She wanted to argue, to beg him to make the call, but she wasn't an officer on this ship, wasn't even a crew member.

No one moved. No one seemed to even breathe.

Tommy only stared at the paper as if it would tell him what to do. From the corner of her eye, Aoife saw the three fae sisters approach from the officers' quarters, but they didn't say anything. They, too, seemed to be waiting for Tommy's direction.

Tommy cleared his throat and bellowed out the order, "Weigh anchor! Gavin, get us underway."

The crew moved at once, and Tommy turned back to Lucan. "Thank you, friend. But you'd best get off the ship, unless you want to come with us."

Lucan seemed to shudder at the thought and ran quickly to make it down the gangway before it was moved, leaving Aoife and Tommy standing in the middle of the deck with the fae still hovering nearby.

Aoife rested a hand on his arm. "Tommy? Where are they taking him? Where's the dagger?"

Tommy ran a hand through his hair before turning to her with what looked like fear in his eyes.

"The Black Sound."

Aoife forgot how to breathe, giving her words no sound as she said, "You mean…"

"Aye. The sirens."

Panic hit, sucking the last of the air out of her lungs, but she managed a breath. "There's no getting past them. Not for any of us."

"That's where they come in," Tommy said, tossing a glance at the sisters. "We'll get to him before they get there."

"I hope so," she said, her gaze turning toward the vast waters that lay ahead.

Sands help him—and everyone on Cregah—if they didn't.

The story continues in

From These Dark Depths

Aisling Sea Book 2
Summer 2022

A desperate pirate crew. An abducted captain. Can they save him before he faces the bloodthirsty sirens or will other dangers of the sea claim them first?

The crew of the Siren's Song race to catch up with the ruthless pirate who has captured their captain. But a sudden storm forces them to choose a perilous route. Desperate to save their captain and retrieve the enchanted dagger, the crew argues over how to survive the waters and what lies beneath.

Declan finds himself in the hands of a cruel and ambitious pirate with no desire to listen to reason or the truth. With no chance to escape, he must buy his crew time to reach him before he falls victim to his captor's deadly scheme.

In a world of myths and mystery, a captain's life hangs in the balance. But it will take more than skill and magic to save him. Can a crew come together to free their captain–or will their stubborn hearts sacrifice him instead?

ACKNOWLEDGMENTS

As a reader, I adore this part of the book where we get a glimpse behind the scenes at all the cheerleaders and supporters who made the author's work possible. As an author though, I dread it. Not because I don't know how to thank people. I promise, my mother did teach me to write thank you notes, even if I've failed to continue the tradition or pass it on to my children. Rather, it's the fear that I won't express my gratitude sufficiently—or worse—I'll leave someone out by accident.

But fear aside, let's do this.

To those who fueled my creativity: Yes, I'm thanking Black Rifle Coffee who kept me caffeinated and New Amsterdam Gin who made writing a book during a pandemic fun. Y'all made this journey all the better.

To my pirate girls: I am trying to keep my swearing to a minimum here, so just imagine all the extra snark in between these words. Beth,

Beth, Beth. I couldn't have done this without you, and you now are stuck being my critique partner for every future book I ever write. Tricia (#teamDeclan), Morgan (#teamTommy), Negan (see what I did there?), Jourdan, Lauren, Crystal, and Moriah. Thank you for all the chats, laughs, drinks, and more. We will all meet one day in person, and it will be epic. Or awkward. Okay, it will be both.

To my publishing team: Maria for the gorgeous covers, Gerralt for the amazing map and illustrations, Emily for your meticulous editing, Carla for your fighting expertise, Sarah for your voice talent. I have thoroughly enjoyed working with each and every one of you to bring this story to life!

To the authors who inspire me: especially Ronie, Danielle, Rachel, Amy, Micheline, Mary, and Holly. Thank you for your friendship, your advice, your wisdom, and your words. You embody everything good about this community of creatives, offering encouragement time and time again.

To my street team: y'all got excited early on for this book and kept that energy going. Thank you thank you thank you for all you did and continue to do!

To the readers: whether you picked up the book because you know me, or because a friend recommended it, or because you had gotten to the end of your TBR and had nothing else to read (rather unlikely), thank you. There are so many fantastic books and talented authors out there, and it is not lost on me that you chose to spend your precious reading time with my story.

To my mom: for fostering my creative side, for saving all my childhood writing, and for getting me back into reading after so many years. It was your recommendation of Care and Management of Lies and The Nightingale that had me revisiting the library after an embarrassingly long hiatus.

To my kids: I know it's not easy having a mom who piles up her plate, stretches herself thin, and chases after crazy dreams, but you've cheered me on all along the way. Getting up early with me to talk to me while I write, asking me about my characters, brainstorming names of locations with me, and singing along to my playlist in the car—you offered your support in so many ways! No matter what you choose to do with your life and your talents, I pray I can be as supportive as you have been. I love you all. Moose wins!

To my husband, Joel: Thank you for all your help in writing this book, even when I claimed you were doing the opposite. I couldn't write these snarky characters without you and your wit being my companion for the last sixteen years. You listened to me ramble and complain and cry. You have obliged my pirate obsession with quiet grace (sorry for all the anchors on the walls—I got carried away, I know). You made sure there was always coffee in the morning, gin in the freezer, and limes on the counter. But most importantly you believed in me and never let me give up. Thank you for your love, your patience, your guidance, and your humor. I love you more than I could ever put into words.

And last but far from least, to Christ Jesus for His saving grace. It took me so many years to find my way back to faith in You, and I certainly don't understand or appreciate fully all the blessings I've been granted. For the gifts of language, story, creativity, fellowship, and redemption, thank you.

From the bottom of my heart to all of you, thank you!

A former engineer and data analyst, Vanessa recently ditched her day job to spend her days writing books and running a small business creating gifts for book nerds like herself. She lives on the plains of Wyoming, with her Army pilot husband, their four kids, and a three-legged dog named Bruce.

Printed in the USA
CPSIA information can be obtained
at www.ICGtesting.com
LVHW050817290823
756437LV00003B/518